COSMIC WIDOW

AN AGENT RENAULT SPY-FI ADVENTURE

JONATHAN NEVAIR

CANTINOOL BOOKS

First edition: November 19, 2024.

Cover art and design by Miblart

Editing: Jonathan Oliver

Published by Cantinool Books

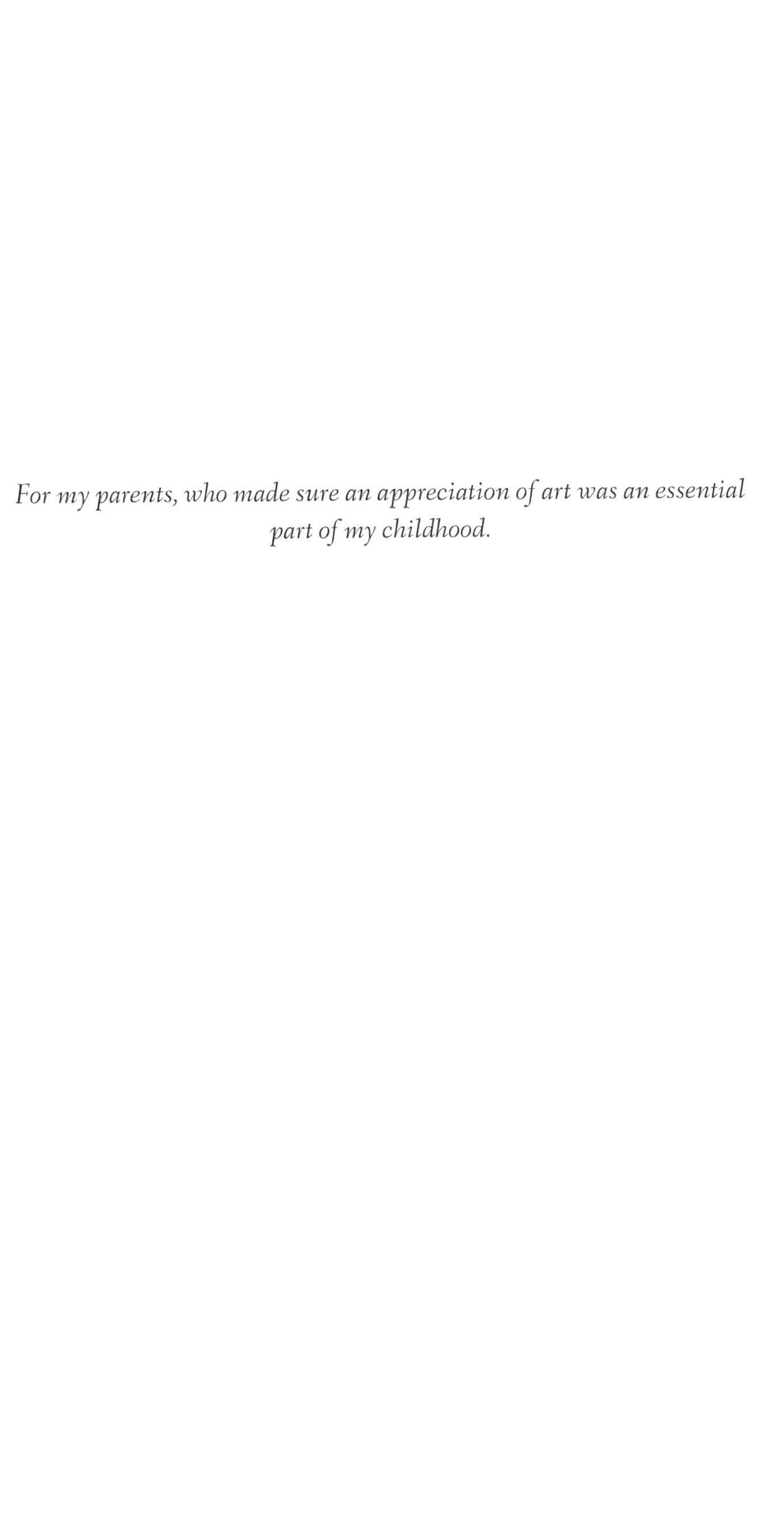

For my parents, who made sure an appreciation of art was an essential part of my childhood.

ONE

Agent Lilline Renault had never witnessed a battle so fierce.

Orange projectiles screamed toward their targets, breaking through a line of enemy frigates. Swirling storms of crimson plumed from mangled hulls. On flight decks, dabs of blue and green served as reminders that uniformed protectors helmed a war-ravaged fleet – career soldiers, call-up reservists, and those with no other choice but to defend against a threat most dire.

And yet, light years away stood unwavering stellar observers. Blueish-white specks flung onto a black background by a god's masterful hand. With infinite patience they waited, a moment of folly playing out within a majestic and boundless galaxy.

"It never fails to lure us in, does it?"

Lilline turned to find a portly Gej-ti human variant smiling at her. Pink cheeks shone like roses in the snow.

"Art, that is," he said.

She glanced back at the painting.

"Reginald Bilarus... Curator of Collections." He extended a translucent, milky-skinned hand.

"Caroline Liro," Lilline said and shook it. "Art appraiser."

"I see you were admiring *The Battle of the Darians*."

"Like you said," she smiled, "it never fails."

"Better that than our lost treasure." Bilarus gestured at a display case in front of the dramatic image.

Lilline let the illusion stand. She'd been caught in a moment's distraction, the dazzling canvas pulling her attention from the vitrine.

The curator stepped forward and peered through the plasma shield. Faint blue light glowed on his white linen suit. "I'm afraid this one was on my watch." He shook his head, eyes on the empty velvet blanket.

Lilline re-read the label: *Venex Horse Pendant. Excavated: Gendari Plain, Pol-9. 5 x 7 x 3 cm. Donor: anonymous (Stolen: 5009).*

She bit down, jaw tightening. Her mother had uncovered that horse. In a rare exception, the archaeologist leading the excavation had offered it as thanks for her prodigious discovery. The famous "Venex Horde" that emerged from the survey team's preliminary digging had yielded unprecedented treasures of a bygone galactic age.

"Did you ever see it in person, Ms. Liro?"

Lilline balled a hand into a fist. Vicarious pointy ears and hooves dug into her palm. Memories rushed back: her small fingers clutching the pendant like a talisman as she fell asleep, its ceremonial position at breakfast next to her plate, and the rhythmic click-clacking as her mother danced the equine across the kitchen table.

"Only in reproduction," she said. Lying stung, but professional obligation usurped all personal facts and feelings.

"It's easier on our institution since the donor remains anonymous." Bilarus sighed. "Saves us the embarrassment of where to direct our shame."

"It's not your fault," Lilline said. The memory of Granny Kissy holding her hand in front of this very case, showing her the horse on display, pushed its way forward. It had been her mother's only known posthumous request, made once as a passing comment, or so her grandmother had said.

Lilline held back an elegiac smile. She knew too well how unexpected deaths left little behind of final wishes and words of goodbye.

"I'm sure the donor understood the risks." Lilline smiled at the curator. "It's the one who took it who should be ashamed." Her eyes went back to the empty vitrine and narrowed. *You're on my list of unfinished personal business... whoever you are.*

"Which brings us to why you are here, Ms. Liro." Bilarus took a handkerchief from his breast pocket and dabbed sweat from his forehead. As with all Gej-ti, his translucent skin revealed the human variant's muscles and nerves closest to the surface.

"Indeed." Lilline adjusted her smart-looking suit. "I'll require close examination of the incident to pass on an assessment to the insurance company." With her dark, shoulder-length hair and modest but costly jewelry, she fit the fashionable style of intelligentsia on Tavi-Prime. That was the intent, even if both she and Bilarus knew it wasn't her true identity.

The curator's attention shifted to an adjacent wall. "Stars, is that the time?"

Lilline followed the Gej-ti's eyes to the digi-clock. The numeric display hovered above a row of electrified paintings glowing with the audacious colors of the early Third Galactic style. Lilline didn't care for the aesthetic. Too bold and garish for her taste, but she respected the anarchic palette that served as a revolt against tradition, one that pronounced a new era of civilization across the stars.

"If you care to come this way, Ms. Liro." The curator gestured toward the hallway leading to the First Galactic collection.

"Were you the first on the scene?"

Bilarus shook his head. "That would be our new curatorial fellow. She happened upon it on her way to our offices." He sighed as if to deny the reality of the situation. "The guard on morning rounds was summoned and called it in."

As they walked, vibrant blues, reds, and greens from the electrified paintings cast a kaleidoscopic glow on the curator's linen suit.

"I understand you've blocked off the entire wing?"

"As a precaution, yes. I requested a section of the museum be closed to ensure the gallery was out of public view." The curator fiddled with his handkerchief. "Much to the resentment of today's visitors."

"I'm sure." Lilline watched as a group of Dendari tourists were turned away from the entrance leading to the museum's biggest attraction. They passed her as she and Bilarus approached the portal, consternation on their furry faces.

"Terrible business," Bilarus muttered.

From what she had heard at the GAM-OPs briefing an hour earlier, it was. If the preliminary facts proved correct, this was an art crime like no other. Bilarus was going to have a fresh crisis to add to a string of existing problems. Anyone who followed the art world in the Inner Core knew of the curator's waning reputation.

"I'm not sure if you are aware, Ms. Liro, but your director and I were at university together." The curator shuffled through the ornate portal to a makeshift barrier with two Kreeli security guards.

"Is that so?" Lilline lifted her gaze to the two oblong blue heads. Both guards had at least a half meter height over her. The pressure band across one of their foreheads glittered. A feature shared by all Kreelis, the device adjusted barometrics so their internal system stabilized with the outside atmosphere.

"Our degrees were in different disciplines," Bilarus said, "but he took a minor in galactic art history."

"Did he now?" Lilline held back a smile. That *was* a surprise. So, her boss, Asher Lauden, and Reginald Bilarus were old college mates? To think that the director of GAM-OPs had a bit of expertise in art. The straight and narrow, emotionally restrained head of clandestine operations had a love for sensuous aesthetic delights. The galaxy was indeed full of surprises.

"Ash had a great eye," the curator said as they passed through security. "Still does, I imagine."

Ash? That's a new one.

Lilline's trendy Gemmelli heels clicked and clacked like a ticking clock in the empty gallery. With each step, a generation of creative endeavor passed like grains of sand through an hourglass. Her eyes went from masterpiece to masterpiece, taking in the collective treasures of bygone eras. A museum was the closest thing she knew of to a time machine, made manifest through visual artifacts that captured the spirit of each successive galactic age.

"She's with me," Bilarus said as they reached the grand promenade. "Let us through, please."

A Rasp, with its signature snake-like neck and small head with a single eye, examined Lilline. Its monocular gaze was earnest, yet nervous.

The icon for the faux private security firm, *Fireline,* was legible in her peripheral vision, imprinted on their jacket. Lilline's agent eye for detail didn't miss the distinctive bulge of a GAM-OPs-issued H-42 hyper-proton blaster at the Rasp's hip either.

Good. The agency had set up a secure crime scene using T# agents-in-training. She recognized this one. A recruit working under her colleague, T5.

The crackling of the Rasp's clay-colored skin bounced off the ceiling as the agent-apprentice reached for a control panel. A three-fingered hand punched a code and undid the security shield.

"Ghastly business, this," Bilarus said, shaking his head.

Lilline had to agree. She expected there to be nothing where the famous work of art hung.

Instead, there was a clock.

TWO

Watchful, long-dead eyes followed Lilline as she crossed the gallery to the crime scene perimeter. An array of painted species, some extinct and others still thriving, mixed with dramatic narratives of space battles and planetary conquest. So much of First Galactic history remained shrouded in mystery.

Like visual cliffhangers, each painting's allure and intrigue pulled her onwards. Together the suite of historical images formed an ensemble, rising to a visual crescendo that culminated with the gallery's main attraction. Even now, focused on her serious agenda, Lilline found it hard not to get swept up in the rising artistic tide.

That was, until a glaring void broke the visual rhythm of artistic masterpieces. Like a screeching halt to a symphonic performance, the empty wall sent a sobering shock wave through her bones. The weight of the crime slowed her steps. The *Cosmic Widow*... stolen. The most famous work in all of galactic art history purloined from the Inner Core's premier art museum. When this hit the public news feeds the shock and surprise would echo like an electromagnetic pulse to the most distant star system. Billions would be stunned. Galactic media companies would cash in on content and associated advertising covering the story. A showboating spectacle by crackpots and amateur sleuths touting far-fetched conspiracy theories would run on popular networks alongside legitimate art experts lamenting the invaluable cultural loss from the theft. In short, it was going to be a major galactic mess.

Lilline glanced at Bilarus. His translucent milky skin flushed, blood rushing through his visible veins. She couldn't blame him. The museum was in for a PR disaster.

Or...

Her eyes narrowed.

A massive opportunity.

It was no secret that the art institution, and Bilarus especially, was struggling of late. Most of the problems stemmed from stubbornness in the face of shifting cultural attitudes. Ideas about the past were changing. New perspectives, alternative histories, and revisions to existing narratives filled the latest programs and educational materials. Popular opinion was that current and future generations deserved to see this reflected in their civic institutions. The public demanded change. The museum's board and curators believed more exposure to tradition should be prioritized.

Lilline held out a hand to slow the Gej-ti's steps. "Mind the barrier, Mr. Bilarus."

Behind the translucent plasma shield, an Oltari examined a timepiece suspended in mid-air in front of the empty wall. The GAM-OPs head of tech hovered a half-meter off the floor, double wings fluttering, and took a series of image captures of the clock's shimmering surface.

Lilline walked around the security barrier so she was parallel with the technician.

"Pin!" She waved a hand.

Futile. The shield was soundproof.

"This is quite unusual," Bilarus commented.

"Not really," Lilline said. *Just standard work dynamic with an*

Oltari. She opened the comm on her wristband and entered Pin's GAM-OPs sequence.

The Oltari halted her examination, dropped down on her two stumpy legs, and with one of her four arms tapped her comm.

"T8, you really should get to the museum. There's a series of adjunct evidence related to—"

"Pin." Lilline mustered her calmest tone. "Look to your right."

The Oltari's mouth curved into a circle and she emitted an unheard sound behind the plasma shield. She flew to a portable hover table and placed down the camera. With a tap on her comm, the shield cube deactivated.

"Apologies. I was in the zone," Pin said.

"Clearly."

"I've been here for an hour." The Oltari picked up a data pad. Lilline recognized the usual array of high-tech GAM-OPs field equipment organized in neat and precise rows on the hovering tabletop.

"Would you like me to get you up to speed?"

"In a moment. Pin, this is Reginald Bilarus." Lilline gestured at the Gej-ti.

Bilarus nodded in greeting.

"He's the Curator of Collections at the museum."

"Yes, I am familiar with the staff list." Pin shifted on her stumpy legs and faced the curator. "Mr. Bilarus, I would like to use this opportunity to pose a query regarding the museum's acquisition philosophy. Is there a justification for the disparity of representation in the Third Galactic collection?"

"Um... sorry?" Bilarus dabbed sweat from his brow.

"I've been auditing the museum's collection, as part of a larger cultural analysis of public institutions on Tavi-Prime. A personal project in my spare time. Judging by the number and type of acquisitions in the last hundred cycles, I can say without question that a bias is at work."

Oh no. Palpable tension rose like a plasma shield manifesting.

With everything else at play the last thing she needed was a GAM-OPs employee critiquing their client. "Pin, this isn't the appropriate time to be discussing personal concerns about the galleries."

"Oh, they aren't personal, I assure you." Pin folded both sets of arms across her chest. "Subjective responses to art and aesthetics are a different matter. I am referring to strategies of curating and the ethics of representation. Specifically, a lack of work by species that—"

"Pin." Lilline held up a hand. "We have a crime scene to deal with. If you have a grievance, you can contact the Curatorial Department. Isn't that right, Mr. Bilarus?"

"Indeed." He fiddled with his handkerchief. "In fact, our new curatorial fellow has a vested interest in this topic. She's a specialist in First Galactic art history. We've hired her for guidance addressing exactly these kinds of revisionist approaches." The Gej-ti's eyes drifted across the gallery and widened. "There she is now." Bilarus nodded towards the far side of the gallery.

A Rasp dressed in a sharp-looking black dress, a narrow gold collar the only color accent, rotated its snake-like neck to and fro. Her monocular gaze searched the room.

"Renina!" Bilarus waved his handkerchief like a surrender flag.

The Rasp halted her search and held up a data pad, indicating something needed his attention.

"Perhaps you should go and check in, Mr. Bilarus," Lilline said. "I'm sure there's a pile of associated items to deal with considering everything that's happened." She gave him a look that said, *Here's your escape route.*

"Thank you, Ms. Liro and most appropriate considering... well, the circumstances." The Gej-ti nodded. "Nice to have met you, Pin. I hope you and Ms. Liro can help us solve this dreadful crisis... quickly."

Lilline followed the Gej-ti as he made for the curator. He moved like an overwhelmed tourist trapped in the galleries, seeking an exit. To be expected. His head would be on the chopping block for this debacle.

The Rasp glanced her way and Lilline smiled vacuously. The curatorial fellow reciprocated and, as Bilarus arrived, handed him the tablet.

"Renina," Lilline said, taking mental note of the name.

"Blackstone," Pin added, providing the curator's surname. "I have already filed her contact information into my personal database. A letter of inquiry will be forthcoming post-haste."

And what a letter it would be. She watched Renina talking to Bilarus. *Good luck with that one, curator.* Although, she had to admit that Pin wasn't wrong. An obvious disparity in the collection existed and needed to be addressed. But not on official GAM-OPs time.

Lilline turned to the crime scene. Pin was sifting through her investigation tools. At some point when they were back at HQ she'd have a delicate conversation with the Oltari about field work and professional boundaries. Again.

Lilline straightened the sleeves on her smart suit. *Alright, let's do this.* She examined the empty wall. *Not my thing, but for some reason Lauden wants me here.*

Why the GAM-OPs director had sent her to investigate an art crime, she didn't know. Not the usual purview for secret agents charged with protecting the galaxy. GAM-OPs wasn't the legal branch of the galactic government. They were, as the acronym stated, a galactic agency maintaining order, peace, and security for billions across the stars - clandestinely, and usually through daring feats and life-threatening gambits in the field. A stolen painting, even one as famous as the *Cosmic Widow*, wasn't typical espionage fare.

"A most intriguing scenario," the Oltari said.

"Anything so far on the portrait?"

Pin shook her head. "Not a trace of evidence on my scanners."

Lilline examined the wall where the *Cosmic Widow* usually hung. She conjured the alluring image of the sitter in her mind. It wasn't hard. Everyone in networked systems had encountered the mystery figure at some point in their lives, most many times over. A tiny painting, no larger than a small book, the *Cosmic Widow* held court over its grander-scaled neighbors like a queen presiding from a god-given throne.

Lilline's eyes ran over the wall's surface, searching for signs of the theft.

"I assume those are the security sensors?" She pointed at faint red dots forming a complex geometry.

"Correct. And those—" Pin pointed one of her four hands up at a thin line on the ceiling. Another aimed down at a matching mark on the floor. "—are the shield barriers. Osmic electro-wave technology."

"Top of the line security," Lilline said, gazing up. "So, it had to be shut off in order to access the *Cosmic Widow?*"

"Seems to be the case," the Oltari said. "But doing so auto-engages the room's blast wall doors."

"And they somehow managed to bypass them as well?"

Pin gestured with all four arms as if stumped. "I'm evidence and tech analysis. Would hate to be in your shoes."

Subtle as always.

"Camera feeds?" Lilline asked.

"All smeared."

"With a substance?" Lilline scanned the walls. Motion bots were there, invisible to the naked eye, cloaked by a veneer of simulation-paint.

"No. Through a jamming system. According to museum security, all footage in the First Galactic Wing is wiped from closing until the missing theft was discovered this morning."

"Impressive," Lilline said. A feat unto itself to get in and out with the portrait and install a hovering clock unseen and without trig-gering any security measures.

"Without question, our thief had access to highly exclusive off-market hacking equipment." Pin shifted to face her. "Even so, you shouldn't be able to pass all those redundancies, no matter what kind of counter-tech you have. It's not possible given the physical space and distances."

"Well, it is now," Lilline said, taking in the various security measures.

No doubt, whoever took the *Cosmic Widow* was an elite professional. One with an odd sense of dramatics. She'd seen calling cards before, but nothing this banal.

"Looks like an old timepiece." Lilline leaned in to examine the hovering object. Circular and encased in golden metal, a simple white face with hour, minute, and second hands displayed the time in illegible numeric symbols. "I'd guess First Galactic by the style."

"Check the back."

Lilline shifted around between the clock and the wall. A single line in elegant script was engraved on the timepiece, written in Galactic Common:

Time is short.

"A bit on the nose, don't you think?"

Pin didn't respond.

She glanced at the techie. Two hands held a tablet and the other two typed with extraordinary speed.

Whoever the culprit was, they had to up their literary game. It fell far short of their thieving skills.

"'Time is short,'" Lilline said and walked back around to the front. "Kind of cliché?"

Pin made an indecipherable gesture.

"I mean, with all the possibilities to be clever or cryptic and you go with this?" Lilline examined the clock's face a second time. She tracked the seconds hand as it rotated around the dial. *Something's weird...*

She leaned in and focused, concentrating on the ticking needle. "Pin, it's running backwards." With each tick, the thin band moved counterclockwise. "That's odd."

"It has you sucked in," the Oltari said, breaking her silence.

"Touché."

Time is short... until what?

Dealing with a master thief was one thing, but the backwards mechanics combined with a statement of urgency added a tinge of...

Games.

She sighed. The job never changed. Whether tasked with stopping devious individuals with dreams of galactic domination, thwarting dangerous megalomaniacal visions of grandeur, or enacting extreme forms of retribution, the enemy always added arrogance through a form of play and taunting.

Lilline stared at the clock, thinking of the thief. *So, which variety of deviant are you?* She stepped back and took in the full view.

"What's holding the clock in place?"

"Gravitron tunnel," Pin said. "A standard one like you can get at any commercial supplier."

Lilline's eyes went to the floor. A black disc the size of a pinhead lay centered underneath the hovering object, creating the suspension channel. As the techie had said, nothing fancy, just a common device used for home decorations and kiosk items.

"Alright, you can give me the full report on the portrait back at HQ. For now, talk to me about this clock."

The Oltari flew over and landed next to her.

"Do we have an ID on where and when this was made?"

"I am afraid not, T8. And I don't think that is the primary concern."

"What do you mean?"

"It's less a matter of when or where and more what."

"Not following, Pin." Lilline scrutinized the clock's surface. "It's some sort of metal, right?"

"Yes and no."

She halted her examination. "Pin, you're making things less clear."

"Not my intention. I'm being accurate."

Deep breaths. After a full cycle working together, understanding Pin's unique personality remained a work in progress. Oltaris were highly intelligent and able to access a broader range of sensory experience than any other species in the galaxy. Their modes of discourse, however, presented a constant challenge. Rhetorical nuances like metaphor, sarcasm, and the like weren't part of their communication vocabulary.

Alright, let's try this again.

"Care to elaborate, please?"

"Certainly, T8."

Lilline faced the techie. Against the backdrop of surrounding paintings, Pin's porcelain skin shone with a hint of iridescence. Her two sets of arms, with their multiple elbow joints, folded across her chest.

"Exterior details suggest standard clock production. As you hypothesized, superficial signs point to a date within the First Galactic Age."

"Even I'm right twice a day, Pin." Lilline smirked and raised an eyebrow.

No response from the Oltari.

She gestured with arms out and palms open. "Like a stopped clock?"

"If it's stopped why not change the battery?"

I give up.

"T8, you are aware that most First Galactic mechanisms such as timepieces run on energy sources or autonomous wind-up systems?"

"Yes, obviously. I was—"

"Either way, there is no reason for it to remain idle, and certainly not for a full day."

"It's a proverb, Pin. I was—"

"Furthermore, this clock is running so the connection you suggest about—"

"You're right." Lilline held up a hand. *So much for a bit of levity.* "Please continue."

"The central material is as you guessed, a metal," the Oltari said. "However..." Pin approached the timepiece. Her double wings fluttered and she rose a half meter off the ground, leveling off at Lilline's line of sight. The techie reached out a gloved hand and touched the clock.

"Wow."

"An appropriate response, considering the surface reaction," Pin said.

That was putting it lightly. "Did it just—"

"I believe it did."

Lilline checked on Reginald Bilarus. Arms waving like a composer, he spoke with his assistant underneath a dramatic rendering of a planetary siege.

Thankfully, Pin's demonstration went unnoticed.

"Okay," Lilline turned her attention back to the hovering clock. "You've got me more than curious. So, what is it made of?"

"Hoo!"

The signature Oltari outburst bounced through the gallery. Bilarus and his assistant halted their conversation and turned. Lilline waved a hand, signaling everything was fine.

"Pin?" Her colleague's face held an unfamiliar and puzzling expression.

The head of tech dropped to the ground. The pinkish tint on her cheeks flushed blue.

"No known geological or synthetic material exists in the database."

"The GAM-OPs database?"

"No. The entire galaxy."

THREE

The Andrews River shimmered with afternoon light. Lilline came in for a landing outside Galaxy Unlimited, Inc., banking the hover bike in a spiraling descent, careful to steer clear of the security bubble extending from the river's opposite bank. Inside that invisible barrier, low-lying stone buildings housing Parliament and the Galactic Ministry stood out from the endless urban landscape. Surrounded by towering spires, scaffolds of greenways, and living units, the government buildings were an architectural anachronism. Their weathered and aged exteriors spoke of the longstanding political power associated with Tavi-Prime, the most populated and prosperous planet in the Inner Core.

Lilline glided the Yilari Lightning down and into the virtual outline of her private parking spot. She'd only had this new speeder a week, but so far she was smitten. Deep purple with a jagged bolt running on one side, the Yilari was like a poisonous viper and handled like one too. The slightest touch to the throttle sent the machine surging forward like a snake striking out at its prey, the cryex crystal infused burner spewing blue and orange flames in its wake.

"Good morning, Ms. Larkin," a phlegmy voice said.

"Jeen, how are we today?" Lilline handed the young Froo her helmet, careful not to contact the valet's fingers. As a cold-blooded amphibious human variant, Jeen and all others of her kind secreted a skin slime that irritated most sentient species. Originally developed to ward off predators on their wetlands home world, the slime contained a virus that disrupted the bacterial balance in the gastrointestinal track, causing a digestive illness that kept unfortunate victims within steps of a bathroom for weeks.

"Very well, thank you," Jeen said and gurgled. Her green lips widened, stretching across a frog-like jaw. "The humidity is delightful." The Froo patted her feet.

"Bit much for me," Lilline said and meant it. She was already sticky underneath her form-fitting black riding suit. As soon as she was through to her office, she would change into fresh and more formal attire.

"Hope today is an adventure, Ms. Larkin."

"Every day at the office is, Jeen," Lilline winked and made her way to the building's entrance.

For twelve cycles, Lilline had been coming to work as Keely Larkin, an expedition scout for the adventure company, Galaxy Unlimited, Inc. The identity had served her well, making for easy excuses when shooting off to remote planets on secret missions and providing convincing justification on her returns bearing fresh scars and strange injuries.

For everyday citizens and visitors to Tavi-Prime, GAM-OPs headquarters lay hidden and unknown, yet hard at work protecting billions across the stars. Its facade was an actual, real-world company offering high-end excursions for those with a wanderlust to explore the thrills of a vast and varied galaxy. Lilline thought it ironic that the company's slogan worked double-duty. *For Those Who Dare* was equally fitting for her true occupation as a T# secret agent. The risks might be different but they were as real for GU as the clandestine agency hidden behind scanner-proof walls.

Lilline passed through the mirrored doors and shivered with delight, the cool air cutting Tavi-Prime's heat and humidity. She crossed the open-plan office toward the elevator. Dramatic holo-advertisements ran in the three-story space over customer stations, displaying a fireworks-like narrative of adventures on land, sea, and sky. Clanks of pickaxes on ice walls, the roar of Hesh-9's legendary Bukki tigers, and the hoots and shouts of rafters shooting Xeret's canyon rapids bounced off the ornate ceiling.

To her left, at a tourist station booking climbing excursions, the familiar oblong blue crown of her colleague, Katar, rose like a prodigious mountain peak above a range of species. Customers, rapt with attention, listened to the Kreeli's first-hand accounts and conquests of the most challenging ascents in the galaxy. She caught the former T# agent's eye and he gave her a knowing nod, his scarred face a reminder of the near fatal mission that ended with Lilline bringing him in from the cold.

A flash of their harrowing escape sent a different kind of chill through her bones. She pushed down the uneasy feeling twisting her stomach. That recon operation had left a wake of trauma and death that still echoed through the agency's halls. Lilline battled her own recurring demons from that nightmare mission - late nights tossing and turning in bed or alone at her kitchen table, a bottle of Gondau doing its best to numb the pain and horror. The assignment had been Katar's last as a T# agent. Now he ran the adventure company and made sure no one, GU employees or the public, knew what went on in the building's interior depths.

Lilline reached the far side of the hall and pushed the call button on the elevator. She entered and with a quick retinal scan and exhalation for a breath print switched the tube's track. Her toes pushed down inside her boots to counterbalance the familiar bump and lean as the directional mechanism bypassed the system's usual grid, taking her to the restricted GAM-OPs entrance.

Whoosh. The portal dematerialized and all the excitement and bombast of GU was replaced by earnest restraint and tradition. GAM-OPs, the galaxy's shadow agency with a centuries-long history of clandestine operations, revealed itself with spartan elegance. Lilline made her way down the hall like a silent cat, her steps muffled by the plush red carpet. Austere yet refined, HQ spoke the same language as the Ministry across the Andrews River. Timeless and unwavering, as if its galactic oversight had always been and always would be.

Ahead, mid-tier administrators and analysts loitered outside the the Octagonal Club, making the most of their lunch breaks. Heads of a variety of species turned at her approach. Lilline smiled courteously as their banter halted, knowing they would wait for her to pass out of earshot before resuming hushed and secretive conversations.

"Granny," Lilline said and nodded in greeting at the sight of Kissy's statue at the club's entrance. For all her cycles as a T# agent, she had lived in the shadow of that bust. A reminder of her grandmother's former accomplishments as a GAM-OPs operative herself, unrivaled in legendary status.

Now that she thought about it, Kissy still managed to needle her way into her own missions, even in retirement. That wasn't all, either. Living together on Tavi-Prime had been nothing short of a GU-style adventure. She never knew what the ninety-plus cycle spitfire was going to do next, or to whom.

Ignoring the hallway leading towards the office of GAM-OPs director, Asher Lauden, she continued down three more corridors and entered her own modest quarters. Facing east, away from the

Andrews River, her windows provided a third-story view of the trendy shops and restaurants of West End. She took a moment to gaze out at the bustling cityscape. Above the rise and fall of terraced buildings and intermittent greenery, a steady flow of air traffic - personal transport pods, air taxis, and hover bikes - created hypnotic dotted lines across the afternoon sky.

Five minutes later she stood in front of the reflection wall in her office bathroom, dressed in a casual two-piece black suit, hair tied in a ponytail. She pushed a loose strand over the small wedge that was all that remained of her missing ear, lost to a Bukki tiger on a dangerous GAM-OPs mission eight cycles earlier.

Lilline ran her fingers over the streak of scars where the tiger's fangs had dug into her skull. A perfect example of the synchronicity between Galaxy Unlimited and GAM-OPs. Too perfect for her liking. Once in a lifetime was enough with that kind of adventure.

Back down the corridors, she arrived at the director's office. Cazshi, the Rasp who served as Asher Lauden's personal assistant, sat at his desk outside the portal. As usual at this time of day, he was absorbed in paperwork.

Lilline opened her mouth to speak.

"Is that T8?"

The question arrived over the audio system like a fencer's parry, cutting off her words before they left her mouth.

Cazshi's one eye rose from the holo-file on his desk, snake-like neck craning left. His monobrow gestured in surprise.

She winked.

"Yes, sir," he said pushing the inter-office comm.

"Well, send her in already."

Lilline met Cazshi's gaze. No words passed between them, but his facial expression made clear they agreed. It was going to be one of those days.

The Rasp pressed a button and the portal to Lauden's office dematerialized.

Waves of toasted nutmeg and burnt leather tingled her nostrils as the savory scent of Queen Yaz Flake wafted through the portal.

Cazshi gestured a three-fingered hand in the direction of the office. "Go on in, T8."

Lilline straightened her shirt sleeves and made for the portal.

"Good luck," the Rasp whispered.

FOUR

Lilline halted at the sight of the empty desk. She expected the GAM-OPS director to be absorbed in the current crisis, barking orders over the comm or entangled in close-study of holo-files. Instead, he stood peering out the office window and puffing on his pipe. How the Gej-ti managed to go from the urgency of his audio remark to a statuesque presence in Tavi-Prime's afternoon light, she didn't know.

"Have a seat, T8."

"Sir." Lilline strode forward and sat.

Along the interior wall stood the only other living entity in the office: an elegant bonsai. Noble and withered, as if shaped by centuries of wind, it rested in a low-lying ceramic pot atop a credenza. The miniature tree's presence was a reminder that the Gej-ti had been at the controls of the galaxy's most powerful clandestine organization for longer than she, and her grandmother before her, had been in the agency's employ.

Lilline's eyes swept back past the desk to the tall and gaunt figure of Asher Lauden. His hawkish nostril-less nose broke the symmetry of his chin and forehead, balanced itself by the Cavinelli pipe that complimented his angular face. The smoker's signature wave-shaped stem, and its wide and seasoned Maluc wood bowl, had been attached to the Gej-ti for so long that Lilline couldn't help but consider it a permanent appendage. When he was without it, he appeared incomplete like a tuxedo without a bowtie.

As for his outfit, today he wore a green and beige plaid suit, the cravat and socks a deep blue the color of an ocean's depths. Lauden had style; austerity was his sartorial language. Only the best and highest quality from the fashion houses in Kersi, a city on an Inner Core planet famous for its sophisticated designs.

"I understand you spoke with Bilarus?" Lauden said, breaking the silence.

"Yes, sir."

The director *humphed*, pipe clenched between his teeth. Through the blinds, Tavi-Prime's afternoon light cast a repeated horizontal pattern on the director's silhouette. The image was visual poetry, a subtle metaphor for his preferred habitat. Like all his fellow Gej-ti human variants, the director descended from a planet world of near darkness.

"He mentioned you two were at university together," Lilline said.

"Indeed, good chap." The Gej-ti took a long pull of Queen Yaz Flake and gazed out the window. Smoke exited his neck gills, sending a thick cloud billowing into the striated light like a desert sandstorm pluming across the dunes.

Lilline shifted in her chair. Why he was being so distant, she didn't know. Moments ago, he was barking for her to enter in haste.

A low and crackling rumble erupted from the director's gills.

That cough sounds worse.

It was no secret that Lauden wasn't well. His malignant condition left him terminal, within cycles of the end. But to look at him from this distance was like contemplating the bonsai across the office. Withered and yet strong beyond measure, driven on by some hidden power while the internal disease ran its course.

"I didn't realize you studied art history, sir," she said, eager to break the tension. "Did you have an area of specialization?"

A milky-skinned finger pointed at the opposite wall.

Lilline focused on the landscape above the bonsai. She'd stared at it hundreds of times while in the office. A historical representation of the founding of the Second Galactic Collective, in the Grinaldi style, hung encased in a gilded frame. Against a backdrop of monumental architecture, a procession made their way ceremoniously to the edge of a broad waterway. Lilline's knowledge of the style was thorough but thin. If needed, she could navigate a casual yet sophisticated discussion of its artistic merits undercover. Grinaldi's layered messages, however, were too dense and complex for her neophyte understanding. Those esoteric meanings were best left to experts with the fortitude and academic drive to delve into the labyrinthine art historical archives and perform close study.

She gazed at Lauden. Now that she thought about it, Grinaldi's dense and cryptic works made sense considering the Gej-ti's chosen profession.

"To business." Lauden crossed the room and sat.

Lilline directed her attention across the wooden desk, meeting her boss's gaze.

"About this museum mess..." Lauden picked up his pipe tool and fiddled with the tobacco in the wide bowl. "According to what Bilarus shared with me, it seems we have an art thief on our hands."

Lilline kept her composure neutral and nodded. The director's personal connection to the curator introduced a backdoor to the incident. Not the usual way things worked during a GAM-OPs crisis. She would need to be extra careful in how she spoke and shared initial impressions.

Lauden clinched his pipe repeatedly, jaw muscles flexing through milky skin. The ambient hum of the office's ventilation system filled the empty silence between them.

Lilline did her best to embrace it. Nothing irked her more than the rhetorical and gestural game Lauden played during these types of meetings.

Screw it. "Sir, I have to ask. Why is GAM-OPs at play on this? Normally the galactic crime bureau handles these types of incidents."

"Quite right, T8. And you are probably wondering why I set up a false security agency in the gallery?"

"That too, but also..." She hesitated. This was already getting messy, with Bilarus being an old college mate.

"You are asking," Lauden said, continuing for her, "with all that secrecy, why Bilarus knew your GAM-OPs role and played along with the insurance ruse?"

"In fact, sir, I am."

The Gej-ti pointed across the desk with the stem of his pipe. "Good show, T8. You're moving the opening pieces as I hoped you would."

What board are we even on? Lilline was still on uncertain ground. *Get to the point, you old fish.*

Lauden locked eyes with her. "How much do you know about the *Cosmic Widow*?"

FIVE

A high-resolution copy of the galaxy's most famous portrait hovered over Lauden's desk. Encircled by glimmering constellations in a clear night sky, a lone figure stood robed in red. The body, cropped at the frame's edge along its lower back, faced away as if walking into the distance. Only one tiny detail of the figure's features was visible: a hand with two thumbs, one at each end of a row of four fingers. The infamous "double pollex," as it was known, had remained an enigma for three galactic ages. Was it some long lost sign language? An omen or ward of protection? Or, as some art historians and cosmic philosophers considered, a secret code that, if broken, would reveal arcane mysteries of the universe?

For Lilline, the figure's hidden identity had always been the portrait's most alluring feature. More so than the artist's signature, which drew much conjecture - a name lost to the sands of galactic time: Azaludarian.

"I'm familiar with the most common interpretations, sir," Lilline said, answering the director's question. She edged up in her seat to get closer to the image. "The most popular is that it depicts the artist's lover, whose identity is hidden to protect them from adulterous accusations."

Lauden nodded and gestured with his pipe to continue.

"Or a representation of some kind of allegory, lost to us, that has a didactic purpose."

The Gej-ti nodded. "Indeed. Most often assumed to be hidden cosmic knowledge, considering what we know of First Galactic iconography." He pointed the stem of his pipe at the robed figure. "Especially red and its associations with tiers of learning in similar surviving Darian images."

Now it was Lilline's turn to nod. Her mother and Granny Kissy had given her a decent art education, and she had continued to pursue interest in a related area, cosmic archaeology, on and off through her own studies at university. That impulse was driven by the Venex Horse. An emotional surrogate, a familial talisman even, her mother's small artifact was a lifeline to a lost past. The more she knew of its history and context, the tighter her grip on a fraying rope to a lost mother became. That was, until it had snapped three cycles ago — stolen, leaving a void that swirled with anger, sorrow, and lament.

"Lastly," Lilline said, "and most tenuous, is that the image is not a portrait at all."

"Oh?" The GAM-OPs director raised an eyebrow.

Familiar with his idiosyncrasies, she knew the translation: he was pleased with her erudition. "Indeed, sir. Although the extent of that theory is best left to others like yourself, who are far more versed in First Galactic art history and its relations to the occult."

"Oh no, T8, not the occult." Lauden shook his head. "That's a categorical designation that is... how to put it?" A bone-white finger touched his chin. "Our crutch. A way of compensating for the lack of knowledge once accessible to those of an earlier, and arguably superior, galactic era."

"You really think the Darians had privileged understanding that we lack?"

"Most certainly." The Gej-ti rose and proceeded to a shelf of physical books behind his desk. A milky finger drew forth a tome. "It's here somewhere..." He flipped through the pages.

Lilline's eyes returned to the portrait. She homed in on the hand with the double pollex. It was odd that none of the present species, especially human variants, exhibited dual thumbs. Whatever evolutionary patterns had brought the rise and fall of civilizations down to the galactic present had bypassed that anatomical design.

She and everyone else in the Third Galactic knew nothing of Darian appearance other than assuming they were bipedal and similar to humanoids, if not actually humans, based on the portrait's veiled figure. All the famous works surrounding the *Cosmic Widow* in the museum were equally mysterious. Interpretations and histories had been constructed, but the fact was an entire age of galactic history had been built on scholarly conjecture.

"Here it is." Lauden rotated, book open to a specific page. "'Within the stars of time are two that open to one. And inside, a reflection of all. The Cosmic Widow, brought to life by Azaludarian, smiles, for the Darians will know the universe through her charms.'"

Lilline stared at the portrait. So much mystery and allure... Even if it was all a hoax, Azaludarian's painting had become a seductive serpent snaking across the sands of time.

Lauden's tall and lean form cast a brief shadow across the image as he sat back down.

"Sir, with respect, I must ask. Why are we so worried about the *Cosmic Widow* going missing? It's priceless, yes. And its precise meaning remains unknown. But you can't do much with a famous masterpiece other than unload it to a wealthy collector. And what else can they do but gloat over owning it in private? Isn't this case more suited for the—"

"The unknown," Lauden said, interrupting, "is a powerful weapon when wielded by a skilled hand. What has us worried here is something far more cryptic."

Us?

"There have been discoveries, T8... off limits to most except those at the highest security levels, of First Galactic relics exhibiting mysterious cosmic phenomena," Lauden said. "They fall outside our fragile scientific parameters and indicate a sophistication that is nothing other than..." The director's head swayed back and forth like a pendulum.

Lilline waited but he didn't continue.

He's troubled.

"Other than what, sir?"

"Terrifying." It came out as a whisper, as if carried on the wind.

Lilline focused on the *Cosmic Widow*. The hand in the portrait, with its double pollex, pulled her with a strange magnetism.

"For now," Lauden said, "locating the *Cosmic Widow* and ensuring its swift return to the Galactic Museum is our top priority."

Lilline scrutinized the Gej-ti's features. The nerves and muscles underneath his milky skin revealed nothing. The director had that familiar expression she knew too well. Pushing back about the relics would get her nowhere.

"Bilarus is doing all he can to stall for time," Lauden said. "He's working a restoration angle. Some nonsense about an urgent conservation issue. That assistant of his... her name eludes me."

"Renina Blackstone."

"That's it, the research fellow. Bilarus has concocted an excuse that she noticed a small section of the painting requiring immediate attention. Fresh eyes and all that nonsense." He waved his pipe in the air. "They're going to re-open the wing tomorrow but the *Cosmic Widow* will be off-view while a so-called minor restoration project is undertaken."

"Renina is aware of GAM-OPs?"

"No. Bilarus told her the Board wants to prepare for the press."

"How much time will that buy the museum?"

"A few days before the tourism board and other cultural organizations push back about impact on business and related commercial losses. Of more concern for us, T8, is the media. The last thing we need is the truth of it getting out. If that happens, the news that the *Cosmic Widow* was stolen will rocket across the stars. Our thief may vanish before the trail is found. Not to mention a PR nightmare would ensue."

The director was right about that.

"This is all quite disturbing." Lauden shook his head. "Outwardly, as far as anyone else but you, myself, and the Galactic Minister are concerned, this is a favor to an old friend."

The GM? A painting concerns the leader of the galactic government?

The director relit his pipe. Orange light from the burning tobacco illuminated his features, casting an eerie glow over his translucent face. The Gej-ti leaned back in his chair and gazed up at the ceiling.

Smoke rose in patient, elegant streams.

Lilline eased back into her seat in a parallel countermove. Here was the game. Her boss was exploiting the tension to purpose. To what end this time, she didn't know.

Her eyes went to the various shelves of ephemera on display in the armoire behind him. All spoke of a lifetime in the shadows protecting the galaxy, each a trophy of the personal sacrifices that were the cost of keeping billions safe.

The slow creaking of Lauden's chair swinging upright cut the silence.

"Your preliminary assessment, T8?"

Lilline took her time shifting her gaze to her boss. Lauden placed his elbows on the desk and clasped his milky fingers together at his chin. When their eyes met, the Gej-ti raised an eyebrow.

He's testing me.

She didn't have much. Granny Kissy had taught her that under these circumstances it was best to be candid. The worst thing was to embellish with half-baked theories. Lauden had spent ample time in the field as a GAM-OPs agent himself. His keen observation skills would see through the fragile boasting.

"T8?"

"Well, sir, it's a three-headed monster," Lilline said. "There's the theft of the *Cosmic Widow* at the heart of it. And then there's the calling card... which I find troubling."

"That damned clock?"

She nodded.

"Head of Tech gave me the gist. I can't say I understand it."

Lilline's agent eyes picked up the same irritation running through him that filled her veins. "And then there's the museum security system, sir."

"What about it?"

"Well for one, Pin suggests it isn't possible for the thief to perform the crime considering the physical layout of the galleries, not with the security hardware's spatial and timing parameters."

Skepticism rose like smoke on the Gej-ti's face.

"From a technical standpoint," she added.

"Well, whoever they are, they did."

"I know." Lilline shifted position in her chair. "I said the same thing, sir. But still, it troubles me."

"You believe there is some new technology at play?"

"Possibly." She wasn't ready to articulate a position on that one. "Something else is at work here. Something we aren't seeing."

Lauden agreed with a gesture of his pipe

"I would like to wait for Pin's crime scene report," Lilline said. "Once the tests come back and she has her analysis finalized, I think we'll gain some clarity."

"Very well. In the meantime, let's get things moving." Lauden swiped a hand over his desk. A blank holo-file manifested, glowing blue.

Lilline waited, the air between them crackling with an invisible energy.

"Operation Cosmic Widow."

SIX

"This one is going to challenge you, T8. You'll need to work outside your usual expertise."

Lilline stared through the blue holo-file. Crow's feet around the Gej-ti's eyes tensed as he drew on his pipe. She tracked the smoke as it spiraled upward like a seductive dancer, creating a second veil through which hid the director's inner thoughts.

As if sensing her close study, he continued.

"I'm assigning this mission to you for two reasons. First, you're our top agent and have the most field experience in clandestine operations. To pull this one off will require a delicate touch, especially in situations where art crosses with affluence."

A compliment? Lilline steeled herself for the counterpunch. A low blow was sure to follow in a one-two combination of praise and critique.

"Second, you're a poet." The Gej-ti raised an eyebrow. "At least an amateur one, as you remain unpublished."

There it is. Lilline didn't flinch. Like a gunslinger in a showdown, her gaze stayed locked on her boss. Loathe to admit it, another rejection loomed. The editors at the *Tavi-Prime Poetry Journal* had been notifying entrants who made their shortlist for the annual open-call all week. As soon as the clock struck midnight tonight that would make four cycles in a row not making the cut. "Time is short" was taking on a second, personal meaning.

Lilline fumed inside at his jab but kept her outward stare cool as ice.

"There's need for a delicate understanding of the power of art and aesthetics on this. Of a kind a bit—" Lauden pulled on his pipe, drawing in a strong hit of Yaz Flake. "—out-of-bounds."

She nodded ever-so-slightly. *If you only knew how often poetry is more powerful than a blaster.*

"What I'm saying, T8, is you may need to allow your creative faculties a measure of liberty to get the job done on this one. If, as I suspect, there is an intent to exploit whatever lies hidden in the *Cosmic Widow.*"

License to kill and *a license of freedom to my methods? What more could I ask for?*

The corner of her mouth rose and she smirked.

Lauden held up a hand as a gesture of clarification. "I am not referring to far-flung conspiracy theories and the supernatural. I'm speaking about approaches to interpretation and understanding of art, especially by a species that remains largely unknown to us from the perspective of the galactic historical record."

"Understood, sir." Lilline sat forward and touched a finger to the holo-screen, swiping the file. Her profile picture and mission objectives appeared in the virtual summary for Operation Cosmic Widow. She placed a palm on the outline next to her photo, initiating the GAM-OPs agent acceptance protocol. Along the bottom of the blue holo-field, red text displaying the mission status switched to green, the word *inactive* replaced by *active.*

"Which trail do I start with, sir?" Lilline leaned back and crossed her legs. "The theft or the painting's purpose?"

"The theft," Lauden said and sent smoke waves out of his neck gills. "Priority number one is to get the *Cosmic Widow* back in safe hands."

"Shall I conduct interviews at the museum?"

Lauden shook his head. Afternoon sunlight set the director's widow's peak afire.

Lilline tracked the Gej-ti's nerves underneath a layer of translucent skin. They fanned outward like a river delta on his forehead.

"A delicate relationship is at play here between the government and the museum. I will let you know if and when that position changes. Until then, work the theft angle from outside that institution. Is that clear?"

"Cryex crystal, sir."

Lilline found herself targeted by the stem of Lauden's pipe.

"Find this thief." The director emphasized each word as if firing shots from his smoker. "And hopefully we recover the painting before they use it to purpose or sell it to someone with plans to employ it to stars-knows what end."

"You can count on me, sir." Lilline nodded in earnest. "We'll get this done."

"In the meantime, archives will open a file on the *Cosmic Widow*. And I will go through my old university notes. Perhaps there's something pertinent to the case. Bilarus will help as well."

"I know you said to avoid an internal focus at the museum, sir, but is it a good idea to have Bilarus so closely involved?"

"I didn't ask for your opinion." Lauden closed the holo with a swipe of his hand. "Dismissed."

Fine.

Lilline rose and made for the portal. Not a moment too soon, either. The field beckoned, even if only as preliminary interrogations to what she hoped would be a straightforward and quick criminal investigation. Regardless, once she crossed the threshold out of Lauden's office, she was in charge. It was her op to run so long as she kept to herself and did her job... and didn't bother Reginald Bilarus.

Lilline stepped into a beam of sunlight streaming through the office window. Thin horizontal bands of tobacco smoke hung like ghostly rivers in the silent air.

"And T8..."

She halted. "Yes, sir?"

The Gej-ti tapped the bowl of his pipe on the edge of the ashtray and placed it in his custom Bartos marble stand.

"Deception isn't only a thief's game," he said. "Art is filled with both allusion and illusion."

SEVEN

There were Dari cakes and then there were Dari cakes from Malardi's.

As far as the Renaults were concerned, no pastry maker could compete with the bakery's mastery of the traditional delicacy. For three hundred cycles, the pink storefront with its ornamental white awning presided over Tavi-Central's shopping district like aristocracy, enduring and impervious to the whims of changing times.

And yet, across the street stood their longstanding and fiercest competition: Madame Enri's. Two rival pastry families had faced off against one another, neither willing to concede control of prime consumer real estate. It remained so for cycles, then decades, and now centuries. The Malardis and Enris existed in a perpetual culinary duel. Generations of chefs wielding ladles and mixing bowls vied for dominance and culinary glory. An age-old question had become standard fare in casual conversation: "Malardi's or Enri's?" For Lilline and Granny Kissy, and the Renaults that came before them, the answer was indisputable: Malardi's.

Lilline checked the time on her wrist comm and scurried down the sidewalk. Even now, in the late afternoon, the pastry shop's display window showed too much empty space.

She scanned the tiers of remaining pastries. Red sickleberry, white cream, the lavender hue of cresh fruit...

No sign of pink cakes.

If they ran out of Granny's favorite before she arrived...

An hour earlier, exiting the mirrored doors of Galaxy Unlimited, a text had pinged on her comm - Kissy, insisting that she join her for Dari cakes and afternoon tea. Lilline had done her best to decline, hoping to hit the mats with her training partner before dinner.

It's a sUrprise, deAr. (Or it waS... until you rUined it) I EXPECT YOU HERE!

That was that. Kissy had muted her comm after the brief exchange, ignoring all her additional voice texts. Why her ninety-plus cycle grandmother didn't use the audio transcriber like everyone else in the galaxy rather than typing by hand was itself evidence of how stubborn the former agent could be. Regardless, Granny had won. Again.

Lilline passed through the portal and into a world of sweet and fresh bready delights. Warm lingering traces of baked dough teased her nostrils and—

"Keely!"

Her grandmother waved from a circular table. Someone had joined her and sat with their back to the front of the shop.

Lilline scanned the target for an initial analysis: human - a woman with a cane and curly brown hair. How to describe the vibe of her outfit?

Dated.

"About time," Kissy said and dabbed her lips with a napkin.

Lilline followed Granny's gaze as it flashed towards the plate.

Cakes lay stacked in a variety of colors, none of them pink.

The predictable Kissy Renault stink eye followed, burning an invisible red juicier than her favorite missing pastry.

"Keely dear, you'll never believe who is here," Granny said and bobbed her head back and forth.

The mystery guest rotated in her chair.

"Oh, now look at you. All grown up. You were a meter high last I saw you... and precocious as ever."

Lilline examined the woman's face. Crow's feet creased the corners of her copper skin. Her green eyes were tired but strong. A round face with pointed chin and strongly arcing brow gave her an appearance like—

"Don't tell me you've forgotten who this is?" Kissy said, raising an eyebrow.

"Mirna?"

The woman smiled. "My, my, Keely." Mirna's head swiveled to Kissy. "She's a grown woman, isn't she?"

That awkward experience when adults talked about you in your presence rushed back. Lilline shrank, converting to a ten-cycle old little girl.

"You're blushing, dear," Granny said and reached for a Dari cake. "Sit and join us."

"Imani tells me you're an adventure guide now?"

"That's right." Lilline sat. Living under their cover names, Keely and Imani Larkin, had become second nature. To everyone outside of work, they *were* the Larkins. "Mirna, it's wonderful to see you," Lilline said. "How long has it been?"

"Twenty-six cycles."

A tinge of sadness rose in the woman's eyes. Now she remembered. Her husband, Simuel, had been let go from one of the major universities on Tavi-Prime and they had moved to a less populated star system.

"You probably don't remember dear, but we bid Mirna and

Simuel farewell at the jump station for the ride to Elaris... along with your mother."

A flood of memories rushed back. Her mother's protective grip as they navigated the crowds on the orbit station. Waving goodbye to a younger Mirna and Simuel as they boarded their ship. And a view of space from orbit, her first. They had followed the Star Cruiser from the observation deck as it made its way across the system for the jump to FTL. She'd stood transfixed, tiny fingers clasping the newly gifted Venex Horse as the ship flashed out of existence, shattering the space-time continuum.

"I do remember." Lilline smiled. "Such a long trip back here to Tavi-Prime. What brings you to the big city-planet?"

"It was time to—"

"Excuse me for interrupting."

A pudgy translucent hand holding a stack of pink Dari cakes broke into view.

"Oh, Vincenti you are pure starlight!" Granny's clapping hands appeared as the Gej-ti pastry chef placed the tray down on the table. Three rosy cakes lay stacked in a pyramid surrounded by ornamental white icing.

"Only for you, Ms. Larkin. My favorite customer." The chef smiled and wiped his large hands on the apron covering his belly.

Granny's head bobbed back and forth with newfound delight.

Vincenti glanced back towards the counter. "I retreat with haste before Grelda spots me." The chef leaned down to Kissy's ear. "I pulled these from a special order going out this afternoon." His cherub-like cheek, intersected by a thick black mustache, shifted and he winked at Lilline. "Good to see you, my dear."

"You too, Vincenti. And thank you." *You saved me days of dramatic lament.*

"I take my leave." The Gej-ti bowed and scurried off towards the counter.

Granny picked up a cake and took a bite, a wide grin breaking across her wrinkled skin.

The galaxy will know peace once more.

"Mirna is here to donate some objects to the museum," Granny said, chewing with delight.

"*And* to visit with old friends," Mirna added, smiling at Kissy. "But yes, I've brought back several objects from our digs. The museum is interested in them and..."

Mirna's expression shifted, tinged with sadness. "I can't have them around anymore."

Kissy patted her old friend's hand.

Now she remembered. Granny mentioned that Simuel had passed a few cycles ago.

"They paid me a good price for them," Mirna said. "At least I know they're safe inside those walls."

Lilline kept the irony of the comment to herself.

"Speaking of which," Kissy said. "Mirna was saying that the museum moved a painting in the First Galactic gallery."

"Did they?" With her attention on the crime scene that morning, she hadn't noticed.

"I noticed the Venex Horse is still missing." Mirna placed a comforting hand on her shoulder. "I am so sorry about that, Keely."

"Thanks, Mirna." Lilline took a cake and bit into it.

"I remember when your mother found that." The woman's eyes brightened. "What a momentous discovery."

"It was so kind of Simuel to offer it to her," Granny added.

"And even more gracious of you and your grandmother to donate it to the museum after... well, you know."

Memories of better times lurked underneath a difficult present in both women's eyes. Mirna's from the loss of a husband and Granny's, a daughter.

"What about that horn, Mirna?" Kissy asked. "The one with the fabulous engravings. Did you donate that, too?"

"The Rhyton?"

Kissy nodded.

Lilline's archaeological knowledge rose out of a forgotten past.

Rhyton. A word from her days at the university. A ritual object, usually a horn, used to filter and ceremoniously pour wine or other liquid.

"Yes," Mirna said, "I donated that one as well."

"I remember all of them, you know," Kissy said. "Keely's mother used to tell us stories at the dinner table late into the night, describing what you and Simuel had in your collection." She lifted her cup and saucer. "Such amazing discoveries."

"Yes, well…" Mirna's words trailed off.

"How long are you staying?" Lilline asked. "It would be great to have you over for dinner."

Granny's eyes lit up.

"My outbound flight leaves in the morning."

"So soon?" Kissy pouted. "Can't you stay any longer?"

"I'm not cut out for big city-planets. Tavi-Prime is far too overwhelming for me. And all the walking…" Mirna nodded at her cane. "Plus, I need to get back to my garden."

"Keely, I don't know if you remember. Our visit was so long ago, but they have the most stunning varieties of—" Kissy caught herself. "Sorry, dear." She gestured an apology to Mirna. "Are you still keeping up the flowers?"

Mirna nodded. "It's taken a toll on my hips, but yes. Nothing like what it was when Simuel was alive, but I keep a modest version going. The climate on Elaris is ideal, with an extended summer season and low humidity, and the cottage and property are quite peaceful."

"Don't you get lonely, dear?" Kissy asked.

"My friends are growing in my garden."

"Please tell me you've not become one of those people who talk to their plants?" Granny sipped her tea.

Mirna laughed and shook her head. "I'm not that far gone yet."

"Well, we certainly are lucky we've got each other, aren't we dear?"

Granny's withered fingers came to rest on her own.

Lilline made a face at Mirna.

"What?" Kissy eyed her, pulling back. "I saw that look!"

"Yes, Granny. I'm the luckiest granddaughter in the galaxy."

"Now if you would find yourself a partner." Kissy bobbed her head. "Mirna, there was this handsome bartender at Tavi-Central that I—"

"Granny!"

"Well, perhaps we could visit you some time, Mirna." Kissy's eyes shot their signature, invisible guilt-laden energy in her direction.

A three-day FTL trip with her grandmother? She'd rather endure a forced expedition with Lauden through a remote planetary rainforest than deal with that kind of confined torture.

"Speaking of travel." Mirna pulled out a burner-comm. "I need to confirm my return hop up to the jump port."

Lilline watched as the woman attempted to navigate through the screen and pull up her flight info.

"Oh, these things are so—"

"Tell me about it," Kissy said, lifting her cake and taking a bite. "These younger generations with their technology." She shook her head.

"Mirna isn't old, Granny."

"I might not be your grandmother's age, but I'm still clueless with all this technological stuff." The woman shook her head struggling to enter data on the burner-comm.

"Would you like my help?" Lilline reached out a hand. She took the device and confirmed the jump flight for tomorrow from Tavi-Central Station. "You're all set. 11:30 in the morning. Make sure to arrive an hour before departure. That way you won't be rushed."

"Thank you, Keely."

"Would you like me to go with you and see you off?" Kissy asked. "I've nothing to do."

"I'm fine, thank you. You are a dear for offering."

Opportunity knocked, like a poem's last lines approaching. "Well,

I should probably get going," Lilline said. "I'm sure you two have more to talk about and I do need to be somewhere."

"Oh?" Granny raised an eyebrow.

"Yes. And I need to stop home first and change clothes." Lilline stood. "Mirna, it's wonderful to see you again. I'm sorry to hear about Simuel."

"Thank you. Likewise." Mirna's face widened in a smile. "And so grown up." Her hand went to her cane.

"Oh no, please. Stay seated." Lilline stepped around, leaned down, and gave her a hug. "Have a safe return jump." At the edge of her vision, the glint of a tear welled in Granny's eye. "And maybe we can talk about coming to visit you."

Kissy eyes brightened. She clapped her hands with glee.

Why do I do this to myself?

"Don't wait up for me, Granny, I'll be late tonight."

"Oh?"

"Yes, and please remember to feed Hiko."

Granny waved a hand as if she didn't need the reminder. She did.

"Off to some nice restaurant and the theater?" Kissy raised an eyebrow.

"I'm going clubbing, if you must know."

"Well in that case, stay out and enjoy yourself with your companion, dear."

"It's not a date, Granny."

Kissy waved a dismissive hand and winked at Mirna. "Your secret is safe with us."

Lilline snatched up Granny's pink cake and stuffed it in her mouth.

"Why you!" Kissy's jaw dropped.

Lilline winked at Mirna, patted Granny on the shoulder, and took her leave.

There were grandmothers and then there were grandmothers like Kissy Renault.

EIGHT

Post-Industrial Quarter | Planet: Tavi-Prime | Star System: Pesari-9 | Inner Core

"Right here is fine." Lilline swiped her transport card.

The AI-driver eased the personal shuttle to a halt.

"Thank you for using AI-Chauffer. Please exit within thirty seconds, my wondrous passenger."

Lilline mouthed the last phrase with the AI and slid over to the wing-door. The blarney tagline never failed to amuse. Through the tinted window, raucous East Enders in trendy fashions clashed with the grimy, oil-colored buildings of Tavi-Central's industrial district. A mix of species, the clubbers shouted and laughed their way towards the sim-bars and augmented reality dance halls, charged with pre-nightlife energy.

Lilline stepped down to the curb and pulled out her face mirror. The aggressively applied cobalt blush that ran from the bridge of her nose across one cheek had fixed as she'd hoped. Its edges near her missing ear streaked like an abstract painter's brushstroke. She'd balanced the bold cosmetic with an elegant touch of black eyeliner and hot pink eyeshadow on her opposite eye. The color combination returned on her lips, applied in reverse. This was *the* new look on Tavi-Prime, having dropped only days prior on the runaway for Vixen's new seasonal line. She'd paid a hefty sum to attend the exclusive event, mingling with stylish trendsetters, but it had paid off. Vixen's local manager in West End replicated the makeup pattern for her days ahead of it hitting the fashion-streams.

Lilline had gone all-in at the stylish boutique. She'd walked out with a far more expensive purchase than cosmetics: the silver form-fitting body suit worn by the model on the hover runway. With its thin diagonal slit across the chest and tight-neck collar, the look screamed style so loudly it cut through the club music echoing down the street. Her physique gave the outfit a novel touch. Toned, and tough, with scars from mishaps on past ops visible on her arms, her combative aura combined with the outfit's refined elegance was like pairing a subtle white wine with a fiery curry. The balance leaned aggressive; asymmetry was her language and given the choice she always tipped the scales towards strength over subtlety.

Lilline flipped the makeup case shut and examined the final ingredient in her sartorial recipe. A pair of white vinyl boots rose to her knees, their sheen surface reflecting the multi-color lights of a nearby street bar. Smitten? That was an understatement. The heels had altitude *and* attitude, the latter more than a mob boss showing up to a sitdown.

"Looking for some Gesh?"

"I'm good," Lilline said.

"Kash-ke, the best. Will keep you running all night... send you to the stars."

"I don't doubt it." She knew this Goosh dealer. He'd been working the street for a few cycles now.

"Anything running in the alleyways?" She pulled a credit chip from her purse and held it between two fingers at her side. The gentle brush of a hairy tentacle retrieved it with the skill of a master pickpocket.

"Trouble with the Zapper gang a few weeks ago. Made a mess inside the Blue Comet."

"Heard about that."

"Not that you have to worry about it."

Lilline cocked her head towards the orange terrestrial cephalopod, making eye contact with the horizontal black bar across their bulbous head that served as a vision field. "You're well informed."

"No one dresses quite like you."

That drew a smile. "Stay safe," she said. "And do yourself a favor and get a legal job."

The signature whine Goosh made when finishing a conversation cut into the shouts of the nearby crowds.

Lilline joined the stream of clubbers heading east. Two blocks deeper into the industrial sector and the unmistakable cerulean glow of the Blue Comet's entrance cast a gritty radiance over the street. A dense line of clubbers ran along the building to the corner and around it, red lasers forming the street-side boundary of the queue.

"Evening, Ms. Larkin."

"Quite the night, Rex." Lilline smiled at the Kreeli who towered over the waiting crowd.

His massive blue hand deactivated the laser blocking the VIP entrance.

"Hey! Why does she get in?"

"Because I said so." Rex bared sharpened gold-plated teeth at the clubber.

The Rasp's eye went wide.

"Problem with that?" The bouncer's deep voice bellowed, cutting into the thumping beats inside club.

A clay-colored head shook like it was being jolted by an electric shock.

"Didn't think so," Rex said. "Maybe I should send you to the back of the line?"

"No, I'm cool."

The Rasp's human companion backed him up, adding a charming smile.

With his signature mirrored glasses, black suit barely containing his bulging muscles, and glittering barometric headband, Rex made for a fashionable and intimidating sight. Those lenses did more than make the Kreeli look chic. Lilline recognized them as standard security fare, scanning for hidden weapons and other potentially dangerous items.

The bouncer leaned down close. "Thanks again for helping me out with the Zappers."

"Anytime," Lilline said. "I'm always up for a nightcap after clubbing."

The Kreeli grinned, exposing razor-sharp teeth. "Adventure company guide, indeed."

She winked.

"VIP coming through." Rex nodded to a host in the club's entrance. "Everything on the house."

NINE

Thumping. Flashing. Sweat and stale booze. The Blue Comet was alive with clubbing energy.

Glitching smoke and flashing dance lights bombarded Lilline's vision inside the packed dance hall. Her agent eyes worked overtime performing an initial scan. Familiar with the exits, she marked the current position of club security as well as two potential individuals at the bar who made her "raised risk" list. In short, a normal night at the Blue Comet.

Avoiding the crowded dance floor, she steered right of a DJ platform hovering twenty meters over the heads of revelers and made for the bar. Professional objectives took priority, but that didn't mean she had to abstain from the club's offerings.

"Highball," she said to the Goosh bartender and placed her bag on the bar. The cephalopod started her cocktail with two tentacles while it worked another order with its opposite appendages.

Gondau, the best red wine in the galaxy, would always be her drink of choice... *if* it was pre-Roncheau. But that elegant elixir was out of place at the Blue Comet. Gondau required quieter settings, like the terrace at the Golden Pheasant on Tavi's moon, Beisho, and needed to be sipped and relished. Cocktails were ideal for clubs and pre-dinner social events. Complex, they held a unique flexibility. Sipped if you needed to extend a flirtation or an engaging conversation, or knocked back if the itch to get on the dance floor or head to the next destination usurped other priorities.

"Highball." A hairy orange tentacle placed the tall and narrow glass on the bar. "On the house." The Goosh's signature whine cut through the raucous chatter as its appendage spiraled off to another customer.

"Keely?" a voice shouted over the music.

Lilline picked up her drink and turned. "Georgette." She leaned in and kissed the Gej-ti's cheek.

"Stars, you look fabulous! Is that Vixen?" The sous chef from Aesté, her favorite local eatery, ran her eyes up and down the outfit while bouncing to the music.

Lilline raised her cocktail in acknowledgement.

Georgette made as if screaming and gestured with both arms. Her eyes went wide when she noticed the boots.

"I know, right?" Lilline held out a leg in display.

"You alone? Want to join us?" Georgette pointed a milky-skinned finger towards a raised lounge area. A group of well-dressed clubbers sat drinking and laughing.

"Thanks, but I've got an AR-meetup." She nodded in the direction of the sim-bar, Retrograde, at the back of the club.

"Too bad they won't get to see you in that outfit," Georgette shouted and picked up two drinks from the bar. "Good luck. Hope they're interesting. Been all pervs lately for me."

"We'll see… you never know, right?"

"If it goes sour and you want to hang, we're over there," the Gej-ti nodded towards her friends.

Lilline raised her glass in thanks. She tracked Georgette as the Gej-ti snaked her way back to the lounge. The sous chef vanished in the flashing crowds.

Lilline checked the time. With one gulp, she knocked back the highball.

Pushing her way through a variety of tall, short, furry, scaly, and human-skinned bodies, she negotiated her way to a row of translucent yellow panes running across the Blue Comet's back wall. Shadowy silhouettes came and went behind the barrier leading to Retrograde. Like immaterial specters, clients headed to meet-ups with one or more parties for anonymous encounters.

The augmented reality scene had taken the Inner Core by storm a few cycles back. A gaming company had branched out, transcribing its imaging technology into a communication package. Of course, the consumer potential skyrocketed. The idea of meeting people without exposing who you were, choosing your appearance from a variety of customizable AR options, and revealing your inner desires, wants, and needs *in person* had potential for therapeutic practices but quickly evolved into a delicious and irresistible social perversion. Often, it involved voyeuristic and psychologically-enhanced sexual pleasures carried out in the presence of others, without physical contact - self-gratification as both voyeur and object of another's gaze through a strange mix of real and virtual encounters. One more step into the world of neuro-sensory stimulation. Lilline wasn't a huge fan, but she respected and understood the appeal. She still preferred her pleasures haptic. It was the same with the job. No doubt, you needed hackers behind a technological smokescreen to get a mission done, but when it came down to it, at some point you still had to pull a trigger and let blood flow.

"11:45," she said to a Rasp at the entrance. "Keely Larkin."

"You have a match?"

She nodded.

"Looking for more to join?"

"No."

The Rasp's head swiveled to an adjacent holo-screen. One of his three fingers swiped a page and tapped a series of icons.

"You know it costs extra for total encryption?"

"Yes," she shouted over the music.

"Your match is already inside."

Good. The sooner this was over the better.

"Booth 8," the Rasp said.

She smiled at hearing her agent number.

"What?"

"Nothing," she said, swinging her hips to the music. "Excited. Feeling good is all."

The Rasp's single eye flashed with reflected light from the nearby dance floor. Completely disinterested. Just another night at work.

Clay-skinned fingers handed her a passcode.

Lilline climbed the steps and entered through the portal. The Blue Comet's cacophony and energy dialed down as she walked the narrow passageway past rows of numbered chambers. Her nose scrunched in response to the odor. Clubs always had a distinct smell. How to describe it? Stale drink mixed with sweat. Tonight, there was more sweat than staleness. As usual in the augmented reality section, the olfactory cocktail was garnished with a sprig of illegal substances, specifically Gesh. When you popped the vial, it exuded a distinctive aroma that lingered: a potent mix of vinegar and citrus. That suited her fine tonight. The more loaded everyone was the less memory of her presence.

Her fingers tapped the entry code on Booth 8. With a *whoosh* the portal dematerialized. She stepped inside and took a pair of wrap-around glasses off the wall. Before donning the eyewear, she got comfortable on the plush red couch facing the plasma shield. Even without the AR system running, the hairs on the back of her neck rose, instinct making her aware of another presence opposite the glimmering and impenetrable barrier.

Lilline donned the glasses.

"Activate," she said and pressed the button on the side of the lens.

The plasma shield went transparent. Sitting across from her on the exact same couch, in the exact same room, as if in a mirror reality, was the galactic minister.

TEN

"Minister Un?" Lilline straightened her posture.

The galactic minister bellowed a deep laugh. "You should see your face!" The AR version of Felina Un, leader of the galactic government, pointed a blue finger and shook her oblong head.

"I swear, you have to stop doing that." Butterflies fluttered in her stomach from the adrenaline rushing through her veins. Lilline settled back into the sofa, working to calm her racing heart. "That's not funny."

"Oh, I assure you it is," the AR version of the galactic minister said.

"Let me guess, you hacked Retrograde?"

The AR Kreeli's arms went wide. "Judging by your reaction, my avatar disguise is pretty convincing." She pointed up at her headband. "Check this out."

Light danced across her metallic headband as the barometric pressure adjusted.

"I'm impressed," Lilline said. "Only because I know you're good enough to keep your intrusion secure."

"My ass is as much on the line as yours when we do this."

Lilline hoped so, otherwise they would both have to answer to serious accusations. Part of her thought Lauden and the top execs at the Ministry knew these kinds of things went on. All GAM-OPs agents had private networks and self-recruited assets. Many of them were shadier than a solar eclipse. Lilline guessed the higher-ups knew better than to ask questions. So long as they got answers and their agents got the job done, the means mattered not.

"I see you chose your usual boring avatar."

"I prefer to be forgettable," Lilline said. To the eyes of the anonymous asset across from her, she appeared as a thirty-something standard human woman dressed for the office. The tactic exploited similarity to promote assumption of difference. Did it work? She had no idea. Considering her contact hacked into Retrograde and uploaded a convincing avatar, she guessed they could infiltrate high-security government servers. Mostly likely, they knew her T#. Maybe even her real name.

The asset checked the time on the digi-clock and edged up on the sofa. "So, what's up?"

"Ever notice something on a budget line having to do with art?" Lilline focused on the Kreeli's expression. There was no way to know if their facial gestures were accurate to non-AR reactions. Her guess was they weren't. Probably they had programed the avatar to read and convert them into alternatives that redirected body language. She had no clue of her contact's identity, only that they worked at a central bank overseeing the Ministry's shadow finances. Transactions covering all sorts of dubious activities passed through their office, needing approval from who-knows-who before being laundered. Sometimes the money went to a member of Parliament on an off-the-record diplomatic assignment. Other times it was hush money or blackmail, and strategic funding for a special forces op or the backing of a coup in an unstable star system.

"Art you say? This is far more interesting than our usual fare."

Lilline kept silent.

"I can't think of anything, no."

It was a long shot, but worth asking.

"Nothing related to the arts or cultural institutions? Galleries? Art dealers?"

The GM shook her head.

"If you spot anything let me know." Lilline stood. "I'll exit first. You can—"

"Wait a minute." The Kreeli held up a hand. "There was one thing..."

Lilline sat back down.

"I've seen a name on a budget file," they said, "but it never passed over my desk."

"I'll take whatever you have."

The minister bobbed her oblong head back and forth.

"What's the matter?"

"This might land me in deep trouble."

"You're the galactic minister," Lilline said playing for charm and wit. "You can't get in trouble. Just pardon yourself if you get caught."

The asset laughed. "Alright. If I remember correctly, the file had a record of payments... substantial amounts."

"To?"

"Someone known as The Forger."

Interesting.

"The account had a 32 designation."

"What's that?"

"It's a prefix used to indicate credits filtered through a secondary financial institution."

"Which bank?"

Thick blue fingers formed a steeple under her contact's chin. "Be careful with this."

"Have I ever not?"

Her asset's oblong head nodded affirmation.

Lilline edged up on the sofa.

"Beisho Trust."

Someone had a good deal of money and influence. Beisho Trust was a quiet financial institution on Tavi-Prime's moon, catering to elite clients willing to pay exorbitant credit fees to have their identities safeguarded.

"Every 32 designation sequence contains an encrypted digital chain," the GM said. "It's a jumble of numbers, but within the full forty-six account code you'll locate the routing number of the end-line institution."

"So, the final payment destination is an anagram of twelve numbers scattered within a forty-six numerical sequence?"

The GM nodded. "And there's more. Beisho Trust uses a self-invented nineteen-digit numeric system. Rumor has it they modeled it off the Coleopterian body part counting system."

They took client security seriously, that was for sure. Good thing GAM-OPs did too. Lilline knew who to give this to at the agency.

"Thanks," she said and stood.

"Hold on. That isn't why I recalled it."

Lilline sat back down.

"It was the other side of the credit trail."

"Who made the front-end deposits?"

"The Galactic Museum."

Even more interesting. "Minister Un, you have secured my vote in the next election." Lilline blew a kiss.

"Hah!" the Kreeli bellowed. The GM pointed a finger in earnest. "Be discreet."

"Always." Lilline winked.

No response.

"Oh, you probably winked, right?"

Damn these AR glasses.

She checked the time. The urgency to leave rose like an unexpected tide. The faster dangerous work got done the better.

"When we retire, let's have dinner. Masks off," Lilline said.

"If we live that long."

The retort hit like an arrow to the heart. The odds were better for someone in the Ministry's covert banking office than a GAM-OPs field operative, but playing with intel was always a roll of the dice. Share the wrong piece of information with the wrong person or have it do more than help an adjacent operation, and you risked everything. Maintaining secrecy and security had a price tag far higher than individual life.

"I'll exit first," Lilline said. "Thanks, Minister. I owe you."

ELEVEN

Finally, a lead. A complicated one with the museum's mention, but a lead, nevertheless.

Lilline pushed through the club's dense crowd, a new swagger to her step. She eyed an open space at the bar.

Why not?

A highball before heading home. Georgette and her friends were still at a table across the dance floor. They looked to be having a good time. She'd join them. One drink and then—

Her agent instinct kicked in. Without adjusting her stride, she scanned her visual field.

Renina?

Near the club's entrance, Renina Blackstone stood speaking with a Gej-ti woman.

Lilline slowed her steps but continued toward the bar. She settled in and observed the curator from the corner of her eye. So, Renina liked to party? And, from the way the two were close-talking romance might be on the menu.

"I'll be right with you," the Goosh bartender said, its tentacles shaking and pouring drinks.

In the seconds Lilline glanced away and back again, Renina's expression had shifted. No more smile. Now, her features expressed concern.

Lilline checked the Gej-ti. Tough. Rough around the edges, dressed in a hip, almost militant clubbing outfit.

A milky skinned, tattooed arm grabbed Renina's wrist. The Gej-ti said something through gritted teeth. Lilline read the curator's face. It spoke volumes over the flashing and thumping inside the club.

Lilline was down the bar and behind the Gej-ti in seconds.

"Renina, right?" she yelled over the music. The Gej-ti released the Rasp's wrist.

"Blast off, mate," the woman said, turning.

"It's Caroline." Lilline ignored the slight and peered past the woman. "From the museum."

The curator nodded and rubbed her wrist.

"I said, blast off."

Lilline eyed the Gej-ti. Tell-tale zig-zag laser tattoos edged out under her rolled sleeves. A Zapper. These punks had their hands in everything from drugs to loan sharking, and smuggling.

"You always flirt through threats?" Lilline stepped closer. She had about eight centimeters on the woman. Another win for the boots. Height didn't matter; her attitude was dialed up to eleven. It said, *You want to go a round? You better be able to go all twelve.*

"This is none of your business, mate," the Gej-ti said. The woman stepped closer and peered up.

"It's my business now." Lilline burned her gaze like a laser into the woman's black eyes. "Time to leave, Zapper. Use your legs. Unless you prefer I break them and carry you out." She smiled her best "fuck you" smile.

"You'll regret this mate," the Gej-ti said and cracked her knuckles.

Security down the bar edged into her peripheral vision.

"I don't think so, *mate,*" Lilline said. "I'd ask your gang pals before you start trouble with the wrong person."

"What the stars does that mean?"

"Everything okay here?" a deep voice said.

Lilline kept her eyes locked on the Gej-ti as a Kreeli bouncer intervened.

"That's up to her," she said, and nodded her chin at the Gej-ti. "This one likes to rough-handle your customers."

"Hey, I know you," the bouncer said.

Lilline raised an eyebrow at the remark, gaze fixed on the Zapper. "Yeah, it's me."

"Let's go, you," the Kreeli said.

A thick blue hand took hold of the Gej-ti and dragged her away.

The Zapper twisted her head and mouthed the words, *You're dead.*

Lilline flipped her the bird. "Are you alright, Renina?"

The curator nodded and ran jittering hands over her face.

"You club much?"

The Rasp shook her head.

"Well, that's a Zapper. Local street gang. Steer clear. If you like strong types, there's plenty more fish in the sea."

Renina smiled nervously.

Good. Levity always helped after a fright.

"Thank you," the curator said.

"Don't mention it. Honestly, it's not that uncommon." Lilline put a hand on her arm. "My advice? Try and come to the clubs with two or three friends. Strength in numbers, you know?"

Renina nodded. "But you're alone?"

Touché. "My friends are over there." She pointed at Georgette and her crew. "Come on," Lilline tugged her along and made for the exit.

Outside, with the noise level lowered, she got a better look at the Rasp. Well dressed, albeit a bit conservative for the locale.

"You want to walk?" Lilline asked. "I was going to take an AI-Chauffeur back to Tavi-Central but I'm happy to stroll."

"No. Thank you again..." Renina eyed her, confused.

"Caroline."

"Right, sorry."

"No worries," Lilline said. Apparently, Renina didn't get out much.

"I have a taxi scheduled," the curator said. "Maybe I can bump it up." She fiddled with her wrist comm.

"Hey Rex," Lilline shouted. "You have any taxis on hold?"

The Kreeli, sunglasses reflecting the urban vista, put two fingers in his mouth and whistled.

"She had a bit of scare in there," Lilline said.

"You're good now, miss," Rex told Renina. "Couldn't be in better hands with this one watching out for you."

A thick hand patted Lilline's shoulder.

"In you go." Rex opened the shuttle door.

"Thank you," the curator said. "I need to be more careful. I'm still adjusting from life on Ornal."

I'd say. That peaceful Inner Core planet was a far cry from the urban hustle of Tavi-Prime.

"So much for starting my new life in the big city, right?" Renina said.

"Everyone new to Tavi gets a free pass. This one's our secret." Lilline winked.

The shuttle fired up and glided off down the street.

"Thanks Rex."

"You sure you don't want a job?" The Kreeli grinned.

"This scene is too much adventure for me." She gestured at the crowd the bouncer was managing. "I'm going to bed." Jumping into an AI-Chauffeur wasn't going to drain the untapped energy from the incident inside the club. She needed to walk.

The clusters of revelers on the streets thinned as the club area was left behind. A few more blocks and the Industrial District would shift to mid-income housing. From there it was another ten minutes to City-Central. At this point, she might walk as far as—

Tiny neck hairs prickled her collar.

Lilline kept her strides at an even pace and popped open her makeup mirror. A hand ran through her hair to finish the ruse.

Well, well, well.

The Zapper from the club was tailing her. Three figures a block ahead leaned against the wall looking as suspicious as teenage rookies - two Gej-ti's and a Kreeli.

So, it was payback time.

Lilline ducked into an approaching alleyway. She reached down and pulled the strap inside each of her boots. The heels collapsed and flat pavement connected with her soles. She tossed her bag behind a trash bin and stood in the center of the alley.

"I'm gonna bitch you up," the Gej-ti said, rounding the corner. Behind her three shadowy figures followed.

"Never heard that one before," Lilline said. "I like it." She bent her legs and placed her arms, wrists bent and hands like blades, in a tiered formation - *Twin Vipers in Tall Grass.*

"Yo, it's her!" the Kreeli said and took a step back.

"Stars, you're right!" Another thug stumbled back and raised their hands in a gesture of submission.

"Heck no!" The third companion grabbed the Gej-ti leader's arm and tried to pull her back towards the corner.

"Get off of me." The Zapper yanked the arm away.

"That's her, Gina. The one from the Blue Comet," the Kreeli said.

"Yeah, idiot. I know. And we're gonna—"

"No, from last time!"

Lilline motioned with a hand, inviting Gina to engage.

"Oh..."

Three shadowy gangsters vanished around the corner. Shouts urging their companion to follow bounced down the alley.

Lilline smiled. "Just you and me now... *mate.*"

"I... um..." Gina took a step back.

"Not going to bitch me up?"

The Zapper turned to flee.

"Not so fast!" In one fluid motion, Lilline's fingers withdrew the dart from her boot and flung it underhanded.

"Arrgh!"

Gina dropped to her knees, hands flailing for her calf.

"Neuromuscular incapacitation is a bitch." Lilline strode up to her.

Teeth clenched and muscles spasming, the Zapper could only grunt.

"I'd say that's enough for today's lesson." Lilline yanked out the taser dart.

Gina toppled forward, smacking the pavement.

"Going to be about fifteen minutes and then you'll be able to walk. Use the time to think about how you treat other people." Lilline slipped the dart back into the boot's hidden sheath. "Now, let's see." She scanned the alley. "Oh, yes. I've got the perfect spot for you, Gina. You'll feel right at home."

Lilline hoisted her over a shoulder and tossed her in the trash.

Crunches echoed inside the bin. "Soft landing. You got lucky tonight. Oof!" Lilline pinched her nose. "Is that rotten fish?"

A grunt from inside the container.

"If you pull anything like that again... *mate.*" She checked her hand. Damn Zapper made her break a nail. "I will bitch you up for real."

Lilline retrieved her bag and made her way back to the street. She tapped the call request on her wrist comm.

"This is your AI-Chauffeur."

"One wondrous passenger ready for pickup."

TWELVE

East End Residential District | Planet: Tavi-Prime | Star System: Pesari-9 | Inner Core

---

Living with Kissy Renault was a never-ending series of surprises. Every day the story unfolded in ways impossible to imagine. As it turned out, this morning's opening line was a real zinger.

"Granny, are you okay?" Lilline shifted up in bed so her back rested against the headboard. Hiko approached from his spot alongside her thigh and purred, demanding attention.

"Everything's fine!"

Granny's high-pitched voice echoed from below. Lilline positioned it at the boundary between the kitchen and living room.

"No need to concern you, dear."

What sounded like broken shards being swept across the floor bounced off the bedroom ceiling.

"Did you break something?" She reached past Hiko to the nightstand, grabbing hold of her wrist comm, and checked the time. Almost 10:00 a.m. She'd slept late. "I'm sorry, baby. Mama's gotta get up." Hiko's chin received a few loving scratches and she slid out of bed.

"You're not answering me," Lilline said as her feet settled into plush carpeting.

"It's nothing, dear. Would you like tea?"

"Granny..." She threw on pajama pants and a tank-top, "We've been living together for how long?"

"Yes... yes..."

The sound of broken shards dropping into the disposal unit followed.

"You drink that vulgar sludge. Really, Lilli, the stuff is like oil."

"It's called coffee, Granny."

Lilline checked her Inbox. Nothing yet from Pin regarding the bank account lead. After returning home at midnight, she'd sent off a request for the Oltari to attempt to hack the Beisho Trust financial database. If she could, maybe it would yield something on The Forger angle. As for the Galactic Museum, that was more complicated, Bilarus being an old friend of Lauden's, she needed more time to think about how to approach that one. Perhaps the curator wasn't involved - merely a bystander to another employee or Board member up to no good. Until she knew more, that one was staying close to her chest.

And as for the other long-awaited message...

Whatever. Move on.

She descended the spiraling stairs with Hiko at her heels.

Kissy swung around from the disposal unit at the kitchen counter. Damn but the woman was still fast.

Her grandmother returned a rogue strand of hair to her bun and straightened her suit. As usual, Kissy was dressed as if heading to the office. In reality, the retired GAM-OPs agent had nowhere to go and nothing to do. That was a recipe for danger *and* disaster.

But Kissy wasn't the only spy in the family.

"What's this?" Lilline leaned down and picked up a tiny fragment of blue glass. "Is this..." She eyed her grandmother. "Was this my serving dish from Tatiana?"

"Accidents happen, dear." Granny swished past her and sat at the kitchen table. "I don't want to talk about it." She lifted her cup and saucer and took a sip of tea.

Lilline hit the switch for coffee on the counter dispenser. In the corner of her eye, a faint streak smeared the polished tile floor. "Practicing again?" She locked eyes with her grandmother and gulped coffee.

"If you must know, these shoes are new. The soles are thicker than my usual brand." She raised her chin in defiance. "My roundhouse kick is fine. I need to adjust for the extra two or three centimeters."

I swear... I should give up poetry and become a novelist. The Life and Times of Retired Agent, Kissy Renault.

Lilline joined her and plunked a leg up on a neighboring chair.

"Well?" Granny set down her tea.

"Well what?"

"How was your date?"

"I told you it wasn't a date. Believe it or not, I do work, remember? I'm the *active* secret agent." Lilline's eyes went to the computer terminal at the far end of the living room. She needed to get online but dreaded another check of her Inbox.

Nothing had arrived before the midnight deadline regarding her submission to the *Tavi-Prime Poetry Journal*. Radio silence meant another rejection. Par for the course. Add another notch to the ever-growing suit of amateur armor.

She kept her disappointment hidden behind a well-honed agent exterior and sipped her coffee. At least that always satisfied. A moment's peace, if such a thing was possible with Granny, and she'd work through the blow to her literary confidence.

"Oh, by the way. This came for you." Kissy indicated a white envelope on the table.

"Really?" She reached for it but stopped centimeters short of picking it up. "Did you run it through the scanner?"

"I'm not senile, dear."

Lilline stared at the envelope.

"Well, go on. It's not going to bite."

An odd expression filled her grandmother's face. Lilline slid the envelope across the table and flipped it over.

Her eyes went wide.

"I've been waiting for you to get up all morning."

Granny continued speaking but her attention was fixed on the return address:

> *Eris Tanaza, Editor-in-Chief*
> *Tavi-Prime Poetry Journal*
> *Center for Galactic Literary Art & Culture*
> *University of Tavi-Prime, West End.*

Of course, the contest jurors had sent a response by hand. Poetry: the last written art to prioritize a textual format... a literary experience meant to be read with the eyes. A rarity in a media age of audio and visual dominance. How apropos to send physical notification. It was like a nod to a noble and ancient tradition, an anachronistic pride shared by a select few across the galaxy.

Lilline opened the seal and pulled out the single sheet of paper. Even more to the point, the missive was handwritten.

Dear Ms. Larkin,

We are pleased to inform you that your poem, "Lost and Found," has been accepted to the Tavi-Prime Poetry Journal's *upcoming special issue. The editors found your choice to mix a traditional poetic form with an uncommon literary device both daring and provocative, successfully conveying the poem's theme while maintaining an artistic prudence not often seen in sophisticated free verse today.*

A second digital message will arrive shortly with forms to sign (and additional information regarding the special issue). Please return your contract as soon as possible, as we intend to publish the issue within the next few weeks.

Congratulations as one of the selected poets representing emerging talent in the galaxy!

Respectfully,

> *Eris Tanaza*
> *Editor-in-chief*
> *Tavi-Prime Poetry Journal*

A rush of emotion flooded her body.

So many cycles of rejections. Always at the most inopportune moments, often in the field on a dangerous assignment, as if the literary gods relished her humiliation. And now, finally, all the hard work and blows to her confidence fell away leaving a flawless and gleaming poetic armor shining with pride.

"Congratulations, dear."

"Thank you, Granny."

"My granddaughter, a published poet." Kissy smiled and patted her on the knee.

"I'm not ten cycles old, Granny. But thank you."

Her grandmother's face softened.

"What?"

"Your mother would be so proud of you." Kissy wiped a tear.

"Oh, Granny..." Lilline reached over and hugged her. The view out the Domus window blurred as her own eyes welled up.

"Well," Kissy said, pulling back and straightening her suit sleeves. "Let's see it."

"The poem?"

Her grandmother nodded.

Lilline tapped a button and called up the table's holo-screen. With a finger, she navigated through her files to the poem and opened it in her favorite holo-font color — magenta.

> *Without and within, nearby and far.*
> *Lost and found under the light of a star.*
> *Too see and to hide, to laugh and to cry.*
> *Life is a rush of time passing by.*
> *In shadow and light, we hide and reveal.*
> *Our journey a search, never-ending.*
> *Open and closed, my heart always sings.*
> *Of a time we were young.*
> *Where can it be?*
> *Lost and found under the light of a star.*

"Look at you," Granny smirked. "I never expected to see the Hyterion form in your verses. I thought you too progressive."

Lilline shrugged. "Tradition has its merits. I'm not opposed to building on it, so long as its use is a choice and not an expectation."

Granny made a face.

"What?"

"I'm impressed."

Wow. A rare compliment.

"About time you came around to the importance of tradition."

"Whoa there." Lilline held up a hand. "Literary traditions, like any other, have their faults too, Granny."

Kissy sipped her tea.

"What?"

The old woman shook her head.

"You have something to say. I know you do."

"I do not. I respect your individual style and poetic expression. That's what makes the soul appear on the page." Kissy's eyes went to the magenta lines of holo-text. "A clever use of merism throughout, by the way. Your phrases of opposites have a nice rhythm. And I like the rhyming free verse."

A strange way to come around to saying something positive...

"In fact, dear, I too believe—"

Ping.

Hiko scurried away at the sound of the chime.

"Guest requesting unit access," the Domus AI's voice said.

THIRTEEN

"Identify," Lilline said.

"Mirna Grochevsky. Human. Retinal scan confirmation. Galactic travel badge provided."

Granny clapped her hands. "I knew she'd change her mind and stay." She reached forward and tapped a button under the holoscreen.

"Entry access granted," the AI said.

Lilline slammed her coffee and made for the stairs.

"We can have her for dinner tonight," Granny's voice followed her as she ascended to the bedroom. "It will need to be on the early side though, knowing Mirna."

Lilline opened a drawer and threw on some casual clothes. "So long as I am not stuck at work, I'll join you."

"Do try and get back, dear. I can always reach out to Asher and request—"

"Do *not* do that, Granny." The last thing she needed was Kissy contacting Lauden like some parent asking if their child can be sent home early from school.

No response from below. Translation: Kissy's head was bobbing back and forth.

Lilline descended the stairs. "I'm sure I can make it. Order delivery. Something nice and fun that Mirna can't get out in the sticks."

"Elaris isn't the galactic sticks, dear. It's on the edge of the Inner—"

Ping.

"Open portal," Lilline said to the AI.

"Mirna!" Granny was across the Domus and at the door in seconds.

Lilline stood, mouth agape, momentarily stunned at the old woman's speed.

"I'm not staying." Mirna held up a hand quelling Kissy's enthusiasm. "Good morning, Keely."

"Morning, Mirna."

Granny pouted.

"I know," Mirna said. "You probably thought I'd changed my mind."

Kissy nodded.

"I still have to make the 11:30 flight. But I brought you a parting gift." Mirna withdrew a pink box with ornamental white lace trim from her bag.

"Oh, you *are* a dear!" Kissy swayed her hips in the style of the Kilari tango, a now dated dance that was hot when the former agent was in her prime.

Lilline chortled.

"I couldn't resist, to be honest." Mirna blushed. "I ate three at the shop."

Kissy broke out giggling and patted her shoulder. "I know, sometimes I—"

"Sometimes you what?" Lilline said, approaching. "Doctor Zeglo gave you strict orders to keep the Dari cakes to no more than two every—"

"Oh poppycock!" Granny waved a hand at her. "I'm ninety-one

cycles." She thrust her hands onto her hips. "I should be able to eat whatever I please."

Lilline rolled her eyes.

"Three pink ones." Mirna handed the box to Kissy. "Make sure you let your granddaughter have one." The woman smiled in her direction. Mirna's presence was more upbeat this morning. Lilline examined Granny. Her too, in fact. Both were in better spirits having spent time together.

Lilline checked her wrist comm: 10:26. "I don't mean to break up the party, but Mirna you really should get going to Tavi-Central. The air traffic lanes can still be slow this time of day."

"Oh, yes. I guess I should."

"Do you have a shuttle waiting downstairs?" Granny asked.

"No, I figured I would call one."

Oh boy. Definitely not a city-planet person.

"You'll never get a standard taxi at this hour," Lilline said. "I'll call you an AI-Chauffeur." She made for the holo-board on the kitchen table.

"Aren't they expensive?" Mirna asked.

"Don't worry about it." Lilline pulled up the live-time chauffeur grid. "It's on me." A green dot blinked two blocks from their location. She locked it in and entered the destination. "You're all set. It'll be here in three minutes."

"You didn't have to do that, Keely," Mirna said.

"Oh, yes she did." Granny said. "It's the least we can do. And besides, it's an experience."

"What do you mean?"

"You'll have a wondrous ride," Lilline said as she tapped open her Inbox.

A new message:

> *Tavi-Prime Poetry Journal*
> *Title: Cover Art - upcoming issue.*

Lilline opened the file. An abstract graphic with dynamic red and blue diagonals formed the backdrop for the journal title, issue number, and...

Oh my stars.

A list of contributors running vertically on the cover's right side.

Her eyes scanned down from the top. There she was. Well, there Keely Larkin was at the midpoint of the alphabetical list.

Ping.

"That's your shuttle, dear. Oh Mirna, I hate for you to go."

Her grandmother's voice was light years away. Lilline stared at the cover. It was so... what?

Professional... an actual publication!

She sprung up and glided to the portal. "Goodbye, Mirna." She gave the woman a hug and a kiss on the cheek.

"What's gotten into you?" Kissy asked.

"Nothing." Lilline did the Kilari tango and bumped Granny at the hip. "Thanks for the Dari cakes. It was great to see you." She snatched the Malardi's box from her grandmother's hand.

"Goodbye, dear," Granny said and hugged Mirna. "Safe flight up to orbit and a good jump back to Elaris."

The portal closed.

Lilline dropped the box on the kitchen table, refilled her coffee and sat. She undid the delicate bow on top and slid her fingernail under the lid to—

Ping.

"That's not the Domus AI," Kissy said.

Lilline's eyes went to her wrist comm.

"No, it's work." A blue alert flashed across the small screen.

"Is that the cover of your poetry issue?" Kissy pointed at the holo screen.

"Yep." Lilline made for the side table and grabbed her H-42 hyper-proton blaster and hog holster.

"You aren't going to have a Dari cake?" Granny sat down and popped the lid.

"Save me one." She snatched up her hover bike key. "Actually, save me *two*. You," she pointed at her grandmother, "are limited to one per day."

Kissy frowned. "What's the rush?"

"Blue code."

Granny's expression made clear she understood.

FOURTEEN

GAM-OPs Headquarters | Planet: Tavi-Prime | Star System: Pesari-9 | Inner Core

———

"T8, meet our forger."

Lilline peered through the two way plasma shield. A well-dressed Froo sat in the GAM-OPs interrogation room. His green six-knuckled finger tugged on the collar of a designer shirt.

"Who is he?"

"According to the scanners," Lauden said, "his name is Yil Abaqati."

The name didn't ring a bell, at least not from the GAM-OPs watchlist.

"Although when we interrupted his beauty sleep this morning he was living under an alias... Smiley Tananger."

"Creative," Lilline said, "if a bit classist."

"Indeed. It's been a busy night." Lauden took out a tobacco

pouch and packed his pipe. "The Oltari broke your code in under two hours."

Of course she did.

Between Pin's penchant for data analysis and the fact that her species had an indigenous twenty-eight-digit numeric system, it was like asking an astrophysicist to solve the orbit pattern of a three-planet star system.

"We've been after this one for cycles," Lauden said, pointing the stem of his pipe at the suspect. "Been a tough nut to crack. An asset with connections to Mr. Abaqati's business and social circles has been working with us to lure him out. We were making progress but every time we got close, he dead-ended us. Your intel gave us the missing link in an investigatory chain involving illegal trading and art sales." The Gej-ti took a pull on his pipe and exhaled through his gills. "Including forgeries."

Lilline studied the Froo. Well-groomed hair, Valten silk shirt and pants, and Petracci shoes. Mr. Abaqati was benefitting from a hefty bank account.

Her anonymous asset had come through big time. "Follow the credits" was a popular saying for a reason.

"I won't ask where or how you got this intel," Lauden said.

Lilline pictured the augmented reality version of the GM at Retrograde. *You wouldn't believe me if I told you, sir.*

"Four hours after head of Tech decoded the encrypted routing number we had the secondary financial institution nailed down," Lauden said. "From there, a residential address was easy work. S.W.A.T. went in and conducted a dark-op abduction, with Intel staffers trailing behind to scour the Domus unit."

"He was on Tavi-Prime?"

The director *humphfed*, puffing away. "Intel gathered a good deal of incriminating evidence in the raid."

Lilline found herself confronted with the laser sharp stare of her boss.

"That previously running operation is now secondary, T8. The cryex crystal ticket is this: Intel mined his home network and personal comm records. An auction is happening... tonight. This Froo is connected with a well-known, albeit secretive, event that pops up when valuable objects are stolen or new archaeological sites are discovered and looted."

The Cosmic Widow...

"Where, sir?"

"That's the problem." The Gej-ti gazed through the plasma mirror.

So, The Forger wasn't talking.

"We have no location and no idea who runs it."

Even if they had those two crucial details in their hands they still needed a way in, whether through an invitation or - more likely, at this late hour - in disguise by disabling someone on the guest list.

"Who is it, sir? The one working with us on this?"

"Someone on Tavi-Prime associated with the arts. And before you ask, no they can't help us from their end." Again, the black pupils locked with her own. "End of conversation."

Lilline held his gaze, her thoughts running back to the club and her asset's mention of the Galactic Museum.

"Has anyone interrogated our suspect?"

"The lads from Intel gave it a go." The director gestured to their right.

In the monitoring office, two GAM-OPs officers sat amidst an array of sophisticated surveillance equipment, waiting to listen in on whatever went down with the Froo. One of them, a Kreeli she recognized, waved a blue hand.

"Let me guess." She eyed the Froo. He sat in the empty chamber grinning, his wide green lips stretched close to his circular cheek glands. "They struck out?"

Lauden nodded.

Not surprising. If this suspect worked with high level criminals he was more intelligent and sophisticated than a thug. Mr. Abaqati would know how to navigate and evade questions. No doubt he had a decent understanding of his rights under galactic law.

But this was GAM-OPs.

Still, there was no guarantee the Froo would talk. If he did, the slippery bastard might lead them on a false trail to stall. Or, spite them.

The Froo twisted his neck, examining the two-way mirror. Green lips arced across his cheeks, stretching his yellow spots in a smug expression.

"Are we working the wrong direction, sir?"

"How do you mean?" Lauden's gaze remained fixed on the Froo.

"Perhaps we should be tracking back, focusing on the crime scene and the thief. Wouldn't that lead us around to the painting?"

"No time, T8. This isn't a murder investigation with a body in the morgue. Our O.T. is on the move, heading somewhere for some purpose. At best, onto the wall of some billionaire's Domus who wants to gloat at having the galaxy's greatest masterpiece all to themselves. At worst..."

He paused and took a pull on his pipe.

Whoosh. A stream of smoke rushed from his neck gills.

Lilline followed the expanding plume in the antechamber's cold light. Thick, gray waves crossed the view of the Froo like fog swallowing a coastal village.

"We need to get it back," Lauden said.

Lilline glanced at the adjacent office. The director had avoided explicit mention of the *Cosmic Widow*. He'd used the field abbreviation: O.T. — operational target — to maintain discretion in the presence of the Intel officers.

"There are layers of concern and pressure here, T8. Not even the metro police have been made aware of this..."

"Can we trust museum security to stay tight-lipped?"

"We've had the guard involved with the morning discovery relieved. Their family is enjoying an all-inclusive vacation at the Gold Coast Resort on Param."

Nice. The white sands and buffet at the posh resort were top-notch.

"And Renina Blackstone?"

The director faced her, pipe stem clenched between his teeth. Smoke rose like a serpent over his face. "It's in her best interest to avoid anything controversial. Bilarus tells me she's eying his position."

"She doesn't know about GAM-OPs?"

The Gej-ti shook his head.

"Fireline Security."

So, Renina was under the impression that an elite security firm had taken on the project under a government sanctioned action. She had to admit, it was a good play.

"We've got a full digital record of Fireline's existence accessible through public networks should Renina decide to do a bit of snooping," Lauden said. "With discretion about its activities... to add credibility. We brought her in for a meeting with Bilarus and the GM's Secretary of Cultural Affairs. As far as Renina knows, she's been made privy to an exclusive inner circle. One that will work to slide her into Bilarus's post if this all works out."

So, Renina gets a potential quid pro quo and an ego boost. Not bad.

"As long as we can keep this under wraps, and out of the public eye. If it breaks on the networks..." The Gej-ti raised an eyebrow.

The old fish was right. They'd need more arms than a Goosh bartender to plug all the leaks and catch all the potential Ministry heads that would roll if this got out. Not to mention, the metro police would be furious. No matter. She'd never been chummy with that bunch. Too gruff and lenient when it came to interpretations of civilian rights.

Not that GAM-OPs was a saint when it came to—

"He's protecting someone," Lauden said.

"Himself, most likely."

"Agreed, but he's keeping his contact and financier under wraps as well."

"We don't have much time to change his mind."

"Indeed. Care to take the lead on this?"

Lilline turned to the director. "You'll be joining me?"

"Why not." Lauden pulled out a pipe tool and extinguished the bowl of tobacco. He gestured to the Intel officer through the plasma shield to open the portal.

FIFTEEN

"Okay, Mr. Tananger..." Lilline said, entering the interrogation room. She pulled out a chair and slid it across the floor.

Screech!

The Froo winced.

She sat.

The director joined her in the adjacent chair.

"Oh, I apologize," she said. "It's Mr. Abaqati, isn't it?"

The Froo's eyebrows rose.

Lilline placed both hands on the table and leaned forward. "Not a very impressive cover name."

"I'm not talking," Mr. Abaqati shot her a cold-blooded stare.

"All I need is a few answers about your associates."

The Froo shook his head. "Not going to happen, Ms...?"

"Jones." She smirked. "That's about as good a cover name as yours, don't you think?"

The suspect shook his head at the dig. "And him?"

"Mr. You Don't Want Him to Get Involved," Lilline said.

The pitter patter of Petracci shoes on concrete echoed off the walls.

"You're not a cop."

"No." She leaned forward and stared him down. "I'm much worse."

"Look, I would help but—"

"You want to spend the rest of your life?" she asked.

The Froo cocked his head. "The rest of my life what, Ms. Jones?"

Lilline chose silence.

"Did you mean to say, 'with full immunity in a star system of my choice and twenty million credits in an unmarked account?'"

She stared him down.

"I assume we are negotiating?" He gestured with long green fingers.

"No, I was finished." Her face remained stone cold. "I imagine you want that? The rest of your life?"

More patter of Petracci shoes.

"You don't know what these people are like," he said.

"Oh, but I do, Mr. Abaqati. I deal with them all the time. That's my job." Lilline stole a glance at Lauden. He sat like a statue. Good. That was what he was here to do - put the fear of death in the suspect through cold-hearted silence.

"It's dry in here." Mr. Abaqati fingered his shirt collar.

"Indeed. Come to think of it," she made as if checking the room, "I believe the humidity is off."

Fear on his face. A Froo's cheek glands never lie.

Good for the Intel crew. They knew to shut off the ventilation to sweat the suspect. "Dry out" would be more accurate. He'd been in here a while by the look of his skin.

"Name of the seller who runs the underground auction?" She locked eyes with him.

The Froo shook his head.

"Location?"

Again, a gesture of denial. A finger went to his shirt collar.

In the cold light from the overhead bulb, cracks ran like rivers across his wide cheeks. Lack of humidity was not conducive to a

Froo's epidermal system. Without an adjustment to moisture level, Mr. Abaqati was entering the danger zone.

She waited, tension palpable in the deafening silence.

Would he break or go down denying them?

Lilline tapped her fingertips on the table's surface, cascading them from pinky to index finger in a drum roll. Lauden picked up on the signal, leaning forward and placing his elbows on the table. Having a director who was a former T# agent had its advantages.

"Make a deal here, Mr. Abaqati," Lauden said. "You give us something. We give you something."

"Like what?" The Froo's eyes went to the Gej-ti.

"Your life."

You are a cold-blooded bastard, Mr. Director.

"The name," Lilline repeated. A trail of blue blood trickled from a bone-dry seam along the Froo's cheek gland.

"Look at where you are, Mr. Abaqati," Lauden said. "You're nowhere. This is a far cry from a metro police station. That should tell you all you need to know."

"*Name.*" Lilline's tone wasn't an ask.

The Froo's eyes darted from the director to her and back again.

"Carmini," he said.

The art dealer? Lilline knew him by reputation. Never caught in the act or able to be proved in a court of law but known to cater to discreet clients with a taste for stolen art, whether pilfered from museums or illegally excavated at protected sites across the galaxy.

"That's a slippery and shady associate, Mr. Abaqati," she said.

The Froo's six knuckled fingers trembled.

Lilline leaned back and smiled.

Click.

Perfect timing. These Intel folks knew their game.

"Thank you." Lilline accepted a wet rag from a staffer who entered. She dabbed her face and sighed audibly. "It really does get dry in here."

"You're sick!" The Froo's bulbous eyes widened.

"I'd really like to attend that auction." She handed the rag back. The staffer placed a file on the table.

The Froo shook his head. "I'm safer in jail."

"That's the thing," Lauden said. A tobacco-stained finger flipped open the folder. "*You* might be safe. But what about your family?"

Lilline kept her gaze cold as ice. She had hoped it wouldn't come to this. Dirty interrogation tactics. She wasn't a fan but she was also no fool. Debriefs and interviews like this one threw out the rule book. These types of sessions provided vital intel to accomplish mission objectives in the field. Still, it never sat well. The ends always justified the means at GAM-OPs, as Lauden always said.

Lilline's moral conscience wasn't sure she agreed, but professionally until something better came along this was the way the espionage game worked.

"Cute little tadpoles," Lauden said, finger sliding a printed image aside to reveal another. "And such a lovely spouse."

"Please..." The Froo's voice was a raspy whisper. The amphibious human variant's head wobbled. He blinked, squeezing his eyes open and shut in rapid succession.

"How do we get into the auction?" Lilline said.

"Okay." Streams of blue blood ran like tears on the Froo's face. "It's a domain with a password." He swallowed through cracking lips. "A digital request via a security wall."

"Virtual address?" Lilline asked.

The Froo fidgeted.

"*Virtual address?*" She directed his attention to the images of his family.

"Z server. Domain is 'parallax.'"

Lilline rotated in her chair and peered at her reflection. She offered an inquisitive nod to the staffers through the two-way mirror.

"*Password?*" The voice from the adjacent office echoed over the audio system.

"My family will be safe?" the Froo asked.

Lilline nodded. *They were never really in danger, but you don't need to know that.*

"Twilight star."

"Enter it," Lauden ordered, speaking to the officers listening in.

Lilline stared at the Froo. He was in too much pain to fight back.

"Wait," he whispered and hacked, gasping for air. "It takes a moment and then—"

"Confirmed."

The Froo's eyes rolled back in his head.

Smack! Lilline slapped the table.

Two bloodshot orbs, like dying suns, returned. Face a paling green, Mr. Abaqati moaned and teetered.

"Get him some water and rags. And hit the air," she said.

Cool mist rushed into the chamber, soothing more than the dying Froo. Relief rose as the guilt washed off of her agent armor.

"My office," Lauden said. "Now."

SIXTEEN

"Get the head of Tech and the twins up here, Cazshi."

Lilline followed her boss through the office portal.

Awkward silence had tested her patience on the lift ride from sub-level 3. As a veteran agent, she knew better than to break it. The director's exterior might have exuded serenity, but his brain was moving pieces on a mental chess board. What had the Froo said to trigger the urgency?

Lauden gestured for her to sit and strode around his desk.

"And make sure they are ready to report," he told his assistant through the portal and sat.

"Yes, sir." The Rasp's words cut off as the office door whooshed shut.

"As soon as Intel sends anything up from the Froo's interview, break in," Lauden added, finger depressed on the office comm button.

Interview... interesting way to put it. Lilline crossed her legs and got comfortable.

"Look at this, T8." The director swiped a hand over a sensor plate. Milky-skinned fingers glowed blue as a holo manifested.

Lilline edged up in her seat and read the comm exchange.

"Update on Grande Dame?"
"Waiting at drop-off location."
"It's not in your hands?"
"No show."
"They're late?"
*"No communication since we provided the
     equipment."*

Lilline shifted down to the second thread:

"Update?"
"Nothing since we last spoke."
"They screwed us?"
*"No idea. Either way, you pay me. This is your
     problem not ours."*
*"It's all of our problems if it doesn't arrive for
     Parallax."*
"As I said, waiting. Can't do much else."
"Do we know if the circus act was a success?"
"No."
*"Check with third party. Carefully. Then send an
     update. I will stall."*
"And my credits?"
*"Another twenty percent will be deposited. Find out
     what the stars is going on."*

Lilline leaned back in her chair.

"What do you make of it?" Lauden asked.

"Is this from the chatter you mentioned?"

He nodded. "Latest surveillance. Intercepted yesterday. Early in the morning and again later, a few minutes after 4 p.m."

No wonder he was quiet on the ride up. This was a solid lead. Combined with the intel from the Froo's interrogation, pieces on the board *were* moving.

"Speak your mind, T8."

A milky-skinned hand performed a familiar gesture, turning from face down to palm up. She and her agency colleagues referred to it as "the thing with his hand."

"I'd say we're looking at a double-cross scenario, sir. Assuming we take this Grand Dame to be the *Cosmic Widow*."

Lauden nodded and took his favorite pipe from its Bartos marble stand. "I agree." He packed and fired up the tobacco. "I remembered it when the Froo gave up the domain name granting access to the auction."

"Well, someone appears to be in a pinch," she said. "You think the painting is meant to go on sale?"

"It's our best lead."

Lilline re-read the exchanges. "And this so-called third party?"

"Our thief, perhaps?" Lauden raised an eyebrow. "Provided with equipment related to the ruse."

That did make sense. Pin's initial crime-scene assessment indicated the robber had employed cutting-edge tech to infiltrate museum security.

Vague and shadowy suspects swirled in her mind. Lilline did her best to transcribe the evidence and players into a focused mental image. All she knew for certain was that they were professionals. These conversations were carefully navigated, with a prudent eye should they be under surveillance.

And they were.

She scrutinized Lauden, careful not to make direct eye contact. Short, repeated puffs on his pipe sent rapid plumes of smoke rising like smoke signals, vanishing into the ceiling's ventilation system. His pupils stared at the holo-screen.

Lilline re-focused her attention on the comm exchanges. "Who's this?" She pointed at the one answering the posed questions. "Driver and delivery?"

"Looks that way, yes."

"Do we have any tracking on this?"

Lauden shook his head. "Encryption is like nothing we've encountered. The best our hackers can do is the local sector. Both parties are somewhere within the Tavi-Prime comm grids." He leaned back in his chair. "But that includes Beisho and the surrounding satellite hotels."

Over a billion civilians within that sector of the Pesari-9 star system. No help there. This was turning out to be—

"*Sir.*"

Lilline eyed the audio speaker on the ceiling.

The director straightened in his chair. "Go ahead, Cazshi."

"*Head of Tech is here. But the twins are off-site.*"

"Where in stars are they?"

"*Attending TAVI-CON, sir.*"

"Tavi what?"

"*The gaming conference. Remember you approved their request two months ago?*"

"Damn it, Cazshi. Tell them to report in as soon as they return." With a swipe of his hand, Lauden made the comm exchange vanish. "And send in the Oltari."

SEVENTEEN

"Good afternoon, Director."

Pin made her way into the office, wings fluttering. She drifted half a meter off the ground, two of her four arms clutching a tablet to her chest. Another gripped the handle of a leather case.

"Oh, hello T8," the Oltari said. "Fortuitous that you are present. It will lessen redundancy."

"Glad to be of service, Pin. Office efficiency is always my priority."

The Oltari dropped down next to her.

"Was that sarcasm?" Pin whispered.

"It was." Lilline winked.

"Alright," Lauden said. "Walk us through it. How did they get this painting out of the museum and what do you have on that damn clock?"

"May I have access permission for your holo-screen, sir?" Pin tapped on her tablet.

The director's finger ran through a sequence on the desk terminal and gestured for her to proceed.

"I would like to start with the thief's calling card."

"That damned clock," Lauden muttered.

He's really ticked off about that thing. Lilline kept the pun to herself.

Pin withdrew the timepiece from her case, along with a tripod stand. She placed the clock on the platform so the face was visible.

"I admit to being excited," the Oltari said and rubbed two sets of hands together. "To review, the device dates to at least the First Galactic."

"At least?" Lilline asked. "What does that—"

Pin held up one of her seven fingers. "Allow me to continue, T8. It will make sense. Or, at the least, it will become clear why I uttered a seemingly illogical statement."

"Proceed," Lauden said.

"I believe this to be one of the 'soft' clocks from ancient history."

"A Darian clock?" Lauden asked.

Pin nodded.

The director rose. "Show me."

Lilline remained quiet, eager to learn where this was heading.

Pin approached Lauden's bonsai on the credenza. "May I, sir?" She pointed to the soil mixture at its roots. "Just a pebble."

The Gej-ti nodded.

Pin returned to the tripod. "Ready? Follow the stone."

Lilline focused on the tiny rock.

The Oltari tossed it at the clock's face.

Blip.

A ripple effect, as if the pebble penetrated the surface of a pond, spread over the dials and numbers to the edges.

"I don't believe it." Lauden leaned down, peering at the device.

"Where did it go?" Lilline asked.

"That, T8, is both an enigmatic and exciting question," Pin said. "Unfortunately, I have no idea."

"It's not inside, I presume?"

"It might be." The Oltari shrugged. "I can't dismantle it. I've tried to open it but so far it's been impossible."

"It will remain so," Lauden said, straightening up and running a hand over his widow's peak. "A Darian timepiece is the stuff of legend. Purportedly, cosmic philosophers of unknown origin made astounding discoveries that allowed them to break spacetime."

Lauden's face shifted.

I don't like that look. Grave and yet... *is that fear?*

"If it is as you say, and the dating is accurate," Lauden eyed Pin, "then this is truly extraordinary."

"Even with the composition of the clock's metal unknown, our available technology confirms the materials have been exposed to atmospheric elements since the First Galactic but—"

"But that doesn't mean it isn't older," the Gej-ti said. "Or... *stars.*"

"What is it, sir?" Lilline asked.

He shook his head, refusing to answer, and returned to his desk. "It's still running backwards?"

"Yes, sir," Pin said. "It's cycled through the thirty-four-hour dial and is now repeating."

That was a relief. Lilline rose. "May I repeat the demonstration, sir?"

Lauden gestured approval, absorbed with something at his desk.

Lilline took a pebble, squatted in front of the timepiece, and tossed it at the face.

Again, it vanished and a wave of concentric ripples passed over the surface.

"Do you understand the physics of this, Pin?"

The Oltari shook her head. "Other than obvious and inadequate conclusions offered through empirical observation, I am stumped."

"Which are?"

Lilline read confusion on the Oltari's face.

"Humor me," she said.

"The objects enter the timepiece and remain inside or, more likely, they disintegrate on impact through some kind of reaction, be it molecular, chemical, or some other unknown force. Both hypotheses have illogical outcomes, however, considering the size and related capacity of the clock, as well as the ripple effect which may suggest…"

"What?"

"They are going somewhere else," Lauden said.

Lilline spun around at the director's response. Again, the grave expression.

"I'm sorry, sir. But I don't have more answers," Pin said.

"I wouldn't expect you to," he said, typing on a virtual keyboard.

"So this is a dead end?" Lilline asked.

"Not entirely," Pin said. "I have a colleague who specializes in extra-dimensional phenomena. With your permission, sir, I would like to consult her on this."

"Where is she located?" He swiped a hand, closing the keyboard, and turned his attention to Pin and the clock.

"The Calostine system."

"Calostine? What in the stars is she doing all the way out there?"

Valid response. Talk about remote. The Calostine system lay at the farthest tip of an Outer Rim spiral. The *longest* galactic arm, in fact. Any further out and you were in the Beyond.

"She received a grant from the Cosmic Exploratory Commission to study what she believes are anomalies occurring inside black holes." Pin extended her two upper arms wide in excitement. "She on the cutting-edge of extra-dimensional studies."

Lilline locked eyes with her boss. They'd been down this road once before, and it hadn't ended well.

"Her work is focused on the nexus point of zero gravitation, where a doubling occurs."

"As in a black hole?" Lilline asked.

"Yes and no, T8."

That answer was becoming too common of late.

"Let me back up and give you both context and go over basic principles," Pin said. "This will only take about an hour."

"We can't spare it," Lauden said.

Lilline read the disappointment on the Oltari's face.

"After we finish this case, you can tell us all about it," Lilline said.

"Really?"

Lilline smirked at her.

"Oh, that was sarcasm?"

Lilline nodded.

"I take it this colleague of yours may have answers for this... phenomenon?" Lauden said.

"Indeed, sir."

"Right. I'll have Cazshi inform Intel. They can run her background and send contractual materials to sign. It's going to take some time to ping all the way out... there." He waved his pipe indicating the edge of an invisible galaxy.

"Thank you, sir. If anyone will have answers it will be Slushie."

"Sorry, did you say 'Slushie?'" Lilline asked.

"Indeed, T8. That's her nickname. She got it at Uni when we—"

Lilline held up a hand.

"Very well," the Oltari said. "I will tell you after the mission, since I know you are eager to learn all the details."

"Well done, Pin," Lilline said.

"That was sarcasm, right?"

"Indeed, it was."

"Next report." Lauden's voice was anything but sarcastic.

"Sir," Pin tapped her tablet's screen. A blue holo-version of a building's exterior manifested. "The Galactic Museum."

An unfamiliar gesture stretched across the Oltari's face. "What is it, Pin?"

"I am equally vexed with this scenario, T8." The head of Tech switched the holo to an interior view.

The familiar architectural layout of the galleries with the empty Venex Horse vitrine manifested, as well as the hallway leading to the main attraction - the *Cosmic Widow*.

Pin enlarged the crime scene so it filled the available space over Lauden's desk.

"Walk us through it," the director said.

EIGHTEEN

"We have no footage?"

Lilline registered the annoyance in Lauden's expression.

"Unfortunately not, sir," Pin said. "All we know is the thief managed to get into the building unnoticed, proceed through the closed blast wall doors... which appears to be impossible, and into the gallery."

"Security activity?" Lilline asked.

"Active rounds all night," Pin said. "They've confirmed the blast doors were shut. Four passes during the twelve-hour shift."

"What about the surveillance feeds?"

"This is interesting, T8," Pin said. "All functioning, under observation throughout the night per usual security procedure between roaming rounds. And yet, as soon as the blast door was opened in the morning, the overnight footage was smeared."

"Set on a trigger," Lauden said, smoking.

"But wouldn't that have been a hack?" Lilline asked. "A set of looping footage overnight to convince them the gallery was empty while the thief was hard at work?"

"Would seem so, yes," Pin said.

"Then why smear it when the doors open?" Lilline moved her gaze from Oltari to Lauden.

Neither had an answer.

"Strange." Lilline examined the virtual mockup. Her eyes roamed the gallery, the memory of her visit the day before filling in physical details. She walked the space in her mind. There was no way to do this. It didn't make sense.

"Continue, Pin," Lauden said. "Begin with what happens from inside the gallery."

"At this point, sir, the thief encounters the museum's most important piece of protection, The Claw and Tail."

Lilline followed as red lines extended from dots on the wall, creating a labyrinth of alarm lasers. They crisscrossed the area in front of the *Cosmic Widow*.

"And beyond, only centimeters from the painting, lies a shield barrier," Pin said.

"Osmic electro-wave technology, right?" Lilline said.

"Indeed, T8. A brilliant redundancy if I may say so. And both baffling and spectacular that someone—"

"Or some *thing*," Lilline said.

"What's that, T8?" Lauden asked.

"I hadn't thought of it until now, but perhaps a drone could—"

"Negative, T8." Pin shook her head. "Anything mechanical emits enough vibration and beta waves to be captured by at least four related museum security scanners."

"What if it was shut down?" Lilline asked.

"Sorry?" Pin said.

Lilline peered at Lauden. "Why couldn't all this security simply be shut down?"

"By whom?"

Lilline shrugged. "Someone on the inside. Renina perhaps? Or..." She eyed the director. "Reginald Bilarus."

His face was as still as an antique bust.

"Renina is logged as leaving the museum after working late in the galleries. The blast door was confirmed as closed by security and the online network when she left," Pin said. "Her alibi overnight is sound. She then arrived early — a pattern that is normal for her according to museum security."

Highly motivated. I guess I would be too if I wanted to become Head Curator. Still...

"This staying late and leaving early..." Lilline said.

"Bilarus says it isn't unusual," Lauden said. "They're in the early stages of curatorial revisions, re-arranging displays, adding works from storage, removing others, and whatnot. All part of the changing politic of museum culture." The Gej-ti waved his pipe around as if he were annoyed at the attack on tradition.

"And Mr. Bilarus was off-site from before closing that day until the discovery of the theft the following morning," Pin added. "With a solid alibi."

"So, someone got inside the museum, avoided notice by multiple parties en route, made their way through security barriers, possibly shutting them down, to the gallery with the *Cosmic Widow*," Lauden said. "Impressive, but if they are a highly skilled professional thief, it's possible with, as you say, the right technology. Difficult, yes. But not impossible."

"Except you still have this problem." Pin pointed one of her four arms at the area closest to the *Cosmic Widow*.

Lilline nodded, remembering. "This is the rub, sir."

"Exactly, T8. The Claw and Tail Security System runs independently of the museum's power grid and is immune to all known EMP devices such as Stumpers, etc."

"Nothing can diffuse it?" Lauden asked.

"The only way to shut it down is by direct call to the Claw and Tail company, which is off-site in the western suburb of Tech Valley. The process involves a voice authenticator and retinal scan, along with a subsequent code provided to the museum security manager."

"So, a staffer and museum security both have to participate to shut it off?" Lilline asked.

"Yes, T8."

"Do we know who has voice and retinal authentication approval for the system?"

"At present, only Mr. Bilarus and Renina."

"Not the security manager?"

Pin shook her head. "They have a live-time security interview with an employee at Claw and Tail who asks a series of questions. If answered correctly, they are provided with the code. Their backup for this permission is the alternative manager who runs the day shift. And before you ask, T8, she is confirmed off-site for the entire night. I will add that the livestream interview must be transmitted through the main security station server inside the museum."

Impressive. As far as protection went the Galactic Museum did their best. Unfortunately, it still wasn't good enough.

"I think it is fair to say that someone managed to thread the needle of the Claw and Tail to the painting," Lilline said. "And somehow back out again with the *Cosmic Widow*."

"I concur," Pin said. "What vexes me is that a negotiation of the grid and sensors in that spatial arena requires—"

"—a high degree of dexterity," Lilline said. How anyone could pull it off though...

"Anatomically speaking," Pin said, "any of the human variants *could* do it. As well as a Rasp."

"Not the other sentients?" Lauden asked.

"Kreelis, Dendaris, Oltaris such as I, and even Coleopterians are too large, wide, or have exoskeletons that would inhibit their dexterity. Either they aren't physically able to perform the maneuvers or fall short of the requirements of spatial containments set by the Claw and Tail grid system to reach the painting without triggering the alarm."

Lilline studied the mockup. She put herself inside the gallery, her avatar jumping and balancing its way through the obstacle course. Each time she attempted to pass through the section Pin highlighted her forward progress stalled.

How do you get through that?

"What is it, T8?" Lauden asked.

"I'm trying to solve this acrobatic puzzle, sir. I think it's more than a species requirement."

Lauden did the hand thing.

"This spot here." She edged up in her seat and pointed near to where the *Cosmic Widow* would be. "I can't figure this out. It leads me to conclude that whoever did this had an extraordinary talent. They must have been—"

"Professionally trained," the Gej-ti said, finishing her thought.

"Exactly, sir."

"A dancer?"

"No, more like a..." The realization hit with cryex crystal clarity. "Circus acrobat."

Lauden's hand froze, pipe midway to his mouth.

NINETEEN

Two clues now linked.

"Good show, T8." Lauden pointed his pipe. "Pin, check for any performative events, traveling circuses, or other amusement-based entertainments in and around Tavi-Central in the last few weeks."

The Oltari shifted on her jointless legs to face the director. "Yes, sir. Although, I am not sure I follow why—"

"If I may, sir," Lilline said, interrupting Pin. "It might be worth checking the GAM-OPs watchlist for anyone with a background fitting these skills."

"I'll have Intel check into it," the director said. "Well done, T8."

A second compliment? Lilline sat back in her chair but kept her smugness hidden. *The afternoon is looking up.*

Lauden placed his pipe on the marble stand. "I'd say we're dealing with a human variant or Rasp."

"Agreed," Lilline said. The problem was, almost every current suspect fell within those parameters. Carmini was still a wild card species-wise, but it was unlikely he was the thief. That one was after profit as a seller.

"Keep working on this," Lauden said. "Have every relevant

department informed. All angles. Somehow, someone got in and out of one of the most impenetrable security systems available... with the most famous masterpiece in the galaxy under their arm." The Gej-ti shook his head in disbelief.

Two of the Oltari's four hands typed furiously on her tablet.

"Where are we on background checks?" Lauden asked.

Pin's fingers halted. "I had trouble accessing a file on Mr. Bilarus, sir."

Interesting. Lilline did her best to hold her exterior neutral.

"I found the administrative assistant in Records to be quite unhelpful. In fact, my persistence was treated with a level of disregard that bordered on a species relations departmental complaint because—"

"Never mind that," Lauden said. "And the others?"

"But sir, in the GAM-OPs manual it states—"

"Noted. End of discussion."

Lilline held back her shock at the Oltari's interjection. Talking back to the director? Pin had a pair of wings on her; she'd almost forgotten.

"The others?" Lauden repeated.

Pin's pink cheeks flushed blue.

In the awkward silence, the ventilation system hummed.

The Oltari shut off her tablet.

Oh no. "Pin," Lilline said. "I have the same problem with Records. Everyone does. It's always been that way. No need to take it personally."

"All the more reason why it should be addressed, T8. If this is happening to all GAM-OPs employees who use that department's services then—"

"You're right."

The voice was Lauden's. The Gej-ti rose and took a copy of the GAM-OPs manual off the shelf and placed it on his desk. A milky-skinned hand, veins and nerves showing through translucent skin, patted the top of the tome. "I'll look into it."

"Hoo."

This time Lilline lost the battle with self-composure and cracked a smile.

The Oltari was right. Records could be a pain in the ass but in this case, she knew something was afoot with access levels and that Bilarus file.

Pin tapped the tablet back to life. "Everyone's records at the museum," the Oltari said, "except for Mr. Bilarus who I can't speak to because..."

Come on Pin, you can do it.

"I was unable to access his file... were clean with no red flags."

Lauden nodded his appreciation for her help in smoothing things over.

You owe me, old fish. Next time I request the company's elite spaceship you better not give me a hard time.

"Except for Renina Blackstone."

Lilline swung her head towards Pin. "What?"

"Yes, T8. Ms. Blackstone was questioned by the authorities in relation to a forgery scandal two cycles ago. No charges were filed."

Lilline checked Lauden's expression. He looked as surprised as she felt.

"Dig into that," the director said, "and report back if anything turns up."

"One thing, sir," Lilline said. "I think it's worth checking on other First Galactic art stolen from the museum, say... in the last ten cycles."

Lauden smoked on, unaffected.

"A few artifacts have gone missing and they could be connected, either to this clock or the *Cosmic Widow*." The Venex Horse and her conversation with Bilarus was forefront in her mind. "Or," she added, "something to do with our thief that might reveal a pattern and help that angle of the case."

The solemnity of his nod spoke volumes. Something was going on that he wasn't sharing.

"I can have the team add that to the request list," Pin said. "I should be able to get you the background follow-up within the next—"

"*Sir.*"

Lauden held up a hand, halting Pin.

"What is it, Cazshi?"

"*Intel sent details on the auction.*"

"Send it through."

"Pin." In a soft voice, Lilline got the Oltari's attention and pointed at the chair next to her.

The head of Tech's cheeks went blue. She approached on stumpy legs and sat.

The holo-screen vanished, replaced by an opaque blue field that blocked the view of Lauden across the desk.

Lilline tracked a trail of smoke that emerged over the block-screen's top edge. It rose like a snake from a basket, accented by several audible *humphfs* from behind the barrier.

"Patch me through to Intel, Cazshi," the director said.

In her mind, Lilline pictured the Gej-ti inserting a comm earpiece.

"Control here," Lauden said. "Can we get T8 in?"

A pause.

The snake danced higher. Soon its seductive path would take it into the ceiling and through the building's labyrinth of ducts until it reached its life's end at the purification filters.

"Thank you," the director said. "Good show, lads."

The opaque barrier vanished. As Lilline expected, the director was removing his earpiece.

"Dismissed, Pin. Thank you."

"Sir," the Oltari stood and gathered her things to go.

"Stay, T8."

"Oh, I almost forgot," Pin said. "Thus far my review of the existing research on the double-pollex has yielded nothing substantial."

The director nodded.

The portal closed with a *whoosh*. Lauden rose and strode to the window. Pipe in hand, he gazed out at the afternoon air traffic. Reflections of sunlight dappled the window where the Andrews River peeked through gaps in the director's lean profile.

"You'll be attending the auction this evening," he said.

A rush of excitement passed through her veins. *The field, finally.* Her spy juices flowed at the thought of an undercover op.

"We're setting you up as a buyer for a wealthy client." The Gej-ti lifted his pipe and inhaled, gaze fixed on the cityscape outside. "It means sacrificing our progress with Mr. Abaqati's associates but we have to prioritize this... you'll need to brush up on your art auction knowledge. I'll have Intel get you a file with the basics. With so little time, make sure the essentials are solid." He turned, half in the light of Pesari-9's afternoon rays and half in shadow. "The rest you'll have to improvise. Wealthy collectors and dealers love artful description and whatnot. Anything to embellish the value of the works on sale. Use your poetry skills, T8. Sprinkle your conversations with alluring language. Ekphrasis will suit well for this."

Ekphrasis. The word rose from the memories of her university days.

Lilline nodded, indicating she understood its meaning: the literary description of a work of art.

"Get us information," Lauden said. "And not just undercover as a buyer. I want you behind the scenes. Break into Carmini's personal office, storage rooms, wherever... do as much snooping as you can."

"Understood, sir."

"I'll have the head of Tech put together a surveillance and equipment package for you." The Gej-ti glanced at the clock. "You won't make it if we outfit you at HQ." He strode back to his desk and hit a button. "Cazshi, set up a second transportation file for the head of Tech. Same station destination as T8."

"Yes, sir," the Rasp said.

"You're sending Pin into the field?"

Lauden bit down on the stem of his pipe, the corner of his lips breaking into a subtle smile. "The equipment officer needs time to get some things together. She will meet you enroute."

This is going to be interesting.

Lilline rose and straightened her shirt sleeves. "Sir, one thing. From what we know on that comm intercept, the *Cosmic Widow* isn't going to be at the auction."

"We can't count on that. Perhaps things have changed."

"And if not?"

"There's an old saying in the espionage game, T8."

"Sir?"

"If you can't fish, better understand the bait."

So, they were indeed tracking backwards, but not from the direction she had assumed. Admittedly, with the evidence they had this was a better lead than the thief's astounding break-in and the cosmic weirdness she'd witnessed in Pin's clock demonstration. A haunting sensation told her that before this was all over, unraveling that enigmatic dimensional puzzle would be essential to solving the case.

For now, she pushed it aside. Lauden was right. They had a set of tracks.

"I've compiled a personal brief on First Galactic art for you. Its primary purpose is to better educate you on the *Cosmic Widow,* but it will serve double duty for the auction as well."

"I look forward to reading it, sir."

"Good luck, T8."

"Thank you." She made for the portal but halted. "Sir, one thing."

Lauden did the hand thing.

"Where am I going?"

"Sky City."

TWENTY

Outbound Flight | Planet: Tavi-Prime | Star System: Pesari-9 |
Inner Core

From her window seat on the *Aspirion Atmo-6*, Lilline fought with
the ferocity of a Bukki tiger. She shifted and rotated, sending a flurry
of strikes and kicks outward at imaginary foes. With intense concen-
tration, her mind flowed through the choreographed sequence. She'd
performed the esoteric form thousands of times at the monastery high
in the peaks of Hesh-9, the movements as natural to her now as if
they'd been embedded into her DNA.

She blocked and passed, entering her opponent's guard. An
attack followed: knife hand to the throat. A knee slammed an inner
leg at a vital point. Her foe responded, involuntarily lowering. An
elbow released, impacting their incoming sternum. With smooth and
circular precision, she positioned a leg behind their calf and
performed a foot sweep, finishing with a joint lock. Inner energy

surged through her limbs, tingling her extremities, and bringing a freshly sharpened and deadly edge to her martial prowess. It didn't matter that her physical body was at rest. The mind labored. Neurons firing, her vicarious practice had become as effective as working with a partner in real time. Honed over two ten-cycles, her body still got its fair share of activity in the workout space at GAM-OPs, but these days progress was defined more in philosophical terms.

Lilline completed the final turn of *Miransa*, a form inspired by the graceful and elegant shore bird of the same name, and bowed, letting go of the inner world. Out the ship's window, ten thousand meters below, afternoon light dappled the billowing clouds like burnt tips of a meringue. At a cruising altitude of fifteen-thousand meters, the sleek and glimmering Atmo-6 raced through Tavi-Prime's high atmosphere en route to its destination.

Lilline peered out the portal, squinting to focus. Still nothing other than a sweeping white blanket and the deep blue of high atmosphere edging into space. Any minute, a titanic upside-down pyramid would break the horizon. Sky City's signature technology, the black object served as a prodigious support system for a population of almost a million, allowing their world to stay aloft. Suspended via cables two thousand meters below the inverted structure, Sky City was known the galaxy over for its unique application of gravitational equilibrium. A floating world full of decadence, corruption, and entertainment rivaling the best resorts and casinos across the stars.

It was all thanks to Iodren, a newly discovered helium isotope. In its gaseous state, Iodren helped maintain a delicate balance with the force of Tavi-Prime's gravity. Complex computers, linked to a myriad of meteorological instruments, controlled a hive of regulators that generated and discharged the harmless element as needed to maintain the Goldilox Effect. Now and then, an abrupt and unannounced dip or rise in the city's elevation occurred. Residents referred to the adjustments as cloud quakes. Subtle but alarming, after notching two or three quakes on their belts visitors grew accustomed and gave them no further thought.

"Ms. Larkin, would you care for a beverage?"

Lilline pulled her gaze from the view. She peered past her neighbor to the drone server hovering in the aisle. A Gej-ti dressed in the blue and white Aspirion uniform smiled in miniature on the ovoid's screen.

"A glass of Gondau please, pre-Roncheau if you have it."

"Certainly." The virtual Gej-ti nodded and the drone moved on.

Lilline checked the window. A black speck broke the monotony of the horizon.

Sky City beckoned.

She'd visited once before, cycles ago. One night at the Royal Loha Suites, on assignment to escort an asset seeking asylum. She remembered the Dendari vividly, a large furry creature common to colder planets along the Outer Rim, with his walking stick and odd gait. He had traded valuable technological secrets in exchange for a new life free from a breakaway planet leaning toward fascism. The stay at the Royal Loha had been exquisite. Lilline still recalled the plate of slip slugs, fresh from the Cimo Sea, and a memorable bottle of '46 Gondau, a pre-Roncheau vintage of particular repute.

A second shape joined the pyramid at the horizon: a frustum, a long cone with its pointed top sliced off. It rose from behind the edge of the world as the pyramid ascended. A shiver of excitement ran through her at the anticipation of arriving. The weather was cooperating. With only low cloud cover over Tavi-Prime, the approach would be a memorable one. *Atmo-6* would spiral the balloon on descent to the frustum's arrivals port, offering a spectacular view of the floating urban world. Composed of alloy and high-pressure windows, most described Sky City as a narrow steel lampshade. But what its exterior lacked in decoration was made up for by the richness of its interior world. A tax-free haven, the hanging city maintained its autonomy from the strict economic regulations enforced across the galactic commons. That exemption had drawn entrepreneurs from far and wide, developing a unique galactic internationalism - a myriad of distant cultures and species combining luxury with an edge of risk that extended to bodily harm should one venture into the wrong sectors.

Lilline leaned back in her seat, reflecting on the unusual nature of the op. A stolen painting, an impossible security maze navigated by a master thief, a nexus of ghostly suspects, and a mysterious dimensional enigma connected to a civilization lost to time. How did it all fit together?

A beam of sunlight broke through the passenger window, streaking the fabric seatback in front of her. Memories of Hesh-9's fiery alpine light at day's end flashed through her mind. The monastery, her teacher, and the cycles of struggle and growth she'd experienced at the remote sanctuary rushed back.

So many cycles had passed since she first arrived at those large and intimidating wooden doors. Led by her grandmother's firm grip, a precocious twelve-cycle old girl had crossed the threshold and embarked on a life-changing adventure. Cycles later, after endless struggle and doubt as a seasoned trainee, it had all fallen into place.

Lilline smiled at the memory. She'd expected it to come under duress, pushed to exhaustion in one of her teacher's training sessions. Battered and bruised, humiliated with her limited technique and fortitude - that was when she assumed awakening would arrive.

But it had been so different.

Alone, mid-morning tending plants at the pond's edge, sheltered by the monastery's rock walls. The crunch of pebbles had faded as a fellow apprentice moved off to other tasks. She'd been left to relish a familiar monastic silence. That's when Hesh-9's early light broke the day, peeking over ancient stone walls. Rising like a solar flame across snow-capped peaks, it sent shimmering waves of golden light over the pond's still water. An urge to pause had taken her and she sat.

Alone with its beauty, the world had opened.

Tolling like the early morning bell, a new spirit echoed through her senses.

And she awoke.

Before her lay all there ever was and all that ever would be. Until the next moment came and usurped it, making itself the same in paradox. She had been circling this answer, seeking it, her entire life. And always it remained beyond her reach. Now, it had finally showed itself and invited her inward.

This was the Way.

She had entered the Now.

Since that day all her tactical decisions in the field and responses in hand-to-hand combat had become... easy. Why? Because there was no past. No future. Liberated from the burdens of those two distractions, all that remained was doing what was needed in the moment.

Summoned from the spontaneity and inspiration that morning came words:

Observe reflections.
Relish in shadows.
Sparkle does the water,
when inner peace rises.

She had penned her first Ho-to, seated on the pond's edge. An ancient poetic form celebrated by those who practiced a path to enlightenment through martial philosophy. Two syllabic lines of five, followed by two lines of six. Each, an evolution toward awakening. The first, one's action. The second demonstrating comfort and security of the current, limited state. The third, a catalyst - provoking awakening through beauty, wonder, or power. And the final line: unveiling knowledge that was there all along, hidden by limitations now understood as illusion.

The Ho-to had no title; it simply was. Lilline had never written it down. It existed only in a present, made manifest by recitation or recalled internally within the mind.

When she shared it with her teacher, the old Rasp had stood

silent. Lilline respected the quiet and to her surprise, had experienced no questioning of self-confidence or anxiousness of self-doubt.

No past.

No future.

Only now.

Waiting was waiting. Nothing more.

It would end and something else would replace it.

"Welcome, Lilli," the old Rasp had said, drawing lines in the pebbles with his staff. He had walked away without another word.

"Ms. Larkin?"

The memory faded like time receding through a dimensional portal.

"Thank you." She accepted a glass and napkin from the Gej-ti, who leaned over her neighboring passenger.

"I doubled the napkin," the attendant said.

And this was the Now. A present of esoteric layers, visible to a select few who understood a different set of illusions.

She sniffed the wine. Indeed, it was pre-Roncheau. A lesser vintage, but with a limited amount left in the galaxy, getting a glass on an Aspirion flight was itself a win. She took a sip, the mixture of berry and smoky leather tingling her tastebuds and slipped the lower of the two napkins down to the window-side armrest.

Lilline checked on her neighbor, a twenty-something human man in a business suit. He sat absorbed in a broadcast.

She slipped her eyes to the napkin.

Sky Lounge, Taborri Sky Lounge. 6:45 p.m.

TWENTY-ONE

The Royal Loha Hotel looked every bit as grand and luxurious as Lilline remembered.

She passed through the old-fashioned revolving door like a time traveler returning to a lost century. A world of marble, dappled with red area rugs and ceramic urns sprouting massive palm-leafed plants, conjured an air of reserved charm. Plush leather furniture, a check-in counter in the deco-noir style, and a thick Maluc wood bar running along the lobby's wall, evidenced the Royal Loha's relentless attention to first-class hospitality.

Lilline paused, bag in hand, taking it all in. Guests climbed and descended symmetrical curving staircases that hugged the reception desk, making their way to and from the establishment's top-end suites lining the second and third floor balconies.

"Madame is checking in?"

A Froo, dressed in the hotel's signature white uniform with gold trim, gestured in the direction of reception.

"Yes, thank you," Lilline said. "Just taking a moment."

"Indeed." He nodded. "The Royal Loha's charm is timeless."

A familiar percussive rhythm echoed off the frescoed ceiling. Lilline homed in on its source: a Goosh bartender hard at work preparing the hotel's signature cocktail.

Check-in time.

She took a step forward but froze as her wrist vibrated. Changing course, she veered to the side of the main aisle. Her eyes went to her comm.

Are you feeling okay, dear?

Granny.

Yes, why?

Oh, nothing.

Lilline bent her head back and exhaled. Two stories above, a starry jungle night, viewed from a palace balcony and rendered in a stylized hand, calmed her rising frustration.

What is this about, Granny? she typed.

I've got a case of the tummies is all.

Well, how many Dari cakes did you eat?

Why is that relevant?

You know there's heavy cream in them. Too much of it never sits well with you.

Yes, dear. I am well aware. I wanted to check if it was only me.

Well it is, and I'm sure we both know why.

Oh, look at that... Hiko spilled his milk. I need to go.

Lilline groaned. Her fingers tapped like rapid blaster fire.

HIKO ISN'T SUPPOSED TO DRINK MILK, REMEMBER???

Delivery failed. Recipient has silenced notifications.

"Unbelievable." She picked up her bag and made for reception.

"We have to stop meeting like this."

I know that voice.

She turned. "Renina?"

"I noticed you come in." The Rasp gestured at a bistro-style seating area by the bar. "Care to join me? Or are you in a hurry?"

"What are you doing here?"

"I got some time off from the museum. Requested it, actually. With everything going on, Mr. Bilarus was happy to approve it." The Rasp's eye shifted toward her table. "I just ordered. Let me at least buy you a drink as thanks for saving me at the Blue Comet."

Lilline kept her exterior casual and social. Internally, she was working undercover tactics and analytics on hyperdrive. One half focused on crafting her Caroline Liro persona in preparation for a conversation, the other was reading the Rasp's exterior.

"Sure, why not." She picked up her bag. "Lead on."

Ten minutes. That she could spare. Plus, a drink was the perfect antidote to the lingering frustration of Granny's unexpected interruption.

"It's even more impressive in here than the tourist brochures," Renina said, sitting. "And that's stunning." She pointed one of her three fingers at a mural behind the Goosh bartender. "I think it's an original Oshilara."

Lilline remembered the famed image from her last visit. Yu-Shek, the lone volcanic peak that rose from the endless jungle of Hesh-9's equatorial region, rendered with thick and juicy strokes of paint. The familiar skyline of Hikesh ran across a natural ledge halfway up the mountain, the only interruption to an otherwise pristine tropical rainforest. Dapples of color indicated low-lying residential districts, as if the artist had flicked a wet paintbrush at the surface. The effect was like visual punctuation, complimented by the bold and confident strokes that brought the skyline's corporate towers to life. At the mural's lower boundary, rows of liquor bottles of various shapes and sizes ran like a haphazard fence of glass, adding an optical illusion that integrated two-and three-dimensional space in a delightful *trompe l'oeil.*

"Your drink, madame."

Renina's one eye widened with delight as the Kreeli placed the cocktail down in front of her.

"And madame, may I get you something?"

Lilline eyed the chilled blue liquid in the triangular glass, its long stem and delicate base a perfect fit for the Royal Loha's aesthetics. A swirl of viscous white, moving with the patience of a cephalopod on a sea floor, hung like a cloud in a clear sky.

"When in Sky City," Lilline said to the server.

"Another Skytini it is. Does madame have a preparation preference?"

"Rattled with ice." She smiled at Renina. "And no cloud for me. I prefer a clear sky."

The Kreeli nodded and retreated to the bar.

"I would have taken you for a sunset," Renina said, sipping her Skytini.

"Too sweet for my taste."

"Not a fan of nuvola-noir?"

Lilline shook her head.

"This is a real thrill for me," the curator said, head snaking left and right, taking in the lobby.

"Quite a leap in lifestyle for you, I imagine... growing up on Ornal."

Renina's clay skin cracked as she nodded. "Yes, I've come a long way."

I'd say.

"Are you staying at the Loha as well?"

"No. I'm at the Wingard Grand."

"Also nice," Lilline said. Cheaper by a good degree, and reasonable for someone on her salary.

"It's not the Royal Loha," Renina said. "This really is exquisite."

"Here you are, madame. A clear Skytini." The Kreeli placed it down. "Enjoy."

"Stars to you, Renina." Lilline held up her glass.

"And to you, Caroline."

Clink.

Lilline eased a bit of the cocktail into her mouth. The crisp liquor stung, but its chill brought a sensory pleasure like entering cold water after a sauna.

An awkward silence rose. But unlike Lauden's office, this time Lilline relished it.

Your move, Renina.

"You're not an insurance agent, are you?"

Lilline sipped her Skytini, weighing options. With the curator in the know, albeit to a limited degree, about the sensitivity of the situation and the Ministry's attempt to keep it under wraps, she was facing down a rhetorical decision.

"No." She placed the Skytini down and eased back in her chair, crossing her legs.

Screw it. I'm all-in. Let's see what cards you're holding.

"You work for the government?"

"I do."

The Rasp nodded, a mixture of satisfaction at guessing and resentment at being fooled hung on her face like the cloud in her cocktail.

"My job is to locate our missing painting." Not a lie, and not a breach of confidentiality about her true occupation. She was playing it safe. Call it a trust-building exercise. Soon, she would strike like a Bukki tiger. Her eyes went to the mural behind the bar. The confrontation with the feline predator on Hesh-9 had done more than cause her to lose an ear. She'd since learned much about that beast's tactics and had applied them several times in the field. Once it had saved her life.

"This is such a mess," Renina said. "Honestly, I'm glad to have a few days off." She stirred her drink. "I've never been to Sky City. I figured this was close enough, and yet different enough, to distract me."

"Less dangerous than the Blue Comet," Lilline said, "if you stay out of the lower levels."

The Rasp raised her glass in appreciation.

Lilline checked the time on the clock behind reception.

"Are you any closer to finding it? The *Cosmic Widow*, I mean…"

"I'm sorry Renina but I can't say."

"Well, anything I can do to help."

"Actually, I do have a question."

The Rasp gestured to proceed.

"I understand you were questioned about a forgery incident a few cycles ago?"

Renina nodded. "I was a grad student. I had no idea what I was involved in. It was a case of looking for job experience and choosing the wrong place at the wrong time… with the wrong people. Typical, I suppose. A naive back-system newbie trying to break into the Inner Core art game. I was questioned and cleared." She sighed. "I've been trying to put that behind me for cycles. I thought I had."

"What do you mean, 'thought?'"

"If this painting isn't found I'll never make it professionally, not with that mark on my record." She shook her apple-sized head. "This is going to destroy my career."

"I understand you have aspirations to be Head Curator?"

"At the Galactic Museum?"

Lilline nodded.

"Absolutely." The Rasp leaned forward. "I'm not sure if you've noticed, but I'm not keen on Mr. Bilarus. I won't hide that fact. But if I can help you, I will."

"I understand you know a great deal about the *Cosmic Widow?*" Lilline sipped her drink.

"And First Galactic art in general."

"Why aren't you a fan of Reginald Bilarus?"

Renina leaned back and folded her arms. "Really?"

Lilline laughed. "Okay, I imagine he can be a bit odd to work for."

"And difficult," Renina added. "The Board too, for that matter."

"Not keen on them either?"

Renina rolled her one eye. "Old cronies too worried about their reputations and not concerned enough about what others need."

"And what is that, exactly?"

"A history that reflects the new galactic world." Renina gestured a three-fingered hand around them. "That whole museum needs re-arrangement and updating. I've gotten them to let me move one or two paintings based on updated scholarship, but changing labels and revising the historical narrative?" She shook her clay-skinned head. "That's going to take some time."

"Why do you think they are so resistant?"

"Who knows. Nonsense about preserving tradition is what they say, but afraid of change is what my ears hear."

"Well, I hope you get a moment's pause from it all." Lilline knocked back the rest of her cocktail. "I'll do my best to get our missing item back. Soon hopefully, before its disappearance leaks."

The Rasp's expression of agreement appeared genuine. Maybe she truly was an innocent bystander caught in art world criminal crossfire.

"Thank you for the drink, Renina."

"My pleasure... *Caroline*."

Lilline smirked at the Rasp's coy choice of words. "And by the way, there's a Gej-ti at the bar interested in you."

Renina's hand froze halfway to her drink. "Really?"

Lilline nodded. "She's a lot cuter than that Zapper at the Blue Comet too."

She winked and headed to reception.

Not an entire waste of time. She'd gotten a small peek at the cura-tor's hand of cards. It wasn't much, and might be nothing, but Renina wasn't as naive and innocent as she made herself out to be.

"Good evening, madame," the human receptionist said when she reached the desk.

"Checking in, please. Keely Larkin."

"One moment." The receptionist tapped her holo-board, pulling up the reservation. "First time at the Royal Loha, Ms. Larkin?"

"No, I've been here before."
And so has Renina.

TWENTY-TWO

"Good evening and welcome to the Taborii Sky Lounge." A human maître d' smiled from behind a black quartz greeting stand. "If you would, please." They gestured to the entry scanner.

Lilline ran her room card across the sensor.

"Ah, Ms. Larkin, your associate is here. I've seated them in Sconce 14." The maître d' stepped out from behind the podium.

Valenti striped suit. Petracci wingtip shoes, freshly polished. And an asymmetrical pixie cut dyed a gleaming silver. As exquisite as the surroundings.

"This way, please." They gestured for her to follow.

Lilline scanned the room. An assortment of species dappled the low-lit lounge, puffing away on snake-like tubes extending from bulbous ceramic vessels. Melted into cushy sofas and wing backed chairs, the patrons released plumes of deliciously scented smoke, enjoying the establishment's selection of world-class tobacco. The Taborii Sky Lounge was as much a business venue as a social space, with credits and more dubious assets traded and exchanged, or bribed, through shared smoking sessions that ended in deals, deadlocks, or long negotiated and carefully considered refusals.

Curious eyes tracked her as she followed the maître d's graceful strides. To be expected, considering her sartorial choice for the galaxy-famous hotspot.

After checking in to the Royal Loha, she'd showered and selected a dress for the rendezvous, opting for elegance. The meetup was a perfect opportunity to strut in her new Vixen sheath dress, midnight black, that folded around her just shy of her shoulder blades. Silver chain links held the two sides together, running in a criss-cross across her bare back. Offensively high, black Gemmelli heels and a single cryex crystal pendant on a tight silver choker completed the look. In the Taborii Lounge, she fit in like any other fashionable and wealthy patron on holiday or important business in Sky City.

Except for one important detail.

Copious scars, visible in the sleeveless dress, told those around her that she was an experienced and particular kind of galactic traveler.

"Here we are," the maître d' said. "Sconce 14. Secluded and... private."

"Thank you."

Their eyes met.

And lingered.

Lilline found the maître d's face to be a beautiful contradiction of angularity and softness.

"Madame may select a tobacco from the inventory, hit the call button, and it will be delivered."

"By you?"

The maître d' held her stare. "Normally requests are delivered by one of our runners, but if you prefer I can make an exception."

"I'd like that."

A smile tipped the balance toward softness. And submission.

"Very well, Ms. Larkin. Shall I make a leaf recommendation?"

Stars, I love flirting. It had felt like forever since she'd done it.

"That would be appreciated."

From the corner of her eye, through the portal, Pin stood with her back turned, focused on the view out the bulbous window.

"Queen Yaz Flake, Limited Edition is our finest stock."

Lilline's heart sank. *So, you're one of ours.*

"Enjoy your session, Ms. Larkin, and if you need anything during your stay..." The maître d's lips, done with the faintest trace of lavender lipstick, curved at the edges. "Anything at all..."

The gentle touch of their hand grazed her forearm.

"Please do not hesitate to contact me."

Oh... so work boundaries are loose in Sky City.

"Thank you, Mx.?"

"Haron." Their hazel eyes sparkled. "But you may call me Alex."

"Thank you, Alex." *I like your eyes.* "I'm Keely."

"Enjoy the view. The aurora are particularly strong this week." The maître d' gestured at the concave sconce and departed.

Powerful magnetism in here as well.

"Was that all code, T8?"

"Huh?" Lilline turned to the Oltari.

"The banter," Pin said, gesturing with all four arms. "I assume that is one of our company assets and you've gathered some important on-site intel?" Behind her colleague, green and red serpentine trails dappled Tavi-Prime's thermosphere.

"You could say that, yes." Lilline hit the ignition button on the Taborii vessel and plopped down on the sofa. "Good show, Pin. You picked up on that."

I mean, it's not like that was technically a lie.

Flirting *was* code. Language filled with allusions and implicit meaning. And often times, innuendo.

"I find it odd that there are a great many aspects of your job that do not appear in the GAM-OPs manual."

"Well," Lilline said, easing into the couch, "think of it as an advantage. There's a freedom each agent has that allows them to work to their strengths and..."

"Tastes?"

She examined the Oltari's expression. Was she toying—

Ping.

"Queen Yaz Flake, Limited Edition," Alex said, entering. "Cellared at 18.3 degrees Celsius in a constant humidity of sixty-eight percent in the Midrift Caves." They held out the tin. "At Heenan & Thorpe Tobacco, Inc. in Gledfordshire."

A brush of Alex's finger as they handed over the tobacco sent a tingle up her arm.

"Oh my!" Pin exclaimed.

Lilline caught a falling Alex in her arms. Their eyes met and the maître d' smiled.

"That was unexpected," Alex said.

"I like surprises." Lilline helped the maître d' steady themself on their feet.

"Was that a cloud quake?"

"Indeed," Alex said to the approaching Oltari. "Your first?"

Pin nodded. "Although I don't understand what all the fuss is about. If you have wings it's quite an instinctual and non-disturbing adjustment in elevation."

"We humans are much more delicate," the maître d' said. "We often need someone to..."

Again the hazel eyes on her.

A warm rush ran through her blood like a dam bursting.

"Gledfordshire," Pin said, taking the tin from Alex and examining it. "That's on Tix. In the Woshon system."

"You know your cosmic geography," Alex said.

"Not really, but I did some background research on this tobacco's history. My boss—"

"Thank you, Alex," Lilline said.

"My pleasure." They ran a well-manicured hand through silver hair. "Oh, and if you need to reach me..."

Lilline's wrist comm vibrated.

"My number." They smiled. "Now please, enjoy yourselves."

Hazel eyes pulled at her.

The maître d' broke contact and exited.

"To business, T8?"

"Yes, Pin." Lilline gazed out at the aurora. The fiery spectacle wasn't cooling the heat in her blood. "To business."

TWENTY-THREE

The GAM-OPs head of Tech sat and opened a suitcase on her lap.

Lilline unhooked a tube from the Taborri and took a pull, drawing in Yaz Flake. She wasn't a smoker, but sometimes the field required it. Although why the GAM-OPs team had chosen a tobacco lounge for the equipment drop was lost on her. She blew out the savory smoke, choosing not to inhale but to take the flavor and nicotine through her taste buds and tongue. An interesting leaf. Pleasant, if a bit bold for her liking. She eyed the tin, flipping it between her fingers.

"Here." She handed it to Pin. "Give this to the director when you return to HQ."

The Oltari took it without a word and continued placing items out between them.

Lauden would be hard pressed not to express his gratitude. Limited Edition Yaz Flake was hard to find across the galaxy these days, and this cellaring was particularly impressive.

"By the way, your boots came in handy the other night."

"Did you employ the drop heels?"

"Oh, I did indeed." Lilline exhaled a stream of smoke and eased back into the sofa. "And that taser dart too."

"Oh, do tell!" Pin's eyes lit up. "Did you find the voltage effective? I set it to fifty-thousand, so about one-thousand five hundred should have entered your target."

Lilline brought her fingers to her lips and made a smooch. "Chef's kiss, Pin."

"Excellent. I will give my team the go-ahead to produce a set for all the T# agents. Thank you for being the beta tester."

The pleasure was all mine... and Gina's.

"One woman's trash..." Lilline whispered and took a hit of Yaz Flake.

"What was that?"

"Oh, nothing. Okay, what do you have for me?"

Pin stood and held out a silver ring. A gem the color of an azure sky glittered, capturing the auroras' lights.

"Are you proposing? You should know, I don't mix work and pleasure." She thought of Alex. *Usually...*

The Oltari eyed her. Her mouth curved at the edges. "Humor! You are making a joke?"

Lilline gestured with the Taborii tube like a baton.

"The ring is for you, T8. But its purpose is to aid in detecting forgeries at the auction."

Lilline edged up on the sofa and accepted it from her colleague. The report Intel had prepared mentioned that Mr. Abaqati signed his paintings on an underlayer. Typical. A hubristic move - stick it to those foolish enough to believe his works were originals. And pay handsomely for them.

"Close and open your finger once to activate it and hold it clenched for two seconds to shut it off."

"What does it do?"

"It contains infrared capability. Emits a ten-by-ten centimeter beam. Aim it at something within ten meters and it will penetrate a surface layer. Just be careful. It will be visible to anyone in the available sightline."

"Interesting." Lilline put it on. "Is there an intensity adjuster?"

"Indeed. Voltage and radiation have three tiers. Close and open your finger sequentially from one to three to increase it. You can analyze multiple degrees of underpainting and penetrate beyond mere pentimenti."

"Look at you, Pin." Lilline leaned back and examined the gem. "Throwing around the art history vocabulary."

"A pentimenti is the appropriate term for a visible correction on a painting that—"

"I know. What kind of stone is this?" She wanted to dive into its clear blue prism.

"Viozite. Quite rare. The agency has a small stash from when we helped topple the Trilon dictatorship and shut down their inhumane and exploitative mining operations."

"Well, it's nice to know it is being used in the cause of justice. What else do you have for me?"

"Speaking of footwear," Pin pulled a pair of shoes out of her case.

"Are those my Gemmelli's?"

"No."

"They look like my Gemmelli athletics, Pin."

"Good. They are your size and color. I noticed you wearing a pair a few months ago and made a note."

"Note for what?"

"To buy a pair and add a feature."

Lilline accepted them. "I don't notice anything different."

"What you don't see is a radar bounce wave system."

"A what?"

"I've inserted a set of weight-activated chips, one in each sole. The right sends a radio wave pulse outward with each step. The left sole has a receiver to accept the bounce back signal."

Lilline slipped out of her heels and tried them on. "What am I using them for, exactly?"

The Oltari reached down and pushed the insteps as if she were a salesperson checking how much room was in the toes.

"Check your wrist comm. I activated the RBW system."

A set of concentric circles with a central circular light blipped onto the tiny screen.

"Walk around."

With each step, a pulse spread outward over the comm's glowing circles.

"Nothing is showing up," Lilline said.

"I wouldn't imagine we would get that lucky."

She sat and removed the shoes, slipping back into her heels.

"What I have not yet shared is that it detects Corellium."

Corellium... Lauden's file mentioned it. "Isn't that a material used in frames for valuable paintings?"

"Not anymore," Pin said. "You won't find it anywhere these days. Not the safest material to be around. But back in the First Galactic..."

Lilline smirked. "So, if I am near an antique painting that has an original frame..."

"Like the *Cosmic Widow*?" The Oltari steepled both sets of hands, twenty-eight fingertips dancing in delight.

"Good show, Pin."

"Thank you. I know it's a long shot considering the status of the case but I thought it worthwhile."

Anything to increase the odds was welcome at this point.

"Range?"

"Not great. Only about fifty meters."

"I'll take it. These will be getting a lot of use," Lilline said, handing back the shoes. A small stone figurine between them triggered an internal alarm. "Pin... did that sculpture move?"

"Oh, right." The Oltari picked up the artifact. "Did your file include mention of the bait?"

It had. Apparently, Mr. Abaqati negotiated a better deal by providing specifics about the auction. She was to bring an item for appraisal with the hope it opened more doors, literally, leading to clues about the *Cosmic Widow*.

Pin held out the figurine.

"Is that real?" Lilline flipped it over in her hand. The size of a narrow cocktail glass, the carving looked akin to Second Galactic idols commonly found in humble domestic shrines of the Lyodic people, a human trading culture that once spread across the galactic Mid-Span.

Two white opal eyes, abstracted to be larger and disproportionate to the face, followed her as she moved her hand.

"Creepy," she said.

"It's not as subtle as I would have liked, but on short notice this was the best I could do. I tried to cause as little damage as possible."

"This is an original?"

"Indeed, T8. Mr. Bilarus provided it to us. I've added a motion-sensor camera with audio that tracks and transmits through an earpiece."

Lilline accepted the prosthetic ear. Good, this would help ensure her identity was disguised. A missing ear tended to draw attention. And questions.

"Bilarus gave us a Second Galactic artifact?"

Pin shrugged. "It's networked to your comm. You can watch the camera capture on your screen and listen in through the earpiece."

Lilline placed it down on the sofa. With its crudely carved wavy hair, large eyes, and folded arms set against its chest, it stood poised in a reverent state of attention for all eternity.

"The small drive inside has a five-image capacity," Pin said. "Snap digi-photos by tapping your wrist comm control screen."

Crafty. And impressive considering the short turnaround time.

"Is that it?" Lilline asked.

"In terms of equipment, yes. But I brought your wrist-action blade and cable. I am sure you will be happy about that." The Oltari took the strap and weapon off the couch and gave it to her.

"I feel better already." She placed it in her clutch. The flight up had forced her to leave her go-to weapon behind, but Pin always found ways to bypass security.

"You will also be relieved to know that I sent an official letter of concern to Renina regarding my criticisms of the museum's current display philosophy."

Waves of relief are washing over me.

"T8?"

"That's great, Pin. Just be patient. She might not read it for a while. Renina is on leave, taking a short vacation."

"I would imagine it will be forwarded to Mr. Bilarus, then?"

Lilline took a pull of Yaz Flake, feeling oddly like Lauden at his desk.

"Don't count on it," she said in the Gej-ti's voice and did the hand thing.

"Hoo!" Pin clapped two sets of hands.

An attempt to blow a smoke ring failed miserably. *Two out of three... good enough.* "Aren't you going to try the Yaz Flake?" Lilline gestured at the Taborii tubes.

"I've had enough already, thank you."

Lilline cocked her head, mouthpiece between her lips. "You never fired up your snake?"

"As an avian species, my respiratory system is more sensitive," Pin said. "And far more efficient."

"No need to gloat about it, Pin."

"It's a fact, T8. I've absorbed as much, perhaps more, tobacco smoke than you through secondhand respiratory inhalation. You might find it hard to believe, but if I were to puncture this window..." The Oltari rose and flew toward the sconce.

"Pin!" Lilline spat the tube out.

"Hoo!"

The head of Tech's cheeks blushed blue. "Human humor... I am beginning to grasp it."

Lilline eased back and took a pull of Yaz Flake.

"If, as I was saying," Pin continued, "we lost pressurization, I would be able to survive the thin atmosphere long enough to descend to the surface of Tavi-Prime."

Interesting. Lilline made a mental note should something ever arise at the agency that needed delivery through thin atmospheric conditions. Not a field-related op of course, but if something was... simple.

And direct.

Without concern for discretion.

On second thought. Not a good idea.

"I find the nicotine to be quite exhilarating." Pin placed all four hands on the window and leaned against it. "It makes me want to..." She spun around, facing her. "Talk."

"Well," Lilline checked her wrist comm, "unfortunately, I'm out of time. If I don't get going I won't make the auction." She tucked away the ring in her handbag. A knuckle brushed the muzzle of her H-42 PB Mini, holstered to the interior. "And you need to get back on the last flight down to Tavi, right?"

"Sadly, yes." The Oltari turned back to the aurora. "This has been a wondrous adventure for me."

Lilline's heart warmed at her colleague's statement. A childlike marvel hung in the room, complimenting the Yaz Flake.

"Flaming Sky Dragons," Pin whispered.

"What was that?"

"A name for the aurora. From an unknown ancient source. My flock leader shared it with the fledglings when we got our wings and left the trees."

"Are the aurora on your home world uncommon?" Lilline followed a green band rise in a titanic arc across the sky.

"Hoo."

The signature Oltari expression reached her ears without its usual bravado. Emotional yes, but more elegiac.

"Sadly yes, T8. So much so that it's used as a legend to deter us from straying too far from the ground."

"And yet here you are, Pin." Lilline stood and approached.

The maître d' was right; the aurora were strong. Majestic green, yellow, and red serpents danced across a canopy of stars. Below at the horizon, a flash of lightning indicated an approaching storm front.

"Being a secret agent does have its perks," Pin said. "I admit to being envious."

"This is the good side of it." Lilline checked the time. "Where I'm heading now—" She followed a red aurora's trail as it usurped its green and yellow neighbors. "—is into the dragon's lair."

TWENTY-FOUR

Lilline strode Sky City's circular promenade looking every bit the art world buyer. Hair up, fastened into a bun with two sleek steel hair sticks and wearing a minimal gray Korobi suit with her white Gemmelli athletic shoes, she could grace the cover of any entrepreneurial digital zine as the latest "Top 100 something or other."

She veered to the open core railing and peered down. A wave of vertigo shot up her legs. Located at the top of Sky City, the Royal Loha occupied a segment of its three uppermost stories. From where she stood, an open-air shaft plummeted to a tiny sparkling vanishing point three kilometers below. Somewhere below, shrouded and hidden in the lowest layers of the floating world, lay her destination.

Each step toward the drop station increased her anticipation. It was always this way with undercover ops. The unknown left her anxious and tense. When she arrived that would all change. Like a dramatist taking the stage, once the curtain rose everything would fall into place and her well-trained and experienced GAM-OPs agent persona would shine. The difference was that she had no script, no stage rehearsals, and no director to guide and hone her character development. That was what made undercover work so dangerous and thrilling. You had to land on your feet and be a master at improv.

This evening's persona had no name and no background. That was a boon of Carmini's auctions. All guests were vetted through his private network and invited via codes. You arrived on site or would bid remotely as an assigned number. Tonight, she would be known only as #19. All done to ensure security and maintain vital redundancies. If one individual was caught and prosecuted, they took the fall alone. Equally to her benefit, the client she represented didn't need a name. Only credits. Lots of them. It meant the GAM-OPs hackers performing a digital sleight of hand, dropping what appeared as half a billion credits into a fabricated bank account to make the ruse convincing. Lilline could only imagine her contact's expression at the Ministry when that one passed over their desk.

Carmini was crafty, she would give him that. The question was: what game was he playing and who else was at the table? Mr. Abaqati was there, dealt in, of that she was certain. He had given them the auction to save his family, but something told her the Froo was hiding valuable intel behind his smug amphibious grin. A forger involved with those who profited from exclusive and well-vetted underworld sales events. No doubt, Mr. Abaqati and Carmini were close pals.

The problem tonight was an unknown of a different kind, one that overshadowed all the perks of anonymity provided by the nature of the auction. She had no idea *what* she was here to find.

The Cosmic Widow *would be nice.*

Possible but unlikely. The mission's trail of breadcrumbs hadn't strayed from the well-trodden path into the forest shadows... yet. Could it end here? Sure. Wouldn't be the first time she wrapped up an operation quickly. But something told her they were still light years away from the painting returning to the walls of the museum.

Lilline weaved through well-dressed guests along the core's railing. Ahead, a red light flashed, indicating the drop tube. She hoped to catch an express, which would skip sectors 2-7, and plummet to the lowest segment of the frustum above the industrial levels housing Sky City's internal servers and energy plant. A rocketing dive into the city's bowels, leaving security and order behind to enter dangerous and unpredictable territory.

Her wrist comm buzzed.

At this hour? I swear, Granny...

The arrival icon for the express tube lit up.

Lilline increased her pace.

Again, her wrist vibrated.

Not looking.

Ping... Ping. Ping.

She froze.

The GAM-OPs priority tone sequence.

A cupped hand shielded the comm and she checked the incoming message.

Lauden?

Lilline tapped the screen to connect the call.

A grave expression on the Gej-ti's translucent face sent a chill down her spine.

"Is there a problem, sir?"

"I'm afraid there is, T8."

Light and shadow at his jawline shifted as he clenched his teeth.

"It's your grandmother."

Lilline weaved through passersby to a bench. "Go ahead, sir."

"Kissy was admitted to Tavi-General an hour ago. With you on assignment, the emergency contact re-routed to the GAM-OPs field desk."

"What happened?"

The tiny Lauden on the holo shook. Lilline gripped her wrist with her free hand and took deep breaths.

"Doctor Zeglo is on site. He's in ICU with the head physician." The director tapped a button on his desk. *"Patching him through."*

Lilline scanned the rotunda. No one appeared to be loitering suspiciously or tailing her.

Lauden's office panned left, replaced by Doctor Zeglo's furry gray face. His bulbous eyes, with their signature Dendari UV-screen, reflected the familiar features of a hospital room. Lilline made out a miniature bed with someone in it.

Granny.

A deep breath to fight the tightness in her chest.

"Go ahead, Doctor Zeglo," Lauden said.

"Thank you, sir. She's unconscious. They've stabilized her. I am going to let Doctor Klitarney speak. She's the chief physician and cleared through our medical desk."

Doctor Zeglo stepped aside. A Gej-ti, with curly black hair and thick Bukki tiger patterned glasses entered the view.

"Her body is fighting something, Ms. Larkin. Temperature is elevated and her white blood cell count is through the roof."

"An infection?" Lilline asked.

"Technically, no. None of our scanners are finding traces of bacteria or other foreign organisms. I would normally default to a virus, but from a biological standpoint, the typical signs are not present."

"Poison?" It was Lauden, breaking in.

Lilline's belly wrenched at the thought.

Doctor Klitarney shook her head. *"Doctor Zeglo and I have access to every known galactic variety, I'm not getting any toxicology hits."*

"We're stumped," Doctor Zeglo said, his furry Dendari face popping into view.

"Regardless," Doctor Klitarney pushed her gaudy glasses up the bridge of her nose, *"we need to treat your grandmother so the developing issue can be halted, and hopefully reversed. Without knowing what to prescribe, I can only treat broadly... which isn't ideal."*

"Did she say anything when she was brought in?" Lilline asked.

"She had complained of not feeling well a few hours ago but it didn't sound serious."

Doctor Klitarney shook her head. *"The medic reported that she collapsed a few blocks from your residence. A passerby said she was mumbling about going to the ER."*

Stubborn woman. Should have called an ambulance.

"Ms. Larkin, did your grandmother ingest anything out of the ordinary in last few days?"

"Not that I can think of," Lilline said.

"Do anything outside of her usual routine that brought her into contact with a new substance or material of some kind?"

Lilline shook her head.

"What about visiting a location not part of her daily activities?"

Again, Lilline had no answers. They'd been to Malardi's a thousand times. Other than that, as far as she knew, Granny had spent the morning at home. "Nothing. But then—"

"Yes?"

"It's just, she's a free spirit, Doctor. She comes and goes doing who knows what around the city."

"So I've heard from your director." Doctor Klitarney nodded, marking something on her clipboard. *"If anything comes to mind, please contact me immediately. I'll give you my private number."*

"I appreciate it."

"For now, we'll do our best to control her symptoms. If we work across a range of medications, we may be able to hit on something that slows or stops whatever is causing this."

"And if you can't?"

The Gej-ti took off her glasses. She glanced off-screen, nodded, then edged backward and out of view.

Dr. Zeglo's furry head re-appeared.

Lilline met his bulbous eyes through the holo. Again, Granny appeared in bed in the optical reflection.

"If this continues," he said, *"based on what we are seeing, her body*

will shut down. At her age, Ms. Larkin, and at the current rate this is working in her system…"

"How long?"

"Days… if we're lucky."

"Thank you, I appreciate your efforts," Lilline said.

"Keep us posted," Lauden added.

The Dendari nodded and cut the feed. The GAM-OPs director re-appeared in miniature at his desk. He clasped his hands and locked eyes with her across the virtual distance. *"T8, you can make the last flight back with the head of Tech if you—"*

"No, sir." Lilline shook her head.

"Lilline."

Her breath caught. In all her cycles at the agency, Lauden had never addressed her by name.

"I won't mince words," he said. *"This doesn't look good. Come in. I have T6 on his way to Tavi-Central to catch the last flight up. He can at least scrape something together after the auction."*

Lauden's face blurred.

Lilline wiped her eyes. "She would never forgive me if came in, sir."

"Nonsense." He waved a hand. *"I'm making an exception. This is Kissy. And I know the unique circumstances with your own parents… you would regret—"*

"I can't, sir." Lilline centered herself. *Still water. Morning light. Reflections…*

Now.

The future is the future.

Clarity of purpose calmed her nerves.

"If I don't attend the auction, we lose our one solid lead. Plus, with my university education, I have the best art background. I'm the most informed of all the active T# agents. And I read your brief on the flight up. I'm ready to do this."

Even through the virtual technology, Lauden's eyes scrutinized her with an invisible force. Like a scanner, they ran over her face with x-ray vision.

She felt transparent, as if he penetrated her agent armor.

Pathos rose on the Gej-ti's features.

"Very well."

His eyes said it all. He'd been an agent once. He knew the score.

"Do GAM-OPs and Kissy proud."

"Thank you, sir." Lilline checked the time. "I have to go or we'll miss our chance."

Lauden nodded.

"And I need to go dark," she said. "I'll report in as soon as I can, hopefully with something solid."

"Contact Station S when you have something." He stood, put on his blazer, and waved off the office lights. *"They'll be in constant communication with the hospital and can provide updates."* He tipped his head in earnest. *"Good luck, T8."*

Lilline cut the feed and made for the drop tube.

"Time is short" was taking on a whole new meaning.

TWENTY-FIVE

"You are #19, yes?"

What in the name of...

Standing against an urban backdrop of neon lights, holographic adverts, and hyper-consumerist attractions stood a giant of a creature. A Dendari by the anatomy but...

Shaved?

"I am, thank you," Lilline said, peering up.

Even through the wraparound sunglasses the intensity of their gaze hit like a laser.

"I work for Mr. Carmini. Follow me, please." Like a bass woofer, each word cut through the treble and mid-level noise of the multi-species revelry. Sky City's lower level was a hedonistic cornucopia, like a high-proof shot of galactic delights - physical, virtual, sensual, culinary, and otherwise. Even now, undercover, its intoxicating lure was hard to resist.

Lilline examined the creature as it took bullish strides through the crowd. Passersby not wise enough to open a space for the Dendari were sent spinning and tumbling by their bulging arms and hips. It was like watching a runaway frigate crash through a docking bay.

None of the pedestrian victims reacted with anger or annoyance. They either scattered or rambled apologies, bowing as if in subservience to a menacing master.

Ahead, at the curb, a gleaming Yilari Lightning speeder with a sidecar reflected the lights of a nearby arcade.

Lilline used the last moments before they reached the vehicle to size up the Dendari.

Rex at the Blue Comet cut an imposing figure, but this brute would bat the Kreeli away with a swipe of their hand.

And speaking of hands...

Those claws. Lilline had a decent knowledge of Dendari from previous ops and had interacted with them often, mainly due to their central role as ice distributors in the Pesari-9 system. She'd been to their remote polar world, Frebu, and spoke a crude version of their indigenous language. This one had the typical thick and yellowing nails, filed down from the standard glacier-penetrating length to more manageable, but no less deadly, dagger-size points. She couldn't reconcile the contradiction of his appearance and anatomy. Either he had a naturally occurring mutation or had been cross bred in a lab with a wild beast, most likely of a canine variety. Add in the shaved body, swelling with muscles, a white silk shirt and tailored suit, shiny bald crown, and her escort had the making of a striking contradiction. To complete the look, the Dendari had left the fur under his nose and trained it into a thick, handlebar mustache. The best description Lilline had was, "a shaved, well-dressed, snoutless werewolf mixed with a carnival strongman."

"Sit, please." Five pointy daggers gestured as the sidecar plasma bubble dematerialized.

"I believe you have something for me?" Lilline used her best condescending tone.

The Dendari reached into a blazer pocket.

"Thank you." Lilline took the card, careful not to contact the razor-like fingers. The code matched the one in her file. She dropped into the sidecar. Roomy and comfortable, more so than she expected.

She'd eyed similar add-on appendages at the Yilari dealership. Granny could fit in there if—

With the sharpness of the Dendari's claws, Kissy's image in the hospital ward cut into her undercover persona. Luckily, the bustling world outside went mute as the plasma shield manifested, giving her a moment to regroup. She bounced as the Dendari's hulking frame sat on the bike, forcing the anti-gravity hover system to rev up.

"How long a ride is it?" she asked pushing the comm button.

"Ten minutes." The Dendari's deep voice crackled, testing the audio system's limits.

Lilline peered out as they rose from street level. Pedestrians that had been parallel walking figures became mere heads as they ascended. To either side, buildings climbed in endless stories, connecting with the level's ceiling. It was a world of urban passages, an architectural cavern forming a labyrinth of excitement and danger.

The Dendari leveled off the bike at the fifth story of the adjacent buildings, idling. Lilline peeked in a window. An old Rasp in a white tank top eyed her from inside a dingy apartment.

She smiled.

He flipped her the bird.

Vroom! Vroom!

Her body shook as the Dendari cranked the throttle. Definitely a larger cryex burner than her Yilari. Gauging by the intensity of the exhaust, she guessed it was the biggest model available, the Elite 3000.

"You have a name?" she asked.

"Gongo."

Fitting. The Dendari word for bull.

"Hold on," he said.

The neon world blurred as they shot off, a roar echoing in their wake.

"#19, welcome."

A young Gej-ti in a dress that fit like gift wrap on an hourglass approached. Lilline recognized it as Coultier's seasonal release. The woman had hair that made you jealous - flowing like a waterfall to mid-chest, perfect texture, and with golden highlights shimmering against a chestnut mane. Her neck and wrists dripped with viozite diamonds.

Lilline shook her hand.

"I'm Mr. Carmini's assistant. I run the auction."

"A pleasure."

Over the woman's shoulder, a variety of well-dressed species strolled around a wide parlor, sizing up paintings and artifacts. The decor was ornate meets art world chic, as if an aristocratic private residence had been renovated with nods to the trendy galleries in Tavi-Prime's East End.

"Thank you, Gongo," the Gej-ti said.

The Dendari bowed his head and moved around them. He had to shift sideways to squeeze through the portal to the parlor. The way the behemoth crossed the gallery gave new meaning to the term "bull in a china shop."

"Please, if you would." The woman gestured with a milky-skinned hand to walk with her. "You can refer to me as the auctioneer."

"So only Mr. Carmini uses a name?"

The woman nodded. "I love your Gemmelli's by the way. I have a pair myself. Hard to put on anything else after walking in them."

Good. Not only was she meeting expectations appearance-wise, but something about the remark told her it was more than a compliment. The Gej-ti's words carried an implicit undertone, as if validating her status. What the auctioneer didn't know, was that with each step she took a radar pulse emanated through the building, seeking a prize more valuable than anything for sale this evening.

"I do have an item with me that I was hoping could be appraised?" Lilline said.

"Is it potentially for sale?"

"If the result is positive, yes." Lilline withdrew the figurine, wrapped in red velvet. More than a few eyes in the room glanced her way.

"Oh, a Lyodic figurine," the auctioneer said. "May I?"

Shit. Pin had switched off the artifact's surveillance system, thankfully. But if the Gej-ti knew her Second Galactic archaeology the modifications might not pass her notice.

Lilline handed it over.

"Gongo."

With surprising grace, the Dendari left his post and navigated around pedestals, politely asking pardons as he crossed in front of guests observing paintings.

"Take this downstairs. Set it with the other smaller items on the central table."

Lilline, eyes on a familiar painting across the room, eased her nerves. Gongo shouldn't have a clue about such things. Hopefully he would place it in a suitable viewing position.

"We have about fifteen minutes, 19. Is there anything specific that has your client's eye? I'm happy to open cases or discuss the paintings to help you with a bidding decision."

"No, thank you. I'm well prepared," Lilline said, stepping closer to the painting that pulled at her.

"That may steal the show today," the Gej-ti said.

Lilline recognized it as the famous battle scene that hung in the Galactic Museum - the one that drew her attention when Bilarus had first approached her. She stole a peek at her wrist comm. The radar on her soles wasn't sending back anything detectable.

One of Mr. Abaqati's copies?

"This looks like a newer frame." Lilline took her best educated guess based on the information in Lauden's file. "Late Second Galactic?"

"You have a good eye."

Why would you auction a forgery?

"Such mystery," Lilline said, pulling up what she remembered from the report. "To think the Darians had a formidable enemy and yet we know almost nothing about who it was." She examined a painterly detail of a battleship. Impressive work by the Froo. Like the original, the surface had the telltale wet-on-wet application of paint distinct to the period.

"Allure makes the bidding soar, as we say."

Lilline chortled. "The *alla prima* technique is exquisite." She leaned in and scrutinized a frigate facing off against the battleship. "I've never seen it duplicated with such accuracy." *There's a shot across your bow.*

"You know your First Galactic, #19. I'm impressed."

Lilline shrugged, making as if anyone in this room would. Or should.

"This will be the last item up for bidding today."

The finale? Not the Cosmic Widow? She kept her exterior cool as ice but inside she was struggling with the logic of this painting's sale.

"Count on me being here for it," Lilline said.

"Excellent. I'm delighted we've added you to our roster. Jerald... oh, excuse me." A hint of rose peeked through the translucent skin on her cheeks. "Mr. Carmini will also be pleased, I am sure."

So, he's Jerald to you? Interesting...

"Excuse me, #19. I need to get ready. The sale commences in a few minutes. Each item will be brought in according to its auction number and staged at the podium." She gestured at a row of chairs and a pedestal. Behind it on the wall, a holo-board listed remote bidders, identified by numbers for anonymity, who had signed on to participate in the sale. "A few items from downstairs not on view will be brought up as well. These are of... lesser value."

"I look forward to it, thank you."

Lilline checked for nearby guests as the Gej-ti moved off. All were occupied elsewhere with pre-auction decisions. It was now or never. Her index finger squeezed closed and open. Only a half meter from the painting, she raised her hand and aimed the ring's gem at the bottom left corner.

Nothing.

She squeezed again, increasing the beam's wavelength.

No signature hiding under deeper layers.

This doesn't make sense.

Lilline circled the area with the beam, careful not to draw attention. To be certain, she ramped the ring to the highest setting.

The canvas showed.

This isn't a forgery!

"Collectors of distinguished taste the galaxy over."

Lilline squeezed her fingers into a fist, deactivating the ring. She turned to find a grotesque, gelatinous biped in a tuxedo at the podium. Her shock about the painting's authenticity, and what that meant for the one hanging back at the museum, clashed with the vision before her: a Jenzara. A species with unnatural long life marked by a unique anatomy. As if the world were upside down, its eyes lay below its nose and its mouth ran across its forehead. Five brains, one in each limb and head, as well as a neuro-nexus nestled in the chest cavity, controlled its consciousness. A hideous being by aesthetic standards, with a constantly sweating, red and gooey epidermis that covered a body with the consistency of uncooked dough.

"For those of you who do not already know me, I am Mr. Carmini. Welcome, you honor our floating city."

TWENTY-SIX

Lilline accepted a bidding button and chose an aisle seat in the second-to-last row. Practical as much as it was performative, her modest choice offered a view of the coming action and quick access to exits. Those consisted of two portals flanking the podium and stage eight rows in front of her. Through the left portal, uniformed kitchen staff prepared small bites and drinks for what she assumed would be a catered reception. On the right, and within a few short steps, was a hallway. A restroom icon overhead indicated a lavatory accessible to bidders, but she didn't miss the well-dressed Kreeli standing at a corner twenty meters further down the hall. Based on the auction-eer's comment about the lower level, and the fact that Gongo took the figurine down the corridor, she guessed it led to the artifact storage room and Carmini's personal offices.

Running a hand through her hair, she made as if socially investi-gating her neighbors. She rotated, noting the gallery that led back to reception. An identical Kreeli stood in the narrow passage at the entrance.

Nodding in greeting to a middle-aged Froo in her row, she turned her attention forward to the podium. Gongo, hard to miss, stood behind Mr. Carmini and the auctioneer, who spoke in hushed tones.

The Jenzara stepped forward. With a tap of the gavel, the audience hushed.

"Welcome distinguished guests, be you representatives or direct buyers." Bone white pupils with yellow irises carried a fiendish aura against his blood-red skin. An air of elitism clung to the dealer, as if those of the wealthiest echelons in attendance would not expect him to treat them as equals. She had to admit the Jenzara's presence was magnetic. Arrogance oozed from his grotesque pores. It wasn't born of classism, nor did she sense its origin in material wealth. An intelligence radiated from his fiery eyes, as if an extraordinary longevity had honed wisdom into a dangerous and effective weapon, one with an intellectual edge sharp enough to slay the most entrenched forms of power and privilege in the galaxy.

How old he might be Lilline couldn't tell. Rumors abounded about the species' life span. It was said that Jenzara lived upwards of a thousand cycles, longer than any other sentient citizen in the galaxy. Intrinsic masters of strategy, one of their five brains took precedence, emphasizing a particular cognitive specialization: memory, perception, learning, language, or problem solving.

"We have an extraordinary selection of works on auction this evening." Carmini gestured in the direction of the gallery behind him. "And while the galaxy's museums are full of art for public consumption, we as the privileged exceptions, are the real aficionados."

Chuckles, in a variety of tones and pitches, rose amidst the multispecies crowd.

Lilline's dislike and distrust of the illicit dealer and this entire ruse soured whatever charm and seduction his words might carry.

"Let us proceed to the event, yes?" A wide grin formed on his forehead. "I leave you in the competent hands of my *lovely* assistant."

By the looks on the faces around her, the emphasis wasn't lost on anyone.

"I am eager to speak with all of you at the reception," Carmini said. "There's an exquisite bottle of '44 Gondau decanting as we speak."

Several guests murmured their delight. Lilline among them. It was a top vintage, her second favorite next to the rare and almost unattainable '42.

"Although…" Carmini feigned regret, "I will admit to lamenting the loss of these exquisite items from my temporary charge." He gestured at the auction list.

Nods from the crowd.

Maybe add bullshit artist to the cognitive list.

"Alas, such is the life of a humble dealer, yes?" He sighed. "We are but a waypoint on a road leading to our client's dreams."

The contrived rhetoric was enough to make her want to vomit.

"Good luck." With a wave of a red hand, the infamous dealer exited down the hallway with Gongo following at his heels.

"Let the bidding begin," the auctioneer said, taking over at the podium.

With the Dendari blocking her sightline, Lilline caught passing glimpses of Carmini. The dealer halted to speak with the Kreeli at the corner before disappearing in a side passage.

"A lovely Second Galactic pendant, excavated from a royal burial chamber in the Okynos Isles of Liransa." The auctioneer gestured at the display table. A dazzling jewel hung on the neck of a stone bust. Murmurs of excitement and anticipation rose. The Froo down the row smiled, thick green lips stretching wide. Lilline reciprocated and fiddled with her controller, feigning eagerness to enter the bidding.

With the auction underway, it was time to test out Pin's figurine.

She activated the device from her wrist comm, careful to make sure her screen remained hidden.

A chime echoed in her prosthetic ear.

Okay, Pin. Let's play with your toy.

A smattering of ceramic vessels, antique utensils and plates, and one human skull on a long table formed from the snowy static on her small comm screen. Vignetted as if peering through a pair of binoculars, Pin's figurine offered a vicarious view of the room in high definition. Lilline's body might be seated at the auction, but her eyes were now inside the miniature statue.

"Seventy-thousand galactic credits offered by #4 in the front," the auctioneer said, pointing at a Rasp. "Who will match it?"

Lilline checked on the Froo and other nearby guests. All were absorbed in the bidding.

"This is a disaster in the making!"

Carmini's voice.

A moment later the Jenzara entered from the right side of the screen.

"I'm risking everything on that damn painting... everything!"

The dealer spoke as if he were his own audience.

Boom!

Lilline jumped in her seat as the Jenzara's fist slammed a table. "Excuse me," she whispered to no one in particular, playing it off with a few coughs as if clearing something from her throat.

A behemoth followed in Carmini's wake. Gongo, quite the good sport, took the Jenzara's words of frustration like a verbal punching bag.

"All my credits are wrapped up in this. I put up everything for the tech to pull this off. This was going to be my swan song!"

Gongo leaned against the table. The Dendari's oversized, custom-tailored blazer consumed the view.

Damn it!

"Sold! #12 is the winning bidder at one-hundred and fifteen thousand galactic credits," the auctioneer said. "Congratulations."

Lilline clapped with the others.

"Next up we have—"

She went back to the feed.

"You have no idea where they went?" Carmini asked.

"No, sir." Gongo's deep voice crackled the audio.

"You've heard no attempt to offload it through your network?"

"No."

"If we don't find this rat and get our hands on the painting so I can sell it, I'm ruined. You hear me? With the amount of money I borrowed for this? Do you know what the syndicate does if you don't pay?"

"I do," Gongo said. *"The problem is the thief never handed off the painting to the Zappers."*

"I know what the problem is you idiot!"

"We've lost them," the Dendari said. *"By now they could be halfway across the galaxy."*

"What about our friend on the inside?"

Lilline's ears perked up.

"They know nothing. Claim they did their part."

"I find that hard to believe," Carmini said. *"They're up to something."*

"They are doing their best to aid us…"

"Have you put the fear of death in them?"

"Believe me, they are in over their head," Gongo said. *"They're terrified."*

"They better be. I won't go down alone on this. I'll take them all with me."

Lilline checked the auction. A portrait of a Second Galactic royal from the Xeret court sat on an easel. The price was at half a million galactic credits and climbing. Several remote bidders were fighting for the top spot with the Rasp in the front row. He rose and asked to examine the painting, pulling out an old-fashioned monocle for his large eye.

"After all these cycles of doing business… a master thief runs out on me like this?" The distinct clicking of Carmini's fancy shoes on the floor followed. *"Acrobat my ass. Double-crosser is more like it!"*

This was definitely starting to come together. But between the vague ranting and Gongo blocking the view she still had nothing solid.

"I still have them on my leash."

A sinister, heckling laughter came over the audio.

"What is that?" Gongo asked.

"An astronomical chart. They need it."

"Why?"

"Stars if I know or care, you idiot! But they want it. I made sure when I acquired it, at great expense, that I would hold on to it until they delivered the Cosmic Widow. *That's why I have five brains. They might be able to jump and flip, but I have the intellect of a sage!"*

Jackpot. So, Carmini *was* the mastermind. And, as she and Lauden had deduced, someone... it sounded like the thief, had double-crossed him.

Lilline's eyes narrowed. *I need that chart.*

"Contact everyone you can through your network, Gongo. Give them our thief's description."

"What about their name?"

"I don't know it. They're a professional, not some amateur."

"What are we offering?" Gongo asked.

"Tell them I'm paying double the usual rate for a contract. Triple, if they find them in the next thirty-one hours."

"But I thought you said you don't have credits now that—"

"I'll have the painting if we find the thief! My buyer will make me the wealthiest Jenzara in history. And, if not, I'll sell this damn chart to some ignoramus with delusions of cosmic treasure."

"Yes, sir," Gongo said.

The clicking of Carmini's shoes returned.

Damn it, Gongo. Move!

As if under the power of her stare, the Dendari shifted. The edge of Carmini's tuxedo as he walked away flashed on the screen, the chart in his hand.

More... move you bull.

The Jenzara was almost at the edge of the camera's field of vision, still blocked by a shifting Gongo.

The Dendari was taking too long!

"Sold!" the auctioneer declared with a strike of her gavel.

Lilline tapped the camera capture five times blindly as the bull cleared the screen. Carmini lifted the map, rolled it up, and tossed it on a table. He vanished out of view.

Her finger shut off the surveillance system and she joined in the applause, nodding at the Froo down the row.

"Extraordinary," he said and gurgled, cheek glands going blue.

"Indeed. Quite the event."

Now to check the images.

She shielded the screen with a cupped hand, finger ready to tap the comm.

"Next up for bidding, the famed Venex Horse."

Lilline's hand turned to stone.

TWENTY-SEVEN

The tiny horse stood proud on a bed of black velvet. Lilline stared, paralyzed. Bidders clicked their controllers. Even the Froo was in on the action.

A remote user broke ahead of the pack, crossing two-hundred thousand GCs.

She snapped back, her thumb squeezing the controller.

"#19, with two-hundred and ten thousand," the auctioneer said, nodding in her direction.

Emotions swirled within her: shock at confronting her long-lost talisman, anger at it being auctioned off in the underworld when it should be in a museum, fear of losing the bidding and having it disappear to another buyer, and the excitement of potentially reclaiming it. Lauden had encouraged her to participate in the auction, going so far as allowing her to purchase something should it prove necessary to maintain her cover. But the director's cap had been set at two-hundred thousand GC. Her first bid was already ten-thousand over budget.

"Two-hundred and twenty-five thousand from #4."

Lilline's eyes darted to the Rasp in the front row. Her thumb spun the number dial and she pressed the button, countering their bid.

"Two-hundred and fifty thousand from #19, thank you."

The Froo down the aisle raised an eyebrow.

"Two-hundred and seventy-five thousand from #4."

You are not getting this. Lilline smashed the button.

"Three-hundred thousand from #19."

A few attendees gasped.

She would have to pull some of her investments to pay the balance on top of the GAM-OPs allowance. The problem was if she went higher—

"Three-hundred and fifty thousand from #11 via remote bidding."

Heads turned to the holo board.

Damn! An ethical battle surged in her belly. One side charged forward demanding retribution at all costs. The cause: personal justice. And if she lost the bidding war, then she would track the buyer and steal it back. Its opposition let out a battle cry, clashing into its opponent's emotional determination with reason and professional priorities, claiming the moral high ground. *"Stealing? That makes you no worse than the one who pilfered it from the museum. Plus, this isn't your assignment. Don't lose sight of your mission "*

Lilline pressed the button.

"Four-hundred thousand GC from #19."

Gasps and murmuring rose amongst those seated.

Jittery from the amount of credits she'd thrown into the pot, Lilline tapped her feet.

Ping.

A chime in her prosthetic ear.

Nerves high, her attention homed in on the remote bidding board. More foot tapping.

Ping.

Why is my comm—

The radar system in her soles... it was picking up a signal!

Her feet repeated the action.

The system was tracking an object. But where?

She pulled up the radar screen.

It's right below me... downstairs.

"Four-hundred and ten thousand is the current bid. #19, do you wish to counter?"

Lilline spun the dial blindly and hit the button.

"Four-hundred and forty thousand, thank you."

Again, the binocular-like view of the room downstairs. The rolled-up chart lay on a nearby table. She swiped the screen back and tapped her feet. A glowing dot was on the move, heading to the epicenter of the concentric field. Her finger panned back to the camera feed.

A floor below, a shadowy figure in black crept into view.

Human for certain. In the mask and hood, the variant remained unclassifiable.

Back to the radar system.

Stars... the thief. And they have the Cosmic Widow!

"Four-hundred and fifty thousand from #11, remotely. Going once..."

Lilline's eyed darted to the horse then back to the screen.

The mystery figure reached for the chart.

No!

"Going twice..."

Her eyes went to the Venex Horse. She thought of her mother and father, murdered in a brutal act of retribution... innocent victims of a GAM-OPs mission gone wrong. The hurt and pain of losing her parents overshadowed the horse. So close to her grasp, desire transformed into shame. What was this selfishness? She was here to stop a crime, one with yet unknown and potentially catastrophic consequences. Tasked with returning a masterpiece to a museum so that everyone, not just a privileged few with dirty money and even dirtier means of accessing art, should have it to themselves.

"Last call on the Venex Horse...."

The thief, chart in hand, made to leave.

The auctioneer met her eyes. "#19?"

Do your job.

Lilline shook her head as the shadowy figure vanished.

"Sold!"

She was already up and moving when the auctioneer's gavel broke through the applause.

TWENTY-EIGHT

"You passed the restroom." The Kreeli's blue finger pointed over Lilline's shoulder.

"I'm having an allergic reaction." She lowered her gaze and searched through her bag but didn't stop walking. "I need my medicine."

"Miss, I can't let you pass this—"

Crack!

Fingers squeezed in a knife-hand impacted the Kreeli's windpipe. The hand with her bag checked his outstretched arm. She reached underneath in a block and pass. Her hips rotated, twisting the Kreeli to expose his kidney and floating ribs. A fist, the strap of her clutch gripped tight inside her palm, drove into his side.

One more move to complete the advanced sequence known as *Dragonfly Dances over Lotus Blossoms*. Her foot drove into the back of his knee joint, sending him down and out of the hallway's sightline. Unable to speak, and barely able to breathe, the guard tumbled down the stairs.

Motion appeared in her peripheral vision.

Shit!

The Kreeli at the front entrance, the one standing watch beyond the auction room and main gallery, peered his oblong head in her direction.

Lilline leaped over the fallen security guard. She took the stairs two at a time, dashing right and making for a portal down the hall. If she had her orientation right, it should lead to the storeroom directly underneath the auction. She drew her H-42 Mini Proton Blaster. With each step towards the portal a ping echoed in her ear.

She burst through the entrance, adrenaline rushing in her veins.

A figure in black spun around.

Lilline squeezed the trigger. The thief, chart in hand, performed an impressive spinning jump, narrowly avoiding her shot. A burst of red splintered off the wall behind them.

Lilline bolted, dashing past life-size statues and the table with Pin's figurine and other valuables. On another day, with a different set of objectives, this room would be a treasure trove, a major criminal bust. Today none of that mattered. Not with a knapsack strapped to thief's back that fit the dimensions of the *Cosmic Widow*.

Shouts behind her echoed from the stairwell: the Kreeli from the front entrance.

"Stop!" Lilline fired as the thief darted through a portal.

Miss!

She barreled after them. This was it. There was nowhere to go but to the stairs ahead. She had them!

Her hand with the Mini-PB rose. She set the sights to the back of their thigh.

"Halt!" The Kreeli behind her shouted.

Bam!

Pain seared through her arm. She spun from the impact, hit the wall, and tumbled. Flowing with the movement, she rolled and came up with the Mini-PB aimed and fired. The control switch on the portal back to the storeroom exploded. Sparks showered the view of the Kreeli in the doorway as it closed.

Burnt flesh singed her nostrils. She checked her arm. A smoking hole clean through her lower bicep.

It'd been three cycles since she'd been hit. Strange jitters vied with the rising pain.

A liquid sensation ran down her forearm as her suit sleeve went red.

Stay calm.

Lilline dropped the blaster and yanked at the hole in the fabric, ripping the sleeve from shoulder to wrist. She grabbed a med-patch out of her clutch, tore it open with her teeth, and slapped it on the exit wound. The same again with the entry wound on the back of her arm.

Thud!

The door ahead at the top of the stairs slammed shut.

The thief... can't stop or you'll lose them!

Her legs were moving, the corridor teetering.

Focus. The dizziness will pass.

She knew what came after that, though. Intense and debilitating pain. The med-patch would help, buying her about thirty minutes.

Booms echoed behind her as the Kreeli's fists impacted the defunct portal.

Lilline tested her injured arm. An instinctual sensation from her nerves and muscles reached her brain. The limb's controls were down; the arm was useless.

She burst through the door into an alley. A shadow rounded a corner to her left.

"What happened?"

Carmini's voice in her ear.

"She took the chart," a Kreeli said.

"Who?"

"The one at the auction."

"It was #19." A new voice like a vocal abyss.

Gongo.

"Get after her!" Carmini screamed, squelching the speaker.

"The portal is jammed..."

Lilline halted at the corner to the main thoroughfare. Back against the wall, dead arm dangling, she peeked around the building's edge. The thief jumped into a two-seater turbo pod. Lilline focused on the getaway driver: an unmistakable and rare insect-humanoid species known for their piloting prowess.

"Stop!"

Lilline responded by rounding the building's corner. Two blaster shots sent sparks over her back, impacting the exact spot where she had been standing. Now there were two problems: a thief with the *Cosmic Widow* and the chart escaping, and Carmini's thugs behind her, thinking she stole them.

The masked and hooded thief rotated in the pod's seat.

Lilline locked eyes with them.

Who are you?

The turbo pod shot off down the street.

Desperate to follow, she scanned for options. Amidst the hustle and bustle of nightlife, she homed in on Gongo's Yilari Elite 3000.

He's not going to like this.

She tucked the blaster into her blazer, hopped on, and fired the engine.

Gongo burst through the auction house's front entrance. Like a beast unchained, he roared and barreled for her.

Her right foot dropped the bike into gear.

The Dendari dove.

She cranked the throttle.

The Yilari launched but bucked.

Lilline bounced in the seat and almost lost her teeth to the handlebars. She checked the mirror. Gongo's massive arms held the sidecar, his nostrils flaring.

She eyed the dashboard. "Where is it? Come on... come on!"

There!

Her palm slapped the emergency release button. The Yilari popped a wheelie and shot forward. Blaster fire whizzed past, exploding on the side of a nearby building. In the rearview cam, a Kreeli stood at the corner of the alley, weapon raised. Three more flashes from his weapon. Lilline veered left, dodging the shots.

Now to catch a thief!

The turbo pod banked into a side passage. Lilline made for it, accelerating. Lights and signs, and a few slower vehicles, blurred. Damn but this Yilari was fast!

She checked the rearview cam. The scene outside the auction house cut off as a gleaming set of handlebars and muscled arms entered her view: the massive shape of a Dendari on a hover-chopper.

Gongo!

Lilline banked into the side passage, following the turbo pod. A dense world of arcades, bars, and storefronts caused her to veer left, down, up, and right to dodge taxis and avoid adverts hanging from buildings. An obstacle course built of consumer spectacle left her frantic to maintain control, her one good arm barely steering and accelerating while her feet worked the gears.

Alleys and larger cross-streets whizzed past. Her head went left and right.

No sign of the thief's pod.

"Where are you?" she yelled, throttling up.

Boom!

The speeder veered, its rear end sliding right. Lilline twisted her head. A wide grin on the Dendari's face caused his mustache to stretch.

The crazy bastard's ramming me!

Lilline leaned forward so her injured arm was on the steering column and worked to steady the Yilari. Her good arm released and reached into her suit for her blaster.

The speeder wobbled. She couldn't risk it!

Boom!

Her bike pitched up, hit a second time.

He's crazy!

Lilline accelerated and checked the rearview cam.

Two more bikes had joined in, creating a V formation in tandem with Gongo's lead chopper. The Dendari, a bull seeing red, snarled.

She scanned the road ahead and passing side streets. No sign of the thief. She'd lost them!

"Alert. Core boundary approaching. Turn back. Alert..." Red lights flashed warning signals in her path. Two Rasp guards at the checkpoint to the frustum's open core stood flanking the passage.

Screw it!

Lilline blew through the gate, triggering the alarms. Her good arm yanked back on the steering column, sending the bike soaring into Sky City's open core.

In the rearview cam, Gongo and the two Kreelis were on her tail in vertical climbs.

Lilline twisted the throttle and locked the grip in the open position. Hair blowing in the breeze, she squeezed her thighs against the seat and took her hand from the steering column. She activated her comm's voice transcription for a text message, lifting her dead arm with her good hand.

"I need you," she said into the mini speaker.

"Wow you don't waste time... or words."

Thank the stars you responded! "No, I mean for work."

"Oh, that's disappointing."

Lilline took out her blaster and sent a few shots down at Gongo's chopper. She tore upwards in the open core, the levels passing in a blur. "No! That too. Just... right now I need a way off Sky City."

A smiley face and a heart emoji appeared.

"Where are you?"

"You don't want to know, Alex."

Bam! Bam!

Two blaster shots whizzed past. Floors of apartments and commercial levels fell away as she rose. Far ahead in the narrowing tubular perspective, the tiny point that was the top of Sky City loomed.

"How are you with heights?"

Lilline peered down. A kilometer or more below, the lower levels were getting smaller by the second. "More than fine."

"*So, you're a risk taker?*"

"What?"

More shots from her blaster down at Gongo.

"*I need to know. Plus, I like dangerous women. It's a thing of mine.*"

"YES!"

Another smiley face.

"*Meet me at these coordinates.*"

Lilline grabbed the steering column and checked her ascent.

Oh no...

Ahead, a plasma shield manifested across the open core. The only passages through were along the walls where elevator tubes shot up and down the floating urban world. The Yilari, and any bike for that matter, wouldn't fit through.

She checked the rearview cam.

Gongo, mustache flowing in the wind, grinned.

Lilline gauged the distance to the plasma shield. She scanned for elevators rising and descending around the core and spotted one on ascent. She leaned left, banking the Yilari towards it along the curving core wall.

Come on... Her eyes followed the elevator's climb.

She slowed, letting it catch up and pass her. A sea of faces, in a variety of galactic species, pressed against the elevator's transparent tube and gawked.

She gazed down at her pursuers.

Gongo raised a hand with a blaster.

Lilline cut the Yilari's engine.

Boom!

It backfired and stalled, slowing her climb.

A young Rasp, no more than five cycles old, gazed at her from the elevator, her one eye wide.

Lilline winked and smiled.

She checked her distance to the plasma shield. Sparkling atomic activity in the meter-thick barrier came into focus.

Seventy meters.

Come on...

Bam! Bam! Bam!

The crackle of bolts passed near her ear.

Thirty meters.

The Yilari continued to decelerate.

Twenty meters.

She met the young Rasp's gaze and released her grip on the bike. Relaxing her thigh muscles, she arched her back like a skydiver backing out an open side door on an aircraft and let herself go.

The young Rasp's expression turned to shock.

Beats siting at a desk all day!

A moment of equilibrium and then the vertiginous drop of her stomach as she plunged, gravity taking her.

The bike collided with the plasma shield, disintegrating in a sparking explosion.

Gongo burned by her, reversing his engines and steering right in a desperate evasion maneuver.

Lilline squeezed her good hand into a fist. She threw the wrist-action blade that released into her palm. It whizzed across the open-air of the core, cable extended, and plunked into the bottom of the rising elevator.

This is going to hurt...

Yank!

Searing pain ripped through her shoulder as the cable caught. She tensed her core muscles, taking as much tension and weight away from the joint as possible.

Whoosh!

Like a fish on a line, she accelerated upward underneath the elevator.

An endless series of passing apartment levels grew closer.

Smack!

Her body slammed the core wall.

Searing pain.

Her guts rattled like a jar of jelly.

She bounced outward into the open air, struggling to ease the sway.

The shield crackled and neared.

Vision blurry from the impact, the opening above her swung like an out-of-focus pendulum.

Grrraaahhh! Lilline summoned her last bit of energy through a spirit cry. Core muscles pulled her legs over her head. She wound them around the cable and slipped through the opening upside down.

Yes!

She'd threaded the needle.

Returning from her inversion, she peered down.

Her elation quickly soured.

A raging bull hovered on a gleaming chopper underneath the plasma shield, Gongo's nostrils flared with fury. He was barking at someone on the comm. As a veteran agent she knew the gist: she wasn't out of the woods yet.

TWENTY-NINE

"You certainly know how to draw attention."

Lilline placed the stuffed animal back on the shelf and followed Alex down the aisle. A toy store was the last place she expected to rendezvous, but maybe that was the point.

"In here." Alex opened a portal to a supply room. "You are aware that you have the bottom-dweller thugs *and* Sky City Security looking for you?"

"I tend to have that effect on people."

Alex opened a duffel bag and handed her a set of clothes. "I grabbed what I could."

"Thanks." Lilline threw off the torn blazer and shimmied out of her pants.

Alex eyed her.

Don't look at me like that.

"What?" Alex smiled.

You know exactly what.

Lilline winced as she pushed her wounded arm through a shirt sleeve.

"Did someone shoot you?" Alex stepped forward and reached for her arm.

Lilline pulled back. "Yes. And let me tell you, it isn't pleasant."

"I have something that will help." They knelt and rummaged through the bag. "Here. It's a pain killer."

Lilline popped it as the lights flashed.

"Come on." The GAM-OPs asset heaved the duffel over their shoulder. "We have to move."

So far Alex was demonstrating top-level field support.

"What's this all about?" they asked, passing through the backdoor.

"Let's just say it's a case of mistaken identity."

"Right." They gestured to a maintenance elevator. "We need to hurry."

Lilline hustled after them.

"Hey!" a voice shouted.

Alex spun and fired two stun shots with a classic XR Panther pistola.

Two Gej-ti Zappers lay crumpled in the corridor. Gongo's crew by the looks of them.

"Get in." Alex hit the elevator button. "You've made some bad people angry."

"I tend to do that. Nice Panther, by the way..."

"Thanks." They holstered it under their armpit. "I prefer older models... more reliable."

Again, their eyes met.

Was it the pain killer kicking in, or was it the euphoria from this flirtation between them?

"You can't use any of the regular ports and exits," Alex said. "They'll all be monitored. That's the thing with Sky City. A hedonistic haven it might be, but the ways in and out are kept tight."

"Something tells me you've got—"

Ping.

Alex checked their comm. "We've got company at the exit. I see you're armed..."

Lilline drew her Mini-PB.

"Left or right?" Alex asked.

"Right." Lilline tightened the grip on her weapon.

"See that? We're a perfect match. I prefer the left."

The portal disintegrated and fireworks erupted in the entrance. Lilline rolled out and right, dodging a barrage of incoming blaster shots. She fired at two Zappers. A Kreeli collapsed with an agonizing scream, her first shot exploding their kneecap. The second missed a Gej-ti and ricocheted off a column. It danced around the spacious open-plan interior and fizzled out. Lilline dashed for the nearest column. The Gej-ti fired. Three blue bolts flashed from their muzzle. She dove and reached the safety of the pillar.

Her eyes scanned the room, performing a swift tactical mapping: an unfinished structural level with support columns and a crude layout for tech stations. Decent cover with the columns but moving between them was a death wish.

Commotion behind her. She spun around, blaster at the ready.

Alex had been busy. Three humans were down from their Panther. The GAM-OPs asset made their way to her, a Kreeli spewing out rounds in chase. Lilline lifted her Mini-PB and took aim. Through the sights, she locked on the blue oblong forehead bouncing in and out of view behind Alex's silver hair.

Up. Down. Up. Down. She focused as her colleague's head moved in a steady rhythm.

Her trigger finger squeezed on the end of an "up."

Bam!

The impact sent the Kreeli off their feet. They were dead before they hit the ground.

"I was right about you being dangerous!" Alex shouted, reaching the pillar. They dropped the duffel.

"Where to?"

"Over there." They pointed to a wall with a ladder.

"Now I understand why you asked about heights," Lilline said. Icons indicated roof access to the open atmosphere atop Sky City.

"Want to know the rest?" Alex shot off a three-round burst to hold off the pursuing Zappers.

"Surprise me." Lilline shifted around the pillar to avoid enemy fire.

"What the stars is that?"

Lilline followed Alex's gaze. "Oh, that's Gongo." She tucked the Mini-PB under her arm and heaved the duffel into Alex's stomach. "Time to go."

Thankfully, the pain killers were doing their work. The ache of her wound had waned and the narcotic added an amusing edge to her emotions. Whatever cocktail Alex gave her had to be a mix of opioids and benzos. If she guessed right about what was coming next, she hoped the dosage was strong.

"You first!" Alex shouted, urging her up the ladder while pouring out cover fire.

Lilline did her best with one arm, blaster muzzle clenched in her teeth. Thirty meters up, at the top, she reached down and took the duffel from Alex who had climbed up after her.

Crack!

Alex screamed as the steel ladder came loose from the wall.

"I got you!" Lilline snatched their wrist before they fell. Below, a snarling Gongo thrashed the ladder back and forth, bending and pulling to bring it crashing down.

Lilline heaved Alex up and over the edge.

"Not too bright, is he?" they said, hands searching through the bag.

The Dendari roared from below at his error.

"This should buy us some time." Alex twisted a canister and tossed it over the edge. "Have fun with that, Gongo!"

Lilline peered down. A red cloud sent plumes of thick smoke billowing.

"There's another ladder not far so we better move." Alex pulled her along and ran to a pressure hatch. "It's only a smoke bomb."

"Good enough to buy us time." Lilline caught her breath as Alex twisted the hatch. With a whoosh it rotated and opened. "Are you coming with me?"

They shook their head. "Only one wingsuit."

Lilline's eyes went wide but the drugs kept her emotions steady. "I'm free-flying off Sky City?"

"GAM-OPs special." Alex smiled. "You said you were a risk taker." They handed her the black suit and oxygen mask. A hand grabbed the tube from the chin area of the helmet and screwed it onto the tank on the back of the suit. "And you need to hurry," they said. "There's a storm front approaching. I checked the doppler after you contacted me." They checked their wrist comm. "We're behind schedule."

"Alex..."

"You'll be fine." They helped her into the suit. "Ever use one of these?"

"I have." *Not in a high-altitude storm.*

Shouts. Gongo and the Zappers had found the other ladder.

"When I close this hatch, put on the mask and give me a thumb's up. I'll hit the button to open the outer door."

"Got it."

"Good luck, Keely Larkin." Alex winked.

Lilline went to speak but stopped, mouth open.

"What?

"Do you like Gibson oysters?"

"What?"

It just came out, from where she didn't know. *Is this me or the drugs talking?*

"Have dinner with me," she said. "At Aesté, next week. It's this great place in the West End. I know the sous chef and—"

Alex's delicate fingers touched her lips, shushing her.

"You had me at Gibson oysters." A cute grin rose on their face.

"Now get out of here or the storm will get you and I'll have to eat oysters all by myself. Wouldn't that be a tragedy?"

Lilline pulled them close.

What is coming over me?

Green eyes sparkled like an emerald sea. She tugged and their lips met. A rush she hadn't felt in cycles surged through her.

Alex pulled back, eyes glittering. "Tease." They pushed her away, playfully.

Lilline tightened the straps on the wing suit. "Thank you... I mean for helping me get out of here."

"You owe me dinner." Alex readied themself at the switch.

"Get out of here, Alex. Don't try and mess with Gongo." Lilline put on the atmo-mask, stepped inside and closed the hatch. She gave a thumb's up.

THIRTY

A rush of air sent clouds of mist shooting into the chamber. The muted creak of a second hatch opening reached her ears.

Silent steps took her out onto the top of the frustum. A steel roof with multiple entry points ran for at least a kilometer. Inside the mask, only her steady breaths and the muffled rumble of the wind in the night broke the quiet.

To her left, a clear sky full of stars. On her right ..

A wall of pitch.

Flash! Lightning illuminated an approaching monster. A meteorological demon arisen from the shadows of night. A second flash revealed the rain and wind wall crossing the edge of the roof. Lilline checked the distance to the opposite side. At least a five-minute run.

With the storm's pace she'd never make it.

She made for her only option - a suspension station - and started up the ladder attached to the nano-carbon cable. Up she went using one arm, leaning her shoulder against the rung, grabbing and pulling. She craned her neck and checked the ascent. The cable ran like a line into the void. A flash of lightning brought half of the black pyramid to life, three kilometers above.

She needed enough lift to clear the roof when the storm took her. A hundred meters would do it. Flying with the dead arm wasn't a problem - the shoulder worked. The wing could be extended. Thank the stars for the pain killer; now she had a chance.

Boom!

Thunder and lightning.

Louder.

Closer.

I'm only forty meters up!

The rain wall slammed the cable. Her fingers slipped on the steel. Boot soles scraped across the rungs.

Blackness.

Like an airborne top, she spiraled out of control.

Swirling winds and pelting rain hit her from every direction. Lost in the dizzying chaos, cold air pummeled her as the storm battled the atmosphere. Up was down. Down was up. The wind chained her arms to her sides. She needed to extend them to get some drag with the wings!

Shoulders strained to expand the suit.

A flash of lightning revealed the roof, solid and waiting for her body to slam it, only meters away.

Again, she tried but it was futile.

The monastery and her teacher flashed through her mind. She was back at the pond's edge.

Realization dawned.

Let go.

She relaxed her muscles.

Stop fighting... let go.

Like a perfect culinary pairing, the drugs effect and her helplessness in the storm met in a friendship of opposites. She acquiesced to the weather's sublime strength.

The storm's fury transformed into meandering currents. Winds flowed like a river downstream.

Be like water.

She thought of Alex and their kiss. Odd how things happen in life. An impulsive act, one she might have regretted. Now, floating helpless on the wind, she was thankful to have done it.

It was a good first kiss.

She spun helplessly. No care. No worry. No regret.

Now is now.

Thousands of meters below, patches of urban lights flashed between dark and billowing clouds. Cold air danced up and down her body as the storm's intensity stuttered.

Whoosh!

The cloud's bottom edge broke into clear sky. With ease, she spread her arms like an eagle majestic. Already the drag of the wings slowed her speed. She aimed on a descent line and soared through the night.

Minutes later, the visor's digital altimeter read 1500 meters. Tavi-Central's Satellite Tower rose from the endless skyline, blinking a steady rhythm of signal lights. She leaned left and pulled her arms halfway in, banking on a course to the east. Passing silently in the night, she crossed over the Ministry and HQ, turning to land in Regent's Park. The trendy shops would give her an easy directional marker once she pulled the chute.

Tavi-General's emergency landing pad, lights flashing, cast an eerie yellow glow.

Granny.

Had Doctor Klitarney been able to stay the effects of whatever was making her ill? Or...

An urge to see her grandmother rushed over her. She gauged the distance.

I can do it.

"Computer, connect to Doctor Klitarney." Lilline banked into the headwind to slow her descent and gain some distance.

"Ms. Larkin?"

"I hope I didn't wake you, Doctor." Lilline's eyes assessed the nightscape for her tactical approach.

"Not at all, I took the overnight shift out of concern for your grandmother."

An uneasy sensation tightened her belly.

"How is she?" Spiraling downward like a passenger pod on a slow descent into port, she aimed for the hospital.

"Good and bad news," Doctor Klitarney said.

"I've just returned to Tavi-Center. I'd like to see her." Eyes on the landing pad, she yanked the chute cord. Her stomach dropped into her feet as it caught, a wave of deceleration rushing through her.

Gauging the light winds, she steered towards the tarmac's bullseye. By making a westward approach, she hoped to avoid using her left arm as much as possible.

"How soon will you be here?"

"A few minutes."

"I'll meet you at reception inside the main entrance."

"Make that the landing pad, doctor."

"Oh... I see. I'll head up now."

Lilline's feet touched down a half meter off center, signal lights spiraling and casting patterns over the landing pad. She pulled in the cords and tucked and folded the chute as it deflated, working with expert precision to collapse it into a body size pile.

One long pull on the zipper and she was out of the wing suit, stuffing the chute and cords inside the empty cavity. The simple outfit Alex had given her clung to her body, the night breeze sending refreshing goosebumps over her sweaty skin. She tested her injured arm and winced. At least this plan was a two-for-one deal. Doctor Klitarney could examine her and patch her up while she was here.

Lilline heaved the wing suit over her good shoulder and, ignoring the pain, raised her left arm with the wrist comm. Scrolling through and typing, she sent the image captures from Carmini's storeroom to HQ.

Let's see what that yields us.

The thief and the *Cosmic Widow* might have eluded her, but she had left Sky City with something valuable and important. What it was, and what it meant to the thief's plans, she hoped to soon find out.

"Ms. Larkin?" Doctor Klitarney, in her usual lab coat and Bukki tiger-patterned glasses, emerged from the portal. Her head went left and right, then up into the night sky.

"You don't want to know, Doctor."

The Gej-ti's eyes focused on Lilline's arm, spotting her injury.

"Let's just say this is a drop-in visit."

THIRTY-ONE

"The good news first," Doctor Klitarney motioned her down a hallway. "Your grandmother's vitals are steady and we've been able to control portions of her nervous system. She's in and out of consciousness, and not very coherent with the medication, but at least we've got her stable and the pain at a minimum."

"And the bad?" Lilline followed the Gej-ti into an elevator.

The doctor pushed her glasses up the bridge of her milky-skinned nose. "Now that I've had some time to observe it, I'm ninety-nine percent certain it's a biological toxin. From its rate of spread, behavior, and impact to her system, I'd label it Class IIa."

Not good.

Lilline knew her toxicology. Every T# agent did, both for practical and strategic purposes in the field. There were any number of categories — chemical, biological, radioactive... the list went on.

"The odd thing is..." Doctor Klitarney motioned her out of the portal at level 5.

The color palette and the nurse uniforms told her where they were: ICU.

"...it shows the characteristics of a hepatotoxin, but it's working like a combination of a hemotoxin with neurotoxic secondary traits." The Gej-ti stopped at a room mid-hallway, her finger deactivating the plasma curtain.

Lilline's heart sank. Granny lay in bed, various tubes and wires running to a set of complicated machines.

"I've never seen anything like it," Doctor Klitarney added.

Lilline's mind was at war, half struggling with analysis and the other half vying for dominance through emotional artillery. "Hepatotoxin... that's typical of plants, isn't it?"

Doctor Klitarney nodded. "But the hemotoxin would be of animal origin... the neurotoxin as well, or algae based."

How did this happen?

"Ms. Larkin, I'm going to be candid with you. If you can stay close, I would. We can put you up here if you'd like to remain at the hospital."

"What are you saying?"

The Gej-ti took off her glasses and fiddled with the stems. "Unless we can identify the source, and more importantly discover an antidote, your grandmother is going to die."

Glowing numbers on med screens, chairs and tubes, and the bed with Granny all blurred. Lilline wiped her eyes.

"How long?" It came out as a whisper.

"It will depend on how strong her system is but no more than three days."

"Three days?"

"I'm being generous." The Gej-ti's features softened. "It could, and most likely will be, sooner."

———

"Analine?"

Lilline stirred. A slow and steady beeping pulled her from the darkness.

"Analine, dear…"

A dim room came and went like a film reel as her eyelids fluttered.

The hospital.

She sat up in the chair, wincing from a stiff neck. Whatever Doctor Klitarney had given her after patching her up must have made her doze off.

"Analine…"

She approached the bed and clasped her grandmother's hand. "It's me Granny… Lilline."

Kissy's eyes opened with the slow patience of forever. A glaze covered their usual fierceness.

"I've missed you so much, dear."

"It's only been about two days, Granny."

Kissy shook her head. "Your daughter… I did my best but…"

Lilline knelt close. "It's me, Granny… Lilline. Mom's been gone for a long time."

"Who?" Kissy's face stretched, her wrinkles taut with confusion.

"It's okay," Lilline said. "Just rest. I'm going to figure this out."

Kissy shook her head. "Not this time…"

"Yes, this time," Lilline said. "You're not leaving me yet."

So frail. This woman, a legend in the GAM-OPs community, the best agent to grace the espionage stage, lay withered and dying. How? And from what? An accident or an intentional and malicious act?

Lilline followed the languid rise and fall of her grandmother's chest as she took shallow breaths.

"Remember that horse, dear? The one you found… so proud of you…"

"Yes." Lilline acquiesced to the hallucination, eyes welling.

"I took little Lilli to see it... just like you would have wanted."

She squeezed Granny's hand. "I know. Shhh, you need to rest now."

"Such a lovely little girl, Ana. So bright and confident..."

Lilline tightened her lips, a tear running down her cheek.

"Take her to see it again. For me."

Oh stars I can't do this. I—

Ping... Ping. Ping.

"One moment, Granny," She let the aged hand go.

Code blue. With a priority message.

Director requests off-site meeting. ASAP. Enter current coordinates for immediate shuttle pickup.

Lilline checked the time. She'd slept for five hours. Out the bedside window, Pesari-9's faint glow announced the imminent dawn. Her fingers pulled up the comm's GPS and entered the hospital landing pad.

"Granny, I have to go." She clasped Kissy's hand. "I'll be back as soon as I can."

"Lilli?"

"Yes, that's right. It's me." Relief washed over her at the return of her grandmother's lucidity.

"A galaxy to save?" Kissy's lips moved but her eyes remained closed.

"Afraid so."

Withered fingers tightened their grip on her hand.

"Goodbye, Granny." Lilline kissed her on the cheek and made for the portal.

"One request, dear."

She stopped.

Slow, persistent beeps of the heart monitor echoed like a metronome.

"Dari cakes at my wake."

A hand covered her mouth to hide a sob.

THIRTY-TWO

Lilline sipped coffee, hypnotized by the endless grid of Tavi-Prime's ecumenopolis three thousand meters below. Alone on Lauden's personal shuttle, she'd breakfasted in style - Myson eggs with two slices of toast, Hisho jelly, and a side of Pan-ti sausages. The meat's tangy spice blend was unmistakable: a highly sought after Koolan mixture originating with the Carfi, a nomadic culture scattered across Outer Rim star systems. Add to that a cup of fresh-brewed dark roast coffee and more than her stomach and tastebuds were satisfied. Her mind got a much-needed caffeine bump to boot.

Lauden's shuttle exuded the same austerity as his office but with an added degree of elegant sophistication. The Senara P-Class was the most up-to-date and top of the line personal transport. Unlike the dark wood and deep red carpeting in his office, a three-tone palette of white, gray and silver cast a clean stateliness over the shuttle's interior. AI-Chauffeurs were nice, but this level of luxury commuting was in a league all its own.

They'd been cruising at a steady altitude for two hours but the view out of the portal hadn't changed. The city-planet ran in monotonous repetition. Low areas of urban neighborhoods broke into rising skyscrapers like mountain ranges, followed by mid-level industrial sectors that fell back into a valley of residential districts to start the cycle over again. She could be anywhere on Tavi-Prime. Gauging by the location of Pesari-9 in the morning sky, Lilline guessed the heading to be northwest.

"Ten minutes to arrival," the pilot's voice broke the cabin's silence. *"Should be an easy descent."*

Lilline hit the seat's controls, rising and angling position to get a better view out the window. Her hand with the coffee froze halfway to her mouth.

Tavi-Prime's sprawl halted at a sharp edge. It was as if a god had slammed a cleaver down and peeled off the planet's urban skin. Nothing but treeless grassland ran to the horizon. Although she'd never seen it before, she knew what would appear next.

U-City.

A top-secret facility located some five kilometers inside a no-development zone, rumored to be a galactic research base. For what, she didn't know. Even as a T# agent this level of secrecy was off-limits.

"Don't worry about the V-Darts," the pilot said. *"They're an official escort... security protocol."*

An elite inner-atmo fighter appeared on their starboard wing. Lilline leaned over and checked the view to port: another V-Dart flying tandem with the shuttle.

Her stomach dipped as the pilot decelerated and initiated their descent. She knocked back her coffee and fastened the safety belt.

Two minutes later, the shuttle passed over neat rows of satellite dishes, a grid of rectangular white buildings, and an opaque bubble the size of stadium. The craft banked right and a landing port came into view. Completing a tight arc, the pilot hovered a few hundred meters over the tarmac.

The V-Dart to starboard titled its wings back and forth. A roar penetrated the shuttle's sound shields as a blue glow to stern sent the fighter rocketing off.

Lilline's curiosity rose to a fever pitch. The images she'd sent to HQ had triggered this?

The pilot descended the last hundred meters and settled the shuttle down without so much as a bump.

A soft hiss and the plug door opened.

"Agent Renault?" A Kreeli in a Galactic Space Force uniform and mirrored sunglasses peered inside. "This way please."

Lilline rose and followed him down onto the tarmac.

"Can I get your print on this?" A blue hand held out a tablet.

Lilline placed her palm on the device. A beam ran over the screen.

"Follow me, please."

Disorienting sensations vied with curiosity as she made her way toward an official-looking building. Its mirrored walls reflected an adjacent bubble dome and endless plains. To think that over the horizon the most densely populated planet in the Inner Core was alive with urban activity. Where they'd landed appeared like an outpost on an uninhabited planet.

"T8." Lauden greeted her as she entered a break room with tables along the walls.

Like HQ's interrogation chamber its sides were two-way mirrors, the neighboring facilities and Lauden's shuttle on the tarmac visible outside.

"I was so close, sir. I almost had the painting."

"Well, what you did get has turned the tide." Lauden gestured to a table down the line.

Reginald Bilarus sat, fiddling with his handkerchief.

The director raised an eyebrow, picking up on her surprise.

"We're waiting on more guests, but in the meantime let's get you up to speed on a few things."

Lilline followed the director down the aisle and sat across from the curator.

"Agent Renault." Bilarus nodded in greeting. "So nice to see you again."

If anywhere in the galaxy existed where top-secret identities and clandestine missions could be discussed openly, U-City was it.

THIRTY-THREE

"Reginald has been working with GAM-OPs to help with an ongoing sting operation," Lauden said.

Of course...how did I not see this?

"For several cycles now," Lauden said, "we've been providing mid-level museum artifacts as bait to lure out Carmini. Mind you, we didn't know he was the one running the auctions until two days ago, but we knew that a good number of historical objects—"

"*Too many...*" Bilarus said.

"Too many," Lauden said, correcting himself, "were going to the underground market rather than to museums or other public institutions."

"This has been something I've wanted to take on for a while,

Agent Renault," Bilarus said. "When your director came to me with a charge from the Ministry's Cultural Affairs Office, I was more than willing to offer my services and position to aid the cause."

Lauden's attitude and previous dismissal of her comments about Bilarus fell into place. She'd been so busy working the suspect angle, concerned that one of her boss's close friends might be involved, that she'd missed the obvious.

"The recent museum thefts?" Lilline asked.

"Staged."

The director fiddled with a tin of Yaz Flake. The red "Limited Edition" font drew her eye. Lauden hadn't wasted any time putting the tobacco Pin brought back from Sky City to good use.

"We made sure the press got wind of them," Bilarus said. "Then, we waited a few months and the director had one of your organization's intermediaries offer it through their underground network."

"And that got you to Carmini's auction?"

"Not that far, no, but we were close. Your financial lead that exposed the Froo closed the loop."

"You willingly sacrificed one-of-a-kind artifacts from the museum's collection?"

"Oh no, Agent Renault."

Lilline switched to Lauden. His face was as stoic as a marble statue, staring at the tobacco tin with an addict's intensity.

"We decided to beat them at their own game." A rare grin stretched across the curator's cherub cheeks.

"I don't understand."

"A simple matter of employing people like Mr. Abaqati to craft replicas," Bilarus said.

Crafty. Clearly this wasn't a simple sting operation. He and Lauden were hoping to beat a magician with their own tricks.

"But the works... the forgeries," Lilline said. "Carmini must have had an appraiser examine them?"

"Oh yes," Bilarus said. "One of the best."

The corner of Lauden's mouth edged into a smirk.

"One of ours?"

Lauden shook his head. "Someone with, let us say, unusual tastes in physical pleasures. Ones that were... how shall I put it?"

"Unsavory," Bilarus said, his rosy cheeks going crimson.

"If brought to the attention of the authorities it would mean a long prison sentence," Lauden added. "Longer than the individual's remaining cycles."

Squeezing an asset. Not her favorite method, but in this case deserving.

"And they falsely authenticated the forgeries?"

The curator nodded.

"Add in a reminder of how easily this asset's family might learn of his proclivities," Lauden said, "and he was more than willing to verify the objects for us." The director put the tin back in his blazer pocket, defeated.

"There was an original at the auction," Lilline said. "A First Galactic painting from the museum."

"The game goes both ways, sadly," Bilarus said. "It's not the first time that has happened."

Lilline's mind raced towards a single point of light. It exploded in an internal supernova. "And... the *Cosmic Widow*?"

"Oh no," Bilarus held up his hands. "That, I assure you, is authentic. No one alive today has the skill to replicate it. Not to mention, the materials in the pigments are unique. There's no way a convincing forgery could be manufactured."

"And thus, we are all here to try and solve a riddle," Lauden said.

"Rest assured, Agent Renault, that with all of the recently staged thefts used replicas," Bilarus said, "there hasn't been an original stolen from the museum for quite some time. Although in some cases, crimes were carried out without anyone knowing, such as that First Galactic painting you mentioned. Whether secretly swapped under our noses or inside jobs, many of these instances remain unknown to museum staff."

"Surely this will have a negative effect on your career?" Lilline said.

"It already has. I'm doing it because I believe in stopping thieves from taking art for personal collections at the expense of the masses. Works from the First and Second Galactic periods deserve to be on public display. As your director will tell you, this was the main reason I got into this field... to preserve the past for future generations. But don't get me wrong," he held up a milky-skinned hand, "I'm no populist. I still believe experts should decide what goes on the walls."

And that was where she and Bilarus parted ways. Renina had a point when she said her boss was problematic. Lilline respected his professional sacrifice to maintain public access to art, but she opposed the traditionalist position. It reeked of egotism and close-mindedness in the face of a changing galaxy. There was no reason scholarly knowledge and expertise had to come at the expense of new voices, revision, and change.

"And I say this knowing some of the work on display isn't what it seems," he added.

Lilline took a moment to take it all in. So, the museum was like a hall of mirrors.

"However," Bilarus held up a pudgy finger, "that Venex Horse was, sadly, an actual theft."

"I saw it last night."

Lauden and Bilarus locked eyes.

"Where?" The question was spoken as a duet.

"Carmini's auction. It was up for sale. I neglected to mention it in my brief report because..." Lilline pursed her lips.

The director leaned toward Bilarus. "T8 thought, rightly so considering the amount of intel she was provided, that you might be off-loading artifacts and possibly involved in this case." The Gej-ti locked eyes with her. "And therefore, a prime suspect. I told her you were helping us out and I would guess..." his black eyes homed in on her, "she was concerned it might reach you through me."

"Ash told me you were the best," Bilarus said.

Lauden's cheek twitched. Probably as much from the praise as being called "Ash" in front of an underling.

If that was the original...

"What is it?" Lauden asked.

Lilline stomach dropped. "So that means—"

"I'm afraid so," the curator pulled his handkerchief from a blazer pocket and dabbed his bald crown. "Gone."

Lilline's emotions were bouncing back and forth.

"I am sorry," Bilarus said. "I know your grandmother donated it. How is she by the way?"

"Not good. How did you—"

"These things get out, Agent Renault. My predecessor was involved with the donation. She shared the details with me in confidence. Please, do not worry over it. Only myself, the previous head of collections, as well as the development team that arrange such things, know."

"Kissy donated an artifact to the museum?" Lauden asked.

"Yes, sir. She said it was a request my mother made before she—"

Ping.

Lauden held up a hand, halting the conversation. He tapped his wrist comm. "Go ahead, Cazshi."

"Sir, patching T5 through from Sky City."

Lauden leaned toward her. "We sent T5 in with a Spec-Ops team to get Carmini as soon as you reported in. I wanted—"

"Sir, I'm here with Spec-Ops."

Lilline recognized the voice of T5, her fellow agent. It was nice to hear the Kreeli's friendly tone. They hadn't crossed paths in almost two cycles.

"Go ahead," Lauden said.

"There's nothing here. It's empty."

Empty? Lilline edged closer.

"Like they were never here, sir. They cleaned house."

Damn.

"And what about Renina?" Lauden asked.

"I spoke with our asset on the upper level..."

Lilline hid her relief at hearing that Alex had escaped after her getaway.

"And?" Lauden asked.

"Surveillance feed has Renina at the Royal Loha lobby from the time T8 interacted with her through the entire op. She remained at the bar with another guest, a Gej-ti. Looks like a social thing. According to our asset the two took a walk on the upper promenade and then proceeded back to Renina's room at the Wingard Grand."

Bilarus fidgeted at hearing the personal information about his employee.

"Our asset checked with reception and her reservation is through tonight."

"She's scheduled to be back at work the day after tomorrow," Bilarus said, confirming.

So, Renina had an alibi for the time of the theft in the storeroom. That made sense. Whoever took that chart had a human body type, not a Rasp's. Still... the idea that her being on Sky City was a coincidence didn't sit right.

"Thank you, T5. That will be all," Lauden said.

"Sir." The distinct vibrato of Cazshi's Rasp voice broke in. *"Intel reports chatter on local networks. Zappers searching for someone who fits T8's description."*

"They think I'm the thief," Lilline said.

Lauden nodded.

"T8's been linked to an incident at the Blue Comet as well."

Lauden's raised an eyebrow.

"I ran into Renina the other night, sir. Rescued her from an agro situation with a Zapper... unrelated."

"It's not like Renina to be at a club in the East End," Bilarus said.

"Thank you, Cazshi." Lauden cut the line. "You think she's connected to this?"

The curator shrugged. "I can't see any reason why she would be."

"According to metro police records she was questioned about an earlier incident involving forgeries," Lilline said.

"T8, do you have any working theories?"

"Something tells me she's involved, sir. How and to what degree…" Lilline shrugged.

"Reginald?" Lauden raised an eyebrow at his fellow Gej-ti.

"I don't know, Ash."

"About them cleaning house," Lilline said. "Carmini is a master strategist. I wouldn't be surprised if this was an established bug-out plan. Call it a pre-set fail safe, considering the number of stolen antiquities and art he deals with. It's possible they reacted out of an abundance of caution."

"Quite agree, T8. Most likely a—"

"I'm sorry for the delay."

A middle-aged Gej-ti in a white clinical suit approached the table. Her gait exuded authority not by rank or post but by a radiating intelligence.

"Not at all," Lauden said and stood. "We needed a few minutes to go over something."

"So nice to see you, Director," the Gej-ti said, shaking his hand.

"Please," the woman said as Lilline went to stand, "No need to get up." She motioned at Bilarus who had risen halfway out of his seat.

"Agent Renault and Reginald Bilarus," Lauden said, indicating each of them. "This is the head of U-City. You may refer to her as Madame X."

"Apologies," the woman said, "A bit too on the nose if you ask me. I didn't pick it but it's necessary for—"

An alert tone broke in, interrupting the scientist.

Lilline followed Madame X's gaze to the window.

"That would be our final guests," Lauden said.

"Interesting aircraft," Madame X said.

A two-seater shuttle with a rear engine like octopus tentacles lowered onto the tarmac. Lilline recognized the craft from Pin's hangar at HQ.

"It's a new prototype," Lauden said. "Biodigester jet propulsion system."

"Biomass?" Madame X said. "I'm impressed."

"Our head of Tech is the one you should praise," Lauden said. "She's piloting the craft and will be joining us as well."

Madame X followed the pod with her eyes as it touched down. "An Oltari?"

"Indeed."

Through the glare on the windshield, Lilline made out Pin at the controls and a passenger in a tweed suit. She adjusted her angle to account for the reflection and the figure's appearance became legible: an elderly Kreeli with a massive salt and pepper beard.

The GSF officer who greeted her on arrival strode across the tarmac, an empty hover-chair gliding next to him.

"They'll be taking a different route. We can meet them in the auditorium. This way, please." Madame X gestured down a hall.

Lauden rose and Lilline, along with Reginald Bilarus, followed suit.

"You're one of the few non-U-City employees to step foot inside this facility, Agent Renault," Madame X said. "You too, Mr. Bilarus. It's nice to see some fresh faces."

"Don't get out much, I imagine?" Lilline asked.

"Not at all, actually." The scientist strode with a measured cadence. "I haven't been off-site since my first day twelve cycles ago."

"Twelve cycles out here?" Bilarus said.

Madame X nodded. "Contractual requirement. We live on-site for as long as we're employed. You give up a lot to become a part of this government project. It's basically a lifelong commitment. Most of us retire to an exclusive Ministry-supported facility on Beisho." She glanced back, black eyes softening. "It becomes hard to return to civilian life... with what we know."

An endless labyrinth of corridors took them deeper into the top-secret facility. At one point, they entered a hallway overlooking a massive hangar. Lilline thought she noticed—

Madame X hit a control switch, a molecular plasma shield blocking out the view.

"Sir." Lilline kept her voice low. "What goes on here?"

"You don't want to know, T8." Lauden gazed ahead, following Madame X. "Trust me. You'll sleep better at night."

THIRTY-FOUR

"I feel like I'm back at uni," Bilarus said and sat next to Lilline.

She shared the sentiment. The raised stage, podium, and wide holo-projection screen was an homage to the hours-long lectures she so enjoyed in her university days.

"You are more right than you realize," Lauden said, approaching.

A soft whir, accompanied by Pin's idiosyncratic voice, rose to stage right.

"I don't believe it," Bilarus said. The curator stood and straightened his suit.

Pin and the Kreeli from the pod, who floated in a hover-chair, made their way to the group.

"But surely you agree with the need for more diverse representation?" Pin said, flying in tandem with the hovering Kreeli.

"Indeed, you'll get no argument from me. Evidence exists of a similar curatorial crisis in the late—"

"Professor Senjara?"

It was Bilarus, his words jittery.

"Well, well, well... Reginald Bilarus." The Kreeli stopped in front of the group. "My favorite B+ student."

The curator's cheeks flushed as he fiddled with his handkerchief.

"Nice to see you," the professor said. "Although, I must say your work of late at the museum leaves something to be desired." He lifted a blue hand from his lap and stroked his beard.

"Yes... well... I..."

"Professor Senjara, welcome," Lauden said, coming to his friend's rescue. "Thank you for joining us. I know it isn't easy for you to travel these days."

"Anything for my *best* student."

Lauden, his best?

The elderly Kreeli's headband glittered with a pressure adjustment. "I still wish you'd taken that post at Winmoreland instead of this funny business with the government." He pulled a pocket watch from his tweed vest and wound it. "You'd be department chair by now." His wrinkled face shifted to Bilarus, giving him the stink eye. "Maybe even dean of the College of Galactic History... with *your* scholarly ability."

"Yes, well, as it turns out," Lauden said, "my current responsibilities have pulled me back to my academic days." The Gej-ti stepped forward. "Let me introduce you to everyone. You already know Mr. Bilarus, and you've met Pin, who is our head of Tech. This is Madame X, head of U-City. Her academic pedigree would please you, Professor."

A tinge of pink flushed the scientist's cheeks. She bowed her head in greeting.

"And Agent Lilline Renault, our T# operative assigned to this crisis."

"A pleasure to meet you," Lilline said.

"This is Dr. Veer Senjara," Lauden said by way of introduction. "Professor emeritus of Tavi-Central University, longtime chair of the Department of Galactic Art History and my former advisor."

"Mine as well," Bilarus raised his hand as if he were a student.

The professor's eyes rolled.

"Dr. Senjara remains the foremost expert on First Galactic art history."

"You flatter me, Asher," the Kreeli said, adjusting his tweed jacket.

"I've asked him to join us as a consultant." The director's expression became grave. "When you all see what Agent Renault discovered yesterday evening, you'll know why." Lauden turned to Madame X. "Is our final guest patched through?"

Final guest?

Madame X climbed the steps to the stage and approached the podium. She fiddled with the controls and the holo-screen came to life.

"Slushie!" Pin's exclamation bounced through the auditorium.

"Welcome and thank you for joining us, Dr. Liguera." Lauden spoke to the three-dimensional virtual presence of a human woman in a cluttered, low budget office.

"Our final guest, everyone. Dr. Liguera who—"

"Slushie, sir."

All heads spun to Pin.

"Excuse me?" Lauden said.

"She prefers Slushie."

Lauden's blood boiled through his translucent skin.

"Try not to interrupt the director, Pin," Lilline whispered.

"But she prefers—"

"Pin?" Lilline raised a hand in a gentle gesture. "It's okay. This is a formal meeting."

"Dr. Liguera is fine for today, Pin," Slushie said. "And thank you, Director. Greetings from the Calostine system, everyone." A virtual hand waved. "I'm an old schoolmate of your head of Tech and currently on a cycle-long grant conducting research in the Outer Rim."

Professor Senjara nodded approvingly.

"Please, everyone," Madame X said, "have a seat."

"Alright, Asher..." Professor Senjara pushed the joystick forward on his hover-chair. He drifted closer and lined up with the rows of seating. "Now what's so important that you pulled me away from my crosswords?"

THIRTY-FIVE

"I've asked you all here today in the hopes of solving an ancient riddle." Lauden stood at the podium, as if giving a university lecture. "One that crosses disciplines as far-reaching as art history, speculative physics, and astronomy. Many of you have been informed of the current crisis, but for those who don't already know, five days ago the famous *Cosmic Widow* was stolen from the Galactic Museum."

Professor Senjara's eyes shot to Bilarus.

The curator shrunk into his seat.

Lauden split the projection screen, adding a virtual copy of the *Cosmic Widow* next to Dr. Liguera.

Lilline, along with the others, edged forward in her seat. This time her eyes ran over the famous portrait like a code breaker attempting to unravel a cryptic puzzle. That lone figure, back turned wearing the crimson hooded robe, taunted her with its mystery and allure. She focused on the one visible portion of the anatomy: the double-pollex, narrowing her eyes.

Why did Azaludarian paint you that way? Did you really have two thumbs?

Like a telescope rising to an astronomical target, Lilline's gaze ran up the figure's robe, past its hood to the night sky. A constellation, strange and unknown, glimmered in the pitch expanse. What was its meaning? And how did it connect to what she had photographed in the storeroom?

"Yesterday evening," Lauden said, "at an illegal art sale on Sky City, Agent Renault witnessed a suspect assumed to be the thief take an additional item." The Gej-ti clicked a remote, replacing the *Cosmic Widow* with a picture that Lilline recognized: an image-capture from the figurine she'd been controlling during the auction.

Professor Senjara gasped. As if to assess its authenticity, he pushed the joystick and drifted forward, staring at the image. "Stars, Asher..."

"Indeed, Professor. I couldn't have expressed it better myself. For the benefit of the rest of our guests, I hoped you might offer a succinct explanation of what this is and why it has brought us all here today."

The Kreeli whirred up and onto the stage and rotated to face the others. "This... I still can't believe my eyes." He shook off the amazement. "This is the legendary Azaludarian Star Chart." He spoke as if in a dream. "A crucial piece of missing evidence sought for thousands of cycles. Believed by most historians to be a fallacy, a false invention bolstering a myth of Darian idealism and allure."

"Chart for what?" Lilline asked.

"It is said to be the key that unlocks secrets in the *Cosmic Widow*."

"And you're certain it's authentic?"

"Its appearance is consistent with all known records," Lauden said. "The professor should be able to verify its content."

"Indeed." Senjara rotated back toward the screen. "Crude sketches and descriptions survive by later writers who chronicled the Darians. I've studied them all, Agent Renault. They speak of a lost document, a diagram produced by a contemporary of Azaludarian named Henestra. As the story goes, it was an unauthorized replica that many claim fell into the hands of their enemies."

Lilline found herself drawn into the alluring narrative.

"Look," The Kreeli pointed. "That vertical writing is Canitu, a pre-Galactic Common language. Zoom in Asher."

Lilline studied the script as it expanded. "Is it some kind of pictographic system?"

"Close to it, yes. It's iconographic. Each element has a reference, but it's important not to impose later shifts in cultural meanings onto the translation. My former colleague, Dr. Furst, spent decades tracking back through the evolution of interpretations to those accurate to the era. She wrote the book on Darian iconography."

"Can you translate it?"

"I believe I can, yes." The Kreeli whirred his hover-chair forward. "What you need to do is look with the eyes of someone who would be a contemporary to Henestra."

Lilline approached and stood by his side.

"*Star chart of Azaludarian,*" the Kreeli read aloud. "'*With this map and the Cosmic Widow, its...*'" he paused. "Not law, that's post-Darian...no, the translation would be 'power', yes." He continued. "'*... its power can be unleashed and the gate between worlds will open.*'"

The Kreeli whirred to face those assembled, eyes wide.

"What's wrong?" Lilline asked.

"Do you know what this is, Agent Renault? This is the star key."

"Star key?"

"According to myth, with it you can unfold the painting's dimensional layers. To access hidden secrets of great power."

"Mystical nonsense," Bilarus muttered.

Lilline turned to face the curator, who was shaking his head.

"Legend speaks of veiled locations throughout the galaxy," Senjara continued, "of extraordinary concentrated cosmic forces. And somehow the Darians knew how to locate them to access hidden dimensions."

"You mean what Henestra describes as gates?" Lilline asked.

The Kreeli nodded eyes scanning the screen. "Somehow the star chart and the painting work together."

"The mere discovery of this overturns thousands of cycles of scholarship," Lauden said, chiming in. "This is the first time, as far as we know, that the actual star chart has been uncovered."

"All of us, your director, hundreds of academic experts, Mr. Bilarus included," the professor glared at his former student, "as well as generations of scholars may be proven wrong through this discovery. And to think, many others who steadfastly believed the scant evidence lost their reputations standing by what we thought was nothing more than contrived and outlandish claims."

"Is there more?" Lilline asked.

"Yes." Senjara whirred back towards the projection, reading on. *"'In the star chart is hidden the road to the gate, where the Cosmic Widow reunites with Azaludarian, her lost lover.'"*

The Kreeli swung towards Lauden at the lectern. "It's true, Asher!"

A dumbfounded expression consumed her boss's face.

"So, she *was* his lover," the GAM-OPs director said.

"Wait, listen to this..." the Kreeli went on. *"Bring her to the Temple of Moz-Darian during the galactic alignment, break the horizon, and two worlds will meet."* Senjara halted, mouth agape.

"I know this," Lilline said. "It's referring to the sacred location purported to be a Darian oracle."

"Indeed, T8," Lauden said. "That's esoteric knowledge, how did you come by it?"

"I located a copy of Professor Senjara's book on First Galactic art in the stacks at Carothers & Elison Rare Tomes. I perused a section on the legend of the *Cosmic Widow* along with your file en route to Sky City."

"A physical copy? That's a rare find," Bilarus said. "Get the professor to sign it."

"Hush," the professor muttered, examining the star chart.

"What does that say, there?" Lilline pointed to a faded line running vertically on the other side of the star map.

The Kreeli's eyes narrowed. "Hmmm, why yes, there *is* something there."

Lilline's nerves crackled with anticipation, as if about to open a treasure chest buried by ancient hands.

"Now give me a moment..."

She checked on the others. All eyes were on the professor, ears perked waiting for him to speak.

"Yes, I have it." He faced the group. "'The key is written in the stars.'"

Bilarus shook his head.

"What's wrong, Reginald?" Lauden asked.

"I've said it before and I will say it again. This is hogwash. You're falling victim to the ramblings of a bunch of scholars drumming up interest and drawing attention to themselves by forcing together loose connections."

"You don't believe this evidence is sufficient?" Lilline asked.

"Of course not. People's careers have been ruined with this nonsense."

"Because you and your fellow naysayers went after them with the relentlessness of playground bullies," Professor Senjara said.

"Because it is *not* possible," the curator's voice was surprisingly bold and defiant. "With all due respect, it makes a mockery of the discipline. This is legend, nothing more."

"Reginald you lumphead!"

Lilline jumped at the volume of the professor's voice.

The Kreeli thrust the joystick forward and charged the curator. "Again with this damn close-mindedness? And you wonder why you're being pushed out of the Galactic Museum!"

Yikes. This was getting intense.

"How many times during your studies did I tell you to respect hypotheses, no matter how far-fetched? Even those most tenuous must never be ruled out. They remain conjecture *only* until evidence is found to back them up!" His blue face went beet red. "Between your pig-headedness and now these thefts under your museum tenure..." The Professor shook his head.

Lilline kept her expression neutral. It hurt to see the curator have to take one for the team about the artifact ruse, even if his bias kept him from accepting a changing galaxy.

"Let's get back to the topic at hand," Lauden said.

"Quite right, Asher," the Professor said. "Some of us are committed to working together... despite the tenuousness of the evidence."

"With respect to Professor Senjara, I have to disagree," Dr. Liguera said.

Lilline, along with all the others, focused on the holo-screen.

"I believe there *is* credible evidence, speaking from a scientific position." The researcher's eyes homed in on Bilarus. "It contains a good deal of conjecture, I will admit, but is backed up by theoretical astrophysics."

Pin's friend now had everyone's attention.

"Proceed, Dr. Liguera," Lauden said.

"Keep in mind this theory is only half-baked," the researcher said.

"U-City is where half-baked theories change the galaxy." Madame X spoke the declaration as if it were a mission statement or company tagline. "Out-of-the-box thinking is what we do here."

"Very well, then. To boil it down to simple language, I've found what I believe to be evidence that whirlpool galaxies, like our own, have what I call 'cosmic pressure points.'"

"Pressure points?" It was Bilarus.

"Yes, channels of energy flowing through a galaxy's spirals that gather at specific locations."

"Where?" Lauden asked.

"That's difficult to answer but trace evidence, combined with a great deal of speculation, points to disturbances of orbital patterns and spacetime at specific galactic locations that, I believe, indicate the spectral remains of black holes."

Murmurs rose from Pin and the others down the row.

"You lost me at 'spectral' Dr. Liguera," Lauden said.

Lilline, along with everyone else, gazed at the screen.

"A Second Galactic astronomer... more of a mystic, whose writings were lost to history, suggested it. I came across them in the archives on Xeret. They've been essential to my current research. Despite no hard evidence, he based a hypothesis on otherwise inexplicable trace residues along galactic spirals in the form of unique radiation. The wavelengths suggest previous cosmic events related to an extraordinarily fast rise and collapse of gravity. He named them ghost holes, since they leave no other trace of intrusions into spacetime."

"Ghost holes?" Lilline asked.

"Indeed." Dr. Liguera's eyes lit up. "There and not there, in too short a time to be explained through our understanding of astrophysics. Much like other famous principles, you have a paradox. I intend to honor the astronomer by naming it after them in my upcoming academic paper."

"As?" Pin asked.

"The Lumsden Paradox."

Pressure points... Lilline narrowed her eyes. "Sir, can you pull up a view of our galaxy?"

Lauden fiddled with the lectern's controls.

The famous image from the Iwara Probe, sent out almost a thousand cycles earlier, appeared on the screen.

"What are you on to, Agent Renault?" Professor Senjara asked.

"I'm familiar with Dr. Liguera's theory from another context. Martial arts systems exploit vital points along energy meridians and other interior anatomical channels, triggered through techniques that either strike with quick, precise force or longer blunt impacts to send a shock wave through the target."

"That's a bit far-fetched, isn't it?" Bilarus asked.

"No, it's not." Lilline didn't turn. Her eyes were transcribing the cosmic diagram into a simile of a body's energy meridians. "My teacher at the monastery is more versed in this but," she faced the group, "to amplify the effect and cause the greatest energy disruption, two or more opposite points are struck in a sequence. It's based on cosmological elements of various cultural origins - water, fire, air, wood, metal... but the same holds true at a galactic scale if we consider a meta-cosmology. The result might—"

"Trigger a cosmic reaction?" Dr. Liguera said. "If a particular alignment were established?"

"Exactly." Lilline said, smiling at the virtual researcher.

"Dr. Liguera, what kind of effect do you assume occurs to the spacetime fabric?" Madame X said.

"My theoretical calculations indicate it would generate two parallel and intense gravitational bursts surging inward from respective event horizons."

"Respective what?" Bilarus asked.

"Event horizons," Dr. Liguera said. "Think of them as boundaries... cosmic thresholds that disturb the laws of physics, and from which there is massive gravitational pull. Technically, that's known as a gravity well. It draws nearby objects with mass, and if they cross the event horizon well... nothing up to the speed of light can escape it."

Lilline stood, eyes on the projection.

"And here's the thing," Dr. Liguera said, continuing. "Based on the more advanced detectors we have today, I believe an unknown matter is given off as a byproduct when these reactions occur." Her virtual face filled with excitement. "One that my calculations suggest has the capacity to temporarily overcome a core singularity." The scientist's virtual eyes shot to Bilarus. "That's where a black hole's gravity is so powerful time and space are pinched," the researcher said. "A point of infinite density and zero volume. Nothing is thought to be able to overcome it. Well, almost... but that's a topic for another day."

"About this byproduct, Dr. Liguera..."

Madame X's white uniform appeared at Lilline's side.

"I assume it is a form of exotic matter?"

The virtual researcher's holo-eyes widened with delight at Madame X's understanding.

"One with negative mass?" the U-City director asked.

"Indeed."

"You've lost me," Bilarus said.

"That means it is repulsive," Dr. Liguera said. "Think of it as a force that pushes things away. Even intense gravitational energy that is squeezing spacetime shut."

"Stars..." Madame X said. "Dr. Liguera it's time to take your theory out of the scientific oven. It's baked to perfection."

"Hoo! I told you Slushie was the best!" the Oltari exclaimed.

"Thank you, Pin. And here's the finale." The researcher put a finger to her chin. "Actually, Madame X would you care to join me in a deductive duet?"

"I'd be honored."

"Delightful." Dr. Liguera edged closer to the screen, face filling the projection. "Following this course of thinking, if the right combination of cosmic reactions, in two otherwise separated and distant galaxies, were to be carried out when what we're calling an intergalactic channel of energy between them were aligned, it might..." The researcher gestured to the head of U-City.

"Create parallel gravity wells in the space fabric," Madame X responded. "And, if exotic matter is a byproduct, then it has the potential to push both sides of the respective core singularities open, creating—" She passed it back to the researcher on the screen.

"An intergalactic channel across folded spacetime." The researcher clapped, the delight of their collaboration visible to all.

"Or," Lilline jumped in adding a third, more vernacular voice to the conversation. "In layperson's terms..." She motioned for all three to speak together as a trio.

"A wormhole."

THIRTY-SIX

"One more time, please. For those of us less scientifically minded," Bilarus said, rubbing a hand over his face.

"Are you familiar with the folded paper analogy?" Madame X asked.

Bilarus shook his head.

"Let's say you have two distant points at opposite ends of a sheet of paper. Now imagine it represents an immense distance across space. Make it two locations in two separate whirlpool galaxies." The scientist made as if bending one side down and under in a gentle curve, aligning it to the other edge with about a ten-centimeter gap. "They appear closer now, right?"

He nodded.

"Good. We'll say one is directly over the other, or if you like, one is directly under the other. It doesn't matter. What does matter is this: you still have a degree of what we'll call 'space' between them. That's where the extreme collapse of gravity in black holes comes in... each side has incredible mass sinking into that area, pulling it inward so they're nearly touching in that empty space between the two sheets. Think of both as 'dropping inward' with one right side up, and one upside down."

Bilarus rattled his head.

"Stay with me," Madame X said. "Hypothetically speaking, a wormhole can appear like a black hole from the outside."

"And you are saying the two sides meet?" Bilarus asked.

"Exactly! Think of it like a god pushing their finger through inter-dimensional galactic skin," Dr. Liguera said. "No, excuse me," she held up a hand. "In this case, *two* gods, one on each side, their fingers pressing through and touching."

"Wait... what did you say?" Lilline asked.

"Think of it like two gods—"

"No, the end about the fingers."

"Breaking the space fabric so their fingers meet."

Lilline took a step forward, closer to the screen.

"Pull up the *Cosmic Widow*, sir."

She homed in on a detail like a laser on a bullseye.

"What is it, T8?"

"Not two fingers..." She faced the group and touched the tips of her thumbs.

"The double pollex," the professor said.

"It's been right there the whole time," Lilline said. "It's a symbol for a wormhole."

"Stars, my heart can't take this," Professor Senjara said. "The interdisciplinary rigor and synergy is—"

"Those stars above the *Cosmic Widow*," Madame X pointed at the constellation in the painting. "Could they be a map of these so-called pressure points?"

"Nothing in our galaxy reflects that star design," Lauden said.

"Maybe Azaludarian made it up," Bilarus said. "It is art, after all."

"Reginald, keep your mouth shut if you have nothing productive to add!" the professor barked.

"You can't rule it out," Bilarus said, defending himself. "Maybe they needed to fill in space... call it artistic license."

"The Darians were a brilliant culture," the professor retorted. "It *must* have a meaning."

"Maybe a star went nova, lost from an earlier night sky somewhere in the galaxy?" Pin asked. "That might account for the difficulty identifying the constellation?"

A rational assumption. Lilline waited, eager to hear a response.

"I've done this..." Professor Senjara shook his head.

"You've gone through the art historical record?" Lilline asked. "No other works include this star formation?"

"None. Believe me, Agent Renault, I've pored over every constellation, from every quadrant, during every age... down to individual star systems. I've searched for planets with that relationship and consulted with astronomers about specific timeframes and passing comets. And as you proposed, I've been through all known First and Second Galactic paintings. After hearing our discussion today, I can only come to one conclusion." His elderly face took on a professorial expression. As if ending a lecture with a final, profound declaration, he said, "this is not from our galaxy."

"That's impossible," Bilarus scoffed. "With all due respect, Professor. How could—"

"Not impossible."

Lauden's voice struck like a gavel echoing in a courtroom.

"Discoveries have been made," the director said. His black eyes homed in on Lilline.

I remember. That day at HQ, the Gej-ti had said there were high-security secrets... ones related to cosmic phenomena. The single-word description had stuck with her. She'd expected him to describe them as profound, or extraordinary, or make use of another term emphasizing excitement at newfound knowledge. Instead, he'd dropped a single-word bomb: terrifying.

"You may speak freely, Madame X," Lauden said.

"What I am about to share is highly confidential," the U-City director said. "Trust me when I say if it leaves this room and the source of the leak is found, there will be dire consequences."

Madame X went from one participant to the next, making each nod agreement. "Two cycles ago, the director and an associate from the Ministry requested we investigate strange and inexplicable resonances emanating from historical objects. While we still don't fully grasp the how and why, I can confirm its existence in surviving First Galactic artifacts."

"What are you suggesting?" Senjara asked.

Madame X. deferred to Lauden, who gave her the go-ahead.

"Our only conclusion is that they do not originate in this galaxy."

"Hoo!"

"Crikey!" The Professor put a blue hand on his heart. "You scared the stars out me, Pin!"

"Apologies, Professor. I find this exhilarating and surprisingly coincidental..."

"What is it, Pin?" Madame X asked.

The Oltari fluttered over and joined Lilline and the scientist. "I ran a composition check on the First Galactic clock from the crime scene and came to the same conclusion."

"Perhaps this explains a great many mysteries." Madame X spoke the words to Lauden at the podium.

Lilline didn't miss him raise an eyebrow.

"And T8..." Pin fluttered toward her. "It would explain why the clock is running backwards. Mirror galaxies!"

"Fascinating. I wonder..."

The voice was the Kreeli's, still patting his chest from the exclamatory startle.

"Something to add, Professor?" Lauden asked.

"Not really, Asher. Just dreaming of what else might have come through a portal if this theory is, in fact, true."

"You mean the last time a wormhole may have opened?" Lilline asked.

The professor nodded. "I imagine anything organic would have long deteriorated, but who knows what other historical treasures lay buried or hidden throughout the galaxy."

"If this is possible..." It was Dr. Liguera.

"Then an ages-old art historical legend has turned into a reality." Lauden's words swirled through the room.

"It's an unprecedented discovery," Madame X said, taking a step forward, "one that overturns the very foundations of our understanding of theoretical astrophysics." She shook her head. "Astounding."

"If I may ask," Professor Senjara said, "what is your degree in, Madame X?"

"Speculative astro-epistemology." She and the professor locked eyes. "And I think a fifth door has opened."

"What could trigger something like this?" Lilline asked.

"You'd need a powerful device similar to a particle collider," Dr. Liguera said.

"You think it's artificial?" Madame X asked.

"Most certainly, it's too site-specific to be naturally occurring, especially considering it requires a synchronized trigger with a mirror galaxy, but the technology needed to produce something of this magnitude is... it's beyond our capability to fathom."

"But maybe not beyond that of the Darians," Lilline said.

"You are talking about something so extraordinary that it's nothing more than science fiction, Agent Renault." Coming from the director of U-City, the words carried extraordinary emphasis.

"I think after what I've witnessed here today," Lilline said, "I'm willing to stretch the boundaries of the possible."

"What in stars does a painting have to do with all of this?" It was Bilarus. "You can't show up at some random coordinates in space and hold up a painting to create a wormhole."

"Don't be facetious," the professor said.

"I'm being realistic. This is a futile exercise."

"Speak for yourself!"

"Be quiet please for a moment, everyone." Lauden walked forward and studied the projection.

"What is it, sir?" Lilline asked.

"Read that line on the left again, would you, Professor?"

"'The key is written in the stars,'" the Kreeli said.

"Could this be a star language?" The director's translucent skin cast an eerie glow in the projection's light.

"Star language, sir?"

"A form of communication invented by the Darians. It relies on a visual gestalt where the size, radiance, and position of a constellation and surrounding stars form a syntax. Think of it as literary stellar music, T8. Words written as astronomy."

"This doesn't show any legible sequences," the professor said, whirring up next to them.

"Do you remember that paper I presented at the Garraffa Conference?" Lauden asked the professor.

"I do. It was one of the most daring propositions made by a graduate student. I was proud of you for that essay."

"Something about this..." Lauden took a step closer, examining a section of the starry design. "Can you read anything here? Even if only in fragments?"

"As I said, it's gibberish," the professor said, head shaking. "It makes no sense."

"Then it leads us nowhere." Bilarus threw his hands up.

"Wait," Lilline said, "I just thought of –"

"It's no use, Agent Renault," the curator said. "We're wasting our time. Cycles of this... round and round."

"Let her speak!" the professor barked.

Lilline stepped forward. "What are you sensing, sir? If I may ask?"

"I can't articulate it, T8. It leaves me..." he sighed. "Topsy-turvy."

Like a sun breaking the horizon, the light of realization rose. *That's it.*

"Pin?"

"Yes, T8?"

"The Darian clock is running backwards, why?"

"It's from another galaxy, theoretically arriving through the wormhole, which runs as a mirror universe."

"It's complicated," Madame X said. "It involves theoretical astrophysics. Do you need a detailed explanation?"

"No. What I need is for the professor to read the stars backwards."

"Backwards?" the Kreeli asked.

"But not yet," Lilline held up a hand. "Let's reverse everything and re-design the map... using ratios." She gestured to Pin. "You can do it, right?"

"Yes, T8. You want a radiance scale where the brightest is dimmest, and so on? With a similar transcription to the other linguistic syntaxes?"

"Exactly."

The Oltari worked furiously on her tablet.

Long, wrinkled fingers squeezed her arm.

"I think you may be on to something." The professor's grip remained in anxious anticipation.

"Done!" Pin said. "Sir, give me access to the screen, please."

Lauden strode to the lectern and hit a control.

The stellar map reappeared.

Lilline's eyes narrowed. A new consistency to the image shone, with a pleasing balance and visual lyricism.

"By the stars, this is it," Bilarus exclaimed. "Professor can you—"

"Yes, yes! I am already translating it!"

The professor's eyes darted to and fro, his lips speaking silent words as he translated the star language. "Hah!" the Kreeli bellowed. "Agent Renault, you are a genius!"

"What is it, Professor?" Lauden said, leaving the lectern to join them. "Tell me you've got it?"

Everyone gathered around.

It was as if the aura of the old Kreeli expanded. He was back at university before bright-eyed and eager students.

He cleared his throat and spoke:

*"Look from the center of empire, to where our reach is
    farthest.
That which shines most distant marks the path.
Bend the stars and the Cosmic Widow will speak its
    secret.
Walk the equatorial chasm on the second planet and
    see with eyes of night.
Between glimmering peaks lies the Temple door."*

THIRTY-SEVEN

"The chart isn't telling us the location of the cosmic pressure points," Lauden said. "It's the instructions on how to find the Temple of Moz-Darian."

"I'll bet there's a device there that works with the painting to trigger what Dr. Liguera is suggesting," Lilline said.

"Good show, T8."

"Thank you, sir. This must be why the thief needed the chart *and* the *Cosmic Widow*."

"Whoever they are," Lauden said, "this criminal or one of their accomplices is well informed on First Galactic art history."

"There's more here," the professor said. "That verse was the outer dimension. There's an inner dimension of text behind it."

> *"Place the pendant onto the chain of time.*
> *Fill the sacred chamber with finger tight.*
> *Let gravity flow.*
> *Bring forth the key.*
> *Aim to the star that shines above the Cosmic Widow.*
> *Collapse the four walls."*

"Sending the professor's translations to the lectern, sir," Pin said.

Lauden strode to the podium and hit a switch.

Lilline read through the projected verses. "These sound like clues to a puzzle allowing access to layers of the Temple, or something like that."

"And possibly activation of a device using the constellation in the *Cosmic Widow*," Madame X added.

"I'm trying to make sense of that initial verse, but I'm vexed." The professor shook his oblong head. "Scroll back to it if you would, please..."

Lauden walked to the lectern and swiped the screen.

> *Look from the center of empire, to where our reach is*
> *farthest.*
> *That which shines most distant marks the path.*
> *Bend the stars and the Cosmic Widow will speak its*
> *secret.*
> *Walk the equatorial chasm on the second planet and*
> *see with eyes of night.*
> *Between glimmering peaks lies the Temple door.*

"The center would be Kalatron. That planet was the capital of the Darian empire," Lauden said.

"But that next phrase?" The professor held out his hands. "Is this a historical reference? Peak of Darian culture was just prior to the early 1400s FG."

"I would venture to guess that 'where our reach is farthest' might imply an astronomical interpretation," Dr. Liguera said. "Perhaps it suggests a directional bearing when Kalatron is at its farthest orbital point from its sun? That would be Insha, if I have my Darian history correct?"

"Indeed," the professor said.

Dr. Liguera swiveled in her virtual seat and entered data on an adjacent holo-terminal.

"But what is this bend the stars riddle?" Lilline asked. "What is that supposed to mean? This galaxy and another?"

"No idea, but we know it is a solar system with at least two planets. Could we narrow it that way?" Bilarus asked.

"You're kidding, right?" It was Madame X.

"That many?"

She shook her head at the futility of the suggestion.

"I've got the bearing of Kalatron at its farthest orbital point from Insha. It would be moving outward from Arm 3 and cutting across two more spirals, Arms 4 and 5, respectively. Pin, I've sent the data over."

Lilline scrutinized the image of a red line cutting across their whirlpool galaxy.

"That narrows it a bit," Madame X said, "astronomically speaking."

Lilline knew by the way she said it there was still a massive amount of galactic space to cover.

"You're crossing Arm 5 there, though," Madame X stepped forward and pointed at an area about two-thirds of the way out on the galactic spiral. "That's uncharted."

"Impossible," Bilarus said head shaking.

"I've been crunching some numbers," Pin said, holding her tablet. "And..." Four hands, totaling twenty-eight digits, typed furiously. "Using the data Slushie sent me... I've isolated the dates when trace particles fitting the characteristics she described have been recorded in our galaxy."

"Let me guess," Professor Senjara said, "one was during the Darian Empire?"

Pin nodded. "1427 First Galactic."

"Incredible." The Kreeli's hushed tone was filled with awe.

Lilline knew that date. It was the cycle every student learned when studying the lost culture.

"That's when all records stopped... stars, it all makes sense now." The Kreeli's head shook in disbelief.

A moment's silence fell.

"Don't you all understand?" he asked, whirring around.

Lilline and the others shook their heads.

"They left."

"Who?" Lilline asked.

"The Darians. That's why they disappeared from the historical archive. They're not from here." A blue finger pointed down as if to suggest their galaxy.

"But that would mean—"

"Yes, Reginald," the Kreeli said, replying to the curator's interjection. "We've had it wrong all these long cycles. They were driven back. And out."

"You're saying whoever, or whatever, came through was..." Madame X paused.

"Hostile."

Lilline, along with the others, shifted her attention to the lectern. The GAM-OPs director's single word was the final touch, like placing down the last and now obvious piece to a complex puzzle.

"Let's just say there's been other, less direct evidence, discovered at U-City that confirms it," he added.

Madame X, tight-lipped, nodded to the group in confirmation.

"It appears," Lauden said, "that the Darians were galactic invaders, colonizers perhaps. Either way, their revered qualities were most likely the result of the fact that they were, literally, extraordinary intruders."

"Stars, Asher. It's been right there before our eyes." Professor Senjara rotated his hover-chair to face the lectern. "All those long cycles unable to reconcile written history with the archive of images."

Shock filled her boss's features. The Gej-ti was still processing this new level of understanding.

"And those baffling battle scenes in the museum's collection," the professor said, rotating his hover-chair to face Bilarus. "They are depictions of our galactic brethren driving them out!"

Lilline conjured the fierce space battle that hung adjacent to the Venex Horse's empty vitrine in her mind.

"I hate to say it," Bilarus said, "but if what you describe is true, then the superlatives about Darian intelligence and technology may be true." The curator spoke as if sharing Lilline's thoughts, and it didn't help ease her concern.

"Those images in the museum are no small affair," the curator added. "They depict an epic confrontation with a threat most dire."

"Let us now remember, and reconsider, that famous surviving description from an anonymous chronicler," the professor said. "'When victory was assured, we wept, for our time was made safe. But should they return, we knew of the power they kept. Next time they vowed no mercy. No negotiation. Only annihilation.'"

"One thing is clear," Lilline said. "None of this is about stealing a painting for fame or riches."

"No, it is not." Lauden's voice grew grave. "Whoever has the *Cosmic Widow* intends to let the Darians back in."

"Excuse me," Pin said. "I think you all might be interested in a second calculation. There's a pattern here. Slushie's data also indicates a date before 1427 FG, with diminished traces consistent with the rate of half-life. I assume that to be when the Darians came through."

"And after that?"

"Well, there should have been two during the Second Galactic Period, and at least three others during our own era, but it appears they did not occur."

"That makes sense if no one had the knowledge to do it," Bilarus said. "So much was lost during those tumultuous cycles in the post-Darian decline."

"Or, if someone *was* privy to this knowledge, they didn't want it opened. For the reasons Professor Senjara articulated." Lauden's words, quietly spoken, screamed with a terrifying logic.

"The Second Galactic is indeed tumultuous as far as epochs go," the professor said. "But quite filled with innovation, as recent scholars have pointed out in revisionist work. Take Dr. Liguera's research built off Lumsden employed here today." He glared at Bilarus. "Don't be too quick to judge."

He was right, some historians referred to the Second Galactic as the Middle Cycles, a designation that cast it as no more than an in-between where the glory of the First Galactic and its renewal in the current age were privileged.

"I fear you may be right, Asher," the professor added. "Something tells me that if this cosmic gate were to re-open—"

"I've determined the next upcoming date." Pin raised her head from the tablet.

Excitement of discovery morphed with an ominous foreboding, creeping into the room like a ghostly fog. Lilline's instinct sensed where this was going.

"Only its beginning, I should add," Pin said. "How long it would remain 'open' for some kind of cosmic activation, I do not know."

"When?" Lauden's earnest voice cut through the tension.

"I would like to state that I had to make adjustments for the lost days after conversion from the Darian calendar and—"

"How long, Pin?" Lauden asked.

"Two days."

THIRTY-EIGHT

"So, we're able to calculate the dates of these galactic alignments but we can't predict where they'll be?" Lilline asked.

The Oltari deferred to Slushie.

"Exactly," Dr. Liguera said.

"Thus, the paradox," Madame X added.

"There's no pattern across sites, Pin?" Lilline hoped the Oltari's extraordinary analytic abilities with a twenty-eight-digit indigenous numeric system might notice something other species couldn't.

"The previous pressure points read like a randomly generated cosmic map." Pin shrugged.

"There's a scientific explanation, I am sure," Dr. Liguera added. "But sadly, it's beyond my capacity to hazard a guess with the available data. We'd need a Darian."

Lauden and Senjara exchanged looks.

"The star chart's verses must hold the answer," Lilline said.

"That document is a riddle," Bilarus said. "Not to mention, we can't crack the painting's constellation."

The Kreeli grumbled from his hover-chair.

"Why would the thief do it?" Lilline's eyes bounced from

attendee to attendee. "If they figured this all out, why go through the trouble to reach the Temple and activate the gate alone? I mean, without sharing the information with the academic and scientific communities. Or the government, for that matter?"

"I don't know." The professor's response was a whisper.

"You say the suspect is human?" Madame X asked.

"If we are correct and the thief from Sky City is also the one perpetrating this larger cosmic event, yes," Lauden said. "Whether they are acting alone or not..." The Gej-ti raised an eyebrow, milky skin creasing under his widow's peak.

"Unless they're from the original invasion?" Madame X said. "Could a Darian be in some highly advanced cryo-sleep system that we aren't aware of? Wouldn't be the first time, that's all I will say..."

That raised some eyebrows.

"I don't think it's plausible," Lauden said. "That's assuming there are humans or a species close to our own in another galaxy."

Lilline read a funny expression on Madame X's face.

"Even so, with the specific astronomical information it's unlike-ly," Lauden added.

"I quite agree," Professor Senjara said. "If Pin is right and there's evidence of previous alignments, odds would be an earlier opportu-nity to return or open a channel would have been taken."

"You didn't happen to notice two thumbs on the suspect, Agent Renault?" Bilarus asked.

"Very funny," she said. "No." Lilline stared at the *Cosmic Widow*. She conjured a mental image of the thief performing a highly impressive acrobatic maneuver in the storeroom.

Who are you?

"Whatever the reason," Lauden said, "it's the unknown waiting on the other side that troubles me most."

Not for the first time, Lilline felt a profound sense of wonder clash with potential danger and threat. Why did galaxy-shattering revelations never arrive with welcome arms? Always, they were linked with antagonism, terror, and the potential for destruction.

She approached the others and took a seat, a mixture of revelation and defeat vying for dominance in her mind.

"Here, you look like you need this." Madame X, who had a refreshment cart brought in for the group, handed her a cup of coffee. She knocked it back in one gulp, eyes fixed on the screen.

"Well, Reginald? What do you make of all this now?" Professor Senjara turned his hover-chair to the curator.

"After seeing this evidence..." Bilarus dabbed his forehead with his handkerchief. "I was wrong."

Senjara's face softened. "Let this be a lesson to you. We must remain open to change, even at the expense of the limits of reason."

Lilline listened, respectfully. An interesting and unexpected statement from the reputable scholar. It was as if this room had turned upside down, mirroring a wormhole.

"Locking and barring scholarly doors won't hold back the future," the Kreeli said, his tone gentle. "It finds a way through, no matter how much we resist it. If I've learned one thing since retiring, it's that you can't keep the next generation's aspirations and ideas back with your own. The sands of time fall through the hourglass whether we want them to or not."

Lilline found herself starry-eyed at the professor's words. She glanced at Lauden. The Gej-ti's face was full of admiration. So, this was her boss's mentor? How odd, to go from an academic discipline like art history to the head of GAM-OPs. And yet, considering the professor's words, it somehow all made sense.

"But we still have a central problem, don't we?"

It was Pin, who by her tone appeared to have missed the emotional moment between student and teacher.

"We don't know the location of the Temple." The Oltari held both sets of arms out in a gesture of futility. "Even with an understanding of what the thief might be doing with the *Cosmic Widow*, and when, we're rudderless to follow."

"Pin's right," Dr. Liguera said from the holo-screen. "Without the location, there's no way forward. We don't have what we need to crack that riddle. As Mr. Bilarus mentioned, that knowledge is lost…"

"Not entirely lost," Professor Senjara said.

Lilline read strange undulations on the Kreeli's wrinkled face.

"There is one who might know how to decode that verse."

"You don't mean…" Lauden interjected.

"I do."

"She won't talk to any of us," the director said. "You, me, or even Reginald" He pointed from the professor, to himself, and then the curator.

"You're right about that," Senjara said. "But the rumors, Asher…"

Lauden cocked his head. "Nothing has ever been verified. Now you are starting to sound like the conspiracy theorists."

"Am I?" The professor whirred onto the stage and approached the lectern. "After you bring me here and show me this? I'd say legends are being verified in short order today."

"It'll never work." Bilarus shook his head.

"Well, it's our only shot," the professor said.

Lauden sighed. "I really need a smoke."

"And who is going to convince her?" Bilarus asked. "She won't trust anyone from an academic field, not since she's gone and joined 'them.'"

Lauden and the professor's faces made clear that for once, the curator was right.

"What about T8?" Pin said.

Lilline felt like a bullseye as all eyes homed in on her.

"She's a secret agent." The Oltari shot her a smile. "Her job is filled with risks and adventure. I've seen you socialize, T8. You can charm anyone. You're an expert at it."

The warm rush of blood filled Lilline's cheeks. *Please don't bring up Alex…*

Professor Senjara whirred down from the stage and examined her.

Lilline held the old Kreeli's stare. There was a depth to his eyes she'd rarely encountered.

"She's a poet as well, Professor," Lauden said.

"Soon to be published," Lilline added to murmurs of approval from those around her.

The Kreeli raised an eyebrow. "Yes, I think you may be on to something here, Asher."

"I'm always game, sir." Lilline said. "If GAM-OPs needs to get this done, I'll deliver."

"Yes," Lauden mused, reaching into his pocket and withdrawing his pipe. "Something tells me if anyone can get her to help us, it's you, Agent Renault."

"Hoo!" Pin covered her mouth cheeks going blue.

"I'll give you the gist post haste, T8," the director said. "There are some complications, to say the least."

"Good luck with those." Bilarus rolled his eyes.

"It's nothing Agent Renault hasn't encountered before," Lauden said. "She's cracked harder nuts."

"No pun intended," the curator whispered.

"You can count on me," Lilline said. She had no idea what she was agreeing to, and something told her it was going to be a doozy, but that's why she did the job.

Pin clapped two sets of hands.

"Madame X, are the upgrades complete?" Lauden asked.

Lilline scrutinized the director's features. *What upgrades?*

The scientist approached. "Indeed. I approved them myself this morning."

"Excellent. Then there's no time to lose. T8, let's get you ready for departure."

"What am I flying, sir?"

"The Racer, of course," Lauden raised an eyebrow. "Did you not see it earlier?"

So, I wasn't hallucinating.

"And where am I going?"
Lauden deferred to the professor, who met her gaze.
"Back in time."

THIRTY-NINE

"T8, if you're successful report in with the coordinates," Lauden said. "Then make haste to the Temple's location. If by bad luck the system is too far from you, hopefully another T# can get there in time. I'm going to send all non-committed agents out in a standard galactic spread. With any luck, one of them might be close enough to arrive before the thief sets things in motion."

"Yes, sir." A palpable tension circulated the group. A mixture of art history, museology, theoretical astrophysics, pioneering scientific technology, and in her case, good old-fashioned secret agent grit formed a unique and powerful invisible current.

"Madame X." Lauden gestured for the scientist to take over. "It's your show."

The scientist nodded in earnest. "This way everyone."

Lilline homed in on the projection, marking it to memory, before following the pack.

"Is there a lavatory nearby?" Professor Sanjara asked.

"To the left," Madame X pointed down the hall. "We'll wait here."

The soft whirr of the academic's hover-chair faded, leaving Lilline and the others in an uncomfortable silence.

"I'm very taken with your facilities, Madame X," Pin said, breaking the tension. "I've only glimpsed what goes on here, but my sensory channels detect an atmosphere of order, earnestness, and regulation much to my liking."

"Qualities we value most at U-City," the scientist said.

"I imagine these compete with innovation and research?"

"Indeed. And speculation. A most important practice."

Pin placed a pair of hands over her mouth and giggled. "U-City sounds delightful! It's been a pleasure meeting you."

"Likewise. I'm eager to hear more about your biomass-digester and anything else you have in the works. We might consider sharing research." Madame X's eyes brightened. "In fact, should you ever decide to leave GAM-OPs, please contact me via Director Lauden. There might be a place for you here at U-City."

"Hoo!"

"No stealing my employees." Lauden pointed a milky finger at his fellow Gej-ti.

No doubt, he and Madame X were well acquainted. And that raised a more profound question: how much did Asher Lauden know about what went on at U-City?

Not for the first time, Lilline found herself humbled by the weight of the director's responsibilities. All that knowledge and confidentiality to maintain the security of billions across the stars... that was a job she never wanted. She'd take being in the dark about the government's coveted secrets to keep her license to roam the galaxy. An open checkbook, Pin's toys and gadgets, and a life of adventure suited her just fine. The chances of getting killed might be higher in the field, but his comment when they arrived grew more convincing by the minute. How the old fish got to sleep at night with all this on his shoulders, she didn't know.

"You need rest, T8," Lauden said. "You're no good to us otherwise. Madame X, is there somewhere Agent Renault can lie down for a few hours before departure?"

"She'll have time to recharge on the Racer," Madame X said. "We've installed a stasis unit with a short-sleep option. Its neuro-control system will lower a user's brainwaves, providing a boost to mental as well as physical rest."

This is getting better by the minute.

"And it will take care of that arm wound." The scientist shot her a wink. "Follow the instructions for the hyper-heal software on the chamber's exterior. Enter the anatomical region and injury type and you'll be good as new when you drop out of FTL."

"Perfect," Lilline said. "Sir, what I do need is to get equipped. Can we hop back to HQ on your shuttle for a quick turnaround?"

"No need, T8." Pin said. "The *Cephala's* aft compartment includes a portable arsenal and equipment station."

Silence descended on the group.

Pin cocked her head. "Why are you all smiling?"

"The *Cephala*?" Lilline said.

Pin nodded.

"As in *Cephala pod*?"

"Indeed, T8." She took a bow. "Homonymic word play."

"Good show, Pin," Lauden said to chuckles all around.

The weight of the crisis and upcoming mission lifted. Lilline suspected the levity gave everyone present a much-needed pause.

Pin had what she assumed to be a smug look for her species on her face. Was the Oltari getting better at social dynamics?

Professor Sanjara whirred around the corner, returning from the lavatory. "What's wrong?" he said, halting a few meters back from the group. "You all have funny expressions on your faces."

"Pin was 'kraken' jokes while we waited for you," Bilarus said.

The group broke out into a second round of cackles.

"Oh, sure. Have all the fun while I'm not here," Professor Sanjara said. "Well, you can try your humor out on me on the return flight,

Pin. I've got a few of my own I think you'll enjoy. Although they got me into some trouble back in my university days."

"Actually, I was hoping to treat you to a late lunch in the Octagonal Club," Lauden said. "You too, Reginald. We can ride back together."

Pin giggled.

"Something else funny, Pin?" the professor asked.

"It's just that an octagonal has eight sides and—"

"Alright, let's move on." Lauden gestured, calling a halt to the humorous word play.

"I'll escort you all back to the tarmac," Madame X said. "Agent Renault, after you finish your inventory check at the..." The scientist hesitated. "*Cephala pod*..." She smiled at Pin. "We'll prep you on the Racer's new controls so you can get up and out of atmo for the jump."

"Excellent, thank you," Lilline said.

The scientist motioned for the group to follow her down the hall. "And Director Lauden, I know you are eager to get aboard your Senara shuttle for the return to Tavi-Central."

"Quite right." He tapped the pocket with his tobacco tin.

"You're not going to smoke on board, are you Asher?" The Professor pushed the control stick forward and zoomed up next to the Gej-ti. "You know how I feel about second-hand smoke..."

Lauden's audible sigh echoed through the corridor. "No, Professor. I wouldn't dare think of it."

"Well, good. In fact, we can use the time on the return flight to discuss strategies for quitting that filthy habit."

Bilarus leaned towards Madame X. "I can't wait to witness this."

Charming though it was to see Lauden reunited with his old university mates, a tinge of sadness ran through her, peppering the mood. The current crisis had provided an opportunity for the Gej-ti to re-connect with old acquaintances, but with his terminal condition it could be their last time.

"I'm sorry to have to ask, sir," Lilline said, as they walked, "but I need a favor. It's a domestic issue. I was hoping someone at HQ might be able to take care of it."

Lauden did the hand thing.

Lilline turned to the Oltari. "Pin, how are you with cats?"

FORTY

Lilline stepped out of the sleep chamber feeling like a million credits. Whatever it was Madame X and the other scientists at U-City were up to with somnic technology, she hoped they didn't stop. It was as if a high-powered vacuum had sucked all the dust and dirt from the corners of her mind. Her mental interior sang with sparkling cognitive clarity, itching to get to work. Her limbs, however, were another matter. It felt like she was standing in a blob of jelly, but somewhere behind her teetering and precarious balance a new energy reserve lay dormant. Her muscles fibers, privy to the equivalent of a vigorous massage and steam bath, were waking with an increase in physical voltage.

Toasty waves of fresh-brewed coffee brought a smile to her face as she made her way up the spiral staircase to the ship's lounge. Everything on the top-of-the-line Racer was in synch. Wake up programs, interior design aesthetics, and all its amenities had been cut from the same innovative cloth. She plopped down on a sofa and took a sip of black coffee.

"*Cilex Racer*," she whispered, blowing on the hot liquid. "Gotta love it."

Worth all the tactical bartering with Lauden. She'd take this over—

"*Arriving in the Sota-4 system,*" the ship's AI announced.

Lilline grinned at the honeyed words. Call it tacky but she couldn't resist the urge to test the newly updated voice inventory. Nothing like the sweet tenor tones of Carton Filatro, the debonair and handsome singer, to accompany her on a solo flight across the stars.

"*Drop from FTL in thirty seconds.*"

Lilline plopped her feet up on the coffee table and leaned back into the plush sofa.

"Ship, play something by Carton Filatro."

"*Solo work or symphonic accompaniment?*"

"Surprise me."

She closed her eyes and let the famous aria soothe and inspire her already tranquil mind.

"*FTL drop complete.*" Filatro's voice broke into his rendition of "From the Stars to your Heart." "*Atmospheric entry in thirty-two minutes and fourteen seconds.*"

Lilline brought the mug to her lips. Warm, savory liquid rolled over her tongue. In the darkness, the blend's profile appeared as a mix of words and colors. She'd always had a touch of synesthesia. Music, especially, came forth as a spectrum of hues. Now, as always, Filatro's arias were a deep crimson. Settings and emotions, on the other hand, tended to bubble up from a spring of word associations. That was where her poetry's internal source derived. Textures manifested as—

Ping.

Her eyes popped open.

"High priority call request. Origin: HQ."

"Stop the music." Lilline stood, placing her mug of coffee down on the table. "Give me a moment." She crossed to her travel bag and threw on some clothes. It wouldn't do to have her talking to Lauden in pajama shorts and a tank top.

"Okay." She returned to the sofa, took a swig of coffee, and got comfortable. "Open the line."

A track of blue lights, like a miniature runway, flashed across the table.

"Connecting," the ship's AI said.

Lilline peered across the galley to the bridge. A distant Elaris, green and blue with swirling clouds, hovered as a distant orb in the darkness of space.

"How was the jump, T8?" Lauden, sitting at his desk at HQ, manifested as a small blue holo over the table.

"Smooth as can be, sir."

"And the sleep capsule?"

"Most impressive," she said. "I have to admit, Madame X really delivered."

Her boss nodded his small virtual head. *"There's something you need to see. But first, I have an update on your grandmother."*

She edged up on the couch. "Any improvement?"

The Gej-ti shook his head. *"She's hanging on, but Doctor Klitarney's prognosis stands. Without a way to identify the source of the toxin they can't turn this around."* He shook his head. *"I'm sorry."*

Lilline nodded. Maybe it was the alpha wave treatment, but the news settled without disruption. The mission objectives remained at the forefront of her concerns. And yet, a glimmer of a third possibility rose to challenge it.

Am I beginning to accept the inevitable?

"I've asked a personal favor of Madame X," Lauden said. *"She and her team have been passed Kissy's medical reports. We're doing all we can, T8."*

"Thank you." Even across the light years, a palpable sincerity in the Gej-ti's tone resonated throughout the cabin.

"On to business," he said. *"Head of Tech got a hit on something. It's quite brilliant."* A miniature Lauden swiped a hand over his desk and the holo split. *"You are going to want to see this."*

FORTY-ONE

"Good morning, T8," Pin said, appearing next to the director. *"Oh... it may not be morning there. Unless you're on Galactic Standard Time. I assume you're not planetside?"*

"Morning it is, Pin." Lilline held up her mug of coffee. "I just woke up, so we'll go with that."

"Pin, show T8 what you've got."

"Yes, sir." The Oltari leaned forward, typing at her desk. *"I remembered the director's report about T5 and our art dealer vacating the premises on Sky City. It got me thinking... Carmini must have taken all those valuable works of art with him."*

Lilline stopped mid-sip.

"And then I thought—"

"He took our little sculpture with him," Lilline said, finishing for her.

"Hoo!"

An miniature virtual eyebrow pulled milky skin upward on Lauden's forehead, satisfaction brightening his black eyes.

"We sent the twins up to Sky City," Pin said. *"They delivered my*

back-up remote to your new friend at the Tobarii Lounge. You remember, the one you—"

"Yes," Lilline said, cutting her off. Warmth spread through her cheeks. "Better not to discuss specifics over this channel."

"But you're on the Cilex Racer, T8. It has the most sophisticated encryption in the galaxy. There's no reason not to speak freely, especially because I was so impressed with how you—"

"The intel, Pin," Lilline said. "The clock is ticking."

"T8 is right," Lauden added.

"Yes, sir. You aren't going to believe this." The Oltari clapped both sets of hands. *"Ready?"*

"Roll it," Lilline said.

Lauden and Pin vanished, replaced by a non-descript room with their old pal, Carmini. The Jenzara's gelatinous red body, still wearing the tuxedo, moved about removing artifacts from boxes and placing them on shelves. The rate at which he sorted the objects, the three eyes on his chin darting about, spoke to the level of intelligence and information processing running through his five brains.

"She's here, sir," a voice out of view said.

"Send her in."

Lilline's eyes widened as Renina entered the screen.

"This situation just got a whole lot worse," Carmini said. *"Do you know who this is?"*

Renina examined a tablet handed to her. *"I do. And now you know I'm not the one who double-crossed you. I did what you asked and got the thief into the museum."*

"Noted," the Jenzara said. He stripped the bowtie from his neck and tossed it on a nearby table.

"I did my part," Renina said. *"I am out. This has gotten way out of hand. I want to go back to the museum."*

"Oh, I don't think so." Three eyes homed in on the Rasp. *"If I don't get that painting back, I'm ruined."* He stepped forward. A screech jolted the audio system as Renina backed up, banging into a table. The mouth on the Jenzara's forehead spoke in slow, sinister

words. *"I will take you down with me, Rasp. Everyone will learn of your part in this."*

Renina held up her three-fingered hands in defense. *"Okay. I can help you. There's something you don't know."*

"What is it?"

"I know who she is."

The Jenzara's three eyes shifted. *"Proceed."*

"That woman works for the Ministry. I don't know for whom exactly, but she's some kind of investigator."

"She told you this?"

Renina nodded.

Lilline winced. Her roll of the dice crapped out. Lauden wasn't going to be happy about it, either. An attempt to woo information out of Renina had come back to bite her.

"Damn!" Carmini slammed a gelatinous fist on the table. Several artifacts teetered and fell over. *"You idiot, she's a GAM-OPs agent!"*

"GAM-OPs?" The Rasp's clay-colored skin crackled as her snake-like neck danced back and forth.

"As in the Ministry's secret agency," he said. *"Stars, but this entire ruse keeps going from bad to worse."*

"But I'm confused. She's not the thief?"

He sighed. *"No, she is not. Now we have two problems."*

"Why is she stealing from you?" Renina asked.

"That is what I hoped you could tell me." He swung around and pointed at the tablet in her hand, indicating she should swipe the screen.

Renina gasped.

"So, you know what this is?"

The Rasp nodded.

"Upstairs." He yanked the pad out of her hand. *"I want to know everything. But I need a drink."*

"I have to get back to Tavi-Prime. I'm due back at work in the morning."

Carmini leaned forward, towering over her, and spoke through gritted teeth. *"You will come upstairs and explain this star map to me, you one-eyed, one-brained, little child. I will drink a Skytini to calm my nerves so Gongo does not rip that apple-sized head off your serpentine neck!"*

Renina cowered, nodding.

"You can catch the last flight down to Tavi. If you miss it, you'll stay the night and take the pre-dawn red eye." He brushed past her, disappearing out of view. *"And you will make sure you close up any loose ends at the museum."*

"Don't worry about my boss," Renina said. *"He won't be a problem soon."*

Lilline made a note about Bilarus and filed it for later.

"This way." The Jenzara's voice grew more distant.

Renina turned to follow but hesitated, examining an artifact that had toppled over. *"My family used to have one of these,"* she said. *"Father kept it on display in our summer estate on Quo."*

"Ms. Blackstone?"

"Yes?"

"I don't care."

Renina placed the artifact down and walked away, leaving a backdrop of stolen art like a historical graveyard.

Lauden and Pin replaced the surveillance feed on the holo.

"That's it," the director said.

"Do we know where they are during this conversation, Pin?" Lilline asked.

"Sky City." The Oltari shrugged, four hands gesturing at her sides. *"That's the best I can do."*

Damn.

"I apologize, T8. It's a crude device made in haste for the auction. There's no tracking or larger sat-comm link."

"Not your fault, Pin." Lilline waved a hand. "It got us a solid piece of bonus intel."

"Indeed," Lauden said. *"According to our asset at the Taborii Lounge, there's been nothing since. They'll keep monitoring but my*

guess is Carmini's jumped ship... or in this case, city. He could be anywhere on Tavi-Prime."

That was a lot of planet.

"Needle in a haystack." Lauden picked up his pipe and lit it.

Lilline agreed. Other than dumb luck being spotted, the Jenzara and those stolen works were long gone.

"So, Renina was their insider?" Lilline said.

Lauden nodded.

"But our conclusion about the thief double-crossing Carmini stands," she said.

The director *humphfed*, clenching his pipe stem between his teeth.

"With this intel, sir," Pin said, *"I should be able to put together a solution to the museum break-in. It takes care of a lot of previous unanswerable questions."*

"But not the final one... where the thief manages to navigate through the laser maze to the painting, right?" Lilline asked, thinking of the acrobatic maneuver at the auction.

"No, not that," Pin said.

"We may yet get answers." The Gej-ti took a pull on his pipe and exhaled a plume of virtual smoke. Thick waves of Yaz Flake billowed from his neck gills, cutting into the holo's blue light. *"As soon as Renina returns to Tavi-Central, I'll have our team bring her in."*

"Actually, sir." Lilline edged up on the sofa, towering over the director's small holo-head. "I think we might try another angle."

"What's on your mind?"

"Let's leave her be. This way we don't tip off Carmini, or the thief, that we've made the connection."

The hesitancy on the Gej-ti's face was unmistakable.

"I'm thinking of your sage advice about bait," she added.

The director pointed his pipe at her. *"Good show, T8. I'll have Bilarus keep an eye on her and report anything suspicious."*

Lilline's mind was two steps ahead, moving pieces on the board. Now she had time to cast a line. If her suspicions were correct, and the bait attracted attention, she could make a gambit. A bold one, but if played right it might turn the tide. The entire game depended on a small hunch, one that her instinct told her was right.

"Oh, and Pin?"

"Yes, T8?"

"Regarding Renina, I need you to check on something for me."

FORTY-TWO

Elaris was known the galaxy over for two attractions: a legendary creature that roamed the moors surrounding Lake Brinsk and the tourists who flocked there for a chance to see it.

From her window seat on the monorail, Lilline's eyes danced over the sweeping landscape. Patches of green, yellow, and brown came and went as the sun poked through low lying clouds. The rolling hills were like a chessboard of light and shadow, interrupted by occasional swatches of thick forest where misty air clung to branches like lingering smoke. Elaris was old as far as galactic habitations went. One of the first planets to evidence a renewed civilization at the rise of the Third Galactic Age. That primitive memory echoed still, nowhere more so than through the legend that drew over a million citizens each cycle.

"How much farther? I'm bored."

Lilline smiled to herself. The young Kreeli in the seat in front of her had boarded with her mother an hour earlier, two hours after the monorail left its initial departure point at the Elaris Air/Space Port.

"Not far now, sweetie. In a few minutes we'll be able to see the Fangs of Brinsk."

"Fangs?" the child asked.

"That's right. Towering rocks like teeth at one end of the lake. And we will hear the howls tonight."

"Howls?"

"Don't worry, we will be safe inside the lodge."

The cycles fell away, the memory of her mother sharing similar words as they rode the monorail to Lake Brinsk returning in vivid clarity. She'd been as conflicted between excitement and nervousness as the young Kreeli. The uncanny wails that bounced across the lake echoed like a haunting terror. The fright as she pulled the sheets in the hotel over her head remained a potent memory. An ages-old myth endured from generation to generation, growing into a well-honed tourist attraction. Nothing more than gusts of wind passing between the crags in the towering rocks - a natural serendipity. Regional gales kicked up as nightly temperatures dropped and, as geological chance would have it, formed the perfect ratio of knots to open channels between spires to produce a whistling effect.

"The Brinsk Beast won't get us, Mommy, will it?"

"No, sweetie. It lives high up in the spires and never leaves its cave. But we will get to take a ride across the lake to view the rocks up close. And then there's the other reason we came here... you know what else Brinsk is famous for, right?"

"Brinsk Beans!"

"That's right. Grandma's credits from your birthday should be enough to fill a whole bag."

A wave of sobering emotion cut through Lilline's nostalgia. The scene out the window transformed into an image of Kissy in the hospital bed, dying.

"*Attention passengers,*" the conductor announced, "*in two minutes we'll be arriving at the village of Carna-Brai. Transfer at the station for westbound travel along Lake Brinsk. Those continuing to eastbound shore destinations please remain on board for our final stop at Brinsk Station. Once again, arriving in Carna-Brai momentarily."*

"Excuse me," Lilline said.

The elderly Gej-ti couple next to her stood and let her pass.

Lilline joined the line of departing passengers at the end of the car. A group of schoolchildren, of a variety of species, fidgeted with excitement, ignoring their teacher's instructions on what to do once they disembarked.

"Now arriving, Carna-Brai."

Lilline followed the group off of the monorail. On instinct, she scanned the platform. Nothing questionable drew her eye. She passed through the village station, ignoring the flurry of tourists and locals offering taxis, tours, and trinkets, and made her way to the street.

Old stone buildings in haphazard positions along the winding cobblestones spoke of a unique and bucolic ease. Crisp, misty air tinged with the scent of farm animals and baked goods filled her nostrils. There was something to be said for country life. It had a charm and visceral quality that was hard to find on urban planets like Tavi-Prime.

She swung her travel pack over a shoulder and made for the local pub.

Honk!

Two blocks ahead, tourists scurried out of the street. A vehicle, its engine rumbling, crawled forward as the crowds opened a path.

When the driver of the hybrid hover/wheel bike came into view, Lilline veered into the shop on her right.

"Welcome to Carna-Brai Candy Beans. Better beans than Brinsk."

Lilline watched through the store window, using the doorway to remain hidden, as the bike rumbled past.

Gongo.

What in stars is he doing here? I went from U-City directly into space for the FTL run to Elaris...

The rumble of the Dendari's vehicle faded.

"I hate those rentals," the shopkeeper said, approaching.

Lilline smiled at the Rasp.

"It's not like it used to be around here. The secrets of the hills and forests are growing forgotten. It's all about consumerism and spectacle these days."

"I came here as a child," Lilline said. "I remember what it was like before it exploded."

The shopkeeper hissed, her throat flap vibrating with delight. She patted Lilline on the arm. "So, what is your fancy, young lady?" Her old legs walked to a section of candied beans in open tiered cases. "I'll bet you remember Olk bark?"

"Do I ever." Lilline accepted the sample from the Rasp's three-fingered hand. The distinct woodsy taste was like a time machine back to her youth.

"What a look in your eyes," the Rasp said and handed her a bag and scooper. "Like the stars of old."

Lilline scanned the copious flavors.

What the heck.

She went from section to section in atavistic pleasure, selecting portions across the available confectionary flavors. In the corner of her eye, a worn book behind the register became legible.

Woodland Stars: A Guide to Elaris's Druidic Traditions.

Lilline topped off the bag and approached the counter. She placed it on the scale. "Interesting book."

The Rasp's one eye met hers briefly before moving on, noting the price displayed on the scale.

"Between us," Lilline said, "that's why I've come back to Brinsk."

"Is it now?" The Rasp confirmed Lilline's payment and picked up a laser stick, aiming it at the bag. A beautiful pattern of stars with the name "Carna-Brai Candy Beans" burned into the paper.

"I'm seeking information from long ago, related to astronomy."

The Rasp's neck snaked back and forth. "What kind of information?"

"A constellation of great importance," Lilline said. "But I don't know where to find the ones I need to ask. I was told by someone who knew one of them that they're in the woods surrounding Lake Brinsk."

Lilline followed the Rasp's apple-sized head as it leaned to the side, checking behind her. The shopkeeper pushed a button.

A click of the door latch echoed in the silence.

"Prove it," the Rasp said.

Lilline didn't miss the shopkeeper's other hand vanish under the counter.

Professor Senjara, with Lauden's assistance, had prepared her the best they could. She'd intended to make use of their information at the pub, hoping to find an old bartender there, but her detour avoiding Gongo into the candy shop had turned into serendipity. Lilline cleared her throat and spoke:

> *"Stars in circles, a stellar crown.*
> *Behold the sky when sun goes down.*
> *We keep the past for future sight.*
> *Our Order alive in the dark of night."*

The Rasp blinked, her one eyelid closing and opening with infinite patience. "Meet me at sundown on Denbaldie Hill south of the village."

Talk about a stroke of luck.

"I'll be there," Lilline said.

The Rasp handed her the bag of candied beans. "Under the lone Olk Tree. You can't miss it..." The shopkeeper leaned toward her. "Cracked from lightning it was. Looks like an old crone whose time has passed her by."

FORTY-THREE

The Rasp wasn't kidding about the Olk. Lilline climbed the hillside in the failing light, making for the withered tree. Against a crepuscular sky, its trunk and remaining limbs cut a silhouette into the dimming light like a bent old witch.

What a strange course she'd travelled on this mission. Every assignment had its surprises, but to go from a crime scene in an art museum, to a floating city, followed by a debriefing in a non-existent government facility, only to end up in the rural countryside atop a lonely hill felt as stretched and distant as the First and Third Galactic Ages.

She halted and gazed at the rising stars.

Like traveling through a wormhole.

A much-needed bite to eat in the local pub had passed the time while she waited for the sun to set. Local Brinsk regional fare: Cairn sheep stew filled with a hearty mix of root vegetables. She'd devoured the generous helping dropped in front of her.

Now, huffing her way up Denbaldie Hill, she was thankful for the exertion. Dinner sat in her belly like an indigestible cannonball. None of the wines on the pub's menu had passed her minimum standard, so she contented herself with two mugs of the local brew - Lake Brinsk Porter. Not that she had much choice. It was either the dark ale or a thin, tasteless commercial beer served the galaxy over. The Porter turned out to be an excellent pairing. The addition of heather in the brewing process gave it a finish that rounded out the stew's savory broth.

"Like fog to a moor," the bartender had said when recommending it with her dinner. He'd proceeded to talk her ear off for the next hour, gossiping about everyone and everything in the small village. She'd nodded her way through it, amazed at his capacity to ramble. The man was more informed than a broadcast journalist for a major news network.

Lilline eyed the Olk Tree about thirty meters further up the hill and started off again.

A light breeze kicked up, its invisible touch gentle and silent on her cheek. Crisp and cool night air carried the scent of musty earth and blooming heather.

Aaaa-ooooooooooooooooooo!

Hairs on her neck pricked to life. She swung around to face the source of the echoing howl. Brinsk's far off twinkling lights dappled the lake's shoreline. Across long and narrow black waters loomed shadowy spires.

A second howl rose, bouncing over the moors.

"The land is alive tonight."

Lilline spun around. The Rasp, dressed in a loose white gown with a single gold star crudely embroidered on its chest, stood next to the Olk Tree.

"Let us hope the stars share tonight's energy." Two hands, splayed wide, gestured at her side.

How did I not hear you?

"Come, we mustn't linger. The stars are climbing." The Rasp motioned her to follow and made for a line of forest down the opposite hillside.

Silently they stepped over moss and damp grasses, punctuated by an occasional crunch as feet stepped on clumped heather.

"We haven't been introduced," Lilline said.

"You may call me Nithya," the Rasp said. "It is my Star Name."

"Star Name?"

Lilline found herself engaged by the Rasp's single eye as its small head rotated one-hundred and eighty degrees.

"Part of a mid-range quadrant in Arm 2, a quiet little system with three planets close to the boundary of the Outer Regions. I chose it because it reflects my personality and the type of community that brings me comfort." Nithya pointed back towards Carna-Brai, and then rotated her head forward, continuing on.

"You may call me Keely."

"Indeed."

The shadowy wall of the forest neared.

Lilline stepped around a small boulder and followed the Rasp into the woods.

"A word of advice, Keely..." In the dark trees, the Rasp's form was ghost-like, a billowing specter leading her deeper into an alluring and mysterious unknown. "If by coming to the Circle you seek an answer to a secret, you must be willing to give up one of your own."

They walked on for a half hour, winding through dense woodlands of old and cragged trees, occasionally crossing rocky streams bubbling with dark waters. The Fangs of Brinsk's howls faded, buffered by the forest canopy. Lilline did her best to maintain a bearing, but she lost it after ten minutes. At this point, each step was a vivid and haunting present, as if the world outside and time itself had been kept at bay.

Following Nithya's ghostly form, waves of mysticism swirled in the quiet night. A world away from the overflowing synthetic technologies and galaxy-spanning communications of her everyday existence, something stirred. Cilex Racers and holo-feeds were replaced by humble footsteps and passing whispers. The galactic reality she knew so well was falling away, leaving a sheltered and comforting alternative full of natural language and haptic encounter. New life breathed in her, inspiring unspoken words.

> *I'm lost.*
> *A ghost of night*
> *my guide through fading stars.*
> *The past a future promise bright.*
> *Dreams stir beyond the pale.*
> *Wake me to time.*
> *Before.*

Lilline knew on instinct the verse manifested in modified Cinquain, a favorite poetic form that she could conjure with natural improvisation. Its ancient structure filled with literary allure, the esoteric mode was rediscovered in the archives of a long forgotten ruin. Something about the exponential word growth and musicality of the syllabic rise and fall through the 2/4/6/8/6/4/2 structure gave it a progression mirroring her method of resolving moments of unique profundity through inner monologue.

Lilline spoke the words a second time, marking them to memory. When there was time, she would put them down in her—

"The Circle gathers," Nithya said.

Ahead, orange firelight danced on tree trunks. Beyond the woodland's edge, white-clad figures moved about in a meadow with the grace of ballet dancers.

Lilline followed Nithya into the clearing. The Rasp gestured for her to halt.

"Welcome to the Circle of Stars," Nithya said.

A multitude of species, dressed akin to the Rasp, flowed in choreographed sequence. Each time they reached a particular formation the figures stopped, raising their arms to speak in unison.

"Tilaris!"

Lilline followed a Kreeli as they weaved through their fellow druids, reaching a pre-determined position in the next formation.

"Karmish the Rider!"

"These are constellations," she said to Nithya, who nodded.

"They are dancing the last of the northern skies before their solstices."

Lilline knew their locations, but they were distant from one another. Tilaris was an Inner Core design seen from the Quinar system, made famous by a legend popularized as a novelization and later in a VR game. Karmish was the fiercest four-legged beast on the planet Ula in the Miom-9 system. She and her rider single-handedly conquered a warring threat in the First Galactic Age and became an icon of noble sacrifice and heroic tragedy.

"You have brought an outsider?"

Lilline pulled her eyes from the mesmerizing dancers. She took a step back at the sight of a Jenzara dressed in flowing silver robes. Loose-fitting fabric sparkled in the firelight, as if dusted with mica. Like Carmini, three eyes ran along the bottom of her face, mouth across a red forehead. The gelatinous hands and feet visible at the robe's edges were bare, displaying the species' signature six digits.

"They spoke the Words of Starlight," Nithya said.

Now the Jenzara took a step back.

Lilline, unsure of protocol, bowed. "I come with respect and humility, seeking someone who I hope can decipher a stellar puzzle."

The druid examined her.

It was as if a scanner ran over her from head to toe. Five brains worked on overdrive, penetrating every layer of her being. Which neuro-specialization this Jenzara possessed, she did not know.

"Whom is it you seek?" the circle's leader asked.

"Rinka Ho. She was a student of Professor Veer Senjara."

The Jenzara shook her head. "There is no one here by that name. Despite knowing the sacred words, I am afraid you have wasted your time. You must leave."

"I'm sorry," Lilline said, pressing. "No member of your circle bears that name?"

Three eyes blazed with the power of starlight. Lilline held the

Jenzara's gaze. She'd come all this way. It was the only chance they had to decode the stars in the *Cosmic Widow*.

"There was, but no more."

"Are you sure?" Lilline asked.

"Quite sure. She used to be me."

FORTY-FOUR

"This concerns the *Cosmic Widow*," Lilline said.

"Even more reason for you to leave." The Jenzara ushered her away from the others. "That painting, and all that goes with it, should be buried alongside the one named Rinka Ho."

Lilline halted, her defiant body language like a glass shattering in a quiet restaurant.

Nithya stepped back, distancing herself.

"Apologies." Lilline held up a hand. "But you have not offered me an opportunity to state my reason for coming."

Nithya's one eye went to the Circle's leader.

"Very well," the Jenzara said. "But it will not change anything. Rinka Ho is no longer."

"It's not her I need. It's knowledge."

"Thus, do we gather here under the stars," the Jenzara gestured around her. "Speak."

"I carry with me a version of the lost chart of Azaludarian."

"You jest."

"On the contrary." Lilline withdrew her tablet and tapped the screen, pulling up an edited and refined image capture from the storeroom. "It's a contemporary copy, presumably by Henestra."

The Jenzara accepted the tablet. Her three eyes moved independently. One examined the Canitu text running vertically down the side, another focused on the central star language, and the third roamed the remaining borders.

"'Star chart of Azaludarian,'" she said, translating the iconographic language. "'With this map and the Cosmic Widow, its power can be unleashed and the gate between worlds will open.'"

Lilline noted the facility with which the Jenzara read Canitu. No hesitating over historic shifts in linguistic associations like the professor had struggled to overcome.

"So, the Star Chart has been found after all these cycles."

"There's more," Lilline said. "The gates are wormholes." She made an improvised version of a double-pollex with her hands.

One of the Jenzara's eyes went to Lilline's digits, observing the linking tips of her thumbs.

"'In the star chart is hidden the road to the gate,'" she continued, "'where the Cosmic Widow reunites with Azaludarian, her lost lover.'"

Whatever skepticism remained on the druid's features transformed into an earnest interest. Her mouth on her forehead spoke.

"I tried telling them for cycles," the Jenzara muttered. "Aza is the root for 'partner' and the use of 'lu' is a gender signifier."

"You read Darian?" Lilline asked.

"I may be the only one alive in the galaxy who still can."

We need a Darian. Professor Senjara's words at U-City echoed amidst Lilline's swirling thoughts. "But you're—"

"I am a Jenzara, yes… and older than you think. Lucky enough to descend from a bloodline that carried intimate and secret knowledge down through generations."

No wonder Lauden and the others sent her here.

"And what do you base this wormhole interpretation on?" the Circle leader asked.

"Cutting-edge cosmic research. The science is sound... in theory."

To her surprise, the Jenzara nodded. Lilline didn't read any skepticism in the gesture. If anything, it communicated confirmation.

"You are suggesting the Darians left through one of these cosmic channels?"

How did she make that deduction?

"I take it by the look on your face that I am correct?"

"Yes," Lilline said, regaining focus. "Driven out, actually."

"Stars... yes, of course." A strange expression rose on the druid's features.

Nithya, standing humbly to the Jenzara's side, remained lost to their discussion. Thankfully, the Rasp's expression had relaxed from her initial concern at bringing an outsider into their cloistered community.

"And what do we have here?" The druid's middle eye narrowed, focusing on the faded lines Lilline had brought to Professor Senjara's attention.

"That is why I have come."

"'Bring her to the Temple of Moz-Darian during the galactic alignment, break the horizon, and two worlds will meet.'" The Jenzara lifted her head. Their gazes met. "'The lost star is the key.'"

"Sorry." Lilline held up a hand. "Can you repeat that?"

The druid respoke the line.

"Our translation was different. A former colleague of yours, Professor Senjara, translated it as, 'The key is in the stars.'"

The Jenzara nodded. "An easy mistake, especially for the professor, but I assure you the correct translation is 'the lost star is the key.'"

That changed things.

"We've interpreted the star language on the chart," Lilline said. "Everything fits together. But a crucial piece of evidence hides somewhere within the *Cosmic Widow*."

The Jenzara handed back the tablet. "Good. Let it stay that way."

Lilline's eyes went to Nithya, who stood at the archdruid's side. Behind the Rasp, the grove members were gathering around the fire.

"Don't you at least want to hear the translation?"

"Very much so, but some things are better kept unspoken, especially when great power is involved."

"I could not agree more," Lilline said. "However, we believe another has decoded this information, and uncovered the Temple's location. We're almost certain they are about to use it... to use the painting... in less than two days' time."

"We?"

The air between them stirred. An invisible tension pushed against Lilline's skin. This was it. Nithya had said that an offering would be expected.

"I work for an old associate of yours, Asher Lauden."

Gelatinous cheeks stretched in surprise.

"I'm an undercover field operative for a clandestine organization that works as a branch of Ministry government, protecting the galaxy from extreme threats."

The Jenzara smiled knowingly. "Why does this make sense? Asher Lauden, the head of a secret organization."

"I guess both of you work in the shadows," Lilline said. It was bold, but true. "I hope you also share similar motivations."

The Jenzara clasped her red hands together. "That was well put. Quite poetic." Her silver robe glittered like the night sky. "The one I once was, Rinka Ho, viewed the galaxy differently." Her head bent back, gazing up. "But she is gone, and I have replaced her. The light of that star's demise awakened me into who I am now." She crossed both arms over the embroidered design on her chest and smiled. "I am Nova."

"Lilline Renault." Lilline handed the tablet to the Druid a second time. "I need you to help decode the Temple's location. There's less than forty-eight hours before something catastrophic might occur. I can offer all we know in exchange for your aid in completing this puzzle."

"Another threatens to disturb an ancient secret's rest? If that is so, then you need not barter. This transcends petty disagreements such as those between me and your colleague. What matters is protecting precious knowledge from those who would abuse it. Besides, my issues when I was Rinka Ho are faint and distant echoes from another lifetime." The druid shifted so she observed the members of the Circle of Stars. "Fate has brought you here. You and I are like two planets whose orbits pass close to one another once in a galactic age."

A wave of relief pulled the tension from Lilline's muscles. Her body settled, and with it a profound sense of respect that left her without words. Once again, Lauden's strange ability to associate with individuals complicated and yet noble left her humbled.

"Thank you," Lilline said. "I'm glad you agree because unless we act, and soon, fate may shift the course of our galaxy forever."

"Ah, fate. Such a cunning and elusive spirit," the Jenzara said. "Always proving its existence through past events, but yet..." The druid locked three eyes with her own. "At the mercy of our freewill. It is the present that directs the future."

The druid's silver robe glittered with the firelight's reflections.

"The stars and their planetary children may be bound to cosmic fate, Agent Renault. But we as petty minions walking their worlds still have the means to alter our future." The Jenzara gestured for her to follow and strode past the others. "Come, let us speak at the Star Pool."

Soft and sonorous song rose from those gathered by the fire as they passed into the trees. Harmonies as light and airy as the celestial canopy to which they were dedicated cast a spell of tranquility and solace over the wood.

"Nithya, inform the others of my absence. You may lead tonight's starlight ceremony in my place."

"Thank you, Nova." The Rasp returned to the circle.

"We will start with the star language in the chart in hopes of uncovering the oracle's location," Nova said, the forest growing dark around them. "As for the painting... that may prove more difficult."

"I have a copy of the *Cosmic Widow* on my tablet." Lilline said, trailing the druid.

"No need." The Jenzara's words carried on the air, harmonizing with the fading voices singing by the fire. "I know the painting as precisely as if Azaludarian painted the sky that cradles us this night."

"How far is it?" Lilline stepped carefully, her eyes adjusting to the dark. Shadowy walls of rock closed in on either side of a bubbling stream that served as their path. She had to concentrate with every step to avoid slipping and falling.

"Only another minute or two."

Nova's silver robe sparkled as she passed through a beam of moonlight.

"You are walking in one of the few remaining old growth forests on Elaris."

"I was here once as a child." Lilline hopped from rock to rock following the archdruid upstream. As they climbed, the channel transformed into a series of stepped waterfalls. "I never forgot the forest."

The uniqueness of the old growth trees, with their majestic trunks and towering branches, was a potent memory untarnished by the cycles. It had been branded into her youthful psyche, both for its natural wonder and the associated familial reminiscence. She and her mother, Analine, along with Granny Kissy had embarked on a galactic cruise to visit Mirna and Simuel a cycle after the two left Tavi-Prime and moved to the quiet planet.

"Be careful on this final ledge."

Under the rush of a waterfall, Nova edged along the narrow rock wall.

Lilline followed, careful where she placed her feet on the glistening stone. Cool mist tingled her skin, softening the water's roar as she passed behind it.

"There's nothing here!" she yelled over the rumbling of the falls.

Nova reached into a slit in her robe. A red hand withdrew a small device.

Waves of mist passed through a blue beam as the Jenzara aimed it at the stone wall. A hidden constellation appeared, glowing bright on the rock's surface.

The druid touched each star twice, moving in what Lilline took to be an arbitrary pattern. A massive slab hinged open revealing a narrow passage.

The druid waved for her to follow.

"How many know of this place?" Lilline asked, passing through the opening. The pounding water faded to a faint echo as they moved deeper into the cavern.

"Only those of the Circle of Stars. So has it been since the dawning of the Third Galactic Age."

The faintest hint of light at a bend ahead illuminated Nova's form. Lilline used it to follow to the corner. She located the source: a pulsing button inlaid in the course rock.

Nova pushed it. With slow and patient scraping, the night sky came into view as the cavern's ceiling retracted. As if in a call and answer, the stellar landscape appeared in a mirrored reflection on the surface of a subterranean pool.

"Stars," Lilline said, her eyes alive with awe.

"Indeed." the Jenzara motioned her to enter. "Welcome to the Star Pool."

FORTY-FIVE

Silent voices echoed through the cavern. Ancient memories lingered. Lilline's consciousness tingled with an indescribable curiosity. No doubt, she was treading on sacred ground.

"It's..."

"Yes," Nova said joining her at the edge of the still water. "The Star Pool never fails us with its sublimity."

A stellar night glimmered on the subterranean waters. Lilline edged closer and peered down. In the available light, a blue void plunged downward and out of sight.

"It's a natural spring, without bottom," Nova said. "The runoff flows through a channel underneath the surface." The Jenzara pointed in the direction where they entered. "That underground tunnel leads to the falls down to the running stream."

"Amazing."

Geological serendipity at its finest. A tumbling and fast-moving waterfall to keep the spring's upper surface remarkably still.

Lilline craned her head back. The oculus, at a one-to-one scale with the pool, connected the chamber to the open air of night.

"When closed, from the outside it appears as no more than a typical bald rock crown," Nova said.

Lilline scanned the edges of the cavern. Here and there, recesses provided gathering areas. Three archways of smooth stone told her there were adjacent chambers. Of what size and purpose, she did not know.

"Hand me your tablet, please."

Lilline offered the device to Nova, who tapped the screen, pulling up the star chart.

Kneeling, the Jenzara brightened the screen to its maximum and angled it. The constellation shimmered on the water.

> *"Look from the center of empire, to where our reach is*
> *farthest.*
> *That which shines most distant marks the path.*
> *Bend the stars and the Cosmic Widow will speak its*
> *secret.*
> *Walk the equatorial chasm on the second planet and*
> *see with eyes of night.*
> *Between glimmering peaks lies the Temple door."*

The Jenzara dipped a gelatinous finger into the pool, dragging it across the surface. As if erasing the sky, the ripples disrupted the reflection.

Lilline waited, silent.

The Star Pool settled. Again, Nova leaned the tablet over its surface.

> *"Place the pendant onto the chain of time.*
> *Fill the sacred chamber with finger tight.*
> *Let gravity flow.*
> *Bring forth the key.*
> *Aim to the star that shines above the Cosmic Widow.*
> *Collapse the four walls."*

"How did you know to do that?" Lilline knelt next to her.

"I didn't until you shared the wormhole theory. From there, it was obvious. My brain system specializes in linguistics, with a secondary cognitive focus on problem solving."

The rate at which the species functioned neurologically left Lilline equally in awe as she was with the setting.

"We deduced that the center referred to in the first line must be Kalatron," Lilline said, "being the capital of the Darian empire at its peak. That is, once we realized it was written in a star language."

"Yes, Professor Senjara would not miss that fact."

"He did, actually. It was my boss who identified it."

The Jenzara's head pivoted, its three eyes homing in on her own two. "Was it now?"

Nova's eyes twinkled.

"Asher always was full of surprises," the druid said, mouth on her forehead stretching into a smile. "Good for him."

"From there it was a team effort," Lilline added. "There were several of us, including another from your past."

"Let me guess, Reginald Bilarus?"

Lilline nodded.

The Jenzara's three eyes rolled. "Who else?"

"My colleague at the agency, Pin, who is our head of Tech. And two scientists. A cosmic theorist working on wormholes and a meta-epistemologist."

"That's a mouthful."

Lilline laughed, her voice echoing off the still water.

"Although we were successful in translating it, we made it no further than the first line decoding its meaning," Lilline said. "The second verse we assume to be instructions on how to pass into and through the chambers of Moz-Darian, but that first verse…"

"Yes, I concur about the second stanza," the Jenzara said. "It reads as a guide. There's a star syntax used for directions, something akin to our second-person voice, that is employed."

"About the first stanza, which appears to be a puzzle to the temple's location, Dr. Liguera, our cosmic theorist, believes the phrase 'when our reach is farthest' implies an astronomical, rather than a political or metaphorical, interpretation."

"I agree." Nova stood. "Come."

Lilline followed the druid around the edge of the pool. The Jenzara entered the first recessed area and placed her hand on the wall. A waist-level platform, with a multitude of controls like a soundboard, emerged.

"The first two lines of the star chart..." Nova's hands worked the board. "...are a galactic-level starting point. Initial assessment of the verse, combined with my existing knowledge of Darian language, tells me this will be a two-stage puzzle."

"Can you unravel it?"

"We shall see."

Nova pushed a button and a holo of the galaxy, its spirals reaching the edge of the pool, manifested over the water,

Cool blue light filled the cavern. Lilline took in the spectacle, her mind struggling with its conceptual scale. Their whirlpool galaxy, home to everything that made up her current universe, reflected off the water. Hints of the night sky penetrated where empty spaces allowed it to pass through, adding stellar twinkles to the pool's surface. Mixed cosmic realities read like a galactic hall of mirrors. So much to decipher and at a level of difficulty that left her feeling useless. She had needed the others at U-City to get over the art historical and astrophysical hurdles. Now the baton passed to a strange linguist and cultural specialist turned cosmic druid. She felt like the last runner, jittering with nerves down a vast and endless racetrack, waiting for the baton to reach her to sprint to the finish line.

The problem was, where to run? And, she had no idea if the baton would be passed to her in time.

"You said you have a sequence of dates for the past and upcoming alignments, calculated by your head of Tech?"

"Yes, she's an Oltari and was able to do the intense calculations with the aid of computer."

"Excellent. May I see them, please?"

Lilline pulled the data up on the tablet. "Dr. Liguera, that's our cosmic researcher, introduced a theory based on a Second Galactic mystic that posits these alignments are energy centers that work as gates between two distant galaxies. She believes the evidence remains of fast-forming and vanishing gravity intrusions... black holes. The key to her theory is a by-product she believes to be exotic matter with the capacity to overcome intense gravity and—"

"Push open the respective core singularities."

"Yes, how did you—"

"I dabble in many things." The mouth on Nova's forehead smiled.

"Dr. Liguera dubbed them ghost holes." Lilline held out a hand. "May I?"

She accepted the tablet from the Jenzara and linked the device to the control board. A mirrored version of its screen manifested over the pond to the side of the whirlpool galaxy.

"Yes..." Nova stepped closer to the water, scrutinizing the dates.

"But while we can calculate the dates—"

"You don't know where they are in the galaxy." The Jenzara faced her. "Quite the paradox."

"Exactly. Somehow when a point is triggered... we assume with a device, and we are hoping one may be preserved at the temple...the two ghost holes link the mirror galaxies."

To her surprise, the Jenzara nodded as if this was the most obvious conclusion and one without any measure of doubt.

"Do you know much about the Darians, Agent Renault?"

"My knowledge is cursory at best. Consider me a well-informed neophyte who has done a little extra reading on the subject."

The back of the Jenzara's gelatinous head rose and fell as she nodded, facing the holo-projection over the pond.

"Their language, like their culture, is full of layers. Implicit meanings abound. It's like a wedding cake. If you scrape off the icing the substantial meaning lies underneath. But even then, depending on where you slice, it will either reveal or veil further information."

Sounds like a nightmare.

"I take it by your silence you acknowledge the problems?"

"Unfortunately, yes."

A shadow crossed the holo of the galaxy. Lilline's eyes shot up just in time to spot the silhouette of a nocturnal bird pass overhead.

Odd how its two-dimensional shadow tracked across the three-dimensional holo. She noticed the Jenzara's central eye aimed upward having also followed the bird's flight.

"If you don't mind me asking, do you and I share the same spatial vision?" Lilline asked. "I encountered another Jenzara a few days ago and it made me curious about your optical capabilities."

"Yes," Nova said. "My vision is binocular using a stereoscopic effect with my two outer eyes. The central eye works independently in two-dimensional rendering. It provides an efficient informational input used for reading and—" Nova held up a hand.

"What is it?"

"Pull up the *Cosmic Widow* if you would. I assume you have a high-resolution image?"

Lilline grabbed the biggest file in her inventory and opened it.

"Wormholes... ghost holes... why didn't I think of this sooner?"

Lilline waited as the Jenzara scrutinized the projection of the famous painting.

"Sometimes, Agent Renault, the answer lies in plain sight. It is the viewer who does not see." The Jenzara motioned for her to approach.

"Those layers of the cake... they can also be an advantage." The druid eyed her. "And even a solution."

A red hand reached for the tablet. Lilline gave it to the druid willingly.

"Bear with me. We are starting from the third line. From there, hopefully we can work our way back." The Jenzara tapped the screen and the projection over the star pool vanished.

"What are you doing?"
"Bending space and time."

FORTY-SIX

"Do you know what anamorphosis is?" Nova asked.

"It's a kind of visual illusion, isn't it?" Lilline leaned closer, curious. "A distortion of perspective?"

"It can be. Quite common in visual works. A skilled artist can create an image that requires a specific, often oblique, viewpoint to make the subject legible and convincing to binocular vision such as ours."

Lilline had seen examples at the Galactic Museum, many from the late Second Galactic period, that required the spectator to stand to the side, or below, a painting to expose an otherwise "hidden" inclusion. It was a big hit with school groups visiting the collections.

"There is also another mode, known as mirror anamorphosis," Nova said. "This one involves a reflective surface, either concave or convex, to view an image that appears otherwise... stretched or distorted."

Now the Jenzara had her full attention.

"And you know, wormholes, in theory—"

"...stretch the fabric of space," Lilline said.

Nova's mouth atop her face smiled. "I have often thought that the way Darians describe the world through language was... how shall I put it?" She finished working on the tablet and tapped a button. "Distorted."

Lilline took in the altered version of the *Cosmic Widow* over the still water.

It was as if Nova had taken the canvas out of the frame and wrapped it around a cylinder.

"All this time, we've been viewing the painting with eyes like the passing black shape of the bird on the water... a three-dimensional world casting two-dimensional shadows. When in fact, the image that appears accurate, is in fact itself a distortion."

Lilline stared at the reflection on the water's surface. It was as if someone had pulled the *Cosmic Widow*, stretching it in a curving arc. Not only did the robed figure appear voluminous, but the double-pollex looked strangely... what was it?

Resolved.

"Let me guess. Professor Senjara has been trying to identify that constellation for tens of cycles?"

Lilline nodded, mesmerized.

"Try it now," Nova said, stepping to the edge of the pool. "The design is different in this anamorphosis."

She was right. More distance between the glittering spheres, as well as the curvature, altered it substantially. "Nova..." Lilline narrowed her eyes. "Are you seeing what I am seeing?" She pointed at the brightest sphere. "Look at the position of the others in relation to that twin star."

"Oh, yes indeed. Well spotted."

"Let me try something." Lilline went to the board. "I learned how to do this from our head of Tech. You can build your own solar systems and program in brightness levels for a star. It tracks the illumination on orbiting objects." She rotated the curving image of the painting, moving as if she were navigating by ship through a solar system. As her view shifted, the computer calculated the light crossing the spheres' surfaces, leaving them half illuminated and half in darkness. "They're planets," she said. "It's a binary star system!"

"We are getting closer to an answer," the druid said. "Follow the equatorial chasm on the second planet." The Jenzara quoted the line of verse. "I think we've found our little Temple's home."

"But... it still doesn't tell us where this system is located."

"One step at a time." Nova left the control board and approached the water's edge. "You have the previous dates your head of Tech calculated, yes?"

"I do."

"Pull them up if you would. You can take down the *Cosmic Widow* for now. But save those files."

Would she ever. She backed them up and sent Pin's list to the holo over the pool.

A strange mumbling resonated from the Jenzara as she read through the data. Nova swayed at the water's edge, her fingers splayed wide and feet tapping. It was as if her whole body was thinking at maximum levels.

"Reverse engineering." The druid made haste back to the control board. "Excuse me." She stepped up and took the controls.

"What are you doing?"

"I'm curious about something..." Red fingers typed rapidly. Nova turned, excited.

A strange sensation as six gelatinous digits squeezed her forearm sent chills over her skin.

"This is it." Nova hit *Enter* on the keyboard.

The galaxy reappeared over the pool. Bright lines flashed and cut through it. Numbers ran in rapid vertical sequence as the computer crunched its way through a complex mathematical calculation.

"Come on... come on," the druid whispered.

"*Process complete.*" The text cast a blood red reflection on the dark and starry water.

Nova tapped the computer key a second time.

From their position, the foreshortened galaxy was a mess of

curving spirals, globular clusters, and solar systems, intruded upon by bright straight lines.

"Tip it up so we have a bird's eye view," Nova said.

Lilline, using a finger on the control board, dragged the galaxy so it appeared like a cosmic hurricane viewed from above. Precise lines radiated outward from a tiny glowing orb, terminating at various points like a crude two-dimensional drawing of a sun's haphazard rays. "What is that?" she asked, homing in on the shining nexus a third of the way out one of the galactic spirals.

"That is Kalatron. Former center of the Darian empire."

Nova scurried off to the nearest archway, opened a hidden portal with a touch of her hand and vanished. A moment later, she returned carrying an old tome. She plunked it down on a crude bench of chiseled rock and flipped through the pages. "It's here... I remember it."

Lilline approached and bent close.

"There!" Nova held the book up, open to a drawing.

Every line matched the holographic radial design.

"I knew it!" The Jenzara's hand grabbed her arm and squeezed it a second time.

Lilline, shocked by the discovery and not grasping its significance, remained speechless.

"Ready?" Nova's three eyes were shining with excitement.

Lilline shrugged, completely lost.

"These," Nova pointed from line to line, tracing their journeys from Kalatron to their ending points around the galaxy, "are your ghost hole dates converted into locations. The lines are trajectories from Kalatron to each coordinate."

Overwhelmed, Lilline took in a legible version of the cosmic points converted from chronological data into a two-dimensional transcription laid over the three-dimensional galaxy.

"'From the center of empire,'" the archdruid said, quoting the opening line.

"How did you—"

"Too complicated." Nova waved a hand. "And not relevant right now. Just follow along."

"I'm overwhelmed."

"Stay with me!" The Jenzara's three eyes were alive. "Even with my five brains, I too feel meek and inferior to such complex modes of spacetime cognition."

"Okay," Lilline said. "We have a star system with the temple's location on the second planet, and now we have the previous ghost hole locations plotted across the galaxy."

"Go on."

"On top of knowing when they occurred and when the next will manifest."

"Correct."

"What am I missing here?"

"All these radiating lines..." The Jenzara gestured at the holo. "Don't you see? I plugged in *all* of them from your colleague, Pin. They aren't only the past events..."

Realization dawned like a rising sun.

"They include the future one about to happen," Lilline said.

Nova placed both hands on Lilline's shoulders and nodded.

Finally, progress.

"Which line is ours?" Lilline scanned the complex design, lost as to how to find it.

The druid walked to the control panel. "Farthest, as stated in the star chart." She mumbled about distances and data and then held a finger over the *Enter* key. "Ready?"

Was she ever. She'd been waiting for this since the day she walked into the museum.

"Hit it," Lilline said.

A line radiating from the nexus point on Kalatron went from white to red. Lilline followed it outward, tracking it to its destination. This was the star with the temple's location. She would be on her way to stop whoever took the painting from triggering the device and opening the gate.

Her eyes reached the line's terminus at its associated solar system. It shone in a grayed-out patch of a galactic spiral. She stepped closer, hoping to identify it.

Her heart sank.

"Nova." Her eyes fell on the Jenzara. "That's Arm 5... in the Outer Region." A flash of Madame X telling the group at U-City that the galactic sector remained uncharted pushed down her excitement and the elation of their discoveries.

"It's the unknown."

FORTY-SEVEN

"This is taking us two steps forward and one step back." Lilline shook her head. "We have no idea where to go in that region of space. Worse, we don't know if there's a star system matching the one in the *Cosmic Widow*. And we're running out of time."

Silence.

"Nova?"

The Jenzara was nowhere to be found.

"This small act may be my undoing."

Lilline followed the Jenzara's steps as she returned from a second archway further around the pool. In one hand she had a portfolio made of...

What is that?

The color and texture were akin to the ancient animal skin covers in the monastic library on Hesh-9. Some of those texts were unclassifiable. They lived in a recessed area in the mountain retreat labelled as *Ancient Catalogs*.

"Come, you are about to be witness to something not seen for an age." With careful hands, the druid placed the portfolio down on the rock bench and undid a fraying strap binding it shut.

"What is this, Nova?" Lilline asked, approaching.

"It is, as you said, the unknown." The Jenzara unfolded the portfolio.

Star charts...

As if pulled by gravity, the ancient document drew her toward its arcane imagery.

"Ours are the first eyes to gaze upon this since..." the druid's words trailed off. She turned a page. Flecks at the corner disintegrated.

"Be careful," Lilline whispered.

The druid nodded. "Here it is."

Lilline shifted from the stars on the page to the holo over the pool. Then back again.

"Nova... this... is this Arm 5?"

"Welcome to the past." She put a hand on Lilline's hip and shifted her out of the way. Two eyes focused on the projection while one remained down on the ancient stellar map.

"Zoom in for me so the—"

"On it." Lilline was already following, the connection clear. She maneuvered the holo, zooming in on Arm 5 in the area that was uncharted. "Nova," she said, pointing at a section over the pool, "see that star cluster? It lines up with—"

"Yes," the druid nodded. "And this one goes with that section that appears like a triangle. It's a bit off. Move the position slightly. I think whoever did this was observing from somewhere...."

"There?" Lilline said, adjusting the holo.

"Yes, that's it. Look!"

Lilline lifted her eyes from the fading map. She and the Jenzara locked gazes.

They'd found it. A binary star system with two planets.

"Tell me you can read this." Lilline pointed at a key on the side of the map.

"It's Canitu. The system is named... Isara. And the planet we identified in the *Cosmic Widow* is..." The Jenzara gasped.

Tense silence like that which greets a conductor raising their baton to ready the orchestra followed.

"What is it, Nova?"

"Moz."

"The Temple of Moz-Darian." Lilline's words were barely audible, more an expression of internal awe than outward communication. She put a hand on Nova's shoulder. "You did it. You..." She didn't know how to express what she had witnessed.

"No, I am only a medium to those who come before me. This..." The druid pointed at the map. "The ones who did this deserve the credit."

"Are there coordinates? Tell me they're in a grid..."

"Of course." Nova went to the control board and entered them.

"Plot a course from Elaris," Lilline said.

The data and FTL track popped up on the holo over the pool.

Damn. Too far, even with the *Racer's* FTL drives.

"I can't make it, Nova. Hopefully one of the other T# agents can arrive in time."

"It won't be you?"

"No." She couldn't deny how disheartening that felt, but GAM-OPs wasn't one person. It was a team. Sometimes you passed the baton to get the job done. And her not being the one to finish this didn't change the unfathomable discoveries that had taken place here and at U-City. At the end of the day, the collective effort was what mattered.

Lilline gathered her things, stuffing the tablet into her backpack. "I need to call this in."

"You won't get a signal out here," Nova said. "You'll have to head back to the village. Or make for a comm box on the roads leading away from Carna-Brai."

"They still have those?" Lilline took out a small camera. "May I?" She indicated the open page with the Darian radial drawing that inspired the druid's calculation.

Nova gestured to proceed. "Not much changes on Elaris. They're still out there on the roadsides like they were when you were here last. Bright red boxes with leaded windows... charming as can be."

"And the star map, if I may?" Lilline said, indicating the second book from the Circle's archive.

"As much as I am troubled by the idea of giving you this it must be done." Nova switched out the tomes, opening it to the appropriate page.

"My agency is good at keeping secrets." She snapped a picture and paused, gazing at the ancient document. "How did you come by these?"

"Astro-cartographers produced them long ago. How they managed it, charting and plotting distant stellar corridors across the light years, is not known. They are treasured possessions of our circle."

"I wouldn't expect it to be possible without technology as advanced as our own. Do you think the Darians provided it?"

"My brains tell me otherwise. Do not be too quick to assume understanding is linked with technological innovation. The galaxy itself is the most advanced form of knowledge in existence... the ultimate computer. It is we who must learn to attune to it and tap its operating system. Only then will its mysteries be revealed."

"You think there are more layers of reality and hidden information to be uncovered?"

"No question. It's amazing what you can see when the walls of knowledge fall," Nova said.

Lilline took a moment to let the Jenzara's wisdom sink in. Such a rare species. So profound in its cognitive capacities. Her eyes went from the holo of the galaxy and back to Nova. Penetrating the druid's outer layer, she conjured her internal anatomy - five brains linked through neurological highways to an epicenter in her chest. It wasn't unlike a constellation of stars, or the radial design with Kalatron as nexus. Holistic cosmic energy driving consciousness and deduction. And perhaps, most importantly, imagination - the ammunition of theorization.

"Why have these maps not been shared with the larger galactic community?"

"For posterity, you mean?"

Lilline nodded.

"The definition of that word is relative, and to be candid, quite dangerous and destructive in the wrong hands."

Blip.

A drop of moisture fell into the placid water. Lilline tracked the expanding ripples across the pool of reflected stars, considering the remark and the potency of the metaphor.

"Plus, do you see this?" Nova pointed at a symbol on the ancient map. "This translates as 'to be left alone.'"

Lilline examined the section of unexplored star systems next to Nova's gooey finger. *Unexplored...* But then again, wasn't that relative? "Unexplored" by *their* galactic civilization. That didn't mean anything more than their own limited position and experience... as illusory as an anamorphosis.

Her eyes went back to the map with its symbol warning off outsiders.

"What troubles you, Agent Renault?"

"I'm conflicted about entering this region."

"As you should be. However, knowing that you are in the employ of Asher Lauden, I imagine you are familiar with his ethical philosophy?"

She certainly was. Lauden was a consequentialist through and through.

"Ends justifies the means," Lilline said. "He's made that a company philosophy." One she found comforting and, ironically, disturbing. Only once had she witnessed him embrace an opposing moral philosophy, and that was a unique circumstance where personal and professional lives crossed.

"We are facing a paradox on a galactic scale," Nova said. "Do nothing out of respect for an ancient clause and our civilization, as well as potentially other worlds in this section of Arm 5, may be under threat of domination or worse, annihilation." Three eyes rose in unison to the night sky above them. "Or we interfere, as morally conflicted as it makes us, knowing that if we succeed the result far outweighs the cost."

There it was, laid bare.

"In my line of work, Nova, I confront this more often than I like."

"And are your choices consistent?"

Lilline's eyes went back to the pond's starry reflection. "Usually, only once did I—"

"Nova."

Lilline swung around to find Nithya hastening toward them.

"What is it?" The Jenzara rolled up the map. With a wave of her hand, the mirror holo-galaxy over the pond vanished.

"There's something out there." The Rasp, robe drenched from the falls, gasped for breath. A three-fingered hand pointed back through the rocky entry.

Lilline's instincts fired. She was up and making for the tunnel to protect the druids and confront whatever threat approached.

"I stopped the ceremony as soon as our watchers raised the alarm. Everyone disbanded following standard protocol," the Rasp said, throat flap vibrating with heaving breaths.

Lilline peered down the passage. "I don't see anything."

"I closed the entrance," Nithya said.

"What do you mean, 'something' is out there?" Nova's voice bounced through the cavern.

"Not sure," Nithya said. "Zin spotted it. He said it looked and sounded like the Beast of Brinsk."

"What nonsense is this?" Nova asked.

"He risked a closer peek. And said it... well..."

"It what?"

Lilline didn't like where this was going.

"It was sniffing and appeared to be..." the Rasp lowered its eye.

"Nithya?"

"A shaved werewolf."

Lilline's neck hair prickled. "Not the Beast of Brisk," she said hustling back to them.

"You know this creature?" Nova asked.

"A mutated Dendari. And it's after me."

Four eyes, three possessed by the Jenzara and one by the Rasp, went wide.

"His name is Gongo."

FORTY-EIGHT

"Is there another way out of here?"

"There are several," Nova pointed past her. "Close the roof."

Lilline pushed the glowing button. Slow scraping of ancient rock ground into the cavern's stillness.

"Nithya, take the downward tunnel to Hare's Den. Wait until dawn's light and then get back to the village."

"What is going on?"

"No time to explain, go!"

The Rasp scurried off to the farthest portal.

Lilline hustled around the pool. A pitch shadow like an eclipse crossed the pond's surface as the roof blocked the oculus.

"We take this passage," the druid pointed at the nearest archway. "There's an exit with a—"

"We?"

"I'm coming with you."

Lilline shook her head. "It's too dangerous. Just get me out of here."

The archdruid tucked the ancient books under her arm and scurried off to the archive. "You need someone with an understanding of Darian language," she said and vanished inside.

"But I can't get there in time."

"I know," Nova said, reappearing. "But we still don't understand the painting's purpose at the temple. At the least, I can help prepare your colleague and, if they are sat-linked then I can be online with you, Asher, and the others."

The Jenzara's robe glittered across the pool, her doppelgänger appearing like an anamorphosis on the water's surface.

"Trust me," Nova said as the cavern's light dimmed. "You will need my expertise to see this through." The druid pulled a glow orb from a sconce. She tapped it to life, sending cool blue illumination onto her features.

Nova was right but having another in tow made things difficult. And slowed her down. Then again if they had a way out of here and dodged Gongo...

"What could go wrong?" the Jenzara said, waving her to hurry around the pond.

Something always does.

The steady scraping of rock halted. No more than a sliver of the starry night, like a crescent moon, remained on the still water. Her eyes went wide as a dark shadow cut across the stellar reflection.

Lilline peered up. Gongo, arm muscles bulging and wearing a vicious and fanged grin, held the roof back from closing.

"Run Nova!"

Splash! Splash! Splash... Splash!

Four Gej-ti, Zapper thugs by the looks of them, surfaced and swam for the pool's edges.

Lilline drew her blaster and fired. Two of her shots missed, bouncing off the surface and scattering like red sparkles in the cavern. The third hit, stopping one, literally, dead in the water.

"Hurry!" Nova motioned her through an archway. The roof's mechanism whirred, struggling against the Dendari's arms. A Zapper's scream bounced off the walls. Lilline turned in time to witness the Gej-ti sucked under and into the channel out to the waterfall.

"Arrrrrgh!" Gongo's deep voice bellowed as she squeezed through the portal.

Boom!

A thunderous echo resonated through the tunnel as it shut.

"Are they trapped inside?" she said, following Nova down the shaft.

"They can get out behind the falls... the way we came in. But we need to worry about that one on the roof."

"Gongo," Lilline said.

Did they ever. Her mind was racing, trying to put together why Carmini's bodyguard was on Elaris and, even more puzzling, how he managed to know she was here.

"Who is he?" Nova asked as they scurried through the narrow passages.

"A thug working for an underground art dealer. The Jenzara I mentioned."

"Carmini?"

"You know him?" Lilline grabbed the back of Nova's robe to help her stay on course.

"There aren't that many Jenzara across the galaxy. At university my studies in art history brought him to my attention."

Thuds echoed up the tunnel.

"Can they open that portal?" Lilline asked.

"With enough strength and boulders, yes."

Not good. At least the beastly Dendari wasn't in the cavern. If he were they'd be through already.

"I don't know why Gongo is on Elaris," Lilline said. "No way was I tracked. He passed on the street when I arrived in Carna-Brai but I dodged him... that's how I met Nithya."

Like a lazy river, the tunnel meandered left and right with no end in sight. Her legs were beginning to burn with the effort.

"It's a small village," Nova said. "Everyone sees and hears everything. And talks about it. Gossip gossip gossip... especially Tapper Pew."

"The bartender?" Lilline said, remembering the name. "At the Wailwind Inn?"

"You had the pleasure of meeting him, I take it?"

A resounding crack travelled up the tunnel. Lilline knew the translation: the Zappers had fractured the door's stone.

Stupid. She'd talked about visiting Mirna and Simuel as a child in their nearby cottage at the pub. And she asked about Denbaldie Hill. But still... unless Gongo overheard, the chances of it coming up in conversation were slim.

"Your silence about Tapper Pew speaks volumes," Nova said, between huffing breaths. "Well, at least I hope you tried the Porter."

Ahead, over the druid's shoulder, Lilline made out shadows where the tunnel widened.

"Almost there," Nova said.

No doubt now, they were climbing.

"Where does this lead?"

"To a cave along a sheer cliff."

"How does that help us?"

"Leap of faith."

FORTY-NINE

A pattern was emerging and Lilline didn't like it. This marked the second time flying on the wind would be her means of escaping Gongo.

Strapped down with cables near an open-air ledge sat a two-seater micro-glider. It waited like a predatory insect sleeping inside a giant's gaping mouth.

Nova unfastened the cables and retracted the bubble top.

Lilline ran a hand along the aircraft's sleek white shell. Other than its diminutive scale, it had all the shapes and lines of the engine-less flyers used recreationally across the galaxy.

Except for one glaring omission.

"Where are the wings?" she asked.

"Like I said... leap of faith." The druid tightened a final strap on the glider's tail system and motioned her to get in.

"As long as it gets us out of here and fast," Lilline said, plopping down into the narrow bucket seat.

"It'll be fast at first, trust me." Nova stepped over the side into the front seat. "Can you fly one?"

"I can." She had learned to handle gliders on Beisho. Dappled with alpine peaks and long valleys, Tavi-Prime's moon contained an abundance of thermals. Soaring was exhilarating, especially when the winds were strong, but she much preferred a cryex burner's throttle and the freedom that came with a proton drive. Nothing beat the rush of speed.

"Well, this morning you get to enjoy the ride. And once we lose your pursuers it should be a spectacular sunrise."

Lilline looked over a set of controls in the second seat. Familiar enough, not unlike the ones she'd flown.

"Ready?" Nova said.

"Born to do it." For all the danger of the current moment, this was far more comfortable ground, even if it was about to give way under her.

Shouts bounced up the cavern. Gej-ti voices. Carmini's thugs were through the portal and making their way up the tunnel.

"Quick... help me get us to the edge," Nova said.

Placing her insteps into the pedal-slips, Lilline rotated the crude chain in tandem with the druid. The glider's tricycle wheels crunched over loose pebbles on the cavern floor.

Out the cliff's opening, beyond a distant Lake Brinsk, pinkish light declared the imminent sunrise.

"Faster!"

Lilline's quads strained as she pedaled.

Gej-ti voices, closer now, echoed up the tunnel.

"Get ready for the plunge."

"But what about—"

Her stomach lurched. The horizon disappeared, replaced by a canopy of dark evergreens a few hundred meters below.

"Nova..."

"I got it...

Wind whistled through cracks in the glider's frame as they rushed downward.

"Nova!"

"Just a little more speed..."

Lilline gripped the edges of her seat, fingers digging into the cushions.

"Now!" The druid pulled a handle and a set of flexible wings extended mid-capsule. She yanked the stick back.

Lilline's stomach plummeted like she was on a roller coaster. Good thing enough time had passed for the cannonball that was the Wailwind Inn's stew to digest in her system, otherwise the capsule would be a mess.

Tips of deep green firs rushed past as the Jenzara pulled them out of the nosedive.

Crack!

They teetered, the druid recovering from breaking the tip off a tall fir tree.

"Whoops!"

Skimming the treetops, Nova banked them hard right toward a rocky crag. Lilline's stomach dropped as the craft caught a thermal and rose into the skies.

"Out of the woods now, I should think," Nova said. "Sorry, bad pun I know but—"

Pat! Pat! Pat!

Blue lights flashed in the trees below.

Lilline grabbed the stabilizer bar as they pitched in an evasive maneuver.

Pat! Pat! Pat!

Sparks erupted on the right wing.

"We're hit!" Lilline said, marking two holes to starboard.

"It's not too bad," the Jenzara pulled several levers at the controls "I need to adjust some flaps and get to this next rise."

A silver light glimmered in the trees.

"Almost there..." The druid banked left, avoiding another round of blaster fire. Rocks along a craggy moor neared. The glider caught the thermal's edge and the trees grew smaller.

"Heading up!" Nova said.

Golden rays streamed across patches of green and beige hillside as the morning sun broke the horizon. Elaris's countryside came into view as a mix of gridded farmland and patches of forest and open moors.

Five minutes later, they were soaring at a thousand meters. Empty backcountry passed, a lone road cutting like a vein through the natural topography. Nova banked the craft to port following the highway northeast.

"Two of my brains have been thinking about something," Nova said. "The *Cosmic Widow* is here for a reason."

"You think it was purposefully left behind?"

"Without question. Now that you shared the new understanding of what transpired in the First Galactic, I have no doubt the painting was not meant to return with the Darians."

"Why leave it behind?"

"Perhaps some of them survived the purge?"

"You mean here among us?"

The Jenzara took a hand from the stick and gestured as if to say "maybe."

"But wouldn't they be long dead?" Lilline shifted position, getting more comfortable in the capsule.

"Would they? Do we really have any way of knowing Darian biology? Perhaps this was a fail-safe left for someone who survived... long asleep, even."

"We had this conversation," Lilline said. "Professor Senjara and the others raised the possibility as well." Now that she thought about it, Madame X had made passing reference to evidence of alien specimens at U-City.

Lilline shook off the thought. This mission was unfolding like an endless set of boxes inside boxes, each one more disturbing than the last.

"Professor Senjara's likeminded thoughts on the matter only add weight to its possibility," the Jenzara said.

Lilline chose to keep Madame X's mention of outside visitors to herself. "But why preserve instructions using anamorphosis? If a

Darian perceived it with their vision or other capabilities those instructions are redundant?"

"Perhaps someone is an ally. Or the Darians expected it to be figured out."

"To what end?"

"That answer remains unknown."

"I don't like this, Nova."

"Nor do I. Despite the immense enlightenment unveiled about our galaxy and the larger cosmos, I fear something terrifying waits in the shadows."

So do I.

"How did the Darians get here?" Lilline asked.

"You mean first contact?"

"Yes."

"That too remains a mystery. I bet that, with time and resources, we would find evidence... buried ruins or other traces of Darian temples at the various terminuses of those earlier radial points throughout the galaxy. Moz may be one of many such locations... or the last."

Lilline peered out the glider's bubble shell, pondering the historical puzzle. A lone road wandered through the countryside. "Is that the A-24?"

"It is. There's a comm station about seven kilometers ahead. Lonely little red booth in the middle of nowhere... on a straightaway. I can put us down right on the road."

"What village is that to starboard?" Lilline noted the signature spire in the center square.

"Filandshire."

"I know it." Lilline edged closer to the capsule window. She followed the highway as it led from the clustered buildings further west to Brinsk. Her eyes went north off the second lane. A half kilometer beyond a small patch of thick woodland, near a creek, she found her target.

Mirna's cottage. Right where she remembered it.

"I have a better idea." She leaned forward and peered through the cockpit. "See that cottage to the north and a little east?"

The Jenzara nodded.

"Make for it. I know the owner. You can land in the field on its western side. It's closer and more secluded."

"Good because I can't get us any higher. According to the nav-board, I don't think we'd make it to that comm booth. It's too early in the day for the atmosphere to—"

Boom!

Like a fuse reaching gunpowder, a sparking explosion replaced the tranquility of soaring over Elaris.

Wind screamed through the smashed bubble top, pulling smoke from the cockpit up and out.

"Nova!" The word vanished in the rushing air and blaring alarms.

The glider dipped, nosediving and arcing to port.

Lilline grabbed her control stick to pull them out of the spin.

She yanked.

"Shit!"

No movement.

Nova's slumped form lay over the primary controls.

Lilline unstrapped, wind whirring and ground approaching, and reached forward.

"Argh!" She heaved the Jenzara back off the board and hit the control transfer button. Grabbing her piloting stick, she sat back and worked the flaps with her feet.

Thigh muscles flexed as she pushed left and right - only half of the usual pedal range. The glider was like a bird hit by shotgun pellets, torn apart along its wings and breast, losing the battle to say aloft.

Counter movements. Stay calm... Counter movements.

Her flying instructor's words rose.

"Feel the glider... feel the sky."

She listened with her body, responding to the spin on instinct. The imminence of the approaching ground fell away.

Feel the glider. Feel the sky.

The glider steadied and leveled off.

Now!

Both hands pulled back.

Like a swallow dipping to nab an insect and rising out of the dive, the glider arced upward into the sky.

Plunk!

Nova's limp body swung upright, sending blood splattering back onto her face. Lilline squeezed her eyes open and shut, fighting through the stinging liquid. A hand wiped her cheeks clean. She needed to stay low and slow down if she hoped to land safely.

Anywhere would do. She gazed to port, fighting to keep the damaged craft steady at two hundred meters. It was no use. The drag from the damage usurped the glider's aerodynamics, and with no nearby thermals they were going down.

A red flash on the A-24 drew her eye.

You...

Riding the rented cycle, Gongo throttled up and fired another round into the sky.

Blaster bolts passed to port.

"Nova?"

The Jenzara mumbled a response.

Thank the stars.

"Hold on, I'm going to put us down."

Lilline kicked the flaps and yanked the stick to port, attempting to arc the wounded glider toward the road. She wanted the safety of a depression ahead. It would give her a bit of time out of sight from Gongo.

Snap!

The glider pitched. A damaged section of the starboard wing tore off, spiraling back and away. Lilline worked to keep them steady, losing altitude.

"Hang in there," she said to the dying craft, "just get me to that dip in front of him."

Gongo, throttle open and firing at her, raced down the highway.

Lilline banked over a patch of purple heather at fifty meters and turned the steering column. This was it. She needed to reverse course. The glider struggled, but made the arc and the A-24, twenty meters underneath her, gave her a landing lane. Somewhere over the rise in front of her, Gongo was racing towards them.

Unless he slowed down, he should be right where...

She eased the stick back, hugging the road two meters off the pavement, climbing the hill.

"Land... put us down..." Nova mumbled.

"Not yet."

Gongo appeared over the lip, his fanged expression furious.

Their gazes met.

"I just need to—"

The Dendari's eyes went wide at the sight of the glider.

"Cut off the competition."

The wing sliced straight through Gongo's neck before he could scream.

The glider wobbled and pitched. Lilline fought back with the flaps.

Pavement rushed past.

Smack!

The hull impacted the road. Her stomach lurched as they bounced in the air.

Lilline steadied the craft over the straightaway and put them down in a scraping slide as the boom of Gongo's vehicle exploding reached her ears.

Veering off the road, she brought them to a slow but final halt.

"Nova!" Lilline was up and out of her seat. She smashed away the remains of the bubble top and unstrapped the druid.

Pink blood covered the Jenzara's silver robe, her face unrecognizable. All three eyes had been seared away, leaving nothing but charred and crispy red skin.

"Nova!" She placed her down on the grass.

"You..." The word was a whisper from the bloodied mouth atop the druid's forehead. "Remember..."

Lilline took the Jenzara's hand and squeezed it.

"Remember..."

"Shhh... I got you. Let me get the med kit." Lilline went to rise but Nova gripped her arm.

"No."

Like a river trailblazing a course, red liquid ran from the druid's torso, staining the yellow grass.

"Remember the reflection..."

In the warm morning light of the now quiet countryside of Elaris, two opposing forces reached mutual resolution. The head of a mutated beast rolled to a stop on the A-24's asphalt as the wisdom from one of the galaxy's oldest living creatures drifted away, returning to the stars.

FIFTY

The cottage hadn't changed in thirty cycles.

Lilline stepped out from the wooded glade. She made for the rickety gate between crumbling stone walls.

A hand undid the rusted latch and childhood memories rushed back: the succulent aroma of wildflowers, buzzing insects darting to and fro, and the clanking of pots and dishes through the leaded window as Mirna and her mother prepared a hearty meal. Hours passed at the lace-covered table, the two women laughing as she ate sweets and occupied herself investigating an array of trinkets scattered about the living room.

Lilline knelt, concealing herself in the meadow's tall grass as an emergency vehicle passed on the A-24. Smoke from the accident shot a towering plume into an otherwise clear morning sky. She didn't want to think about the first responders' shock when they arrived nor what kind of narrative would result when they found Gongo's head. Local legend and the tourism industry were about to experience a new and disturbing modern take on the Beast of Brinsk.

And then there was the Jenzara's body in the grass.

Nova...

The loss of the druid was a major mission setback and, her tragic end left Lilline with that not unfamiliar feeling of personal responsibility for another's death in the field. Yes, it came with the job. And the truth of it was she did sometimes get people killed. The only solace for the present was that familiar philosophy, one that Nova herself had touted only hours earlier: sacrifices had to be made for the greater good.

But so much still didn't make sense. Something told her that when it did, it would hit with the force of an unmoored frigate.

The sirens faded. She rose and made her way to the front door. Mirna would be shocked to see her. That itself would take finesse, and she didn't have time to nuance her urgent need to use the comm. This might be one of those field situations when she had to peel back Keely Larkin, like she had with Renina Blackstone on Sky City. It didn't mean revealing her true identity or occupation. Just the usual, "I work for the Ministry," company tagline. That spoke volumes to anyone with the sense to put two and two together. Mirna wasn't a fool. Over the cycles, Lilline had often worried that the woman knew what she, and Granny before her, did for a living.

"Ew!" She veered around a dead hare.

It lay in a tuft of grass in the early stages of decomposition. Only a meter away ran a beautiful line of flowers along the path. Lilline paused, fascinated by their potent color and unusual petals. Deep violet, like sword blades the size of a human hand, with bright yellow pistils shooting upward on narrow green spindles, the plants stood almost two meters high. Around the blooms were other more familiar varieties, the entire garden making for a striking display of color and adding rustic charm to the already bucolic surroundings.

"Mirna?" She knocked and the cottage door creaked open.

Lilline peered inside. "Mirna... It's Keely Larkin."

Nothing.

She entered and, like a time capsule, was transported back to her youth. Everything from the smell, the morning sunbeams shining through the uneven glass, and the fraying furniture, had barely changed. Reproductions and original works of art hung on walls and stood in cases, now posthumous artifacts of Simuel's many decades excavating sites around the galaxy.

"Mirna? Are you here?"

Still nothing.

Lilline spotted the comm station next to the stone fireplace and made for it. A push of the button and—

The same ancient self-charging comm box from when she had visited as a child sat on the table. The device worked via a sat-link in the nearby tower in Filandshire and was the communication equivalent of rubbing two sticks together to make a fire.

"You've *got* to me kidding me." She grabbed the handle on the side of the box and spun it, activating the charging mechanism. Red light flashed on a set of horizontal bars: fifteen minutes to generate enough juice for a short conversation with HQ.

"Mirna!" Lilline's shouts were more obligatory than expectant of a response. The woman must be in the village or somewhere else nearby. *Not a bad thing, actually.* With a little luck, she might be able to contact HQ, delete the comm records, and be out the door without her presence being known.

She went to the washroom and scrubbed the soot and dirt from the crash off her face. A few nicks and scrapes here and there but only one deep cut on her arm. That she washed and patched with a small med kit from the cabinet. She may have made it out of the accident alive and largely unscathed, but this wasn't her first crash rodeo. In twenty-four hours, everything was going to hurt.

Back to the living room to check the charger. Two bars loaded. Seven more to go.

The cottage's old floorboards creaked as she ascended to the second floor. A familiar print of an unknown First Galactic ruin still hung, too high, on the wall at the top of the stairs.

Her eyes went around the hallway.

It's like time standing still in here...

She peered into the guest room. Same as when she had visited except for a new set of linens.

Simuel's old office, door closed, pulled at her with the same allure it had cycles ago. On her first visit, she had imagined it filled with rare and strange objects... treasures and magical items like potions and other exciting and forbidden oddities.

As if drawn by some unknown force, her feet crossed to the entrance. Hesitant fingers gripped the handle. To her surprise, with a twist, it opened.

If ever there was a mise-en-scène portraying an old university scholar, this was it. The office had what appeared to be a lifetime of academic endeavor memorialized through copious books, documents, objects, and various ephemera, all surrounding the nexus: a dark-stained Olk desk and chair. Dust had come to rest in familiar crevices, as if a squall of gray snow had blown through an open window.

Lilline went to the desk. Her agent eyes came alive, scanning.

A set of fingerprints and smudge marks dappled dusty notebooks and portfolios, and one or two books, scattered atop the desk.

Those marks are recent.

She picked up the nearest tome and read the title. A strange sensation tingled her spine.

The Collected Works of V.L. Lumsden: Cosmic Mystic of the Second Galactic Age.

"Lumsden?" It came out a whisper. She flipped through the pages, arriving at a double page spread: a crude drawing of energy points scattered about a whirlpool galaxy.

Dr. Liguera's source for her research into ghost holes...

She put down the book and opened a portfolio.

Her gasp sucked the silence from the office.

Two galaxies drawn as mirror images, one above and one below, were dotted with funnels at stellar locations. Hastily scrawled dates accompanied the markers.

Her eye went to Galactic Arm 2.

The cycle, month, and starting date for the current alignment was written below a point. Next to it, in caps: *MOZ!*

"Simuel cracked it," she said. The office absorbed the statement in silence, as if already privy to hidden secrets.

She sifted through various notes on the desk.

"But how?"

A small notebook, a journal by the look of it, caught her eye. She snatched it up and turned to the first page.

Entry #1: Genmarrow City Central, University Archives. Elaris, TG. 5007

Vindication. Finally... A lifetime of conjecture flipped from ridicule to truth. Just like a mirror's reflection... I was right all along. The instructions I've found confirm everything.... All that is needed is Azaludarian's Star Chart and then, those who mocked me will rue the day.

Entry #2: Filandshire. Elaris, TG. 5008

A turn of events. I've made a most disturbing discovery... The star chart has been destroyed. Only the copy by Henestra remains. I must find it... More time is needed to grasp the implications, but the Darians... stars. It just can't be! I must consider how, what, and when... and, though I loathe to say it, "if"...

Entry #3: Genmarrow City Central, Windstream Hotel. Elaris, TG. 5008

I have a lead on Henestra's copy of the star chart.... A dealer named Carmini claims he can access it for the right price.

Lilline flipped forward, scanning more entries.

There was no doubt. Simuel knew about the wormholes. He had cracked the evidence for when and where the *Cosmic Widow* could trigger a link opening the Darian gate.

But whose fingerprints lay scattered on the books and documents?

Someone came here for this information. And... A pit with no bottom dropped open in her stomach. *Stars... they took Mirna.*

Ding!

Like a crack of thunder, the alert smacked her out of a dream.

Lilline snatched up a handful of notes and rushed downstairs. Fingers worked the call box, entering the bounce number that would take her through four false destinations before jumping to the AI terminal at HQ.

The light went yellow, connecting.

Tonal squawking, like an electronic insect chorus, came over the speaker followed by a click.

"You have reached Galaxy Unlimited, Inc. How may I direct your call?"

"Keely Larkin requesting secure line to back office. Access code: 7AL9B448."

Lilline peered out the cottage window. Still no sign of Mirna, or anyone else for that matter. She didn't want to think about what someone interested in this mess would do to the poor woman.

"Access granted," the AI said. *"One moment, T8."*

Lilline picked up Mirna's cane which had been leaning against a chair and examined it. *Bastards didn't even let her take this.*

The comm light blipped green.

"T8?"

Lilline sat and knocked over a framed photo.

"Shit."

"Excuse me?" Lauden said.

"Yes, sir. It's me," Lilline said. *Damn it. Great way to begin a conversation...* She bent down and picked up the photo. "Apologies.

Equipment on this end is rustic at best." The picture was of a young woman. Lilline brought it closer, examining the figure.

She knew those features. It was Mirna and she was—

"Were you successful with Rinka? Do you have the Temple's location?" Lauden asked.

Lilline's eyes went wide.

Mirna posed proudly with a medal around her neck.

Behind her was a trapeze.

"T8?"

Lilline read the small inscription in the bottom corner: "Mirna Trelano. First place, Inner Core Galactic Acrobatics Finals, Tavi-Prime. 4953."

Stars...

"T8, are you there? Report..."

"Here, sir. I have the location... but it came at a terrible price."

It's all making sense now.

"There's something else."

"What's that?" Lauden asked.

"I know the identity of our thief."

FIFTY-ONE

"You say her name is Mirna Grochevsky?"

Lauden's authoritative voice penetrated the cottage's eerie silence. A space so intimate to her own family history and childhood now imposed upon by sobering professional obligations. Clashing realities blurred her focus and challenged her ability to stay centered.

"Yes, sir," she said. "But her pre-marriage name was Trelano."

"Cazshi, let Pin in," the director said. *"She's in the call waiting room."*

The familiar click of the third-party connection came over the line.

"Hello, T8," the Oltari said.

"Pin, check this name and background: Mirna Trelano," the director said.

"Trapeze Trelano?"

"You know her?" Lilline said.

"Oh yes, T8. She was an amazing acrobatic competitor in her younger cycles. One of the few humans able to do a triple..."

Silence.

"Pin?" Lilline eyed the speaker box.

"Hoo!"

"What is it?" Lauden asked.

"Sorry, sir," Pin said. *"It's... that maneuver, the one Trelano made famous. I think... let me just run something."*

Lilline examined the photograph. Mirna's body was lithe and tight, like a slender bodybuilder built for speed.

"It would be risky and requires extraordinary skill but looking at the grid and considering the motion of the maneuver, yes. It works."

"What in blazes are you getting at, Pin?" Lauden said.

"Sir, if executed with near-perfect precision, the Triple Trelano would allow a human to pass through the alarm system to the Cosmic Widow... *undetected."*

"And this Trelano was married to Simuel Grochevsky?" Lauden asked.

"You know of him?" Lilline said.

"Of course. Everyone studying First Galactic history would. Remember at U-City when the professor mentioned that Bilarus and a group of colleagues made it their mission to undermine his credibility? Their relentless critiques of his theories, albeit far-fetched as they were, about the painting and the Darians more broadly, shamed him. An endless barrage of scholarly articles and public lectures led to the poor man's eventual firing and early retirement."

"Well, in an ironic twist of fate," Lilline said, walking past the kitchen table to the window, "Simuel Grochevsky turned out to be right." She checked the road to the cottage. In the mid-morning light, the countryside was coming alive with color and wildlife.

"And you are certain Mirna took the painting?" Lauden said. *"The acrobatic connection gives you enough evidence?"*

The director had that tone in his voice. She knew, even across the light years, that his face held a skeptical expression.

Good thing she had a zinger locked and loaded.

"We met after I was at HQ that day, sir. Malardis with Kissy. Mirna had mentioned something, and I remembered it coming up again when I spoke with Renina at the Royal Loha's bar. She told

Kissy a painting was moved in the main gallery housing the *Cosmic Widow*."

"*And?*"

"Renina informed me that she stayed late the night the *Cosmic Widow* was stolen and had moved it. Yet, Mirna had been with Kissy all morning. Which means..."

"*She would have seen the new arrangement only if she was there after the museum had closed the night of the theft,*" Lauden said.

"*Hoo!*" Pin interjected.

"*Good show, T8.*"

"Thank you, sir."

"*If I may, why did Mirna take the painting?*" Pin asked.

"I discovered copious notes upstairs," Lilline said. She pulled a handful out of her pocket and sifted through them. "Her spouse, Simuel, knew everything, Pin. He had the alignments, the wormhole theory, and even the location. Which, by the way, is in Arm 5 in the uncharted sector. I'll transfer the coordinates. It's a planet called, not surprisingly, Moz."

"*I'll alert the travel office and work out which agent is closest,*" Lauden said. "*I believe it's T5, but she is still going to have a long ride. The chances of her getting there in time are slim.*"

"*Excuse me, but my question got lost in the conversation,*" the Oltari said.

Lilline read through the note from Simuel's office. "My best guess is revenge, Pin. From what I can tell, Simuel figured out the Darians were driven out. He had all the information to open the gate but didn't. According to his journal, he destroyed the original Azaludarian Star Chart."

"*Then how did Mirna locate the copy by Henestra?*" Lauden asked.

"There's a line in his notes about it, sir. It even mentions Carmini. If she went through his things maybe that tipped her off to contact him."

"*If I may,*" Pin said. "*On a whim, I ran some tournament history through the computer while you were conversing, cross-referencing it with some of the well-known art thefts of First Galactic objects."*

Lilline stopped scanning Simuel's notes.

"Four artifacts vanished from museums at the same time competitions were being held on those Inner Core planets. And, the dates line up with tournaments that Mirna participated in. In fact, I have her as officially on the roster for all of them."

"Well done, Pin," Lauden said.

"Thank you, sir."

Lilline's eyes narrowed. "And then, an acrobatic thief meets and marries an art historian involved with First Galactic history and culture."

"Indeed. The pieces of the puzzle are falling into place," the director said. *"And she was a family friend you say, T8?"*

"Yes. She's struggled since this all happened with Simuel. Mirna was recently on Tavi-Prime to sell back a few works from their excavations for a financial boost. And that visit overlaps with the theft of the *Cosmic Widow*."

Lilline ran back through the memory of Granny and Mirna at Malardi's.

You crafty thief.

"Sir, she had both me and Kissy duped." Lilline picked up the cane leaning against the sofa, examining it in disgust. "She played off a longtime hip ailment that affected her walking."

"Or, maybe she injured herself during the heist," Pin said.

"Could be," Lilline said. "Either way she was performing when we met her. Add in acting confused with any high-tech devices and—"

Layers were unfolding like Nova had said about the Darians.

Craftier than I imagined. Play the innocent rural visitor to the big city planet.

She stared at the comm speaker. Somehow, she was going to have to break the glider crash to Lauden.

"What is it, T8?" the director asked.

"Pin, check the official manifest on the flight at 11:30 out of Tavi-Central the day after the theft. It would be connecting to the cruiser heading to Ortor hub."

"What am I looking for?"

"Mirna. Either last name."

"What's your angle, T8?" Lauden asked.

"If my instinct is correct, sir, I may have put something together. All my offers to drive Mirna to her flight were refused."

"No record of her on the departure manifest," Pin said.

"Now, do a full search of passengers that day to Sky City... out of Tavi-Central."

Lilline strode to the window and gazed out. Such a beautiful property and cottage. Her eyes went to the kitchen table and chairs. All those cycles Mirna too, had been living a double identity. Kissy, Mirna, her... everyone but her mother had a well of secrets.

"Hit! T8, I'm impressed with your cognitive capabilities."

Pin's remark sent uneasy waves bouncing through her stomach. A flash of Nova dying in her arms interrupted her thoughts.

"So that puts Mirna at the auction, stealing the star chart?" the Oltari said.

"It does," Lilline said. "And explains the acrobatics exiting the storeroom."

"So, if we put this together with that chatter we intercepted," the director said, *"then Mirna set up some kind of deal with Carmini for the star chart, perhaps in exchange for the* Cosmic Widow, *and then double-crossed him."*

"Makes sense. She fails to show up with the painting, probably meant to be handed over to the Zappers for delivery. That sets off a chain reaction from Carmini's thugs. And, then Mirna has the nerve to break into the auction and take the chart right out from under him." She had to admit, it was impressive.

"Thus, she gets away with both the Cosmic Widow *and Henestra's copy of the star chart,"* Lauden said.

"Everything she needs, with Simuel's research and discoveries, to get to Moz and open the gate."

"*Stars...*" The Gej-ti's voice faded, leaving an eerie silence in the cottage. "*And the clock is ticking.*"

Lilline returned her attention to the view out of the window, taking in the flower garden.

"*You should know, T8 that things have gotten messy here,*" Lauden said.

Lilline swung around, eyeing the comm station speaker.

"*It's Bilarus. The metro police picked him up for questioning.*"

"Why?"

"*Apparently someone tipped them off that he was trading in stolen artifacts. And they went so far as to plant one in his office at the museum.*"

"Renina," Lilline said.

"*What was that, T8? You're breaking up.*"

"Renina, sir." Lilline raised her voice. "It had to be her. She wants his job. This must be a way for her to frame him. My guess is she's trying to distance herself from this mess with Carmini."

"*Bilarus can handle himself, so I am going to let it play out... for now. I don't want our involvement known. However,*" The familiar click of the Gej-ti's lighter, followed by a whoosh of his neck gills exhaling smoke, came over the wire. "*Renina or whoever it was, also alerted the press about the stolen painting.*"

Damn. Now it really is going to blow up all over the galaxy.

"*As you can imagine,*" Lauden said, "*it's turned the Ministry upside down. The GM and her cultural minister are scrambling to do damage control before someone finds out it was being held back from the public.*"

As if they didn't have enough problems. And, limited time.

"My guess is Renina either got Mirna in or created safe passage through security," Lilline said. "She may have shut down the alarm systems."

"I think it's time we picked her up and brought her to GAM-OPs for interrogation," Lauden said.

"I agree, sir."

"Give me a moment," Lauden said. *"Continue. I'm here but on mute... trying to reach someone."*

"Oh, T8," Pin said. *"About your grandmother..."*

Lilline squeezed one of Simuel's notes into a crumpled ball.

"We've made some progress on the toxin. With Madame X's help at U-City lab, we are certain it is of organic origin. Most likely plant based."

Lilline uncrumpled the note. Scribblings by Simuel about an old Darian excavation site... like a hastily scrawled inventory list. Something about an urn containing seeds and—

"Did you say plant-based, Pin?"

"Yes, T8. Akin to the kinds of responses after exposure to the swordshade family," the Oltari added. *"I must admit I'm not a fan of its orange petals."*

Orange? Lilline's view homed in on the strangely menacing violet flowers blooming along the path.

"It's extremely poisonous," Pin said.

Lilline tracked the thick stems to their base.

In the grass, amidst swarming flies, lay the festering brown and furry lump.

"Hold the line!"

FIFTY-TWO

Liline rushed back to the cottage, the stem of one of the tall flowers gripped with a towel she'd nabbed from the kitchen.

"Pin! You still there?"

"Of course, T8. Why wouldn't I be? We're on a GAM-OPs call that the director—"

"Listen to me..." She placed the two-meter-long stem onto the table. Dirt speckled the floor from its snakelike roots. Violet sword-like petals with yellow centers slumped from the pull of gravity. "Pin, the toxin in swordshade..." Lilline leaned down and examined the plant from one end to another, "does it come from the flowers?"

"The entire plant is poisonous, including the roots."

Nibble marks oozed a clear liquid near the base of the stem.

The hare.

"In small doses it can induce what is known as a 'shade sleep' from which someone can fully recover. But larger amounts trigger acute reactions. It has quite an infamous history, especially in the First Galactic Age, as a means of disabling political foes," the Oltari said. *"Its juices are colorless and odorless to all sentient species. There's a disturbing story about the ruler of—"*

"What does it look like?"

"I already told you."

"No, I mean give me specifics... how do you ID it?"

"There are points along its petals. Five small ones and then a larger one."

Lilline squatted next to the table, careful not to touch the flowers.

One, two, three, four, five... larger point.

"These match the pattern, but the petals are deep violet... I think I've found the source of the toxin that poisoned Kissy."

"Hoo!"

"Hold the line." Lilline charged up the stairs two at a time, snatched up Simuel's journal, and dashed back downstairs. She matched the date on the note to the closest one in his journal.

Day 242, Galactic Calendar Standard. Fotia Palace excavation (Kalatron, Moon #2), 4991 TG.

...discovered a sealed urn filled with seeds in antechamber 5A. Neither Mirna nor I are familiar with their kind. Similar to swordshade. Will either consult botanist or experiment with planting them ourselves....

She approached the window. Her eyes swept across the myriad flowers along the path. No other variety was familiar to her. A finger flipped through the journal. A sketch matching the plant appeared in an entry a cycle later. Underneath it was a note:

Day 71, Galactic Calendar Standard. Filandshire. Elaris, 4997 TG.

...strange and beautiful. Mirna has been growing it. Similar to swordshade... we have been careful not to touch it. Unfortunately, our favorite fox got into it. We found him dead two days later. He had eaten an entire plant. Most of the animals know on instinct to leave it

alone. To think we are growing a plant lost to time, brought back from the First Galactic!

How wrong that turned out. Far more than time separated this plant from the present. Lilline stood, awed by the sight while terrified at what it had done to her grandmother. An extra-galactic organism, an alien to their world.

"As crazy as it sounds, Pin. I think Mirna was growing an alien form of swordshade, or something in a similar genus, in her flower garden."

"But... how did she—"

"A sealed urn from a Darian excavation site, with seeds inside." The thought of it was unreal. What other alien varieties of fauna and flora were out there?

"If what you say is true, T8, then that suggests your family friend poisoned your grandmother?"

"Yes..." She stared at the flowers. "I am still not sure why. But right now, what matters is this must be the source of what is affecting Granny."

"My immediate analysis of the current mission circumstances, along with the tangible evidence, confirms this to be a strong possibility," Pin said. *"T8, if you can get us that plant, we may be able to work out a counter treatment or antidote to the toxin."*

Lilline took in the cozy cottage interior. *Mirna... how dare you? What evil... what malicious force would drive their lifelong friend to do this?*

A hidden monster stirred - a beast that lurked deep within her forbidden psychic depths. Not even her assassination missions brought it forth. Those were carried out with cold, unemotional precision as a trained GAM-OPs agent. This was personal beyond measure; a clan-like protective instinct strengthened by the bond of love.

Mirna will die at my hands.

She balled her fist, fingers digging into her palm as a vengeful fire clouded her vision.

And if we can't save Granny in time, I will make it slow.

And painful.

And violent.

An ugliness she didn't like to acknowledge, one usually kept at bay, would be unleashed.

"How soon can you get back to Tavi-Prime, T8?"

Pin's voice hit like cold water.

"What?"

"I asked how soon you can get back to Tavi-Prime?"

The anger receded taking the shadow with it.

"I... I don't know. That depends on our situation with—"

"I'm back," Lauden said, unmuting himself. *"Excellent work you two. I've been listening in while working on plotting a course to Moz. Nav-tech checked all the T#'s current locations and distances. T5 is the closest."*

"Yes, sir," Lilline couldn't hide the disappointment in her voice. Despite wanting to see this one through, time and space was going to win out on this mission. Besides, the swordshade was her new priority.

"But we have a problem," Lauden said. *"T5 may be the closest, but between going exo at her current location and the FTL jump, she is still twenty-two hours out from arriving in that star system."*

"That's too much time, sir," Lilline said. "If Mirna left for Moz after Sky City she might be there by now. Even if she traveled here first, then took a star cruiser to the Outer Rim and transferred to a private ship for hire..." Lilline shook her head. "She'd be arriving within hours."

Lauden mumbled, speaking to someone in his office.

"Sir," Lilline said, "with T5 in FTL there's little room to get her up to speed on mission specifics."

"That's the fastest possible, T8," Pin said. *"Time and space are*

still time and space for us, at least. Oh... oh dear me! Sir... T8... oh dear!"

"What is it?" Lilline rushed to the comm box. "Pin, are you ok?"

"I... the Darian clock. On my desk in the lab... it just—"

"Just what?" Lauden broke in.

"Melted into thin air."

"You mean someone took it?" Lilline asked.

"No, T8. I mean it literally *melted into thin air,"* Pin said. *"It's gone."*

"Not good." Lauden's voice was like a judge delivering a verdict. *"Do your best to find an explanation. Use anything and everything at your disposal and keep me posted."*

"Perhaps I need to retract my statement about time and space," the Oltari said.

"Speaking of which," Lauden said, *"I'm patching through a familiar voice."*

Again, the click of a line added to the group link cut in.

"Hello, Agent Renault."

"Madame X?"

"Indeed."

Lilline strode to the comm station. Why was Lauden patching the U-City director in?

"We may not be able to open wormholes, yet..." Madame X said, *"but at U-City we do have one or two other tricks up our sleeve."*

Lilline was all ears.

"How do you feel about adding test pilot to your resume?"

"Will it get me to Moz in time?"

"If it works," Madame X said. *"If not, you may end up... well... stretched."*

"Bring it on," Lilline said. She didn't know what the scientist meant by stretched... best to ignore that for now.

"We have a prototype of an FTL Distortion Ring. Out here in the labs we refer to it as 'the cosmic rubber band.'"

"And it speeds up travel time?" Lilline asked.

"More like it compresses space... and you inside of it."

"Has it been tested?" Pin asked.

"Twice with an empty craft. We don't believe in using living beings, of any type, in our experiments."

"So T8 would be the first?" the Oltari asked.

"She would. I won't lie. It's a big risk," the scientist said. *"You will be the inaugural sentient species taking this ride."*

"It's your call, T8." Lauden said. *"From what Madame X tells me we can cut travel time to mere hours if it works."*

Such a strange world they lived in. Here she was in the simplest of abodes, on a rural planet speaking through a hand-charging comm station, being asked to test pilot what was probably the most complicated form of technology of the current age. And one utterly secret to billions across the stars.

This was the job. And, if it worked, almost no one would ever know. But if it didn't...

"What do you say, Agent Renault?" Madame X said.

"As our thief's calling card said, time is short," Lilline said. "Let's compress it. I'm in."

"Sir," Pin said. *"T8 has a potential antidote for her grandmother's condition. If she can hand it off before she makes the rubber band jump, we might be able to save Kissy."*

"Madame X, will this slow us down?" Lauden asked.

"We can break it into two runs. One standard FTL to a rendezvous point and a second Distortion Ring haul out to the far-end of Arm 5. I was going to suggest this, actually. Otherwise, I worry about malfunction pushing it over too far a distance."

"Sir, if this slows us down, maybe I should travel straight to Moz. I wouldn't want..." Lilline squeezed her eyes shut, fighting the tears. It broke her heart but she had to offer. Granny was one person; this was about the entire galaxy. "I wouldn't want to risk the operation to save one life."

"How long of a delay, Madame X? Precise numbers if you can." Lauden's voice emerged over the wire cold and earnest.

"Using the two-stage approach I suggest? Thirty minutes, maximum. Big picture, it's a drop in the bucket of cosmic time."

Lilline didn't share how as a T# agent mere seconds made all the difference.

"We meet in international space off Quo," Lauden said. *"It's exactly halfway from you to us. We make the exchange and proceed with the elastic jump using the Distortion Drive to Moz,"* His lighter clicked. *"This is my call."*

"Thank you, sir." A wave of relief rushed through her, but its water quickly muddied with a rising tide of dread. Now was as good a time as any to do it. "Sir, I have some bad news about Rinka."

"Save it, T8. There can only be one reason why she isn't with you."

Her dread ebbed.

"You can give me the details when and if this ends well. If not... there will be far more important things to worry about."

"Yes, sir."

"The issue now is," he said, *"you are going this alone. You need academic guidance. It may prove essential to gain entry to the Temple or solve some cryptic Darian puzzle."*

He was right. She didn't have the esoteric knowledge and odds were, she would need it.

"The only option is that I come with you."

Lilline bit her tongue.

"I would suggest Professor Senjara but he can't handle this at his age." he added.

Admittedly, Lauden would be resourceful with the art history but in his condition? Plus, what she really needed was someone expert in the specifics of Darian culture and art. Literally, a specialist on the *Cosmic Widow* and its milieu.

"Actually sir, I have another idea. Bring Renina to the rendezvous."

"But she's the enemy, T8," Pin said. *"A conspirator."*

"You think we can cut a deal?" Lauden said.

"I think she wants to go, sir. The problem is, she doesn't know where to head. Renina has been chasing after this painting since Mirna failed to deliver it. I can't put it all together, but I'm convinced she was in the hot seat with Carmini when it failed to show up for delivery. It would make sense why she was being harassed at the Blue Comet, and why she appeared on Sky City at the time of the auction. If given the chance, I bet she jumps at the opportunity."

"A degree of immunity from prosecution with the hopes to save her career and keep herself out of prison?" the director said.

That was generous. But under the circumstances… "Sure. At this point, we have nothing to lose other than everything."

"Oh, T8?" The Oltari's voice carried a nervous edge.

"Is this about my earlier request, Pin? Was I correct?"

"You were," Pin said. *"I will send the info to your personal comm. It will pop up when you re-establish a connection to the broader sat-link network."*

"What's this?" Lauden asked.

"Nothing, sir. We're past it already."

"I'll have Renina brought in ASAP," the director said. *"Hopefully we can hand her over at the rendezvous."*

"One mystery plant from another galaxy in exchange for a Darian specialist," Lilline said. "It's a deal."

"Are you sure you will be ok, T8?" Pin asked. *"Renina could turn on you or attempt an escape. She might be dangerous."*

"That's my business, Pin."

"Hoo!"

"What concerns me far more than Renina is getting to the *Racer*," Lilline said. "I estimate at least five to six hours lost covering the distance. I'll have to trek to the village, find a ride to Carna-Brai, then catch the next departing monorail to the space port. That may spell disaster for us, even with the Distortion Ring Drive."

"Not an issue," Madame X said.

"But it's too much time wasted on the front end," Lilline said. "The gate could open in twelve hours and—"

The cottage walls rattled. A pewter pot on the stove swayed and toppled over.

Lilline swung the leaded window open and peered up. A familiar sleek hull grew in scale as it descended. She shielded her face from hot gusts as it touched down in the meadow.

The roar of the *Racer's* cryex burners lessened and the nearby trees and grasses slowed their waving dance.

"New feature." Madame X said. *"AI pilot. First time I've tried it. Glad it worked and didn't crash or this whole thing would be a wash."*

So the Distortion Ring Drive is on the Racer...

"Next stop is the rendezvous off Quo, T8," Lauden said.

Lilline eyed the ship. *I do love this job.*

FIFTY-THREE

Orbit | Moon: Quo | Parent Planet: Missan-2 | Star System: Ci-Tan |
Inner Core

Lilline parked the Racer off Quo. The moon, in a close orbit to its parent planet, lay dead ahead in three-quarter shadow. She'd been there once on an op. A diplomatic assassination involving, ironically... poison.

She shifted a hip, adjusting her position in the bucket seat. Every part of her body was refreshed and full of energy. Two of the three hours in FTL were spent in the chamber and the machine had dissipated the lactic acid and healed the burst blood vessels from the glider crash, leaving her as good as new. She had to hand it to Madame X and the U-City crew. Their tech was in a league all its own.

"Let's hope you are too," she said, tapping the Distortion Ring control panel. The color-coded button system waited, hidden underneath a secret panel that had eluded her on the outbound run from Tavi-Prime to Elaris.

A mini-frigate dropped out of faster-than-light travel off the bow, blocking the view of Quo.

Lilline hit it with the *Racer's* scanner, pulling up the specs.

Three weeks out of the assembly line at the space docks off Kersi. She scrolled through to the registration.

"Well, well, well... it wouldn't be a proper mission without you showing up." She hit the throttle and maneuvered into position.

Eight minutes later she was lined up and down at the space bridge.

The pressurization indicator dinged and she spun the hatch's wheel.

"Hello, Gribb."

The Froo emerged from the tunnel.

"Nice ship," she said. "So new it doesn't have a scratch."

"Thank you, we're on its maiden voyage."

"I see you put all those credits we pay you to good use."

"Supplying last-minute equipment to those in need is a rare profession. But yes," he gurgled. "It's a beauty."

"Name?"

His cheek glands morphed from a reddish green to blue. "*Long Game.*"

Lilline nodded approval.

"I have some things from your head of Tech," he said.

She accepted the duffel bag, careful not to make contact.

"I threw in one or two extras that might be helpful."

"Oh yeah, like what?"

"Consider them a surprise."

"Can't wait." Gribb was the fixer you wanted. The field supplier you needed when desperate somewhere in the stars and about to save the galaxy from impending disaster. If he said she would need it, she was certain she would.

"Oh, and there's a bottle of '44 Gondau in there."

"Really?" That brightened her day. Not the penultimate vintage, that was the ultra-rare '42, but a pre-Roncheau '44 was top tier, a rare find. "What's that for?"

"You've made me a lot of credits last few cycles. Another client had a case of collectable wines pass through their hands... well, claws. Right place at the right time, I guess. Pop the cork after you get this done... whatever it is."

"I appreciate that, Gribb."

"Interesting one, that Oltari of yours..."

"You're not kidding," Lilline said. So Gribb and Pin had met. That must have been something. "Where's my passenger?"

As if summoned by her words, Renina rounded the corner escorted by a familiar face.

"Alex?"

"Hello again." The GAM-OPs asset smiled, leading the Rasp forward. "Oh, are those for me?"

"No!" Lilline yanked the flowers back. "Deadly," she said, making an apologetic face, "even to the touch." Carefully, she passed the long stems to Gribb.

"And to think I traveled all this way to see you." Alex pouted.

"I... what are you doing here?" Lilline nodded at Renina and motioned her to come on board.

Alex stepped forward next to Gribb. "I work for the same company as you, remember?"

"I know, I just... wasn't expecting, well... you."

"It's been an interesting ride," they said. "Gribb has been telling me *all* about you."

"Has he now?" Lilline eyed the Froo, who patted his feet.

"Lots of tales about your time together. I heard about how that Bukki tiger took your ear on Hesh-9."

"Well, seeing that you two are getting on, I'll be heading back," Gribb gurgled. "Don't dally." He held up a hand, green spotted fingers clasping the wrapping around the swordblade's stems. "Time is of the essence, yes?"

"Thanks, Gribb." Lilline eyed Renina. "You can go up to the main floor. I will be right there."

"How long to our destination?" the curator asked, heading to the ladder.

"I have no idea," Lilline said, eyes on Alex and smiling. She literally didn't. "But it's going to be interesting. And... dangerous." She winked at her colleague.

"So..." Alex took a step closer and touched a slender finger to her chest. "I am glad you managed to not fall out of the sky."

Their touch sent a spark of electricity through her chest. The urge to pull them in and—

Lilline's waist surged forward as Alex tugged her and kissed her.

Second time was a charm. The initial curiosity of their first time, of two mouths meeting and whether there would be an intimate connection, had given way to more important and stimulating secondary desires.

Supple, soft lips peeled away from her mouth.

Alex's sparkling eyes held her like a tractor beam.

"Good luck, secret agent." Alex slid a hand down her arm before walking around the corner.

Lilline fell into the ship's wall, legs like jelly.

Libidinous energy surged through her veins. Impulsively, she lunged for the hatch and leaned out and into the tunnel. "Tease!"

Alex, their slender and lithe figure gliding back to Gribb's ship, didn't flinch. A moment later they were through the *Long Game's* portal and out of sight.

***

"Ground rules." Lilline pointed to the sofa in the *Racer's* work area.

Renina sat, a puppy dog look in her eye. Lilline guessed that someone at HQ, maybe Lauden himself, had worked her over good before cutting a deal.

"You do what I say, when I say, without questioning me. Understood?"

The Rasp's clay-skinned head bobbed up and down.

"You so much as twitch the wrong way and you'll rue the day you chose to get involved with all of this."

Renina's one eye went wide.

"I don't know what your part is in this, *Renina*, but I will find out before the end." Little did the Rasp know that she already knew her big lie. Pin's query, based on a small piece of evidence overheard with the surveillance statue at the auction, had paid big dividends. The report the Oltari sent after their call at the cottage proved her instincts were sharp as a knife. Renina was living under a false identity. What's more, her stake in this ruse wasn't professional. It was personal. And tragic.

Lilline was like a card shark with an ace up her sleeve. It was just a matter of where and when she'd make the switch to ensure a winning hand.

"For now, consider yourself lucky," Lilline said. "You help me with whatever I need to get this done and I might sweeten whatever deal you managed to cut. Got it?" Lilline leaned in and gave her the "don't fuck with me" stare.

"I understand."

"Good. Now, sit there." She pointed at a jump seat behind the cockpit. "And strap in because things are about to get interesting."

"What do you mean?" Renina made her way to the chair and buckled up.

"You wouldn't believe me if I told you."

Lilline strapped into the pilot's seat. She steered the *Racer* away from Quo and into the coordinate lane Madame X provided.

"We're about to make scientific history," she said. "But it will never make it into the official records."

Lilline hit the green button.

Stretched? That was putting it mildly...

———

Time?

Gone.

Space?

Lilline wasn't sure. It was like her body had turned to wet paint. Any movement she made left a wake of skin and interior flesh and bones like a paintbrush across an invisible canvas.

She checked on Renina. The rotation took a lifetime but felt like an instant. The Rasp was a blur. In fact, everything around her was out of focus.

Zoooooop!

And then it wasn't.

She was whole again. And breathing. Her body had mass.

"Renina?"

Blah!

Vomit splattered from the Rasp's throat flap. A chunky mess like an abstract painting streaked the floor.

Understandable. The distortion jump took the award for most far-out bodily experience. How long it had lasted, she had no idea. Lilline lifted her eyes to the ship's clock.

Three hours and thirty-eight minutes.

What had she done during all that time?

"You alright?" she asked, swinging around.

Renina nodded and wiped her throat flap.

"Good. Stay strapped in. You can clean that up when we are down." A tragic sight back at the coffee table stabbed her like a knife through the heart. Red liquid saturated the duffel's fabric, as if a someone had stuffed a bleeding corpse inside and zipped it up.

My '44 Gondau...

"What's the matter?" Renina asked.

"Keep quiet." Lilline eyed the Rasp, releasing her frustration at the oenephelic tragedy through a burning gaze.

Out the cockpit window lay nothing but distant stars. Lilline activated the dashboard holo-screen and pulled up the star grid. Before going into the resting chamber, she'd updated the Racer's computer with Nova's chart images of Arm 5.

Following the virtual yellow arrows directing her to port, she fired the burners.

A bone white planet broke the edge of the cockpit window. It loomed large. Like a knife plunged into its surface, a chasm ran along the equator... massive to be visible from space.

"Where are we?" Renina asked.

Lilline hit the burners and barreled towards the planet.

"Moz."

FIFTY-FOUR

"This sand is like needles!"

Lilline nodded and double-checked the *Racer's* exhaust shields. She adjusted her goggles and braced herself against the hull as a gust pelted her exposed skin with grains of sand.

Under the night sky, the desert's barrage was a counterpoint to the silent stellar blanket. Moz's moon, rosy and full, hovered near the horizon. Across an empty expanse of white dunes, cool lunar light dappled the crests like an ocean at night.

"Let's go!" Lilline shouted and pointed east.

She'd spotted a crude switchback two-thirds of the way along the chasm during their descent. The landing had been rough in the high winds. During the worst of it, Renina's usual clay complexion had gone a dusty gray. Luckily, the curator had avoided a second round of vomiting. The look in her eye when they exited the *Racer* made clear the Rasp was coming to terms with the sobering reality of her deal. Being sent to the farthest edge of the galaxy might sound exciting from a hard steel chair in an interrogation room, but when you got down to it, adventure was a two-sided coin.

Lilline, fighting the gusts, motioned for the Rasp to follow.

Welcome to my world.

And what a world it was. How long had this planet stood in silent isolation? A scan of the immediate area with the ship's advanced computer system yielded nothing organic. That boded well for their trek, but beyond that what lay further on was unknown.

"Look!" Renina pointed ahead.

Lilline shielded her goggles with a hand. Nearer to the ledge, an object peeked over a dune's rise.

"I think it's a ship!"

Lilline nodded and made for it, careful to cut a path that kept them out of view.

Ten minutes later they were prone, one rise back, and peering over the edge. Lilline pulled out her zoomnoculars and targeted the craft.

An independent charter by the looks of it, not unlike the ice runners she'd encountered in shadier parts of the Outer Rim. A finger rotated the zoomnocular's dial, toggling to the IR wavelength. Mild traces of heat glowed from the ship's twin burners. Mirna, and whoever else was with her, had a head start but no more than a few hours.

Thank the stars for Gribb. His goodie bag had included a few surprise items, and the zoomnoculars was the first to prove useful.

"Let's go." Lilline pointed to a boulder she'd marked along the chasm. They made for it, giving the ship a wide berth.

Five minutes later the lip of the chasm loomed. She stepped closer and the full scale of the narrow and gaping slice in the planet's surface hit home. Raging wind at her back, a sublime sense of awe at the canyon's scale gave her pause. As if through some out of body experience, her mind rose into the sky and she looked down on two small specks in an endless white void of blowing desert sand.

"Are we going down there?" Renina said, her long thin neck arcing over the edge.

"Follow me. Down these steps." Lilline motioned to the set of crude rock stairs cut into the white stone. She descended to the first turn and yanked off her goggles and headwrap. Stillness was a welcome change from Moz's tempestuous surface. She bent her head and gazed up. Dusty streams of white passed overhead, creating a strange and haunting song that bounced through the canyon.

"That's better," she said.

Renina followed suit, unwrapping and removing her monocular goggle. "Do you see that?" The Rasp pointed below.

Lilline checked through the zoomnoculars. "It's a body... a Coleopterian."

"Coleopterian?"

"Yes, quite rare but some of the best pilots in the galaxy."

"Is it dead?"

"Definitely." A splattering of multi-colored liquid surrounded the insect-like species' smashed carapace. Lilline peered up at the ledge and then back down to the canyon floor. Her fingers made an arc through the air from the lip of the chasm to the corpse.

"You think it fell?"

Lilline shook her head.

"Oh..." Renina covered her throat flap with a hand.

As I said, welcome to my world. Her best guess was Mirna needed to get here, but after that? Either she would make her own way out, or have help from someone... stars forbid, the Darians.

"We need to get moving." Lilline targeted the Coleopterian with the nocs. She switched to hyper-magnification and made a sweep around the corpse.

Nothing.

"Which way do we go at the bottom?" Renina asked.

Lilline repositioned the 'nocs to where the switchback steps hit the sandy canyon floor.

Hello.

Human tracks. She followed them through as they passed wide of the Coleopterian and vanished out of sight.

"East," Lilline said, putting away the 'nocs. "You first, Renina." She gestured for the Rasp to go ahead. *I don't need you pushing me off the edge.*

Fifteen minutes later, they were at the bottom and making their way east. The Coleopterian was a mess of a sight. Lilline had given it no more than a passing glance. Renina, on the other hand, had gasped and muttered something incoherent.

Whether or not it was an act or genuine... was another matter. The vomiting when they dropped out of the Distortion Ring run was authentic, for sure. But all of this? Her eyes narrowed.

We shall see soon enough.

Ten minutes in silence following Mirna's tracks and Lilline could wait no longer.

"How much do you know about what we are doing here, Renina?"

"I know that there's a ruin, and I need to help us get inside."

"And?"

"And the *Cosmic Widow,* and someone... I assume the thief, will be there."

Right...

"A bit different from your home planet of Ornal, isn't it?"

Silence.

"You're quite the galactic traveler now."

"Yes," the Rasp said. "I've come a long way, for sure."

"Do you know why she is doing this?" Lilline asked.

"I don't even know who 'she' is... I assume you mean the thief?"

"That's right."

Renina halted.

Lilline's hand moved close to her blaster holster.

The curator's ball-size head went up, gazing at the starry night far above.

Lilline waited, the eerie whine of Moz's winds singing in haunting suspense.

"No," the Rasp said and started off again.

Lilline shifted the pack on her back. The butt of the second blaster she carried dug into her side.

She had a decision to make. It was going to—

"There's stairs ahead," Renina said.

Lilline peered over the Rasp's shoulder. At the chasm's eastern wall, carved dead center in the living rock, a narrow staircase rose. Sheer cliff faces climbed in tiered geometric levels eventually ending where the organic rock of the canyon continued to the surface.

"Here." Lilline handed her a version of the lines from the star chart.

"What is this?"

"A translation of Azaludarian's star chart."

The Rasp's small head rotated, twisting her snake-like neck. "Seriously?"

"Seriously. The last two lines. Read them and figure it out."

The curator spoke the words aloud.

> *"'Walk the equatorial chasm on the second planet and*
> *see with eyes of night.*
> *Between glimmering peaks lies the Temple door.'"*

Lilline examined the facade, coming up with nothing.

"It's there." Renina indicated an area of crude stone and rubble to the left side of the canyon.

"But the stairs are there?" Lilline pointed, stepping next to her.

"Yes, however you aren't considering the glimmering peaks." The Rasp gestured that she should look overhead. A dry and scaly finger traced an imaginary pair of pointed mountains, following a pattern of stars forming a constellation. Lilline followed the digit as the Rasp lowered it dead center between the two triangles to the canyon floor.

"Between the glimmering peaks," she said.

That's why I needed you here. Her belly tightened. *It should have been Nova.*

"Darians have a different way of speaking and thinking," Renina said. "It carries over into their designs. I'm sure if we inspect that area, we'll locate the entrance."

"Well get going then." Lilline shoved her forward.

Make yourself useful.

FIFTY-FIVE

Renina was right. There was a door. What's more, by the fresh footprints in the sand, it had been opened.

Lilline ran a hand over its surface, gazing at her reflection in the onyx glass. "What is this material?"

"I'm not sure."

The Rasp's head appeared in her peripheral vision. The curator placed three fingers and palm on the surface. "Do you feel that?"

"I do." Although it appeared smooth, the surface felt course and rough to the touch.

"It's like an illusion," Renina said.

After everything Lilline had witnessed at U-City and the Star Pool, something told her this was more about perceptual differences, or limits, than sleight of hand.

"Here." She reached into a pocket and handed Renina a note. "Can you open it?"

The Rasp read through the verses. "This is amazing," she whispered. "Who translated this?"

"Don't worry about it."

The curator's large eye softened, tinged with pathos.

Lilline, in spy mode, on the job with the clock ticking, paid it no mind.

She was sure the emotion was genuine, but feeling sorry for her despite what she now knew about her past wasn't going to affect her. She had one goal and one goal only.

Renina was a means to an end. No more.

"'Place the pendant on the chain of time,'" the Rasp said, repeating the line as she read it.

"Something's happening," Lilline pointed at the surface. "Look," Green tinges undulated like a reflection.

Both she and Renina turned.

"It's starting," Lilline said.

"What is?"

High above, a greenish ring like an electrified aurora brewed in the night sky.

"What is that?"

"You don't want to know." Lilline swung the curator back around. "Think, Renina. Get this door open now or nothing else is going to matter."

"Okay, okay..." The Rasp's eye went from the verse to the portal. "Time for Darians would be stars... it must be something with the sky." She pointed to the strange phenomenon reflected on the surface. Around it, circulated the night's constellations. "They track across the surface as the planet spins in orbit."

"And the chain and pendant?" Lilline checked on the growing greenish ring. *I've got a bad feeling about this.*

The Rasp stared at the portal.

"Think, Renina!"

"Back off!" The curator pointed a finger. "You're suffocating—"

Her snake-like neck danced to and fro and a tongue emerged.

"What?"

"Pendant. Chain... your neck." She stepped back and examined the ground. "I think..."

"What are you doing?"

"Look around! Search for something like a piece of jewelry…"

"Are you serious?" Lilline brushed her foot back and forth, moving it in a search pattern.

"There's a famous pendant from the First Galactic. It was stolen about thirty cycles ago. It's known as the Darian Choker."

"And why would it be—" Gold like the clock at the museum glinted in the sand.

"That's it!" Renina snatched it up. "This," she said, displaying the dangling teardrop, 'is a priceless artifact. But look." She opened the clasp.

Lilline gestured. "It's empty."

"Yes, I know that." The Rasp shook her head. "Someone used it already to get in."

They stared at each other.

"You can't be serious?" Lilline said.

Renina pushed on the portal.

Lilline took in a grand atrium radiating in an ancient splendor.

"I think we found the Temple of Moz," Renina said.

If it was only this easy all the time.

FIFTY-SIX

Any expectation Lilline had of a snarky remark from Renina vanished as soon as she stepped inside. The curator stood by her side, awestruck.

"Astounding," Renina said. "I can't... we're in the lost temple."

Lilline pushed down her rising wonder. She scanned ahead for any indication of Mirna's presence, the *Cosmic Widow*, or a device capable of triggering the wormhole.

"Do you realize the magnitude of this discovery?" Renina said.

Lilline grabbed the curator's arm and pulled her forward. "I do, but right now if we don't keep moving you can kiss it all goodbye."

"What is happening?"

Lilline pulled her on in earnest.

"You're not going to tell me?"

She ignored her, scanning their surroundings. A three-story interior, akin to a basilica and cast in gold and black exuded grandeur and majesty defying description. It took all her willpower not to be swept away by the marvel of an ancient past.

"Those lights," Renina said, pointing at ornate sconces on the columns and walls. "They're like insects dancing inside of—"

She yanked her, hustling them through the entrance hall.

"I think they're molecular."

Lilline allowed herself a glance. *Atomic, maybe?* This place wouldn't stay lit for thousands of cycles unless the magnitude of energy was... she caught herself. *You can't explain something not from our universe with the limits of our universe.*

"All this should be documented." Renina was like a child at their first carnival.

"There," Lilline said. "You see that?" She pointed at an open archway beyond a set of magnificent altars. "Stay quiet."

Like time bandits sneaking through a lost age, silent footsteps passed by treasures without disturbing their infinite rest.

Lilline peered into the second room. In keeping with the entrance hall, it was devoid of any living presence.

"I know that object," Renina whispered, crossing the chamber to a second portal.

Lilline followed, navigating around a circular pool oddly off-center, decorated with a beautiful gold trim. In the blue glow of the Darian lights, the artifact grew legible. "It's a Rhyton."

"Not just any Rhyton," Renina said. "*The* Darian Rhyton... from the excavation at Pios. This is in all the art books. I've never seen it in person. Almost no one has. It's been in a private collection since its discovery."

And I know whose collection.

What's more, a secondary puzzle was coming together and she didn't like its solution. The uneasy feeling it triggered pulled her back to a more vernacular and personal crisis. Granny had mentioned the Rhyton in Mirna's presence. At Malardi's, in fact. Rambling about recognizing it and all the other objects that her mother had talked about over the cycles.

"What's the matter?"

"Huh?" Lilline snapped back.

"You look like you saw a ghost."

"I'm fine." She pushed on the portal but it didn't budge. So much for the easy way. "So now what?"

Renina pulled out the translation.

"'Fill the sacred chamber with finger tight.
Let gravity flow.'"

"'Let gravity flow...'" the Rasp repeated. "Easy, the sacred chamber is the Rhyton. It's used to pour ceremonial liquid, and to purify it."

Lilline took it from the sconce.

"Careful!"

She eyed Renina.

"Sorry," the Rasp held up a hand. "It's more valuable than... well, credits."

"Yes, it's priceless." Lilline went to the pool and filled it, plugging the bottom of the rhyton with a finger. "So is life as we know it in the galaxy."

She nodded at the ground below the sconce with her chin.

"Interesting." Renina bent down. "It's the same material as the portal outside."

An inlaid piece of Darian onyx glass, the size and shape of a large coin, lay directly under the mounting on the portal.

Lilline placed the Rhyton into the sconce, careful to keep it plugged.

"Ready?"

The Rasp nodded.

She removed her finger.

Water fell from the opening.

And vanished.

"Whoa," Renina said. "Where is it going?"

"Not sure but look at the portal."

The material danced with ripples as if water was dripping onto its surface.

Remember it's not an illusion...

Whatever spatial or dimensional event was unfolding had her and Renina mesmerized.

Lilline reached out a hand and pushed, half expecting it to plunge into the watery ripples. Fingertips hit the surface and the portal opened as silent as the night.

"Well done," the Rasp whispered.

Lilline peered down a long tunnel. At its far end, hints of a vast cavernous interior loomed. The view was only a sliver, but what lay in sight was alive with activity. Light and shadow danced across a far wall, and the pitter patter of metal hitting metal echoed down the corridor.

"We're in," Renina said.

Lilline eyed her.

Yes, Renina we are. And I think it's time...

"What now? It says something about following the words of Azaludarian."

"Listen," Lilline said, rummaging through her pack. "I want you to stay here while I go ahead."

"You're leaving me?"

"You ever use one of these?" She handed her the second blaster.

"I... uh...."

"I'll take that as a 'no'." She took it back. "Look, this is the safety." Her thumb flicked a switch back and forth, emitting audible clicks. "When there's no orange bar the safety is on and the blaster won't fire. You switch this off... now, see that orange line?"

The Rasp nodded.

"You are live. Pull the trigger and the weapon will fire. It's a heat round, Renina. That means it kills." She locked eyes with the Rasp. "Not a stun shot... a kill shot." She flipped the blaster around and handed it to her butt first.

"I understand." Three fingers clasped the weapon snugly.

"It's a Rasp-specific model. An H-42 Proton Blaster. I had my assistant at the agency pack it for you."

Renina had a funny look on her face.

"Hey." Lilline gave her a shake. "We good?"

The curator nodded.

"There's no time. I need to stop that thief before they do something more dangerous than you can imagine. I'm talking galaxy-altering threat level, Renina."

"They have the painting with them?"

"I think so, yes. And I am not sure what else. Stay put no matter what you hear. If anything goes wrong, and I don't come back, or someone else heads this way, defend yourself and get back to the ship. Use the AI nav-system to go exo like I showed you."

"I understand."

"If this works out, I will put in a good word for you when we are back."

"I'm really sorry for what I've done to—"

Lilline held up a hand. "No time and, frankly, I don't care." She turned her back on the Rasp and made for the tunnel. "Remember, if I don't return get out of here. Once you are clear of the atmosphere on the Racer, hit the call number that I showed—"

Click.

Lilline knew that sound better than anyone in the galaxy.

"Slowly," Renina's voice behind her was earnest. "Undo the belt and let the holster drop to the floor."

Lilline did as she was told. Pivoting, she confronted a blaster's barrel aimed at her face.

"Now you'll do as *I* say."

FIFTY-SEVEN

"Thank you for being useful." Renina motioned for her to take a step back. "Now that you've brought me here, I can finish this."

Lilline put her hands up. "That's what I am trying to do."

"You have no idea what this is about!"

"Actually, I do... *Felicia.*"

The Rasp's monobrow rose. "How did you..." She tightened her grip and aimed true. "You little—"

"You thought you had me fooled with the whole 'small planet Rasp in the big city' routine? I'll admit, I bought the sob story at the Blue Comet. But then you slipped up, *Felicia.*" Lilline smirked.

"You have guts and nerve, I'll give you that," the curator said. "A blaster pointed at your face and you mock me?"

You haven't seen anything yet.

"Anyway, I have no idea what you are talking about."

"Come now, *Felicia.* Allow me to walk you through it. First, you invite me to join you for a drink at the Royal Loha. Then, when I ordered my Skytini clear, rather than sunset, you acted surprised."

"So?"

"That's impressive knowledge of a specific and sophisticated cocktail. And then, you mentioned nuvola-noir. So much for the little country Rasp from Ornal on her first trip to Sky City. They don't make Skytinis anywhere else in the galaxy, and only the bar at the Royal Loha uses nuvola-noir."

"Maybe I had one before you arrived?"

"No, I had my associate check the receipts."

"You little—"

Clangs echoed up the tunnel.

"Put the blaster down," Lilline said, voice bold. "Let me do what I came here to do while there's still time."

"You know nothing about what I am here to do! All my life to get here... since I was fourteen."

"Yes," Lilline nodded. "Because the thief killed your younger sibling."

The Rasp's grip on the blaster faltered. "How did you..." The curator's one eye narrowed in malice. "I am going to kill her."

"It's a tragedy and for that I am sorry." She was, Mirna had stolen the Darian clock from Renina's family collection. During the break-in her younger sibling accidentally stumbled upon the crime. And Mirna eliminated witnesses. As Pin's inquiries revealed, the sibling had been knocked unconscious and given a dose of poison. Not the swordblade toxin, that hadn't been discovered yet, but another substance that was fast working. And plant-based to boot. Mirna had a penchant for letting organic toxins do her dirty work.

"He was only five cycles old." Tears welled along the bottom of the Rasp's eyelid.

"Yes, and one Felicia Blackwater, a wealthy child and heir to an invaluable collection of First and Second Galactic art, with multiple family estates and properties around the Inner Core, became Renina Blackstone."

"What of it?"

"My guess is you did that to ensure the thief, who you've spent cycles chasing down, would not put it together, especially if you were lucky enough through your art world connections, and internships with shady underworld dealers, to make contact. With one goal: revenge."

"My entire life... my education and career path, all for Binto." Renina wiped her eye on an elbow. "He was just a child."

Lilline nodded. No denying the tragedy of it, but Renina had chosen a series of forks in the road on her life of retribution that caused others harm... and death.

"And you had no morals about how to do it," Lilline said. "My agency has far-reaching eyes and ears. We hear and see all kinds of things. Like a Rasp and a Jenzara talking in a room full of artifacts."

"What?"

"Your summer estate on Quo sounds nice." Lilline cracked a snarky smile. "Some digging by my colleague brought the rest to light. Including your recent ploy to frame Reginald Bilarus. He was your insurance policy once things went south with Carmini."

"I could care less about the *Cosmic Widow* and the other stolen art," Renina said. "I was going to kill her that morning in the gallery. I used the special device he provided and did what I was told. I shut off the security when I left the previous night, like Carmini instructed me. But when I arrived early the next day intent on walking in on the crime, this 'she' as you call her, was already gone. And like a knife in my heart, what did she leave behind? The clock that she stole when she killed poor Binto."

"You didn't let her in to the museum?"

The Rasp shook her head. "She must have entered the previous day as a visitor and stayed overnight, out of sight and away from security patrols and scanners."

"So it would have appeared like you stumbled upon a crime and saved the day had she been there?"

"Very good. A two-for-one. Actually, a three-way deal. I get revenge, save the *Cosmic Widow*, and throw Carmini under the bus to boot. He had nothing on me other than a word-of-mouth agreement. But I had evidence that Bilarus was doing shady business with the Jenzara on the side. Once I gave that to metro police, any attempt by that red bastard to accuse me of being complicit would look like desperation."

Big risk. Messing with a strategic mastermind like a Jenzara...

"You had a lot of dancing to do after the *Cosmic Widow* vanished," Lilline said.

"Sure, his Zappers bullied me, thinking I was in on it with the thief who double-crossed them. But they quickly realized I had no reason to benefit, and so they pushed me, forced me through threats, to help try and locate it. I did that, using you."

Lilline nodded. "Well played. Find the painting and hopefully find the thief you so badly wanted. I imagine that if the *Cosmic Widow* never showed up again Bilarus would take all the heat and you step right in as head curator. Leaking its theft to the press... that was a nice touch."

"A little chaos can go a long way," Renina said.

So, it was you...

"I met with Carmini that day we had our Skytinis if you must know. Paid him for an artifact I planted in Bilarus's office. I had it all worked out... then your secret government cronies picked me up. So, I cut a deal and you led me right here." She gestured with her weapon as if conducting an orchestra. "Now, that I have my sibling's killer in my sights, I don't need you anymore. Frankly, you've been a thorn in my side since the beginning... *Caroline Liro*." Her one eye narrowed. "Who are you, really? Not Keely Larkin, that's for sure."

"Wouldn't you like to know?"

"No matter," Renina shrugged. "In the end, I knew enough to get here. Although I almost lost you after Sky City. Luckily, I remembered my buffoon of a boss rambling about a fellow student at university who knew everything and anything about Darian language and culture. He went on and on about how she'd walked out on her studies and joined some cult near Brinsk."

"Yes, well she's dead because of you." The memory of Nova bleeding out in her arms sparked anger and impatience.

"I figured that might be the case when your Gej-ti boss

demanded my help," Renina said. "How ironic... Carmini's failure turned out to be my success."

More activity down the tunnel. This time a deeper grinding as if a massive mechanism was being shifted.

Time was slipping by. This game had to end now.

There's nothing for it.

She stepped forward and bent down, a hand going for—

"Don't!" Renina aimed the weapon with renewed purpose. "I'm here to kill her but I can't have you coming back with me. I'm sorry. You need to be collateral damage. Don't worry. I'll return the painting and make sure your agency labels you a hero. Your gill-necked associate will hear all about how you stopped the thief from whatever is going on here but died saving it. I was an innocent bystander who helped you get inside."

"You have no idea what is happening here, Renina," Lilline said. "Give me that blaster!"

"Threats won't work on me. And your little agency will be hard pressed to hold me on anything when this is done. Not with the press screaming across the galaxy about the missing painting, unless you want everyone to know about... what is it? GAM-OPs. What does that stand for anyway?"

"Something you couldn't understand, it's above your intelligence level." *And you have no idea what GAM-OPs will do to keep a secret.* Lilline extended her hand towards her blaster.

"One millimeter closer and I will shoot."

"I don't think you will, Renina." Lilline kept her eye on the Rasp. "But maybe I'm wrong... in my line of work I don't have a choice when these types of situations arise."

"Please stop moving." The Rasp's voice was a whisper.

"I think you're bluffing. But if not, then I die. I am here to do one thing: stop that thief."

"Tell me her name! I want to know who she is!"

"Can't do that," Lilline said.

The holster was so close, but the time it would take to grab the weapon and draw it was a life's gamble. "It's funny isn't it, ironic even," Lilline said. "We both used each other to get here. But one thing separates us." Lilline's eyes narrowed. "Your actions got good people killed." *And a few bad ones as well.*

"Stop moving... please," The Rasp's voice was a whisper.

"You can wait here in a pair of electro-cuffs while I finish this," Lilline said. "Then, I'll take you back to serve your time for everything you've done. And for attempting to interfere with an agent."

"I'm the one with the blaster!"

Lilline reached for the holster.

The Rasp fired.

Lilline's hand froze centimeters from the handle.

Click. Click. Click.

Lilline locked eyes with Renina, an invisible laser of retribution burning into her. "Did you really think I'd give you a working blaster?"

Stunned, the curator examined the weapon.

"There is no Rasp-specific model, by the way. That's a five-credit child's toy." Gloating, she added, "Ages ten and up."

"You—"

Lilline drew her blaster and fired a stun shot.

Renina collapsed on the floor.

"That'll keep you quiet for a while." She grabbed her holster and turned to—

Crack!

Hard stone smacked her cheek. Through hazy vision, a shadowy figure loomed. Eyes blurry, Lilline made out a glimmering object swinging back and forth.

"Time is short," a familiar voice said.

She fought the dizziness and pain, head throbbing.

The view stretched and pulled.

No... I have to...

A blurry arm wound up and swung at her face.

Darkness took her.

FIFTY-EIGHT

Lilline woke to a blurry figure dressed in red. She squinted. The *Cosmic Widow*, still in its frame, sharpened into focus a few meters distant.

"I thought you might want a last look at it."

Mirna...

Head spinning, Lilline struggled to get her bearings.

On the far side of a pillared octagonal chamber sat the shadowy form of her captor. Eyes adjusting in the dim light of molecular sconces, she made out a banquet-style table and no other furniture. Not even chairs. Mirna had employed a large bag as a temporary seat.

Powerful in its splendor, the chamber maintained an air of mystery and reserve. Portals composed of the now familiar onyx glass lined its eight walls. Constellations, speaking in an unknown stellar language, covered the surfaces between black and gold panels that shimmered with other-worldy spatial illusions.

"How are you feeling?"

Lilline ignored the question, continuing her sweep of the interior. Each portal was at least five meters in height. Something about that didn't bode well. Were the Darians larger than common sentient galactic species?

Renina was nowhere in sight. Her best guess was the Rasp lay, paralyzed from the stun shot, somewhere back down the passage.

Lilline explored the back of her head, fingers locating a tender bump.

Hiss! Clang!

Flashing lights and odd sounds echoed from a larger tunnel to her right, sending streaks of pain through her throbbing skull.

She forced herself to a knee. Biting down to stay the pain, she managed to get into a seated position on the stone tiles. From there, she pushed herself up, swaying.

"Careful." Mirna, seated with her back to her, pointed up.

Lilline craned her neck and stumbled. A flashing geometric prism made of red metal hovered two meters overhead.

"I marked you with it. The device doesn't take kindly to you leaving the illuminated perimeter. It's a new security system. First chance to use it. No idea how it works, but if you move outside that circumference it does terrible things... burning things."

Lilline checked the tiles. A faint red circle ran roughly a meter around her.

"So," Mirna rose and approached, clasping her hands in front of her. "Of all the planets in all the star systems..."

"Hip all better?" Lilline said.

Mirna waved her off, dismissing the dig.

"I thought perhaps you injured yourself stealing that." Lilline pointed at the *Cosmic Widow*.

"Not a chance. It was almost too easy."

"How dare you poison my grandmother?" Lilline took a step toward—

Mirna pointed at the perimeter. "She'll be fine. It's a temporary sleep."

"She's dying, Mirna! She may already be dead."

"Oh, dear. I feared that might happen after you refused a Dari cake. That is too bad and was not my intention. Your grandmother likes those pastries too much for her own good." The woman shook her head. "One of them was for you."

"She ate them all." Lilline's words were like fire.

"I only wanted to temporarily disable you both."

"Well, I figured it all out. A mystery plant from your garden, of Darian origin and like swordblade, planted from seeds you found in an urn."

"You were at the cottage?"

"I was, and I found out everything."

"There is no cure for that toxin," Mirna said. "I am sorry."

"Why Mirna?" Lilline held out her hands.

The thief strode to a nearby column and leaned against it. "Because she would have gotten in my way. Your grandmother's memory is sharp as a tack, and you..." she raised an eyebrow, "because I needed my space to get this done."

Lilline's eyes went to the *Cosmic Widow* and back to the thief.

"Oh yes, quite the family legacy. Two government agents."

She knows about GAM-OPs?

"All your grandmother's long absences when Analine and I were friends, and then after her death, leaving you for months at a time at some bizarre school on Hesh-9. Strange excuses, always dashing off somewhere at the oddest hours. Once I witnessed her put some drunk Kreelis at a pub in their place. The clues were all there, plain to see. But more than that, I confirmed it after my former teacher was caught."

"Former teacher?"

"The Undertaker."

The famous jewel thief. A grave robber turned master pilferer who stole more precious gems and jewelry than any other criminal in galactic history. And, with a unique calling card: a sprinkling of dirt and a flower.

Granny had finally nabbed him after over a ten-cycle of other T# agents and galactic police forces failing to apprehend him. Geroli

Silk, a Froo with a tiny white mustache, spent his remaining days inside a maximum-security prison on the Isle of Blackill, isolated on the inhospitable and stormy planet of Mobar. That accomplishment had garnered Kissy the first of several personal audiences with the Galactic Minister.

"Considering your line of work, and the fact that you remain single... as your grandmother loves to bring up," Mirna said, "something told me there might be a passing of the torch. When I came to take this," she pointed at the *Cosmic Widow*, "I wanted to be sure and visit both of you. Our conversation at Malardi's made clear you had been at the museum that morning, and my suspicions were confirmed."

Lilline's eyes narrowed, but she remained silent. *Mirna knew about Granny all those cycles?*

"When Imani... I know that isn't your grandmother's name... asked about the artifacts I was donating, going on about remembering each one with vivid clarity and detail, I had to make sure she didn't start snooping or worse, get asked to provide information about the case based on her previous assignment. The last thing I needed was her putting together something from one of the Darian excavations, or stars forbid, one of the pieces I'd stolen that she or your mother had seen at some point and getting it in her head that there was a connection with me and the museum thefts."

"And me?"

"Obvious." Mirna held out both arms. "I needed you out of the way for the same reasons, but more so because I knew you were assigned the case."

"You played a pathetic sob story to my grandmother," Lilline said. "She bought into all of it. You should be ashamed."

"Yes, well. Some things must take precedence. It took me three cycles, and many thefts, to put this together. That wasn't the first time in the Galactic Museum, either. Although on my previous trip I decided to slip in and out without letting either of you know I was on Tavi-Prime."

"The Venex Horse..." Lilline's heart broke in two. "*You* took it."

Mirna held a hand up defensively. "I am sorry about that. It had to happen. Carmini demanded a trial run to establish trust after such a long hiatus. Otherwise, he wouldn't agree to a deal for me to steal the *Cosmic Widow*... which as you know I never intended to deliver. I assure you, I attempted to negotiate another object because I knew how much it meant to both of you, but he insisted. The fact was, that horse was close enough to the main gallery and had the added benefit of being one of the most valuable objects available, and so it fetched him a high price. A test run so the Jenzara was certain I could handle myself with the museum's new security upgrades."

"How dare you?" Lilline took a step but stopped. *I am going to kill you with my own two hands.*

"That job made me enough money to get by after Simuel passed and helped fund expenses for the rest of this." She gestured around her. "Apparently it came up on the market the day you and I crossed paths on Sky City."

"So, you hocked stolen First Galactic artifacts from the excavations with Simuel?"

"I needed credits to hire a pilot for the trip here. And I contributed twenty percent to Carmini's buy-in and loan to obtain the needed security hacking equipment. The pilot came in handy when I slipped away from you on Sky City. Lost you real easy on those bikes in the bowels." She smirked. "I did double duty that day. Took the star chart I so desperately needed, and certainly wasn't going to pay for, and contracted the Coleopterian. You cost me extra money with your interference. I had to find an alternative way off the city." She shook her head. "More palms to grease...."

"And then you killed your driver?" Lilline pointed in the direction of the temple's entrance and the chasm. "Pushed them off the cliff after you landed?"

"Loose ends." Mirna shrugged.

"Why are you doing this? You have no idea how powerful and dangerous the door is you are opening."

The thief strode back to the table and picked up the Darian clock.

The two hands neared a common point on the timepiece's dial.

"Simuel was never the same after we left Tavi." Mirna's eyes glazed with sorrow. "But his last few cycles... something changed. He grew more distant. Isolated. He lived in that office, day and night."

A fractured heart thudded in Lilline's chest. Half of it was broken for Granny, for her mother, for herself, and for the man Mirna married and what had been done to him. The other? Contempt and curdling rage for the woman who had taken out her so-called wrongs on bystanders, innocent or otherwise, setting off a chain reaction leading across the galaxy to Moz. Could she empathize with the sentiment of what happened to Simuel, and therefore her as well by association? To a degree, but like Renina, Mirna's road of retribution was carved by choice, not fate.

The thief strode forward, nearing the edge of the red perimeter. Like a storm rising, her eyes darkened. "He died in disgrace because of *them*." Through gritted teeth, her words forced their way out. "A broken shell of a man. Mocked and laughed at for his ideas. And, as it turns out, he was right."

The woman balled her fists.

"Tell me, Mirna. How did you find out?"

"That Simuel solved it?" Tragic and sorrowful features morphed into a hardened, vindictive criminal. "Being a professional thief, even a retired one, has its benefits. I'm craftier than all of you. The metro police, your Ministry agents... private security firms... none of you see what I see."

"See what?"

"I went through his notes, cleaning up after he passed. Simuel had his own secrets. And I found them."

Lilline edged close to the red light. It wouldn't help, but on instinct she placed every advantage possible into place should an opportunity arise.

"A hidden drawer in his desk. He must have had it custom made in Brinsk when we moved back. I almost missed it. Everything was there. A journal and supporting evidence. His work, proven, with all the necessary parts fitting in place. Including a date for a demonstration. It was then I knew that he was going to surprise me... surprise everyone... and then, my poor Simuel." She covered her mouth, holding back a sob. "Left me before his life's work came to light."

Lilline's mind was racing. Something wasn't adding up. If Simuel had finally worked out all the Darian interpretations, and located the chart by Azaludarian, why was he so morose and languid at the end? And why destroy it and seek out the copy by Henestra if he already knew the location?

"But you needed one thing," Lilline said.

"The star chart by Henestra so I could find the location. As fate would have it," Mirna said, "Simuel's notes mentioned a dealer."

"Carmini."

"And thus, our second recent meeting on Sky City. I eluded you with ease, of course."

"Yes, impressive. Trapeze Trelano using her talents."

Mirna nodded. "So began a quest that would take me across the galaxy, ending here." Her gaze went around the room, taking in the Darian wonders. "Oh, if my Simuel could have seen this."

"You were able to interpret the star language from his notes?"

Mirna swung around. "I'm not an idiot. I spent cycles at his side in the field. My knowledge is on par with most who study the Darians."

"If you were so determined to restore Simuel's reputation, why not contact the university? You didn't have to steal the painting and do all of this."

"You think they would take me seriously? I would be made as much of a fool as he. They would have stolen the scholarship and taken all the credit." She lunged forward to the perimeter's edge. "Fools!"

Mirna's word spit like venom, a reminder that her poison was working on its next victim in a hospital bed light years away on Tavi-Prime.

"Then why not the museum?" Lilline said. "Or the Ministry of Cultural Affairs? It would have been a glorious turn, and one that didn't require theft and death."

"Share it with Reginald Bilarus?" She scoffed. "Stealing the *Cosmic Widow* out from under his nose and leaving that bumbling idiot a message was far more satisfying."

"Time is short." Lilline said.

"And it is for you, too... for all of us."

"I hate to ruin your victim routine, Mirna, but your criminal resume extends back far before any of this started. You cast this as justified revenge but you're a longtime thief... and a killer."

Mirna walked back to the column and leaned on it, folding her arms. "What of it?"

"That Rasp back there, the one I hit with the stun shot, is the older sibling of someone you murdered... poisoned taking that clock." Lilline indicated the famous Darian timepiece on the table.

"Is she now?" Mirna raised an eyebrow. "Tragic, another unanticipated situation like your grandmother I did not intend to happen."

"Is that supposed to excuse you? A twisted victim of circumstance?" Lilline's insides boiled. She wanted action. Now *she* wanted revenge. "You are nothing more than a cold-hearted murderer, Mirna. You think the galaxy has wronged you? You have no concept of how your actions have destroyed the lives of others. And like you, driven them to evil acts of retribution."

"You know nothing about me or where I come from!"

"And this is your solution?" Lilline gestured to the tunnel leading to the massive chamber. "You're doing this for what?"

"For revenge!" Mirna's voice echoed in rage. "They deserve to be made a mockery! All of them!"

"And what then? Once you open that gate, to prove your point, you expect the Darians to come waltzing through with a peace offering?"

"Let them do what they wish." She waved a hand. "If that is to be our fate, so be it. I believe otherwise. Who is to say what our world would be if they had stayed all those cycles ago."

"Do you hear how mad this is?"

"There are wonders you could not fathom in the ruins." Her eyes burned with a new fire. "The beauty and advancement the Darians showed is..." She trailed off, lost in a distant memory.

"Haven't you figured it out?" Lilline said. "The Darians didn't mysteriously die out or vanish. They were driven out. The First Galactic fleet forced their retreat. Our ancestors hid the secrets of the *Cosmic Widow* for a reason. It was to protect us from a second invasion."

"You wield wild fear mongering to try and stay my hand. It will not work."

"I'm trying to save billions of lives. And more, everything... planets, worlds. All life as we know it."

"With what proof? Conjecture based on a logic? The problem is you, like all the others who Simuel studied with, fear anything that isn't fully rationalized and scientific. If it doesn't fit the available evidence, and your institutional bias, you either push it off the table or use it as fodder to bolster your age-old positions. You're as bad as those antiquated displays in the museum!"

"That's not true, Mirna. Professor Senjara, a colleague of Simuel's, respected his ability to speculate."

"There is knowledge out there," Mirna said, pointing in the direction of the tunnel, "and in the name of progress we need to give it entry. We are being held back by intellectual dogma. It killed my husband. If he had been taken seriously, and not shamed and mocked to the point of professional ruin..."

"You are letting grief and anger overshadow reason, Mirna."

"Think of the knowledge... of what might open to us. How can you deny an opportunity to commune with a culture, a species, so ideal and advanced compared to our own? It's like the Gods descending to our plane..."

That sounded like madness, but Lilline had to admit there could be truth to it. The problem was the evidence pointed to diabolic definitions of guidance and inspiration. These were dark lords intent on domination and destruction.

"From what we know, they want more than power," Lilline said. "They want to annihilate us, Mirna. Eradicate the entire galaxy."

"You think I care?" Her eyes glimmered with an uncanny, almost hollow delight. "There is no turning back for me now. I know that."

Their eyes met.

Shit. Lilline knew that look.

The thief walked to the table and opened a bag.

"The galaxy will learn the truth, no matter what lies behind the curtain," she said and removed a thermos.

"Mirna..." Lilline watched as she gulped down blue liquid, emptying the container of its contents.

"And I will join my Simuel." She held up a small holo-recorder and tapped it. A tiny version of the thief, recorded at the cottage in Simuel's office, introduced herself and went on about his work and who was to be given credit.

Lilline had been in tough spots before, but this? A criminal intent on self-sacrifice holding the keys to a portal to immense and unknown danger. Without any concern for consequence, only retribution and the smug satisfaction of getting their wish, it left no room for negotiation or counter-threats.

Only one option remained: get out of her constraints and stop Mirna.

The thief checked the Darian clock. It spun on its chain, clasped in the woman's fingers, the two hands about to meet.

"It is time. Azaludarian is arriving."

Azaludarian?

"Oh, I see." Mirna's face lit up with new life. "I take it by your expression that you didn't know?" She opened her bag and removed a larger container, pouring a second helping into the thermos.

"Because I am a compassionate person, I will leave you a healthy serving."

Mirna knelt, placing the poison down out of reach.

"No idea what will happen from here. But if you find yourself alone after all this ends, and the perimeter fails, the darkness and silence may prove too much for you. There is always an escape."

"You have no idea how much I can take."

"Who are you really?" Mirna's eyes swirled in the blue glow of the cavern's lights.

Lilline held her stare and pushed back.

"Unmask yourself. Or, will you deny me your secret?"

Lilline wanted to tear her to shreds. As much as her focus needed to be stopping her from opening the gate, the drive to violently end Mirna's life consumed her.

You want to know? You got it.

"I'm Agent Lilline Renault, granddaughter of Agent Kissy Renault, of GAM-OPs... Galactic Agency Maintaining Order Peace and Security."

"Kissy?" Mirna chortled. "Quite a name. I think I prefer Imani."

"We stop the likes of you all the time. She took down your teacher and I will take you down."

"Not from inside there you won't." Mirna pointed at the perimeter. "It's good to be honest with one another. Confession before death is cathartic, or so I've read. I feel better having talked openly, don't you?"

"I have no intention of dying."

"You will, Agent Renault... you will."

FIFTY-NINE

No comm signal.

Less than a meter of space to move about.

And T5 was still hours out from Moz.

It's over.

One woman's personal revenge would start a galactic war... or worse. Would this end in the enslavement of billions across the stars? Who knew what lay in store if the Darians broke through.

I'm going to die here, in this circle, while she carries out an arcane ritual within earshot.

Mirna... so much anger and resentment. Her old family friend hadn't revealed the details of her childhood or the cycles leading up to and through her acrobatics career. It was clear that life had been difficult prior to meeting Simuel. Even her tutelage with the Undertaker had ended poorly, thanks to Kissy's hard work.

To think that the woman they had known as a mild mannered and gentle soul had been living a double life. Everything about this mission had been distorted, reversed as if in a mirror's reflection.

Like Nova had said at the end.

And yet, something would not rest inside of her. It rose during the rhetorical sparring match with Mirna. And lingered still.

She shut her eyes, calling back their conversation.

The star chart. Something about that part of the narrative didn't fit snugly.

Think...

Lilline traveled back to the cottage, rifling through Simuel's notes in his office.

The tome with the work of V.L. Lumsden. The catalog of Darian discoveries. The cosmic points.

Her fingers flipped through the pages of his journal. And found what she sought:

A turn of events. I have made a disturbing discovery... As a result, the star chart has been destroyed. Only the copy by Henestra remains. I must find it... More time is needed to fully grasp the implications, but the Darians... stars. It can't be... I must consider how, what, and when... and, though I loathe to say it, "if."

Her mind spoke in internal debate:

Why would Mirna need the chart if Simuel had figured out the location of Moz?

Because he destroyed the original...

Why would he do that? And why would he seek to locate the copy by Henestra?

To make sure no one else had access to it. Because that way he ensured he would be the only one to be credited for the discovery.

Something flickered. A distant light.

It vanished back into the darkness.

Find stillness. Forget the past. Forget the future. Only the now.

The cycles rolled away. The memory of standing at the water's edge in the monastery's gardens returned as a vivid mental reality.

With it, and the water's reflection, rose tranquility.

He already had all the answers. He was waiting for the alignment date to prove it.

Nova and the star pool overlapped the setting, the starry night on still water adding a cosmic layer to the vision.

Reflections... reverse your perception and thinking.

It dawned like the morning sun over Moz's white sands.

He wasn't waiting to prove it.

The water's surface and the starry reflection shattered in her mind.

Simuel knew. Stars, he knew what would happen and he kept it secret!

"Where is she?"

Lilline jumped, arms in a fighting position and opened her eyes.

Renina stood, wielding her fully working GAM-OPs H-42 Proton Blaster.

"Stars, it's you," Lilline said. "Get me out of here."

"What is that?" Renina still wobbly from the stun shot, pointed at the thermos.

For a moment, she hesitated. *No. Not the answer. You aren't a murderer, plus it's too slow acting. And you might need her.* "It's poison. From a Darian flower that Mirna planted. She used it to try and kill my grandmother and me."

"Poison?"

"She may still succeed, Renina. My grandmother is at death's door."

"You said her name is Mirna?"

"Yes, Mirna Grochevsky. Formerly Mirna Trenato."

"As in Simuel Grochevsky? The retired art historian and archae-ologist?"

"The same. And what's more he knew, Renina. He knew what the danger was. He hid away the means to open the gate because it spelled disaster in the wrong hands. Mirna found it. She is doing this for spite and revenge."

"What?"

"I don't have time to explain. But the Darians left. They didn't mysteriously vanish. Opening this gate will let them back in. It's a wormhole, and not the first. If it happens, it could spell our doom."

"Our?"

"The entire galaxy, Renina."

"How do you know this?"

"It took a group of minds and a great deal of evidence. And luck, but it is true beyond a reasonable doubt."

Renina stood, stunned. "The Darians are not from here... yes, that makes sense."

"This is an alignment," Lilline said. "A link between galaxies. It is opening and we must stop it. Mirna is going to use the *Cosmic Widow*... I don't know how, and as crazy as it sounds, meet with Azaludarian to—"

"Azaludarian?"

There was so much to explain, and half of it she didn't understand herself.

"Listen," Lilline said, "I am being honest with you. I need you to get me out of here. If we don't work together to stop her the Darians are going to come through a wormhole. Remember that greenish glow in the sky above the Temple? If she triggers this thing and it forms a link, you can say goodbye..." She stepped close to the red light. "*To everything*, Renina. I need you to get me out of here."

"Mirna... so she was Mirna Trenato when she killed Binto." The Rasp appeared to be light years away.

"Hey," Lilline said. "I need to get in there and stop her."

Renina made for the tunnel.

"Renina! There is nothing to go back to if she isn't stopped!"

"I have nothing to go back to!" The Rasp's snake-like throat vibrated, emitting a strange flapping sound. She spun around. "What waits for me if I go back? Life in prison?"

"Don't you have family, loved ones you care for?"

"They're all dead."

This was worse than Mirna.

"Think of what you are saying, Renina. Look, I get it. My mother was murdered. My father too. Together. I've spent my life dedicated to stopping others who try and do harm, but not only for *me*. For everyone."

The Rasp's head spun to the tunnel.

"You can't bring your sibling back," Lilline said. "I am saying this as a daughter and not an agent. From one victim to another."

Renina's one eye met her two. "I want immunity. From everything."

"I can't promise you that. It's not right of me and you know it." Lilline raised her chin, defiant. "You need to take responsibility for your actions, but I assure you," Lilline placed a hand on her chest, "as I said earlier, if you aid me, I promise to speak on your behalf."

Renina's head went to the tunnel and back to her. She raised the blaster.

Lilline found herself staring down the barrel of her GAM-OPs issued weapon.

"You do realize who I am, right? My director is on a first name basis with the Galactic Minister. I know the GM. Trust me; it *will* make a difference."

Renina's hand with the blaster lowered. "I want the clock. If it isn't destroyed."

"Absolutely. It's yours."

"And she dies."

"On that you and I are in full agreement."

Renina's clay-skinned chin rose and she examined the device on the ceiling. "How do I disable this?"

Thank the stars. Lilline had a solution at the ready. "Break one of the portals with the butt of the blaster." She pointed at the nearest onyx surface. "Bring the biggest shard you can here."

Renina hastened to the closest portal, smashed the glass, and returned with a chunk the size of a small suitcase.

"Lay it flat. Then, slide it over a portion of the ring of light."

"What will it do?" Renina pushed the black shard closer to the red illumination.

"Hopefully bounce the shielding rays in another direction."

The Rasp's three-fingers nudged the glass to the edge. "Ready?"

Lilline nodded.

Renina brought it up and the reflected beam rose, giving her room to crouch.

"Is that enough space?" the Rasp asked. "I think it's too small for you to get through."

"Hold it just like that."

Time to thread the needle. Lilline got into a fetal position, and like a snake uncoiling, extended her arms through the opening.

"It's working," Renina said. "But it's getting heavy."

"Hold it no matter what..." Lilline reached the point where her shoulders passed through. She scraped over the tiles edging her way out.

"I can't hold it much longer."

"You have to, or I die."

With her head and torso out, she took an arm and helped hold the shard up. "Better?"

The Rasp nodded.

"Your hips..."

"Not you too," Lilline said. "My grandmother says they are too wide and make me look..." She exhaled, removing the air from her lungs. Using a breathing technique that she had learned at the monastery, she contracted her pelvis and groin, tucking and pulling everything inward at her body center.

"How are you doing that?"

"I need you to hold it on your own so I can pull myself through."

A drop of sweat from the Rasp's monobrow landed on the tile in front of her eyes.

"Here we go," Lilline said.

She reached both arms forward, palms flat. With one motion, heart pounding from lack of oxygen, she pulled.

Smash!

Renina fell back, narrowly avoiding the red beam as the onyx glass shattered.

Lilline gasped, filling her lungs with precious oxygen. "You good?"

The Rasp nodded.

"That was close... too close." Lilline rose and grabbed the blaster off the floor and flipped through its settings. She dashed to her bag and pulled out a wrist-action blade with a cable extension and equipped it on her arm.

"What do we do now?" Renina asked.

Lilline winked as she walked past her heading for the passage to the main chamber.

"Save the galaxy, of course."

SIXTY

"You're too late, Agent Renault!"

Lilline reached an arm out, halting Renina.

From the tunnel's ornate archway, she and the Rasp had a commanding view of the Temple's main chamber.

Down a set of concentric stairs, Mirna was working feverishly on a circular stage. The thief darted about, appearing like an ant on a plate next to the scale of the surrounding architecture.

"Look!"

Lilline followed Renina's clay-skinned finger.

Streaks of blowing sand passed in the open air of a massive oculus. Moz's high atmosphere crackled with energy, alive and dancing in cosmic disturbance.

"Search the room," Lilline said. "Focus on the upper level and keep out of sight. Look for anything that can close that." She pointed at the oculus. "Got it?"

Renina nodded.

"Leave the rest to me." Lilline dashed down the stairs two at a time. If she could cover half the distance before Mirna reacted, her blaster would be within range for a kill shot.

Eyes like scanners, she swept the interior. Mirna stood, her body glittering in the light of a strange crystal. Atop an onyx pedestal, the glowing stone aligned with a rifle-like device interwoven with spiraling wheels and intricate dials. Lilline followed the barrel's trajectory: dead center on the *Cosmic Widow*. The painting, removed from its frame, sat snugly in a more elaborate version of the now familiar portals scattered throughout the temple.

"Mirna! No!" Lilline bounded down the steps.

None of it made sense, but what concerned her most lay beyond the painting. A majestic throne decorated with strange symbols stood like a monument to a lost empire.

Flash!

Lighting illuminated the chamber. Catastrophic thunder boomed.

Lilline lost her footing. Hip, elbow, and head smashed against the carved rock. Waves of pain shot through her body with each impact as she tumbled down the stairs.

Bam!

Her forearm slammed a stair's edge and she came to a halt. The rattling of her blaster sliding downward echoed in the thunder's wake.

Splayed out on her back, Moz's swirling green skies danced overhead. It was as if a cosmic god waited, ready to pry apart space and time with mighty hands.

She pushed herself up and shook off the pain.

One thing at a time.

She retrieved her blaster and launched down the remaining steps.

Mirna continued her preparations in earnest. The thief's eyes went from a note to a set of dials that aimed the rifle-like device at the painting. Leaning over, the woman picked up the Darian clock by its chain, examined it face, and adjusted the mechanism.

Inlaid channels on the stage came alive with blue light. Lilline focused on the crystal's radiance. Could the glowing object be the so-called "key"? A trigger to initiate the cosmic point on this side of the wormhole?

She crossed the halfway line of her descent. Her thumb flipped the blaster's high-power switch. She halted and took aim.

"You can't stop me!" Mirna shouted without turning from her work.

The indicator light along the barrel flashed green: kill shot range confirmed. No negotiations. No time for demands to stand down. Through her sights, Mirna's head lay dead center.

Lilline squeezed the trigger.

The red bolt shattered a meter from the target, a translucent bluish dome flashing once and vanishing.

Shit!

Renina dashed past on the upper level, head swiveling left and right as she searched for a way to close the oculus.

Lilline locked eyes with the Rasp who halted and gestured in frustration.

"Take a seat for the show," Mirna said and pulled a lever. "There's no going back now."

Lilline gasped as a beam shot from the crystal. It passed through the barrel mechanism to a precise point on the painting's surface. A hitherto dark star manifested, radiating. Even at her distance, it made for an ominous addition to the painting's enigmatic constellation.

Flash!

Lilline shielded her eyes as crimson light streaked from the stellar point.

Like a painter mixing colors on a palette, the star's fiery rays clashed with the sky's green light. Hues blended, sending golden beams shooting through the temple's interior.

Lilline dropped her blaster, awestruck, as a second sight usurped the painting's spectral fireworks.

A mass of molecular energy, like a swarm of flies, swirled on the throne.

Azaludarian...

She rushed closer, edging up to the boundary where the barrier had manifested. "Mirna! Listen to me. Simuel didn't want this!"

"You lie!" The thief's eyes were like fire.

"He knew, Mirna. He knew about all of it. Even the location... here on Moz!" Lilline pointed at the ground. "It's why he hid everything away and destroyed the chart!"

"You'll say anything now to stop me."

"Don't you understand? Simuel was a hero. What he did was noble. It took courage... and willpower. He knew how dangerous this would be. He was protecting all of us by sacrificing his reputation!"

Mirna swayed. She caught herself with a hand on the pedestal, blinking to focus. "He wouldn't. Not after what we went through. The humiliation. The mockery." She shook her head to stave off the coming swordshade sleep. "Not just in public. The letters we received at home..." The fire rekindled in her eyes. "*You* did this."

"You're falling victim to the very thing he was guarding," Lilline said. "Simuel was protecting us." The sight of a gleaming form materializing out of the molecular swarm made her eyes go wide. "Turn it off while there is still time!"

"Never!" Mirna grabbed her stomach and winced. "It's done."

This is madness! Lilline scanned the upper level. No sign of Renina. Had she fled?

Bam!

Sparks exploded around her. Lilline dove to protect herself.

"Renina, no!" She held up a hand.

The Rasp stood; the H-42 Proton Blaster aimed at Mirna.

"You killed my sibling!" the curator shouted.

Mirna was on her knees, retching.

Crack!

Green lightning flashed. A second round of thunder echoed over the planet.

All three gazed through the oculus. The sky above Moz had torn open. As if pulled by immense suction, an ever-narrowing tunnel stretched to infinity.

The ghost hole...

A blip disturbed its deepest reaches. Blue light shot forth, emerging like an electrified smoke ring. It passed over the planet and raced outward through the cosmos.

The innermost point, flaming with white light, widened in the night sky.

Exotic matter... it's pushing open the singularity.

Like a galactic window on the wall of space, a flat and translucent sheen interrupted the surrounding stars.

Lilline, stunned, stared at the cosmic phenomenon. The gate between worlds was a myth no longer.

Objects came into focus through the fracture in space and time.

A chill shot down her spine.

"It's just like the paintings... in the museum," Renina said.

A fleet of ships, beyond count, ran in formation back to infinity.

"You were right," the Rasp said. "They're here to conquer."

Or destroy us...

Lilline shook herself free of the spectacle's terror. She gripped Renina's arm, pulling her attention back planetward. "This shield is keeping us out," she said. "We have to find another way to stop this."

"There is no other way," Mirna said, eyes growing lazy. "It's done." The set of instructions fell from her hand. "The portal will open and the Darians will unlock the gate between worlds."

"She gets to die, like this?" Renina pointed at her sibling's killer.

"Forget her!" Lilline tugged the Rasp. "We need to find a way to shut off—"

Renina's eye went wide.

A shadowy reflection tinged the Rasp's wide pupil.

Azaludarian...

Lilline rotated, haunted by what would confront her eyes. A startling presence formed from the molecular storm. Humanoid, skinned in glimmering silver and red like a fish's scales, the entity stepped down from the throne.

Lilline gasped at the sight. The exposed areas of its body - neck and head, hands and feet - appeared anatomically similar to human variants but at almost two-times scale. Supple and blemish-free skin shifted in hue as if reacting to the light.

Lilline's eyes were pulled to its flawless features. It was as if the being was an idealized reflection of their lesser selves, a work of art rendered through a mirror of perfection.

A Darian...

"Stars..." Renina spoke the word with a terrifying slowness.

Mirna, kneeling and with a hand on the floor to balance herself, turned to the new arrival. "I greet you, Azaludarian," she said, slurring from the toxin flowing through her veins. "It was Mirna and Simuel Groschevsky who—"

The Darian's arm extended. Through some unseen force, Mirna slid across the floor to his feet. Palm open, he lowered his hand as if to silence an audience.

The woman screamed as the Darian summoned an invisible force, crushing her body into itself.

Lilline covered her ears. It didn't help. By some strange transmission, physical and emotional pain penetrated her core. She dropped to a knee, fighting to hold back the suffering. Renina's expression made clear she too, was experiencing the woman's death with vicarious intensity.

Azaludarian folded Mirna into crumpled layers like an accordion until she was no more than a neatly stacked pile of flattened flesh and bones.

A horror so vivid, a power so beyond comprehension... Lilline's mind was numb with shock.

This ability, this weapon, must be born in some greater dimension of time and space. The Darian had literally penetrated physical barriers and bent three-dimensions at will.

"None shall command us," he said. "It is we who command."

That voice... A strange and beautiful music seduced her ears. A chorus speaking in harmony through a single tone.

And the language. Lilline's poetic mind sensed the phrase's

artistry. Five syllables followed by a line of six, with tinges of esoteric literary devices like hyperbaton and diacope. Eloquent and direct. As if someone with mastery of Galactic Common had improved upon it through an arcane and secret linguistics.

The Darian strode across the stage. Shifting like a material shadow, his body traversed three-dimensions as if present here in a lesser form, submitting itself to an inferior world.

"I have waited an eternity, my love," Azaludarian said.

Lilline followed the Darian's gaze. No longer was the *Cosmic Widow* set in the portal. It had dematerialized, the entryway now transformed into a swirling spectral wall.

Without hesitation, the Darian stepped through and vanished.

The crystal's light dimmed. Lilline checked the channels on the floor - they were fading.

"Get back to the Racer!" She snatched up her blaster and dashed up onto the platform. Thankfully, as she suspected, the barrier had deactivated. "Use the AI pilot. Get up in the air and circle the temple."

The portal's sparkling surface dimmed.

Her hand grabbed the crystal.

"What are you doing?!" Renina shouted. "There's no way—"

"Leap of faith."

She sprung through the portal.

SIXTY-ONE

A hooded figure stood, observing a starry blanket. Red fabric billowed despite the silent night.

Lilline raised and aimed her blaster. The movement rolled like honey from a jar, the world around her bending in a slow-motion dance.

This scene... I'm in the painting. That meant the figure before her was

The lone observer rotated and lowered its hood.

"Mom?" Lilline reared back. A pulse of light emanated through the landscape as her foot landed. Like a wave crossing an empty cosmos, it rolled to infinity.

Analine had aged. Crow's feet at the corner of her eyes and the settling of her body frame suggested she was in her early sixties. Accurate, should she still be alive.

A red streak, like a ghost, passed over the woman's shoulder.

"I can't believe it's you," Analine said.

"I'm..." Lilline blinked and tried to focus. "Mom?"

"Of course. Who else would it be?" Her warm smile sent the

cycles rolling back. Comfort, love, and security returned as her lips stretched wide.

This can't be real.

Analine stepped closer.

Lilline found herself pulled to her eyes. They were as she remembered: bluish-gray, radiant, and glimmering with intelligence.

"My how you have grown." A hand reached out and caressed her cheek.

Warm, fleshy. *Real.*

"I don't understand," Lilline said.

"You will. We will have all the time we want. Together." Analine gestured at the crystal. "Give me that."

Lilline's fingers tightened around the orb.

Again, she caught sight of the red shadow.

"What is it?" her mother asked.

"There's something behind you."

Analine nodded. "The Darians are waiting. Come with me and unlock the gate."

"They're not to be trusted."

"The Darians need the crystal. That is all. Oh dear, it has been too long."

"How do you remember me? How can you know me if you're from..." Lilline wasn't sure how to finish the thought, or how to properly express it.

"The galaxy where I exist is more evolved than your own."

"Do I exist there, too?"

"Of course. You are everywhere. You exist in all of them."

"All of what?"

"The mirrors, of course."

Lilline followed the red shadow as it danced behind her mother.

"The crystal." Her mother raised her hand, palm open.

Strange emotions stirred in her belly, vying for dominance. "Why are the Darians so intent on returning to us?" she asked.

"Don't worry about that. The important thing is we will be together."

Lilline held up the crystal and examined it. In its blue radiance, a distorted version of her mother stretched and bent.

Something is off...

"What is this place?"

"The boundary. The place where worlds meet. What matters most awaits you on the other side." Analine gestured to her right. A world, not unlike the one Lilline knew, manifested. It was no holo-simulation, but a scene as physical and vivid as if she were back on Tavi-Prime. "Your lives have followed different courses in each mirror."

My lives? Lilline stared, hypnotized. She, her mother, and Granny strolled through a park not unlike the one near her Domus unit on Tavi-Prime.

Her grip on the blaster loosened.

"I can go there?"

"You already are there." Analine smiled.

Comforting waves, like a drug, relaxed her muscles.

"There are no limits when the four walls collapse," Analine said.

The red phantom neared and hovered. Its crimson shadow cast an eerie and intrusive light. Her mother's reflection flashed on the curving orb.

Lilline gripped it tighter. And then, her mind froze.

Analine stood before her, but what the crystal reflected...

Whatever limitations had distorted Azaludarian's appearance in the Temple, presenting him as a radiant avatar, were unveiled by the crystal inside the portal. Another like him, standing before her, was laid bare. Fierce and angular features with eyes like the Temple's onyx glass were set on a face both regal and terrifying.

The Cosmic Widow.

"You are strong for someone from a world so weak."

Analine's features transformed into the terrifying visage from the reflection. A Machiavellian queen, waiting for her Darian lover, revealed herself.

"Give me that." Unlike Azaludarian's voice, the queen's words slithered into her ears. Each syllable stung like a serpent's fangs releasing venom.

Lilline's heart sank, the illusion fractured. Trauma boiled over and a rush of sobering anger and rage flowed through her veins.

"Give me that," the Cosmic Widow repeated.

"No." Lilline drew her arm back like a bully refusing to return a stolen item.

Bam!

An impact like a concrete block slammed into her and plunged her backwards. How far the invisible force threw her, she didn't know. Writhing in pain, the sight of the queen standing defiant, arm extended in the same position Azaludarian had used to kill Mirna, sent a chill through her bones.

"I will not ask again." The Cosmic Widow strode forward. "Your entry here with the crystal has disrupted the gate. We are trapped. It must be taken to the Darian side." She pointed back in the opposite direction.

Lilline's eyes widened at the sight of her hand. *The double pollex.*

"The longer you wait, the more devastating our wrath will be."

Lilline shook off the pain and struggled to rise. Her body squeezed and stretched like taffy. When her vision cleared, a reflection on the undulating floor drew her eyes. She tracked its source overhead. A swirling mass of energy, not unlike the phenomenon over Moz, rotated in a strange multi-dimensional void.

Tiny whirlpools and other familiar galactic designs lay scattered and interconnected within the spiraling energy, as if the entire universe was held fast in a glowing cosmic soup.

Could this be the core, the energy center linking all galactic worlds?

"You will suffer for your insolence."

Words of venom filled her ears.

Lilline rose. "I will not do this."

"Oh, but you will." The Cosmic Widow smiled.

Red light swirled around the queen.

"I will release you soon, my love," the Darian said to the phantom.

The Cosmic Widow rushed forward. Her mouth ripped open and wide layers of fangs, sharp and glistening, threatened.

Terror flashed through Lilline. She fumbled for her blaster. With a trembling hand, she fired.

Red bolts pelted the Cosmic Widow.

Lilline covered her ears as the fury of the Darian echoed through demented space and time.

The queen shot her arm forward.

Lilline's fingers bent, searing with pain. The blaster tore from her hand. Like Mirna's body, the metal handle and barrel crumpled into a ball. With a wave of her arm, the Cosmic Widow shot the weapon off into the void.

"You are a fool! Do you know what we offer you?" The queen's robe billowed like an anemone. "You would deny the opportunity to join a vast universe? To see your other selves and live in the full dimensions?"

"At what cost?" Lilline backed away.

"Cost?" The Darian surged forward. "You of limited knowledge. So ignorant and foolish. *We* are the supreme beings. *We,* in our generosity, offer you access to hidden knowledge. It is our wisdom that you receive."

"And in return?" Lilline continued her retreat.

"Servitude."

Lilline raised the crystal over her head as if it were a weapon. Strange warmth made her fingers tingle. The hovering core of energy pulsed.

"No!" The Darian froze, hand in a defensive gesture. "We will be trapped."

So, I am not powerless here.

"It must go to the Darian portal to release us."

Lilline stared into the creature's strange and mesmerizing face. "Servitude is what you offer for access to a greater universe?"

"You are worthy of nothing more. It is for the Darians to know its charms."

The queen's final word struck a chord. *The famous lines...* the ones she and Lauden, and everyone familiar with the *Cosmic Widow*, could recite by memory. *Within the stars of time are two that open to one. And inside, a reflection of all. The Cosmic Widow, brought to life by Azaludarian, smiles, for the Darians will know the universe through her charms.*

A sinister curve stretched across the queen's alien mouth.

As if hit by a counterspell, the Darian's deceptions came into focus. Lilline's eyes flashed through the liminal space, taking in the ruse and its purpose. "I don't think so," she said. "We possess a gift defying that cost."

The Cosmic Widow cocked her head, fangs dripping. "Gift? You jest."

Lilline shook her head. "You wouldn't understand."

"You mock me?" The queen's onyx eyes narrowed.

"We are weakened by it. It's something that you can't fathom being, as you say, superior and perfect," Lilline said. "But it gives our life purpose."

The Darian stepped closer.

Lilline threatened to toss the crystal up to the glowing core, halting the queen in her tracks.

"Of what do you speak?"

"Absence," Lilline said.

"Useless." The Darian waved a hand in dismissal.

"The driver of true wisdom," Lilline said. "And compassion."

"We have all knowledge already," the Darian said. "Our destiny is to gather more power. Compassion is for inferior beings."

"Without it, *you* are weak," Lilline said. "Memory serves you no purpose in a world where time and space are limitless."

"I know what was."

Lilline sensed the battle line shifting. Power gained through weakness. It all made sense now. "It binds us to our world... gives us motivation to love, to change, to defend in hope of preservation. Without the past, and our memories, we have no present and no future. We lose purpose. And become heartless monsters... like you."

"Silly, petty minds."

"Victims of fate," Lilline said, acknowledging the accusation, "willingly."

"There will not be another chance."

"More alignments will come," Lilline said. "Try us again." She stepped backwards.

"You do not have that luxury, fool! If this gate is not opened, we and all our connected worlds will be lost to you."

A weight dropped into Lilline's legs, halting her steps.

"Too long has the energy between our galaxies sat idle," the queen said. "If not re-connected now, our two worlds will fade from one another beyond recovery. We Darians will remain networked across the universe. It is you who will be isolated. Cut off and lost. Forever."

Our last chance?

"If you step back through the portal with the crystal, you risk everything. It must go to the Darian side," the Cosmic Widow said. "Otherwise, the ghost hole may consume your galaxy." The Darian's face grew earnest. "Yours wouldn't be the first."

Her leap of faith into the portal hadn't provided hope to stop the Darians. All it had done was make everything worse.

The walls of decision closed in. How did she, of all people, end up here? No individual could make a choice like this - forced to unlock dimensional evolution and a broader connection across the universe only to become another oppressed and dominated galactic civilization. Or, return and be cut off forever at the risk of the galaxy collapsing into the ghost hole. She wasn't the one to make this choice.

These decisions were for councils, and experts in various sciences. Where was Madame X? The GM? Or Lauden?

What kind of fated road to evolutionary change and connection in a greater cosmos was this?

"The others came willingly?" Lilline asked.

"Conquered." The Darian waved a hand, dismissing entire galaxies as petty inferiors. "They knew our power and did not resist."

"We're a bit tougher. And smarter. Wouldn't be the first time we kicked you out."

The Cosmic Widow's features shifted.

Lilline readied herself for the attack.

"I am here, waiting for you," Analine said.

Lilline's strength faltered. It was *real*. She knew it. A version of her mother standing before her.

Fingers trembling, as if controlled by another version of herself, Lilline reached out. Would they really be together in this strange co-dimensional reality... the thought was exhilarating beyond the limits of her mind. What potential did this hold for others in her galaxy? Maybe a Jenzara, like Nova, might grasp the significance and know whether it was worth the price.

But what would be lost? Was it better to live with the emotional pain or have something that transcended it? Look at what loss had done to Renina. And Mirna. Had their personal tragedies, and hers, and the natural cycles of life and death, been worth the suffering and consequences? Granny's words about her mother, and how proud she would have been... wasn't that somehow meant to be?

But the scientific side... Entry into a reality of unfathomable and limitless knowledge and potential. How could she turn that down?

Her mind grappled with the puzzle, pieces fitting into place and yet leaving cracks of light between their edges, casting doubt.

She was there.

And here.

The galaxy is at risk if I go back. And if we survive, cut off forever... She would either be responsible for a galactic cataclysm or, if they were lucky, be the sole reason her world's future would roll on divorced from a vast, networked cosmos.

"The Darian gate is closing," the queen said. "The link must be initiated before the alignment ends."

Lilline stared at the Cosmic Widow. She thought of Nova. How had she and her companions gained their knowledge? The druids had chosen to embrace their world, to humble themselves before it and learn to understand it. To live in harmony with the environs and earn access to its secrets through intelligence. Isn't that what Madame X was doing at U-City as well? And wasn't it the purpose of her own poetry? Change and growth through self-realization and self-actualization. Otherwise, what were they other than servants to another master?

The calm and stillness of the monastery's pool returned. And with it, the Ho-to she had written when, after longs days of struggle, new understanding had risen.

Her eyes narrowed. *I'm not giving this to you.* "Better we remain free and inferior, learning slowly and with mistakes," she said. "And if this is one such mistake. I will live with it."

"You are a fool!" the Cosmic Widow said. "A mere single dimensional civilization. So ignorant and isolated. You will suffer the ravages of time. And lose billions of lives and endless worlds."

The Cosmic Widow charged. Lilline dashed to the portal leading back to the temple.

"You think you have conquered time," she said, halting mere centimeters from the gate to face her foe, "but time has conquered you."

The Darian queen roared, fangs bared. Her hand rose, palm open, summoning her power.

"Time waits for no one," Lilline said. *Please work... I am risking everything to preserve our path.* She hurled the crystal up at the glowing core. "Not even Darians."

"No!" The Cosmic Widow's ghoulish voice echoed through the void. "You will trap me—"

Lilline fell back.

The visage of the Cosmic Widow faded as the portal closed.

Forever.

SIXTY-TWO

Smack!

Lilline crashed down, slamming the Temple stage.

Green light and deafening roars bombarded her eyes and ears.

She struggled to her feet.

Renina stood, clutching the Darian clock.

"What are you still doing here?" Lilline screamed.

"You just left!"

"Where's the ship?"

The Rasp's monobrow rolled in confusion. "You've been gone all of five seconds!"

Lilline checked the portal. Its face was a fractured plane of onyx glass. The Cosmic Widow's shadowy silhouette visible within.

Crack! Boom!

She and Renina gazed up. Glitches flickered across the two-dimensional plane between galaxies. The Darian fleet streaked and smeared as the ghost hole faltered.

Lilline yanked Renina along. "We have to go. Now!" Fingers tapped her wrist comm, switching the *Racer's* AI into recon mode. A tiny pulsing icon marking the ship on the surface grid flipped to green. She switched displays and a set of numbers broke into double digits as the Racer's altitude indicator confirmed the ship was rising and heading for the temple.

"This way!" Lilline dashed up the steps, making for the tunnel back to the surface.

Pop!

Like paper scrunching into a ball, her ears crackled in response to a shift in pressure.

"Keep moving!" She lunged up the steps, thigh muscles flexing, taking them two at a time.

"What's happening?" Renina yelled.

"The gate is either closing or…" She didn't want to think about the alternative.

"Or what?"

Lilline glanced back.

The Rasp was struggling, losing pace.

How do I answer that?

Her silence spoke volumes.

Renina's eye made clear that she understood. Lilline checked the sky through the oculus. The glitching window holding back the Darians had shrunk to half its size. So far so good. The cosmic point was diminishing and with it, the ghost hole's link to the menacing world.

Reflections like fireworks consumed the temple. Prodigious thunder shifted from resounding booms to terrifying crackling like glass shattering. Each wave echoed, bouncing around the interior as if hundreds of hands were smashing mirrors simultaneously.

Lilline pulled the Rasp up the stairs. The top was only—

Whoosh!

As if yanking a parachute cord, Lilline's shoulders flew back. Her feet left the ground. Renina joined her, flailing in her peripheral vision. All around the chamber, unsecured objects rose in the air.

Familiar with low-G maneuvering, Lilline twisted and contorted her body so she faced the oculus.

The Darian world had vanished. Only a tiny white point remained.

Streams of sand funneled from Moz into the high atmosphere, sucked upwards like a ghost in a vortex.

Oh no...

The Cosmic Widow's words had been prophetic.

Renina tumbled past, clutching the Darian clock.

"Grab my arm!" Lilline yelled in the chaos.

The Rasp reached out. They locked wrists. Lilline checked her wrist comm. The *Racer* should be about—

Vrooom...

A shadow like an eclipse blocked out the cosmic storm.

Stars, I love that ship.

Lilline's skin tugged, her muscles and bones drawn to the oculus's east edge as if by a magnet. The pull of the ghost hole... she tapped the remote control on her wrist comm, edging the *Racer* down close to the oculus.

"We're going to crash into the side!"

"No, we're not," Lilline said. But the Rasp was right. Zero-G had given way to a growing gravitational pull and now the ghost hole tugged on the planet. How strong it would become, she didn't want to know. Could it take all of Moz? The whole system? A quadrant? Or, stars forbid... the entire galaxy?

"I'm slipping!" Renina screamed.

Coarse clay skin scratched down Lilline's forearm.

"I can get us to the ship, Renina! But you have to hold on." Lilline activated the wrist-action blade in her free hand, advancing the steel knife with its cable extension into her palm.

Above, the *Racer's* hull hovered like a solar eclipse. Edged with green light from the ghost hole high above, a drop-platform descended from the torpedo-like hull. The ledge lowered through the opening and halved their distance.

"I'm losing my grip!" the Rasp shouted.

Like a surreal dream, Lilline watched as the Darian clock,

gripped in Renina's other hand, drifted upward leading the Rasp higher.

"Use both hands!" Lilline said. She gauged the time and distance until the cable would be in range. "Only another few seconds!"

"No!" Renina shook her head.

The look in her eye said it all. The clock was everything. It was all she had left.

"Let it go, Renina."

The Rasp shook her head.

Clay fingers loosened their grip.

"I can't hold you!" Lilline shouted. Two more meters. That was all they needed. Lilline eyed the platform. *I can make that shot.*

"Renina, let it go!"

Lilline drew her free arm with the wrist-action blade back. She had to use enough force and get the trajectory right with the added pull of gravity. It was no different than calculating for strong winds with a sniper rifle. Or was it?

She shot the blade off, cable trailing, towards the drop-platform.

Coarse finger pads dragged down her forearm and then...

Twang!

The blade hit home.

Lilline tapped a finger on her palm, activating the mini winch.

"Renina!"

The Rasp's one eye locked on her two, hands clutching the clock to her chest, as she drifted up and away.

Eyes on Renina, Lilline rose towards the *Racer*. The Rasp floated through the lip of the oculus, narrowly avoiding the edge. Moz's white sand caught her and sucked her up into the vortex. A flash of light sent a final glitter from the clock's metal through storm. Then, like a star burning out, it vanished.

SIXTY-THREE

The Racer's engines roared.

"Come on!"

Like an expert technician at a soundboard, Lilline's fingers danced over every possible button along the dashboard and overhead controls, summoning as much thrust as the ship could muster.

In the growing dawn, Moz was like a lake drained of all water. The world of sand had vanished. Now, stark rock valleys and arid wasteland ran to the horizon. Boulders rose, breaking off along the landscape's weaker points.

The Racer fought the ghost hole's pull, edging away at a snail's pace.

Like an ill-formed brick of half-dry clay, a crack emerged along one side of the planet's massive chasm.

Stars no....

Lilline veered east, banking halfway into the ghost hole's pull like a sailboat tacking in the wind.

A titanic chunk of Moz broke free and rose from the surface in an eerie and unreal spectacle.

"Collision alert. Collision alert."

"I see it! I'm not stupid!" she said and called up the nav board's evasion route.

"Negative. Evasion impossible. Collision imminent."

"Screw that."

Through the dust and debris along the chasm, the lower edge of the titanic slab hit the sun's morning light.

"I can't go over. I can't go around." Lilline grabbed the controls and took the ship off auto-AI. "We're going under."

Fighting the ghost hole's pull, she hit the turbo reserve.

All in now.

The *Racer* plunged.

"Collision alert. Collision alert."

"Come on, I would think Madame X made you smarter than that."

She pushed the stick forward and dove the *Racer* underneath the slab's edge.

Pang! Ping! Pang!

A hand drew back an overhead handle. "Shields," she said. The blue glow of a barrier radiated over the visible portion of the *Racer's* bow. Fiery explosions bounced off the osmic barrier as debris collided with the ship exterior.

"Collision alert. Collision alert."

"Still?"

Her eyes went to the nav board. "Oh..."

A crack of light spread below the slab. It edged along the planet near the chasm.

She aimed for it.

"Come on... thread the needle."

Blinding sunlight streamed into the cockpit. Lilline covered her eyes just as the *Racer* entered the chasm and passed underneath the slab. She peeked at the board, flying blind, following the altimeter, and waited.

Not yet... not yet...

She wiped the sweat from a palm on her sleeve and reset her grip.

"Now!"

Pulling back, the *Racer* soared skyward out of the chasm.

"Yes!" Lilline slammed a fist on the dashboard and ran through the controls, securing a course away from Moz. She hit the boosters and blasted out of the atmosphere.

Banking the ship away from the ghost hole's gravitational path, she slowed to a cruising speed and checked the view. Her elation morphed into horror. Sand from Moz along with massive chunks of the planet, were tracking inward making visible an otherwise sightless gravitational phenomenon.

Her eyes went to the system's sun. Like a fiery comet rocketing through space, the solar ball's edges pulled towards the ghost hole in a long orange tail.

It's taking the whole system...

Lilline switched to autopilot and opened a comm line back to Tavi-Prime, connecting through the security barriers to GAM-OPs HQ.

"Lauden here."

"The gate is closed, sir."

"So, it's over. Well done, T8."

"Renina, or Felicia, which is her original name, didn't make it. Neither did our thief."

"Understood," the director said, tone as cold as his blood.

"The ghost hole collapsed, sir." Lilline eyed the cosmic event out the cockpit. "It's taking the whole system... at least. Maybe more."

"Stars," the director muttered.

Literally.

"But the Darians are shut out," she said. *Do I tell him all of it?*

"I knew you could do it, T8."

"It took a galaxy, sir." It really did. Without Madame X, Professor Senjara, Nova, Dr. Liguera, Lauden, Pin, and many more they would have never been successful.

"And the painting is safe?" Lauden asked. *"You have it?"*

"I'm afraid I wasn't able to retrieve it."

"It's still on Moz?"

"That's complicated, sir. Best leave it for my report."

"Right. Good show, T8. What matters is we are safe until the next alignment."

Lilline hesitated. She opened her mouth to speak but Lauden broke in.

"I'll inform the GM and get Madame X to send a team out and secure what's left at the location."

"There's nothing left, sir. It's all been taken into the ghost hole."

"I see."

How long until the phenomenon dissipated? Or, would it remain, attaining a local equilibrium?

"Can you scan it? Check for its range of pull?" Lauden asked.

Why didn't I think of that?

"One moment."

Lilline banked the ship. Her fingers programmed a system scan.

"Scanning now..."

The holo-board popped up on the dashboard.

Was she a destroyer of three epochs of galactic civilization and billions upon billions of living beings?

Ping.

Lilline read the data. Finger shaking, she shut the screen, unable to keep the report in her sight.

"T8?"

"It's going to take the Moz system, sir." She exhaled. "But nothing more. How long it will remain before dissipating is unknown."

"Thank the stars for that."

The click of Lauden's lighter echoed over the line.

Her toes and fingers tingled. A storm was brewing in her stomach. Lilline knew the signs. Early stages of shock setting in. She needed to set a course for Tavi-Prime and lie down in Madame X's sleep chamber. At this point, she'd trust the AI for the Distortion Ring Jump. There was no way she could handle being a rubber band through time and space after everything that had happened.

"T8, we have an update on your grandmother."

Lilline's stomach twisted. She had to swallow to keep down the bile.

Stars, I can't take any more. I'm at my limit.

With each second of silence that passed her abdomen wrenched tighter.

"Hold a moment," Lauden said.

"Hello T8."

"Pin. Talk to me." Lilline wiped a tear from her eye and did her best to keep her voice steady.

"Madame X and I just heard from Doctor Klitarney. The sword-shade arrived through your courier. It took us the full night at U-City, with a full staff, but we were able to identify an antigen and develop a prototype antidote close enough to consider trying."

"And?"

"We had a close call last night and almost lost her. Doctor Klitarney decided we had no choice but to administer it and hope for the best. The first dose was injected two hours ago."

Lilline squeezed the steering column. *Please let it work.*

"It's early still but Doctor Klitarney is cautiously optimistic," Pin said.

Lilline broke into tears.

SIXTY-FOUR

"Noble of him," the galactic minister said.

The Kreeli's blue hand closed the holo-screen over her desk. Silence filled the office as the latest development sank in.

Lilline shifted in her chair. For the past thirty minutes, she and Lauden had sat across from the leader of the galactic government reviewing the details of Operation Cosmic Widow. This new evidence added a tragic layer to the mission's narrative.

"It arrived yesterday," Lauden said, "two days after the alignment ended."

"Interesting tactic," the GM said.

"Simuel knew how dangerous this was in the wrong hands," Lauden said. "The missive was sent using preset software in case he didn't make it to the date. Sadly, that was the case."

Lilline glanced out the office window. Across the Andrews River, the mirrored exterior of Galaxy Unlimited, Inc. reflected lines of passing air traffic. Pesari-9's shimmering rays bounced off the water, dancing across the building's surface.

"The letter's contents?" the minister asked.

"A summary of all his discoveries related to the *Cosmic Widow*, the alignment, and the Temple of Moz," Lauden said, "including directions on where to find a hidden compartment in his desk containing vital information on how to trigger the ghost hole and open the portal. He didn't trust anyone with that knowledge nor the power that came with it."

"Can't say I blame him." Minister Un's headband glittered with a barometric adjustment.

"I do wish we could untarnish his academic reputation," Lauden added, "but there's no way of doing it without compromising the secrecy of our operation."

"Quite," Minister Un clasped her blue hands together on the desk. "Speaking of academic reputations, where does this leave Reginald Bilarus?"

"He's been released from custody. Metro police have dropped the charges."

The GM nodded.

"However," Lauden added, "with the previous staged thefts under his tenure, along with the debacle surrounding the loss of the *Cosmic Widow*, the Board's patience was tested."

"He's stepping down?" Lilline asked.

"Not that gentle, unfortunately," Lauden said.

Lilline wasn't sure how she felt about that. On the one hand, Bilarus had done a disservice to Simuel with his relentless efforts to discredit him, and yet he had been willing to sacrifice his professional reputation to work towards a better future... all in the cause of art preservation.

Strange how this business worked. Ends justifying means certainly got complicated.

"As far as the public knows, the *Cosmic Widow* remains missing. Stolen by a master thief," Lauden said.

"And the discoveries of Simuel, as well as those by your team," the GM said, "will remain behind closed doors."

"Agreed," the director said.

Lilline watched blood pump through the veins on Lauden's neck. His face held no clues as to his feelings on the matter, but the increase in his metabolic rate was undeniable.

"And your grandmother, Agent Renault?" the GM asked.

"Doing much better. Thank you for asking, Minister."

"I thought it might be a nice gesture if I called her."

"She would like that."

A blue finger pushed a button.

Now?

Lilline looked at Lauden.

He raised an eyebrow.

The audio pinged as the call connected.

"*I don't recognize this number.*" Granny's voice had that familiar scolding tone. "*You better not be one of those pushy AI sales bots trying to take advantage of an old lady.*"

Lilline winced.

"Kissy, this is the GM."

"*Oh, Minister Un. What a delightful surprise!*"

Lilline rolled her eyes.

"I wanted to check in on you. Glad to hear you are on the mend."

"*I'm feeling quite better thank you, Minister. And so nice of you to send over the care package.*"

"Well, I imagine you'll be avoiding Dari cakes now. I thought something savory might be an enjoyable substitute." The Kreeli winked at Lilline.

"*Good gracious no, Minister. Dari cakes aren't a problem. In fact, I've had three today.*"

Lilline's eyes narrowed.

"*Vincenti, the pastry chef and owner of Malardi's brought me a* stack of pink ones, personally," Granny said. *"He's such a dear. You know we are on first name terms..."*

"Is that so?" the GM muted the mic. "I'm a Madame Enri's fan myself."

Lilline shook her head, as if saying, *"Don't tell her that. Ever."*

"You are getting on well, then?" the Kreeli asked. "Are the staff taking good care of you?"

"Well, if you must know, Minister... the accommodations here leave much to be desired."

Here we go... Lilline pictured Kissy's head bobbing back and forth in the hospital bed.

"And don't get me started about my granddaughter."

What?

"She's barely visited me."

I was just there for two hours.

The corners of Lauden's mouth curved upward.

Is he enjoying this?

"I've got the director and T8 here now, actually." The GM motioned for Lauden to speak.

"Good morning, Kissy."

"Asher... always a pleasure. Thank you for the flowers. It's nice to know some of you care enough to attend to my recovery."

"Hello, Granny," Lilline said. "Are you still the same as you were one-hundred-and-twenty minutes ago when I was there with you?"

This time the GM's earnest expression broke.

A mumble came over the line.

Thought so.

"Well Kissy, as you know there's always business to attend to at the Ministry. I know I speak for everyone when I say we're glad you're pulling through. And of course, we can't thank you enough for your cycles of service as a T#."

"Thank you, Minister. My statue outside the Octagonal Club is quite nice."

Give me a break with the statue routine.

"Take care now." The Kreeli cut the line.

Lilline let out a silent sigh of relief.

"T8," Lauden said, "what are your thoughts regarding informing Kissy of the source of her poisoning?"

Lilline nodded her appreciation. A delicate situation and one that had been weighing on her all morning. "If there are no objections, I think it best to give my grandmother some space to recover first. She will have a tough time of it when she learns the truth about Mirna."

"Quite agree," the GM said, oblong head nodding. "Back to the art. What about the other artifacts, Asher?" the Kreeli asked. "Was anything salvaged?"

"Some were recovered but most were not, unfortunately," the Gej-ti said. "Most of what Carmini had in his possession or related to the auction have vanished."

The Venex Horse flashed in her mind. Lost. It could be anywhere in the galaxy by now.

"And this Carmini?" the GM asked.

"Now that tale, Minister, has an interesting epilogue," the director said.

Lilline perked up. She hadn't heard a report about the Jenzara's fate.

"Whoever Carmini had funding his ruse grew impatient with a lack of delivery. Local authorities found him in one of his resort homes on Giro-5, along the Lacosta Coast. They'd made a spectacle of his body parts throughout the villa. Messy to say the least."

"Any idea who it was?" the minister asked.

Lauden shook his head. "Oddly enough, all five brains were removed and..." he raised an eyebrow, "not recovered."

"This does make for a strange conclusion. Quite the operation," the GM said.

Lilline had to agree. Was it the right decision to keep her confrontation with the Cosmic Widow out of the report? Surely Madame X at U-City would be consumed with the possibilities of what she had experienced inside the portal. And yet, she had gained a new sympathy and kinship with Simuel. She was now the only living being in their universe privy to knowledge of a multitude of realities running parallel to their own. What had Nova called Darian culture? A wedding cake, decorated with icing and deeply layered, hiding or revealing mysteries depending on where you sliced it.

"Once again the galaxy is in your debt," the minister said. "Well done, both of you. Especially you, Agent Renault."

"Thank you, Minister," Lilline nodded her thanks, but something wouldn't settle. *So we go back to the way things were a week ago?*

"What is it, Agent Renault?" the GM said.

"It's nothing, Minister. Just that the gravity of this mission's intel is, well…" Her eyes went from the Kreeli to Lauden. "I've kept secrets before, but nothing like this."

A silence descended in the office.

And you don't know the half of it.

"How many are privy to the specifics?" the GM asked.

"The three of us," Lauden said, "as well as our head of Tech, Madame X, Dr. Liguera, Professor Senjara, and Reginald Bilarus."

Closer to home, it was a shame that a discovery contributing newfound perspectives and knowledge to cosmic science, art, and understanding of the galaxy's past, would remain inaccessible. Perhaps the strangest part, scholars would continue to build off a false historical platform about the Darians, constructing a mountain of interpretations and understandings of a history that never happened. Why couldn't they share that, at least?

Lilline shifted in her chair.

"I see you are uncomfortable with this, Agent Renault," the GM said. "That pleases me."

"Minister?" Uncertainty pushing through her agent exterior.

Minister Un's eyes fixed on Lauden. "Too often we ask those in the clandestine service to put aside emotions and personal feelings. And yet, I believe they are essential for us to make the right decisions."

Lauden nodded.

"I am not sure I follow," Lilline said.

"Precisely the point." The Kreeli's face softened. "If you weren't conflicted, I would doubt your competence." The minister locked eyes with her. "It is precisely because you remain unsettled that tells me you made the right decision on Moz... and that we are making the right one now in this office." Her lips broke at the corners into a subtle but gracious smile.

"It's just..." Lilline stopped herself. The scope of this mission's impact resonated far beyond the present and an elite circle of players.

"Continue please, Agent Renault." The Kreeli gestured with a blue hand.

"We're talking about an entire historical narrative," Lilline said. "One that will continue to shape a misinformed understanding of the past, and therefore impact the way we perceive the present and future."

"Isn't that the way it is most of the time, though?" the GM said. "We always access the past through the eyes of those privileged to leave us stories about it. Subjectivity is center stage."

"Certainly, Minister. I will admit the scope of this makes it more difficult to swallow," Lilline said.

"True," Lauden interjected. "Once again, we at GAM-OPs find ourselves in a familiar position. There is no denying we're in the deception game." He nodded, accepting the ruse. "It is unsettling, T8, I know. But we must make choices. This is one of those that doesn't sit well but must be done."

"Agreed," the GM said.

Lauden rose and approached a Second Galactic painting on the office wall, examining it. "As I said to you at the beginning of this mission, art is filled with allusion and illusion. In this case, we have wielded both to stop an unfathomable threat. GAM-OPs must put the safety of the galaxy first, even at the expense of science and discovery." The director ran a milky-skinned hand over his widow's peak. "Would making this knowledge public contribute to our understanding of the past? Most certainly. Would it help shape a different, perhaps better future? I expect it would. And yet..." he trailed off.

"The possibility of someone making a connection that leads to the ghost holes is too great a risk." Minister Un shifted her attention to Lilline. "Blame the decision on me if you like, Agent Renault."

"I don't blame you, Minister." Lilline said. "It doesn't sit well."

The GM nodded her oblong head. "The longer I serve as head of the Ministry, the heavier these secrets weigh on me. And yet, it must be done."

A softening revealed the burden in the Kreeli's eyes. It was such a strange game they all played. Profound discoveries and privileged knowledge kept under wraps to maintain safety across the stars.

"Thank you, Minister. We'll be going," Lauden said. The Gej-ti stood and motioned for Lilline to follow.

Minister Un rose and came around from behind her desk. "Asher, if you wouldn't mind, I'd like a moment with Agent Renault."

"Of course," Lauden bowed his head. His black eyes went to Lilline briefly before he made for the portal.

"No need to sit back down," the GM said. "This will only take a moment." The Kreeli gestured for Lilline to proceed with her to the office window.

"What do you see out there, Agent Renault?"

Lilline scanned the air traffic over the endless urban skyline. "A busy morning on Tavi-Prime."

"Come now. I hear you are a poet." The Minister looked her in the eyes. "A soon-to-be published one, according to the director. Congratulations, by the way."

Lilline smiled in thanks.

"So, tell me. What does the poet see?" the Minister gestured at the view.

Is she asking me to pen a verse here and now?

"Look with your literary eyes," the GM added.

Lilline gazed at the vista. She wasn't used to intentionality when writing poetry. It was more a spontaneous eruption under duress or extreme excitement in the field.

She took a breath and settled. The world became metaphor, analogy, and alliteration.

> *urban gaze alive*
> *the city thrives*
> *a building's reflection*
> *secrets shine in plain sight.*

The GM stood, waiting patiently as quiet words whispered in Lilline's mind.

A Ho-to. The first to rise since that day at the monastery cycles ago.

"I think, Minister," Lilline said, voice soft and measured, "that some poems are best kept to oneself." She faced the leader of the galaxy.

"Your strength of self-respect is admirable, Agent Renault. Few in our employ are bold enough to take a stand when presented with such a charge."

"It's sacred to me, Minister," Lilline said. "Poetry is the one thing under my complete control. Some verses I share, and some remain…" She hesitated, uncertain about how the statement would land.

"Secret," the GM said.

Out the window, layers of meaning manifested before Lilline's eyes - poetic verses superimposed over the endless urban skyline. A world of individualism flowed into a collective galactic society. One planet, filled with secrets, among millions the stars over. She'd never spoken of her poetry so intimately before. And yet, she hadn't really said anything. The statement was a declaration of a position… a choice.

"I think we understand one another, Agent Renault. It is quite comforting knowing you are in our employ."

"Thank you, Minister."

The Kreeli gestured toward the portal.

"And I'm relieved that your grandmother is making a speedy recovery," the GM said as they reached the office entrance. A blue hand rose from her side.

Lilline shook it.

"I have one more assignment for you."

"Minister?"

"Take a trip back to the Galactic Museum. This afternoon." Minister Un smiled. "Say, two o'clock?"

Lilline nodded.

"Reginald Bilarus will meet you there."

SIXTY-FIVE

"Do you have a favorite, Pin?" Lilline gazed around the gallery.

"In here?" The Oltari hovered off the floor and rotated 360-degrees. "No." She plopped down on her stumpy legs.

"Like them all then, do you?" Lilline smiled.

"Hoo."

Heads turned from First Galactic paintings around the room.

"I believe that is sarcasm, T8."

"Indeed it is, Pin."

"Actually," the Oltari said, "I would like to revise my answer."

"Oh?" Lilline faced her colleague.

Pin pointed her double-elbowed upper arm at the wall to their right.

A glaring empty space where the *Cosmic Widow* had hung stared back.

"That makes sense," Lilline said. "I assume you are being literal and not sarcastic this time?"

"I do not employ sarcasm. It is difficult to grasp as an expressive component of language, but more than that I find it..."

Lilline waited, amused.

"Trite." Pin held up her two lower arms and made a square with her seven-fingered hands like a viewfinder. She scrutinized a painting across the room through the negative space. "But I do respect its ability to prompt laughter among my fellow galactic species."

"Quite gracious of you, Pin."

"These paintings are awful."

Lilline laughed. She waved to Reginald Bilarus as he entered the gallery. By his side, to her mild shock and surprise, was another Oltari.

"They're not my favorite either," Lilline said. "I would suggest keeping that to yourself unless asked. For social etiquette."

"Good afternoon," Bilarus said, approaching. "Thank you for coming on short notice, especially with everything that has happened. I'm happy to hear your grandmother is doing better."

"Thank you," Lilline said. "She should be discharged in a day or..." Bilarus's face held a strange expression. His eyes were on Pin. Lilline checked on her colleague.

"Is everything okay, Pin?"

The Oltari, and her brethren who arrived with Bilarus, were rocking forward and back, their double-wings flared open.

Whoosh!

The two shot up into the air in a spiral-like storm. Ten meters overhead they halted their ascent and looked to be...fighting?

"Pin!" Lilline looked to Bilarus, who shrugged.

Fragments of translucent wings fell to the floor as the two wrangled mid-air.

"Hoo!"

In unison, both Oltari's exclaimed the now-familiar utterance before dropping down next to them.

"Pin?" Lilline asked.

The head of Tech gestured with one of her four hands to her species companion.

"Allow me to introduce myself. I am Aru-i. The new Curator of Collections."

"My replacement," Bilarus said. "Aru-i, this is Pin and..." The Gej-ti gestured at Lilline but hesitated.

"Keely Larkin."

"Nice to meet you both."

"It is very nice to meet you as well, Aru-i," Pin said.

"Are you two okay? You've lost some bits of your wings," Lilline said.

"Oh yes," Pin said, wiping additional fragments from her chest. "We were establishing dominance. Standard social custom for members of different flocks."

"I see." That was a new one. Lilline assumed that Pin waiting for Aru-i to speak meant that the other Oltari took the lead position.

"Pin," Bilarus said, "I forwarded your letter on to Aru-i."

Oh no. What new conflict was this going to spur?

Aru-i nodded and lifted a data pad in one of her four hands. "I am most eager to discuss your requests."

"You are?" Pin said.

"Absolutely. My priority as the new head curator is to address the disparity in representation in the galleries. Your audit is flawless, not that I expected otherwise, but I would like to walk through all 13,215 data lines with you in earnest."

"Sounds like you two have an exciting time ahead," Lilline said. She didn't miss Bilarus doing his best to keep a straight face.

"Don't be sarcastic," Pin said.

"Is that sarcasm?" Aru-i asked.

"Oh, yes," Pin said. "I've identified a linguistic consistency when it appears in casual conversation. It's taken me a while, but I now believe I can isolate it and," the Oltari looked at Lilline, "perhaps begin to employ it."

Wow... game changer.

"You must share this with me," Aru-i said. "It would be most useful for staff meetings."

Pin's pink cheeks flushed blue. "Of course."

"Shall we proceed to the data in the audit?" Aru-i gestured with her tablet towards the portal.

Lilline caught Pin's eye.

"I'll see you back at the office."

"Good luck in retirement, Mr. Bilarus. It's good you are no longer in charge of the collections," Pin said and fluttered off with the new curator.

The Gej-ti's milky face turned to ice.

"It takes some getting used to," Lilline said. "Don't take it personally."

"Oh, I won't. Although I respect the truth of it." He gestured towards the void where the *Cosmic Widow* used to be on display. "And there it is. The cause of my career's end."

"I'm sorry," Lilline said, staring at the wall.

"Don't be. I wasn't planning on staying much longer. But more than that, I was able to take all the heat on this one. Between the artifact ruse and the loss of the *Cosmic Widow* on my watch, the Board deflected all museum responsibility onto me."

"I hope it isn't too hard on you."

"The press will destroy me, but only until the next delicious target usurps my 'fall from grace.' Besides, I don't intend to hang around Tavi-Prime and let myself be a made a public mockery. I've bought a quiet estate on Quo."

"I've been there," Lilline said. "Only for a day but it was lovely moon." She kept the fact that it had been to assassinate a devious politician to herself.

Bilarus took in the gallery. "So many works in a museum aren't what they seem."

"I guess you and I are right at home, then?"

He laughed.

It wasn't only the knowledge she'd learned on Sky City about museum originals replaced by forgeries. Lilline had seen paintings in extravagant villas while undercover that were too perfect to be copies. They had an aura about them. Confronting one was an instinctual response, like knowing whether someone was being authentic or disingenuous.

And yet, Reginald Bilarus left her puzzled. Was he merely an asset brought in by Lauden to help them with the art thefts? Or was there more to the curator?

She scrutinized him as he admired the works on display.

One more secret left to whisper through the ages.

"All part of the job, right?" Bilarus said.

Lilline scrutinized the Gej-ti's face. A mixture of pride and sadness spoke through his eyes.

"Living with false identities. No one knowing who you are and what you really do." He faced her. "How do you handle it, if I may ask?"

Lilline's eyes went around the room. Visitors clustered in front of grand historical paintings, taking in scenes of a lost galactic age. Some engaged in intense conversations and others stood taking in the beauty with awed reverence.

"Poetry," she said.

The word hung in silence between them.

Lilline took one last look at the empty wall. She closed her eyes. Voices in a range of tones and pitches bounced off the gallery ceiling. A palpable shift in the room's energy resonated through the ambient sounds. The paintings relegated to a rising crescendo leading to the *Cosmic Widow* were coming into the light, free of a dangerous and powerful shadow.

"I want to show you something."

Lilline opened her eyes.

The Gej-ti gestured towards the archway leading to the central collection.

Lilline followed the former curator out of the gallery. They walked along the corridor leading back to the display areas near to the museum's central rotunda. Bilarus kept moving without waiting for her to catch up.

Regal portraits of galactic leaders, scholars, and prominent citizens eyed her in silent stillness from the walls. Few museum visitors stopped or spent much time observing these images, intent on reaching the gallery that formerly housed the *Cosmic Widow* or, returning afterwards with haste to the more popular modern works alive with dazzling colors and conceptual puzzles.

Bilarus passed through the next portal and halted in front of the row of early Third Galactic electrified paintings. Again, as when they had first met at the beginning of the crisis, his linen suit glowed in the paintings' spectral auras.

Of all the things to want to show me, he chooses—

Lilline slowed her steps. A familiar blue and red design in the hand of a human at one of the portraits caught her agent eye.

I don't believe it.

The unmistakable cover of the Tavi-Prime Poetry Society annual contest issue peeked out from under an arm, clutched against the woman's side. She spoke with a Froo companion and pointed at a portrait, discussing an aspect of the representation.

Oh. My. Stars.

A swirling breeze rose in Lilline's soul. How to describe it? Excitement, disbelief, anxiety, and pride all vied for dominance. She feigned interest in the portrait across from them. A moment passed and a new contestant entered the psychological arena: accomplishment.

She kept her exterior cool but inside she was screaming.

MY POEM IS IN THERE!

Exhilaration spiraled and transformed. Her stomach dropped. *That means she is going to read it...*

The woman glanced her way. Lilline shifted her gaze to a nearby painting, heart pounding, and ran her eyes over it as if deeply engaged in its scrutiny.

What if she doesn't like it? What if it's awful? What if—

"Are you coming?"

Bilarus's pudgy face was looking up at her.

"If you would, please." He gestured for her to pass through the portal to the next gallery.

"Sorry. I was… this one caught my eye." She pointed at the portrait.

"Ruleni?" He shrugged. "Not my favorite but to each their own."

Lilline followed the Gej-ti to the next gallery, passing by the couple. A final peek at the journal brought a smile to her face and a swagger to her step.

A published poet.

Endorphins rushed through her veins, the corners of her mouth breaking into a smug smile. She had to hold back from giggling.

"By your expression, I assume you share my enthusiasm for early First Galactic style?"

Lilline took in the garish and crude aesthetic of the rebellious painters who pioneered the beginning of the modern age and grimaced.

"To be honest, it's not my thing."

The Gej-ti strode between her and the works on the wall.

Oh no.

He had the look of an art historian about to launch into a lecture billed as a tour that veiled as missionary artistic conversion.

Bilarus held up a hand. "No matter. Taste is, of course, subjective. Perhaps this will be more to your liking?" The Gej-ti nodded his chin, indicating she should turn around.

Twenty meters back, on the other side of the gallery, the vitrine and familiar blue plasma shield surrounding the empty—

It's not empty.

Bilarus's pink cheeks went crimson.

"You might want to take a closer look," he said.

Step-by-step, she made her way across the room. With each passing meter she expected the small object to become legible in surrogate - a cut-out, a hyper-realistic hologram, or some other form of a replica.

Lilline halted a meter from the display case. A horse, like to the one she knew as a child, stood on the velvet blanket.

"What... Reginald, what is this?"

"While you were returning to Tavi-Prime, we conducted a raid on Carmini's residence. Several priceless objects were recovered."

"And this was among them?"

Bilarus fiddled with his handkerchief. "Oddly, no."

Her eyes went to the horse and back to the Gej-ti. "I'm not following?"

Bilarus took a step closer and checked to make sure no one was in earshot. "A collector who had purchased it at auction contacted the authorities and offered to sell it for a reasonable sum." He spread his arms wide and smiled. "And here it is, back home and safe."

Lilline's eyes went to the small figurine inside the plasma shield. "Who was the buyer?"

"No idea. As usual for those sales, the transaction was anonymous."

Her mind ran through the faces from Carmini's underground event. The buyer might have been anyone in attendance, or a virtual attendee. Now that she thought about it, an interested party bidding remotely had cast the highest sum as she exited to pursue Mirna in the storeroom.

"And the new purchaser, the one responsible for its safe return?"

"That, Ms. Larkin, remains a mystery."

The Gej-ti's pink cheeks flushed and he dabbed his forehead with a handkerchief.

"You're certain this is the original?" She leaned down and peered through the faint blue barrier.

"Oh yes. Dating and material has been confirmed by the museum's appraisers."

She glanced at the former curator.

"Let's just say that I am sure of it." He winked.

Lilline's eyes went back to the figurine. She knew it too. Like meeting an old lover or intimate childhood friend, an unseen aura pulled her to the object.

"Well, I guess this is goodbye." Bilarus held out his hand. "Fitting that our first meeting was here and it will also be our farewell."

Lilline shook his hand. "Thank you."

"Please," he waved his handkerchief like a magician. "It's the least the museum can do."

"No, I mean thank *you*... for giving up so much personally to maintain the security of all of this. And a narrative that... well," she gestured at the surrounding collection. "You know..."

"Oh, I've been at art's mercy for longer than you have." He stepped up and peered at the Venex Horse. "It really is a remarkable piece."

Lilline joined him. The miniature horse stood proudly on its velvet blanket. Like the ebb and flow of a tide, time collapsed. Distance squeezed, as if a wormhole opened a portal to potent childhood memories. Analine smiled across the breakfast table, click-clacking the horse, dancing it in front of her daughter's precious eyes. Sound. Smell. Touch. Sight. All suddenly vivid. And through them laughter, safety, and love. Life returned across immeasurable distance through internal space and time.

Bilarus sighed. "It never fails to lure us in, does it?"

"No." Lilline wiped a tear. "It never does."

"Farewell, Ms. Larkin."

The Gej-ti's shuffling steps faded.

Alone with her heirloom, Lilline took a breath and settled. The Froo, poetry journal tucked under an arm, strolled by with her partner.

A celebration of some sort was in order. Hiko and some ice cream sounded—

Her wrist vibrated.

Asté, 7p.m.?

She checked the message ID.

You're in town? she typed.

I can be. I've got the next three days off.

Her eyes went to the gallery's digi-clock.

Tonight?

Why not? Curious about these Gibson oysters you say are all the rage.

Butterflies fluttered in her belly. She started to respond but stopped, fingers hovering.

Why am I hesitating?

The galaxy had been patched, time and space flowed undisturbed once more. Granny was on the mend, in hospital. Lauden had even told her to take some time, that she deserved it.

This IS the number of the risk taker I met last week? Or was that all a work thing?

Lilline shook her head, typing rapidly. *Yes! I mean... no, it is the right number. And not just a work thing.*

Your communication skills need some work.

A smile broke on her face. Something about Alex made her feel at ease, like the warmth of family.

I'd love to.

Great. 7 p.m, then. According to my colleague at the Royal Loha, they have a great cocktail menu.

One condition, Lilline typed.

What's that?

No cocktails. We're drinking Gondau.

***

A NOTE OF THANKS

Thank you for taking the time to read my books!

If you enjoyed _Cosmic Widow_, and have a moment to leave an honest rating, it would make my day! It helps me reach readers and share my stories.
Many thanks, Jonathan Nevair

Agent Renault Spy-Fi Adventures:

To Spy a Star

Stellar Instinct

Wind Tide: A Space Opera Series:

Goodbye to the Sun (Wind Tide #1)

Jati's Wager (Wind Tide #2)

No Song, but Silence (Wind Tide #3)

ACKNOWLEDGMENTS

Well, here we are again. The acknowledgements for *Cosmic Widow* are distinct from previous books in the Agent Renault series. The story's focus on art history meant that I drew inspiration and influence from famous works and scholarly examples that have contributed to my understanding and appreciation of visual art. There's a few additional easter eggs in the book as well, especially for fans of fantasy and martial arts. So, without further ado:

Much of the concept for, and perceptions of, the Darians as an idealized culture was built from art historical writings and interpretations of European Antiquity. I was thinking specifically about the legacy and influence of historians and writers at the rise of neoclassicism such as J. J. Winckelmann (1717-1768) and his 1764, *The History of the Art of Antiquity*. That work shaped ideas and discourse on the Greeks, contributing to a set of idealized aesthetic standards and even a myth of intellectual, philosophical, political, and physical superiority bordering on utopia.

The complexities of illusion, reflections, and other visual distortions in *Cosmic Widow* were inspired by examples such as the famous anamorphosis of a human skull in Hans Holbein's *The Ambassadors* (1533), as well as the stereoscopic experiments and paintings of Salvador Dalí. Worth noting is the Spanish artist's ideas about nuclear mysticism which played a role in the finale with Azaludarian's manifestation on the throne at the Temple of Moz.

On the topic of dimensional phenomena, I made passing reference in the scene at the Star Pool to the idea of four-dimensional objects casting three-dimensional shadows. This was inspired by a comment attributed to the French artist Marcel Duchamp: "Since a three-dimensional object casts a two-dimensional shadow, we should be able to imagine the unknown four-dimensional object whose shadow we are. I, for my part, am fascinated by the search for a one-dimensional object that casts no shadow at all." I always associated this comment with the well-known and fascinating sculpture by the Italian futurist Umberto Boccioni, *Unique Forms of Continuity in Space* (1913). I can't remember if it was made in reference to that or if one of my graduate school professors linked them together. Regardless, it was this statement and sculpture that inspired the reference.

Direct inspiration for the small figurine Lilline used for surveillance at the auction was a nod to Sumerian civilization and surviving Early Dynastic stone worshippers common to Mesopotamia (2900-2600 BCE). And then there's Madame X, Director of U-City. A nod to the famous portrait by John Singer Sargeant, whose sitter remained anonymous at the artist's request. Lastly for the art historical inspirations, I appropriated the title of a scholarly article by Rosalind Krauss for Asher Lauden's remarks about art to Lilline: "Allusion and Illusion in Donald Judd," from *Artforum* in 1966.

Within the realm of astronomy and astrophysics, the concept and type of wormhole employed in this story was built on the idea of the Einstein-Rosen Bridge. "Flaming sky dragons," a line spoken by Pin on Sky City, is a phrase by Hesiod in a beautiful description of the aurora from his *Theogony* (8th century BCE). The radial design that Nova discovers through esoteric calculations is based on Incan astronomy. The lines that emanate from Kalatron, which served as the nexus for the Darian empire in the story's galaxy, are a loose interpretation of the *ceques*, where sacred astronomical points are linked. Learning about the correlations between the *ceques* and constellations led to additional creative solutions for the stellar aspects of the Darian puzzle, including the idea for the Temple of Moz, inspired by the Incan's Temple of the Sun.

Finally, some random easter eggs of sorts: J.R.R. Tolkien's description of the Mirrormere (Kheled-zâram) at Dimrill Dale in Middle Earth, which the dwarves believed to be sacred, has always been a particular love of mine. As Tolkien described it in *The Fellow of the Ring*, "There like jewels sunk in the deep shone glinting stars, though sunlight was in the sky above. Of their own stooping forms no shadow could be seen." I've always been filled with wonder at the idea of starry reflections on the water during daylight, and when I learned that Durin had leaned over , observing a crown (made of stars) above his head, taking it as a sign, it swept me away into stellar realms of imaginative possibility. Thus, when it came time to write this book, the Star Pool was born. Fellow author Melanie Phillips gave me wonderful advice on druidic practices and groves which helped conjure the scenes in the forest outside of Carna-Brai. And those of you who are classic science fiction fans may have picked up on Nova's map containing the line, "to be left alone." That's a nod to my gateway sci-fi author, Arthur C. Clarke, from his *2010: Odyssey Two,* which includes the famous message, "ALL THESE WORLDS ARE YOURS EXCEPT EUROPA. ATTEMPT NO LANDING THERE."

Finally, Lilline's inner voice, reminding her to "be like water," is credited to the martial artist, Bruce Lee. Of course, the idea has a much longer history in martial arts philosophy but for this context I appropriated it from a statement Lee made in an interview, and also on the TV show *Longstreet,* in 1971. And yes, there's a nod to Mr. Han from *Enter the Dragon* at the auction as well, via the welcome greeting by Carmini.

Because of the art historical backbone of *Cosmic Widow,* writing it was, at times, delicious.... *at times.* As a mystery-leaning spy thriller, I spent a good deal of effort researching the genre to familiarize and educate myself with narrative structure, story beats, and typical progressions that exploit clues, alibis, red herrings, etc. for suspense and other effects. Call it a labor of love... well, maybe more labor than love. It wasn't easy keeping track of a complex mystery plot, and much of the revisions to my early (and messy) drafts are the result of the wonderful, insightful, and honest beta readers and critique partners who took time from their own busy schedules to read early drafts and offer feedback. I always bow down before these literary allies in my acknowledgements, and this book is no exception. It takes a village, truly.

First and foremost, I would like to thank my wife, Mallary, for her endless support and patience. To my mother, Nancy, thank you yet again for being the first reader of my stories and my constant champion. I hope this book delivered on some of the requests you pushed for in earlier Agent Renault stories. You read *Cosmic Widow* as each chapter came to life over the summer (and had to wait after each cliffhanger!) and as with earlier books in the series this has been a wonderful opportunity for us to grow closer and spend more time together. Additional thanks goes to family members who supported me: my father and stepmother, Bill and Betsy, for their endless enthusiasm and my stepbrother, Mark Milone who has a knack for texting me cool technology, gadgets, and gizmos at the most opportune writing moments.

Beta readers and critique partners... what an elite team assembled around this book, as talented as the T# agents at GAM-OPs. Each of you brought unique perspectives and specializations to your critiques that were enormously helpful. Veteran readers like Sharon Burke, who always keeps me on track with issues of narrative clarity and tone, and of course Lilline's fashion choices - the boots in this one were for you! Jean-Paul Garnier, both friend and professional colleague, thank you for your advice and guidance on poetic form and science, as well as minutia that tightened all the knots of plot and character development. My critique partners, Lindsay and Michael Wells, continue to amaze me. Truly, you are like the dynamic literary duo, superhero authors fighting to rid my manuscript of the narrative villains holding my story back from being its best. You've been with me since the beginning (six books now!) and you deserve a medal. I want to recognize your honesty... it is so important and I really appreciate it. Rowena Andrews, longtime book friend, who covers my action thriller territory as perhaps the world's leading expert on Clive Cussler (lol) and now, apparently, is keeping me up to date on all things Scottish to boot. Krista Pimpinella and Tina Hagmann provided me with honest and important feedback and editorial advice. I very much appreciate the way you balanced the "inside" and "outside" of this story and its relationship to the rest of the series. Finally, Laura Morgan, book friend, fellow Andor fan, and podcaster/book reviewer extraordinaire at OWWR (On Wednesdays We Read) – thank you for reading and offering such thoughtful feedback. I hope you will stay on board with the others and help shape future Agent Renault stories with your insights.

Jonathan Oliver has been with me as my editor since the beginning, and once again answered the call. Thank you for your copy edit of the manuscript. MIBLart did a great job on this cover, as they did with *Stellar Instinct* and *To Spy a Star*. (I might have the next cover in the series sitting in a folder on my laptop...).

I would like to thank the following writers for their endless support and advice: T.A. Bruno, Marian L. Thorpe, Peter Hartog, Dani Finn, Rex Burke, Adrian M. Gibson, Tessa Hastjarjanto, Jeffrey Speight, Krista Pimpinella, M.A. Phillips, Douglas Lumsden, Angela Boord, Karen Heenan, Gary J. Mack, and Andrew Jackson. There are a lot more of you - you know who you are.

I am very thankful for the gracious generosity and support of the following #WritingCommunity individuals, who continue to support me as I navigate my way through this creative journey: Jean-Paul Garnier at Space Cowboy Books, Rowena Andrews at Beneath a Thousand Skies, Tina S. Beier at Sound & Fury Books, Alex at Spells and Spaceships, Scarlett at Scarlett Readz & Runz, Shazzie (Reader at Work), Sara and Lilly at Fiction Fans Podcast, Laura and Hannah at OWWR Podcast, Adrian Gibson and M.J. Kuhn at SFF Addicts, Sue Bavey at Sue's Musings, Lorraine Bondi (The Book & Nature Professor), Alyssa at Into the Heartwyld, Jamedi (Jamreads), Jodie at W & S Bookclub, Isabelle W. at The Shaggy Shepherd, Robin at the

Book Wormhole, KDS, Ziggy Nixon, and The OG Bookbeard. There are many more. Know that I see you and appreciate all of you.

It looks like a pattern is emerging where I write one Agent Renault book a year. So now, I am off to start that process again. Stay tuned dear betas, critique partners, fellow authors, and reviewers... *Undercover Moon* is soon to rise.

ABOUT THE AUTHOR

Jonathan Nevair is an award-winning science fiction writer and educator originally from Long Island, NY. After two decades in the classroom, he finally got up the nerve to write fiction.

For more information visit: www.jonathannevair.com

Join the mailing list: sign me up!